THE ALZHEIMER'S
CURE

THE ALZHEIMER'S CURE

PETER VAN OOSSANEN

atmosphere press

© 2025 Peter Van Oossanen

Published by Atmosphere Press

Cover design by Kevin Stone

The moral right of the author has been asserted.

All characters and events in this publication, other than those clearly in the public domain, are fictitious and any resemblance to real persons, living or dead, is purely coincidental.

All rights reserved. No part of this publication may be reproduced, stored in a retrieval system, or transmitted, in any form or by any means, without the prior permission in writing of the publisher, nor be otherwise circulated in any form of binding or cover other than that in which it is published and without a similar condition including this condition being imposed on the subsequent purchaser.

Atmospherepress.com

For my family

1.

MONACO

The 2021 Monaco Yacht Show closely mirrored its pre-pandemic editions, following a one-year hiatus due to COVID-19. As always, the event took place in the third or fourth week of September, running daily from 10 a.m. to 6:30 p.m. More than a hundred superyachts were on display, moored stern-to along the quays of Port Hercules to maximize space in the compact harbor.

Securing a spot at the show was a process that began up to a year in advance, with builders and brokers working closely with yacht owners to ensure their vessels would be available for inspection by prospective clients and guests. Many owners opted to stay on board, limiting access to their private quarters. Such was the case aboard the 240-foot motor yacht *Artemis*, owned by Jacky and William Lassiter.

Jacky inherited Morgan Pharma, a multinational pharmaceutical conglomerate, after the passing of her first husband, Alfred Morgan, in 2013. In 2015, she married William Lassiter—Bill to those close to him—who served as chairman of the board. The couple settled into an expansive Beverly Hills estate, with Bill widely regarded as an industry authority and the undisputed leader of the company.

Jacky had a daughter, Lucy, from her first marriage. Lucy's relationship with her father had been strained; she was headstrong and outspoken, often clashing with him over her desires. Upon her mother's remarriage, she adopted her stepfather's surname, having formed a strong bond with him.

On the second day of the show, Lucy arrived aboard *Artemis*, having flown in from New York on the family's private jet. Armand, the yacht's bosun, met her at Nice Côte d'Azur Airport and escorted her to Monaco. It had been over a month since her parents last saw her—their most recent meeting had been a dinner in New York where she introduced them to her latest boyfriend. However, her apparent disinterest in him reassured them that no impending engagement announcement was on the horizon. Lucy thrived on attention, constantly seeking admiration for her beauty. At twenty-five, she cycled through relationships, never considering that many of her suitors were drawn more to her wealth and status than to her as a person.

After unpacking, Lucy joined Jacky and Bill on the sundeck beneath the shade of the Bimini. The warm afternoon sunlight bathed the yacht in a golden glow as they settled into plush armchairs. From her vantage point, Lucy observed the passing crowd, scanning for attractive men. Having ended her most recent relationship just the previous week, she was already on the lookout for her next admirer.

"Would you do us a favor, Lucy?" Bill asked her after a pause in their conversation.

"Sure."

"We have a visitor coming to spend a day with us. He arrives at Nice Airport this evening at a quarter to eight with Air France flight AF7708. One of us needs to accompany Armand to pick him up. We wouldn't be setting the proper tone for his visit if we didn't. Would you accompany Armand to collect him?"

"He must be important for you to invite him on board with us and for me to pick him up at the airport. Is he one of your board members?"

"No, he's one of our employees."

"Isn't that rather unusual? We've never entertained employees on board, or as a family somewhere else. Why would we now?"

When Bill didn't immediately respond to her question, Lucy directed her inspection of the men walking along the quay to her stepfather.

"He's important to us in a way I can't explain just now."

"It's true, Lucy," Jacky added. "He's important, and we want to treat him accordingly."

"Why can't you explain why he's important? It seems like you're trying to keep that from me."

"We are for now," Bill answered. "I know we've never kept secrets from you before, but the circumstances we're in require we do. You'll understand when we tell you later."

Lucy was upset at not being told why their visitor was important, but more so because of her parents' secretiveness. She decided to accompany Armand to Nice to question their visitor on the drive back to Monaco to find out who he was and why he was visiting.

"Okay, I'll go to pick up your visitor."

"We'll have a bite to eat when you return."

Lucy had lost interest in scanning the crowd for attractive men. Her mind kept circling back to the visitor her parents had mentioned. Whoever he was, the visit had to be important—likely something concerning Morgan Pharma, given how consumed her parents were by the company.

***

At 6:45 p.m., Armand came to take Lucy to Nice. She had changed into a more striking outfit: a colorful print skirt paired with a white crop top that left her midriff bare. Her long, light blonde hair was curled and cascaded loosely over her shoulders. Black mascara emphasized her lashes while blue eyeshadow framed her icy-blue eyes. Her lips, painted to match the red in her skirt, added the final touch. A wide-brimmed straw sun hat and open-toe wedge heels completed the look. As they made their way out of Port Hercules to where Armand had parked the Mercedes, the lingering glances from passing men confirmed she had achieved exactly the effect she wanted.

The arrivals area at Nice Côte d'Azur Airport was filled with people waiting to pick up passengers, most of them tied to the yacht show. The signs they held—bearing the names of brokers, builders, and crew—made it clear who they were expecting. Lucy, however, had chosen not to carry a sign. Her plan was simple: Once the crowd dispersed and all the other passengers had been collected, only one man would remain. That would be her pickup.

She had been waiting for less than five minutes when passengers from the Air France flight began filtering into the terminal. Expecting to meet an older gentleman, she studied the men in that age group—until her attention was drawn elsewhere.

A tall, striking man emerged from baggage claim. He wore a light blue shirt, its sleeves rolled up to just below his elbows, paired with dark blue slacks. His jacket hung casually over his left shoulder, and he pulled a rolling carry-on behind him. But what stood out most was his unruly, sun-kissed blond hair, as if it hadn't seen a brush since his last swim. Dark eyebrows and long lashes framed piercing blue eyes, and a neatly trimmed beard added to his effortless charm. Lucy guessed he was close to her age, maybe a year or two older.

He paused briefly, scanning the sea of waiting faces. Then, without hesitation, he walked straight toward her.

Lucy instinctively glanced left, then right, wondering who had caught his attention—only to realize, too late, that it was her.

When he reached her, he smiled and extended his hand. She hesitated, caught off guard.

"Hello, Lucy Lassiter. You shouldn't have come to pick me up if you have. I'm fully capable of finding my way to Monaco on my own."

Lucy didn't know what to say. She shook his hand and then haltingly said something about her parents having asked her to pick him up. She looked at his face far too long for him not to notice her curiosity.

"Come with me. The car is in the five-minute drop-off zone."

They walked to the Mercedes. Armand opened the back door, allowing Lucy to slide into the back seat. Their guest shook his hand and gave him his bag before joining her.

"I hadn't realized it before, but your name, Lucy Lassiter, has a nice ring to it."

"What do you mean?"

"Well, it's a name a poet would use for the woman the hero of his poem is in love with."

Lucy looked at her companion, wondering if he was flirting with her.

"So what do I call you?" she asked, lost for a witty reply.

"I'm sorry, I should've introduced myself when we shook hands. The surprise of seeing you waiting for me caught me off guard. My name is Oliver Corbyn, very mundane compared to yours."

Lucy looked at the man sitting next to her to determine if he was making fun of her or what his demeanor was otherwise. He was smiling at her in a very captivating way. She had never met a man who had fascinated her as much as he had in the space of just a few minutes.

"You'll have immediately guessed my name is very British. You'd be right if you had. What can you tell me about your name?"

"Not much, apart from changing it from Lucy Morgan to Lucy Lassiter after my mother married Bill."

"Why would you do that?"

"My relationship with my biological father wasn't particularly good. I discovered what I'd missed in how Bill treated me, so I decided to take Bill's name."

"Do you realize the tabloids love writing about you?" he continued.

"Yes. What's your take on that? Is that good or bad?"

"I believe it doesn't offer advantages, only disadvantages."

"I haven't thought about it in terms of advantages and disadvantages. Do you care to elaborate?"

"Sure. When practically the whole of the Western world knows who you are because of what the tabloids write about you and your escapades, you're attracting the wrong people."

"I'm not sure what you're getting at."

"May I use the example of why you've broken up with all of your boyfriends ever since you started dating?"

"Please do."

"The publicity you receive is very one-sided. It doesn't do you justice in the sense that no one gets to see your more serious nature. One of the consequences is that you become a desirable woman to men who are basically shallow and superficial. They're attracted by your wealth and popularity. Your history with men reveals you're quick to enter into a relationship with them. But the novelty of being with them wears off after some time because they can't give you what you're looking for. The type of man who can give you what you want isn't attracted to you because of what he perceives you to be, and you never get to meet him. Does that make sense to you?"

"Aren't you being unnecessarily critical of me?"

"No, I don't believe I am. You'll turn twenty-six on December tenth, and you've had a string of boyfriends since you graduated from college. As far as I know, none of them were able to make the relationship last. That in itself is an enigma because you're a very beautiful and impressive woman."

Lucy blushed and turned her head away from him. She understood his criticism, and it caused her to become agitated, but his statement that she was beautiful and impressive left her flustered. She realized she was out of her depth and, at this point, unable to be a worthy adversary in the discussion they were having.

"Who *are* you?" she asked.

"Don't change the subject just yet. Let me say I know about your continual search for the man who can give you what you're looking for. He's elusive because of the parties you frequent and the people you mingle with. Please forgive me for being so candid, but I need to be forthright and truthful when explaining why you've had to break up with all of your boyfriends, as I see it."

Lucy decided that his criticism now outweighed the compliment he'd offered.

"Who are you to be so disapproving of me?"

"Someone who has your best interests at heart."

"You're obviously obsessed with me to know about my boyfriends, the people I associate with, my age, and my date of birth."

"I have a photographic memory, Lucy, and all I did was look you up on the internet when I started to work for Jacky and Bill. That doesn't mean I don't find you interesting."

"What's that supposed to mean?"

"Precisely what I just said. Your looks and sparkling personality draw most men to you, including me."

"Are you hitting on me?"

"Heaven forbid. No, definitely not. You're out of my league. I'm just stating an obvious fact."

Lucy was confused. She realized she was more than interested in the man sitting next to her, but she was angry with him for having dissected her problem with men as accurately as he had. She felt vulnerable.

"I'm somewhat uncomfortable with you knowing as much as you do about me, while I only know your name."

"Yes, I realize that. But I mean you no harm, and I have your best interests at heart, as I said before."

"That doesn't change the way I feel. You need to tell me who you are and why you've come here to be with my parents while they're on their summer holiday."

"I can't just now. Your parents need to decide what you're allowed to know about my visit."

"You're infuriating. I'm starting to dislike you."

"It's your prerogative to like or dislike me. I was going to say I don't mind which, but for some reason, I actually do. I'd like us to be friends."

***

They had reached Parking de la Condamine on Boulevard Albert, where Armand parked the car. After identifying themselves to the security guards at the entrance to the enclosed area set aside for the show, they walked along the quay to where *Artemis* was moored. They crossed the gangway and deposited their shoes in a basket. Lucy then led their visitor to the main salon, where Jacky and Bill had made themselves comfortable.

"How was your flight, Oliver?" Bill asked as he and Jacky stood up.

"Cool, thanks. I slept most of the time during the flight from Boston to Paris. Thanks for the first-class ticket."

"We were initially planning to have you picked up in Boston and flown here in the family plane, but when Lucy wanted to join us for a week on the same day you were set to travel, I needed to give that priority. I hope you don't mind."

"Not at all. Thanks for asking Lucy to pick me up. We had an interesting conversation on the way here, although I believe she would now prefer not to have had that conversation."

"Why is that, Lucy?" Jacky asked.

"He made me feel uncomfortable. He knows practically everything about me, and when I asked him to tell me something about himself, he refused. One minute he tells me something nice about myself, and the next something that infuriates me."

Jacky and Bill smiled. They suspected that Lucy wouldn't have met someone like Oliver before.

Dorothy, the head stewardess, and two of her helpers brought them several plates of wholesome delicacies and set them out on the large coffee table they were sitting at. She asked what they wanted to drink. Lucy was quick to order a martini, while Jacky and Bill wanted the Chardonnay they had the evening before. Oliver asked for a Bud.

When the plates had been cleared away, Lucy said she wanted to change into something more comfortable while Dorothy offered to show Oliver the guest cabin she wanted him to use.

"You won't be able to use the cabin during the day," she said. "It's part of the area accessible to the guests who've been invited by the builder to inspect the yacht. If you leave the cabin before nine-thirty, I'll ensure it's cleaned and in tip-top condition at ten, when the first visitors are scheduled to arrive."

"That's fine, Dorothy. I want to swim in the Olympic pool here in Port Hercules tomorrow morning. I'll return for a shower and a change of clothes before nine."

When Oliver returned to the salon, he broached the subject he needed to discuss while Lucy was away.

"Is Lucy allowed to know why I'm here, given the socialite she is?"

"I can understand why you'd ask that question," Bill said. "But I believe that once she knows how important the matter is, she won't mention it to any of her friends."

"Is there a way of ensuring she won't?"

"There is a way," Jacky answered. "She wouldn't tell anyone something that needs to be kept secret if she were to take a meaningful role in what we're to discuss."

"I'm yet to tell you about my findings and their consequences. There is a role for her in what I want to talk to you about tomorrow."

"Who is the person you're referring to?" Lucy asked as she joined them.

Lucy had changed into blue leggings and a short, sleeveless yoga top in the same shade. Oliver couldn't help but notice how the outfit highlighted her figure, leaving little to the imagination. When Bill nodded, Oliver quickly pushed the thought aside, taking it as his cue to bring Lucy into the discussion he needed to have with them.

"Jacky and Bill agree to your presence tomorrow, Lucy, when we need to sit down to discuss something important. You'll then understand why I hesitated in telling you why I'm here."

"I'm sorry if what Oliver just said bothers you. Please understand that the matter we want to discuss tomorrow is of great importance, and if it were to be leaked to the press, even by a slip of the tongue, the value of the shares in the company would plummet."

"Okay, Bill, I had no idea something could be that important. But my presence during the discussion with our guest tomorrow won't make me feel differently toward him. As I said before, he infuriates me."

"I was just about to invite you to go for a swim with me in the Olympic pool at eight tomorrow morning, but if you feel that way, I'll go alone."

"We have a pool here on *Artemis*. You don't need to go to the Olympic pool."

"But I do. I like to keep fit, and I try to swim a minimum of two miles as often as I can...and the pool is a short walk from here."

"I've been meaning to go there myself one of these days, so yes, I'll go with you."

"Okay. It's getting late," Oliver said. "I won't keep you any longer."

They said good night, and Bill, Jacky, and Oliver retired to their cabins, leaving Lucy alone in the salon. She sat there staring at nothing in particular for a long time.

2.

OLIVER CORBYN

Oliver had been waiting on the aft deck for a few minutes when Lucy appeared from the rear sliding doors of the main salon.

"Good morning," Oliver said as they started their walk to the pool. "Did you sleep well?"

Lucy was wearing a see-through beach dress and a black bikini underneath, Oliver a T-shirt and his swimming trunks. Both were wearing flip-flops and carrying a towel.

"Not as well as I'd hoped. You're to blame."

"I apologize. I didn't mean to upset you, but when you allowed me to use the example of having to break up with your boyfriends to pinpoint one of the disadvantages of being a socialite, I had no option but to explain it as I see it."

"I accept your apology. I shouldn't have allowed you to use that example."

"But you did, and I'd like to hear your reaction to what I explained."

"Are we having a serious conversation, or are you being smug?"

"As serious as any conversation I've had."

"Well, in that case, I want to say that the men I've been

dating have all disappointed me in one way or another. You were right when you said that the reason for breaking up with them was that they weren't able to offer me what I was looking for. Your explanation that another type of man would interest me more touched a nerve. It hadn't occurred to me that he might not be interested in me because of thinking I'm the person the tabloids make me out to be."

"What would make you interested in him?"

"He would need to be sincere and truthful for a start. Most of the men I've dated weren't. He would need to be good-looking, tall, and physically strong to provide that special feeling of being safe when we're together—the feeling I would often have when in the company of Bill when I was a teenager, before he married my mom… And he must be able to take care of himself and not depend on me financially."

"Haven't you left out the most important thing?"

"No, what's that?"

"Butterflies in your stomach?"

"Not necessarily. I've found that a relationship can be satisfying without feelings of affection."

"Do you mean to tell me you've never been in love?"

Lucy was shocked he would ask this question. She suddenly realized he had led her to tell him about her past relationships with men—relationships that failed for reasons she hadn't even told her closest girlfriend about. She felt out of her depth again.

"I don't like the direction our conversation is taking," she said. "You already know too much about me. You've cleverly led me to explain why my relationships with men have failed and what a man needs to be like for me to be interested in him."

They had reached the Olympic pool, where Oliver paid the entrance fee non-Monegasques needed to pay. They walked to two unoccupied sun loungers, where Lucy took off her beach dress and Oliver his T-shirt.

"Can we finish our conversation after I swim my laps?" Oliver asked her.

"Sure."

Lucy watched as Oliver walked to the deep end of the pool. She noticed he had a swimmer's physique—broad shoulders, well-developed abdominal muscles, a thin waist, and strong legs. He dove into the water and adopted a forward crawl. He was a strong swimmer, and she wondered if he'd be able to keep up the pace he adopted on his first lap. She was amazed when he did, lap after lap.

Lucy also dove into the pool and swam up and down several times at a leisurely pace. She left the pool after fifteen minutes, dried herself, sat down on her sun lounger, and watched her companion. He kept swimming up and down for another fifteen minutes before also getting out of the pool. She was surprised to see several teenagers walk up to him with one of the lifeguards, each holding a pen and paper. He scribbled something on each piece of paper thrust at him.

"What was that all about?" Lucy asked him when he reached the lounger next to hers and had begun to dry himself.

"Nothing for you to worry about."

"That's not an answer to my question. I'll ask the lifeguard if you won't tell me," she said, getting up to talk to the lifeguard, who was about to walk by them.

"Don't, Lucy."

"Then tell me!"

"They wanted my autograph."

"Why would they want your autograph?"

"Is that important?"

"It is to me. It would give me great satisfaction to learn you're as much a celebrity as I am and to be able to accuse you of the same things you accused me of last night."

"I haven't accused you of anything. The point of what I said yesterday is that there are disadvantages associated with being as popular as you are because it draws the wrong type of people to you. Men, for example, who can't give you what you're looking for."

"But it's left me feeling bad about who I am if the type of man I'm looking for isn't interested in me because of what he thinks I am."

"I've been waiting for you to draw that conclusion," he said while wrapping the towel around his waist. "Let me explain while we're walking back to the yacht.

"I need to say, first, you shouldn't feel guilty about who you are. You have a sparkling manner about you. I used the words 'beautiful' and 'impressive' yesterday to describe who you are. You're intelligent, witty, feisty, and beautiful. You have everything anyone could want.

"But you're mingling with the wrong people. The paparazzi have a field day every time they take your photograph when you're partying, and while you might not be into drugs or excessive drinking like many of your so-called friends, you're nevertheless associated with them. I'd be happy if the only thing you remember about our conversation is that you're mingling with the wrong people."

"I now get the distinct feeling you care about me."

"I do. Of course I do. Believe me, I have your best interests at heart, as I told you several times already, and I'd like us to become friends."

Lucy didn't know how to reply to his last statement. They continued their walk back to the yacht, side by side, very conscious of each other.

***

Lucy and Oliver went to their cabins to shower and dress. When Oliver met Dorothy in the corridor as he was leaving his cabin, she told him that Jacky and Bill were on the sun deck having breakfast and that he and Lucy were expected to have breakfast there as well.

Oliver wished Jacky and Bill good morning. One of the stewardesses asked him what he wanted for breakfast. He asked for bacon and eggs, toast, and strong coffee.

"How was your swim?" Bill asked him.

"Good... I hadn't realized the water in the pool is filtered seawater and that it's heated to more than eighty degrees."

"Did Lucy go with you?" Jacky asked him.

"She did."

"We were discussing whether she would or wouldn't before going to sleep because she's a slow starter in the morning, usually because she goes to bed rather late."

"Don't tell him anything about me, Mother," Lucy said as she joined them. "He already knows too much."

Oliver helped her to her seat.

"It's been a long time since a man stood up to help me sit down," Lucy said, looking at him.

"There are still men everywhere who would do that, Lucy. Do I need to say more?"

Lucy was quiet, realizing what Oliver meant. She ordered scrambled eggs, toast, and coffee. They discussed the weather, where Jacky and Bill wanted to take the yacht for their vacation, and the pros and cons of having the yacht in Port Hercules during the show. Oliver asked for a second coffee while he waited for Lucy to finish her breakfast.

"Can we go somewhere else for our discussion, Bill? We can be easily overheard from any of the apartment buildings overlooking the port using a long-range listening device."

"Unfortunately, most interior spaces of the yacht are accessible to visitors, the exception being our private quarters. My private office might just be large enough. We'll have to find two extra chairs."

Extra chairs were quickly found, and when Bill's office had been turned into a little meeting room, they sat down. Because of the space constraint, Bill sat behind his desk, and Jacky, Oliver, and Lucy in a row, close together, across from him. Dorothy brought them a pot of coffee, cups, and a tray with pastries, which she placed on Bill's desk before leaving, closing the door behind her.

Bill, Jacky, and Lucy looked at Oliver as if to prompt him to start explaining why he had come to visit them.

"Do you remember reading or hearing about the computer hack on Friday, July second?" Oliver asked Lucy.

"I do."

"More than a thousand computers were hacked. All of those computers were equipped with software supplied by Kaseya Corporation in Miami. That software allows IT specialists to maintain computers from a distance using the internet. The point is that, like so many companies, Morgan Pharma has adopted the software to allow specialists to maintain the servers in your offices and labs around the world.

"The software, however, contained a flaw allowing hackers to embed a piece of code into an executable module after gaining access. It caused those computers to lock up. That was the case with every one of the Morgan Pharma servers except for one. The server at the Boston laboratory didn't. The software that was embedded instructed it to upload the files in the document folder to another computer elsewhere.

"When the staff at the Boston lab discovered the upload, they informed Bill about the anomaly, and Bill contacted the director of the CIA. I believe you know the director, Bill?"

"That's correct. I'd met him at a fundraiser."

"Okay, now that Lucy knows as much as you both do, I'll tell you what I've found out.

"I discovered that the instructions the hackers had embedded on the Boston computer weren't different from the software that was embedded on other computers.

"On studying the code, I found it was looking for documents containing the word *Alzheimer*. Since the Boston lab is almost entirely dedicated to research on Alzheimer's disease, the frequency of that word appearing in the document folder on that server prompted the command to upload its contents rather than the command to lock it up. The conclusion that the hack was intended to obtain the files related to Alzheimer's disease is inescapable. The hackers' subsequent demand for seventy million dollars to unlock the affected computers was a secondary reason for the hack."

"Why haven't those facts been discovered by others as well?" Bill asked.

"Because the part of the code related to Alzheimer's disease was brilliantly encrypted. I suspect none of the IT specialists investigating the hack took the time to minutely study the code. After all, it was presumably obvious to everyone that the hack was intended to install ransomware on those computers.

"Any other questions so far?"

"I'm good," Bill said, while Lucy and Jacky shook their heads.

"Let me now refresh your memory of what the lab in Boston has achieved. The research carried out over the last five years was aimed at developing medication preventing the abnormal buildup of proteins in and around brain cells. One of the proteins involved is called amyloid, deposits of which form plaques around brain cells. The other protein is called tau, deposits of which form tangles within brain cells. It's fair to say that the scientific staff at the Boston lab will soon finish developing medication that will prevent the buildup of amyloid and tau deposits. Since Morgan Pharma is far ahead of other pharmaceutical companies in developing this cure, it will eventually earn the company billions of dollars and, more importantly, offer millions of people around the world a future devoid of Alzheimer's disease.

"On studying the files and documents that were uploaded from the server in Boston, Will Bryce, the chief pharmaceutical scientist, and I concluded that even a mediocre pharmaceutical company would be able to produce the medicine if they studied those files and obtained assistance in taking the last steps. If they were to be first to provide the cure, that would lead to their supremacy in the fight against Alzheimer's, earning them an unimaginable sum of money and boosting their standing in the pharmaceutical community."

Oliver paused to pour himself another cup of coffee.

"Do we know who's responsible?" Jacky asked.

"The hack itself was carried out by a notorious group of hackers that call themselves REvil. It's an acronym that stands for Ransomware Evil. They are based in Russia. But because of the nature of this particular hack, I believe a pharmaceutical company in Russia is ultimately responsible. They will have negotiated a deal with REvil to do what they did."

"Wouldn't the patents we have on the process we use to make the medication keep other companies from copying it?" Bill asked.

"I took the liberty of contacting your patent attorney about that. Since the European Union, Japan, and the United States introduced sanctions against Russia after it annexed Crimea in 2014, patents that Morgan Pharma hold in Russia are virtually of no value."

Oliver took a swallow of his coffee and looked at Lucy, who had been quiet during his report. She returned his look but said nothing.

"So what can we do to stop this?" Bill continued.

"I've given that considerable thought. There's a conference on Alzheimer's disease in Moscow in November of this year. I want to present a paper there on what the Boston lab has achieved without giving away key information. I'll author the paper with Will Bryce. While there, I'll behave in a way that suggests I want to leave Morgan Pharma to work in Russia in exchange for a greater remuneration.

"I would like Lucy to accompany me and for us to pretend we're in a relationship, that I love her and her lifestyle, which requires more money than I earn at present. I suspect that the company ultimately behind the hack will contact me at the conference and propose I work for them.

"As I just said, they need assistance in taking the last steps from someone with knowledge of what the Boston lab has developed. I'll infiltrate their lab and sabotage whatever it is they're doing."

"Isn't that dangerous?" Jacky asked him.

"It can be if they find out what I intend to do. The other element of danger is associated with my escape afterward."

"I don't know what to say, Oliver," Bill said. "Why would you want to do this for us?"

"I have my reasons, Bill. Let's not discuss that now."

"Explain to me more specifically why I should accompany you to Moscow," Lucy demanded.

"To help me convince the Russians I'm willing to defect in exchange for a higher salary, which I need to stay on equal footing with you. We'll need to pretend I'm in love with you."

It remained quiet in the office after Oliver had outlined what he wanted to do.

"I think we need to talk this through, just the three of us, Oliver. Do you mind stepping outside while we do? Make yourself comfortable on the sundeck. Lucy or I will see you there when we're ready to resume the meeting."

"Sure," Oliver replied, standing up to leave.

***

"I insist that you now tell me who he is," Lucy said, addressing her stepfather after Oliver had left. "What he's proposed isn't something an employee would do for his employer. How long has he worked for you?"

"He doesn't actually work for us, Lucy. He contacted me the day after I spoke to the director of the CIA. He said he wanted to meet me in Boston the following day. Jacky and I spoke to him at length at the lab. He told us he wanted to investigate the hack and its consequences. He said he'd graduated from Harvard with degrees in computer science and medicine and that he'd specialized in the causes of and possible cure for Alzheimer's disease while completing his PhD.

"Jacky and I felt good about what he told us. When I offered to pay him for his services, he declined without saying why. He started his investigation the day after. We hadn't spoken with him until a few days ago, when he said he wanted to report to us in person on what he'd found."

"Isn't all that odd?" Lucy asked.

"It wasn't at the time," Jacky replied. "We hit it off with him. We were pleased to have found a competent person to investigate the upload. The fact he's uncovered the real purpose behind the hack proves he's very capable."

"I Googled him late yesterday to see what I could find. But there's nothing on a person named Oliver Corbyn who looks like him. Yet, this morning at the pool, a group of teenagers and a lifeguard asked him for his autograph. I asked him about it, but he avoided the question. I suspect he's not who he says he is. I wouldn't be surprised to find he's an imposter with an agenda that differs entirely from what he's told us. If that's the case, I'll make life very difficult for him."

"I think we should give him the benefit of the doubt," Bill countered. "He's as concerned as we are about the information on the Alzheimer's cure ending up in the wrong hands. We have no other option but to let him do what he's proposed. I believe he's been honest with us."

"I trust him," Jacky added, "but I would feel a lot better

about what he wants to do if you were not to accompany him."

"I'm worried, too, but I'll go with him to observe his every move."

"Thanks, Lucy," Bill said. "I'll tell him we're ready to resume the meeting."

"No, let me, Bill," she replied.

***

Oliver stood when Lucy walked up to him. He had been watching the show come alive as hundreds of visitors poured into the port.

"Sit down, Oliver. I need to talk to you before we return to the meeting. Bill and my mother trust you, and we've decided to let you embark on your plan. I will accompany you to Moscow and take up the role you want me to. Although I now know a little more about you, I find it difficult to accept you would do what you've described after just a single meeting with my parents in Boston without wanting payment of some kind. I believe you're an imposter with an agenda that differs entirely from what you've told us. It would need to be connected to the Alzheimer's cure in some way since that would make you rich if you were to be involved in producing and selling it. If my suspicions are correct, I'll become your enemy. We're a powerful family, and I will be relentless in making you pay if you hurt us in any way."

"I'm sorry you feel that way. I'd hoped to be able to gain your trust as well. Have the conversations we had yesterday and this morning adversely affected your feelings about me?"

"On the contrary; they eventually made me feel good about you. But now I know you don't actually work for my parents, at least not in the normal sense of the word. I don't understand why you'd want to risk your life to carry out your plan. I can't get my head around that. I can't see the incentive for you to do what you've described."

"There are many reasons why we might want to do something for others without being rewarded in terms of money."

"You might say that, but in my circle of acquaintances and friends, that's rarely the case."

"That tells me that the people you associate with are self-centered and not considerate of others."

"I'll grant you that, but why surround yourself with an air of mystery—as if you're hiding something?"

"I'm not sure what you mean."

"Okay, why won't you tell me why those kids and the lifeguard at the pool wanted your autograph? Why haven't you told my parents who you work for and what your motive is for investigating the nature of the computer hack? And what's in it for you when you say you're willing to go undercover to infiltrate the organization ultimately responsible to sabotage their plans?"

Oliver looked at Lucy for a long time. She thought she saw a worried look on his face when she returned his gaze.

"There's nothing I'd like more than to be able to answer those questions, but I can't because of the consequences."

"What consequences?"

"I can't say."

Lucy sighed. She had become increasingly frustrated with their conversation, and Oliver knew he needed to say something that would provide a satisfactory answer to her questions. He leaned forward to take her hands in his.

"You must trust me. I'd never do anything that would hurt you, Bill, or your mom. Let me just say I work for the CIA and I was assigned to help you and your parents deal with the computer hack. People in high places want to see Morgan Pharma produce the cure as soon as possible. The reason for choosing me is that I'm well acquainted with the research that has gone into its development. Can you live with that explanation for now and not tell anyone what I've just said?"

The look on his face when he took her hands and said what he had made her believe him.

"Okay...so if Bill were to call the director of the CIA, he would tell him you were assigned to assist us in retrieving the stolen information."

"That's somewhat unusual, but in this case, he might just do that."

"I believe and trust you. Please don't abuse that trust."

"I won't."

"Would you mind if I told my mom and Bill who you work for?"

"Do you think that's necessary?"

"They trust you as things stand, but I'm certain they'd feel more at ease with the situation if they knew what I now know."

Oliver nodded. He would have preferred not to have needed to tell Lucy he worked for the CIA. He was still unsure about her ability to keep what she knew secret, considering her social status. On the other hand, she had revealed a side of herself that belied the picture the tabloids painted of her. That, and the companionship he felt during their visit to the pool, had put his mind at ease to a certain extent. That, more than anything, had made him decide to tell her who he worked for. Knowing that Bill and Jacky would be informed was less troubling.

***

"You were gone a long time. Would you care to tell us what you talked about?" Bill asked.

"I wanted more assurance that what Oliver wants to do

isn't a cover for a devious scheme he's implementing. I'm satisfied he's been truthful with us, and I wholeheartedly support him in what he wants to do. He told me he works for the CIA and that his present assignment is to help us deal with the computer hack."

"I thought as much, Oliver. I couldn't help but think you were asked or ordered to investigate the hack because of my conversation with your director," Bill said.

"I'm glad you now trust him as we do, Lucy," Jacky added.

"Thanks, all of you," Oliver said. "Please keep the information about my employer to yourselves. Now, if you don't mind, I have to return to Boston to start working on the paper I want to present at the conference. It needs to be submitted to the conference committee a week from today."

"Why can't you work on the paper here for a while?" Lucy asked him.

"Because I need to confer with Will Bryce on several topics the paper is to address...and because you would distract me too much."

Jacky and Bill noticed Lucy's disappointment to hear that Oliver needed to leave.

"Have you booked your return flight?" Bill asked.

"Not yet. I was planning to do that at the airport."

"Our plane is sitting at the airport until Lucy wants to return to New York. The crew is in a local hotel. I can get them to fly you to Boston if you like. That will save time."

"That's an appealing offer I can't refuse."

"Let me call the captain to arrange the flight."

When the flight had been arranged, Oliver packed his bag and walked with Bill, Jacky, and Lucy to the aft deck, where Armand was waiting.

"You and I need to communicate about travel arrangements for the trip to Moscow, Lucy. Give me your phone number."

"Hand me your cell, and I'll input the two numbers at

which you can reach me."

Oliver handed his cell phone to Lucy, and she handed hers to him. Oliver then said goodbye, and as he did, Lucy kissed him on the cheek.

3.

MITCH BANNISTER

Armand drove Oliver to the General Aviation Terminal at Nice Côte d'Azur Airport—the terminal frequented by people traveling by private jet. Oliver stepped out of the car, retrieved his bag from the trunk, thanked Armand, and entered the terminal. A man in a captain's uniform walked toward him. Oliver judged him to be about fifty-five. He had dark hair and dark, piercing eyes, was clean-shaven, and looked physically fit. His hair had turned gray at the temples.

"You must be Oliver Corbyn. I recognized the car and its driver. My name is Mitch Bannister. Bill asked me to fly you to Boston."

"Hi, Mitch. I'm not imposing, am I?"

Their handshake was firm.

"On the contrary; we prefer to be in the air rather than in a hotel."

"But you're on the French Riviera, one of the most beautiful and intriguing locations in the world."

"I know, but we've seen it all. Jacky and Bill come here at least once a year to stay two or three weeks, and we've visited all the places people go to. We've been there, seen that, and done that, as they say."

They had, meanwhile, walked to passport control and security. There was no holdup of any importance, and they continued their walk to the Lassiter jet parked nearby. Mitch introduced Oliver to his copilot, Dave Cassidy, who was waiting near the baggage compartment to stow any baggage Oliver might have. Oliver judged him to be about thirty. A tall, handsome man with brown eyes and short, dark hair.

Oliver was introduced to Annette, the flight attendant, when he entered the passenger cabin. She was particularly pretty but in a different way to Lucy's beauty, Oliver thought. He judged her to be in her early twenties. She had tied her long red hair in a ponytail and applied heavy mascara and dark-red lipstick. She was cheerful, laughing and giggling at the slightest thing. Oliver immediately took a liking to her.

"I need to talk to you about something, Mitch. Can you leave the cockpit for a while later?"

"Sure."

Oliver settled into one of the comfortable seats. On reaching their allotted altitude, he asked Annette for coffee and a glass of water. He asked her to sit in the seat opposite him when she brought him those. His request startled her.

"It's okay, Annette. I just want to talk to you."

"Sure," she said with a smile.

"How long have you been employed by the Lassiter family?"

"Nearly five years. I came on board with Dave when they purchased this plane."

"Do you like your work?"

"I do. We travel the world and meet interesting people."

"I suppose you fly Bill Lassiter more often than his wife or his daughter?"

"No, we fly Miss Lassiter much more often."

"Is that because she's responsible for PR and marketing?"

"Yes, she regularly travels to each of the Morgan Pharma offices."

"Has she ever been on board with her friends to fly to parties?"

"I don't know if I should answer that question, Mr. Corbyn. We were told never to talk about the family."

"I'm sorry, Annette. I don't mean to pry. I've just spent a day with them on board their yacht. Miss Lassiter is to accompany me to Russia later in the year, and I wondered if she is really the person the tabloids have made her out to be."

Annette smiled. "Your interest in her tells me you have feelings for her. I don't blame you. She's beautiful, intelligent, and wealthy. I suspect you don't like it when she goes to parties and sometimes misbehaves, as we've heard she does."

"I don't know whether I have feelings for her or not. I just think she's throwing away part of her life when she does what some people write about her."

"We've never seen evidence of the party life she is said to lead. She has never used this plane for parties or to go to parties."

"Thanks, Annette. That's what I wanted to know."

"We'll be arriving in Boston at around five in the afternoon local time. Shall I prepare sandwiches for lunch?"

"That would be nice. Thanks."

Oliver settled down for the flight. His thoughts focused on everything he had discussed with Lucy. He smiled to himself when he decided that, if she were interested in him, she might not want to continue living a party life. Oliver decided to follow the society columns during the coming weeks to find out.

***

Mitch joined Oliver two hours into the flight. He sat down in the seat opposite him.

"You said you wanted to talk?"

"Yes, I do. I want to ask you a few things about the Lassiter family and about needing your help with something. Please tell me if you feel I'm too inquisitive."

"I will."

"How long have you worked for the family?"

"Eighteen years. I started when Alfred Morgan purchased his first plane. I stayed on after his death."

"What did you do before that?"

"I was employed by the CIA for sixteen years."

"May I ask why you left the CIA?"

"Of course... Monetary reasons, primarily. Alfred paid me considerably more than the going rate, a practice Bill has continued."

"What did you do for the CIA?"

"I flew operatives to secret destinations and picked them up later. I've probably landed and taken off from the most obscure landing strips around."

"That's right up my alley. I'll explain why if you promise to keep to yourself what I'm about to say."

"I think I already know."

"That's not possible."

"I believe you're involved with the CIA in investigating the upload of information about Alzheimer's disease from the central computer in the Boston lab during the worldwide computer hack earlier this year."

"Who told you?"

"I put two and two together."

"Explain."

"It's simple. I flew Jacky and Bill to Dulles after the hack. Bill had scheduled an appointment with the director of the CIA. He told me he wanted to discuss the upload with him. I arranged ground transportation to and from Langley. We flew them to Boston a day later for a meeting with someone. I later found out you were that person. That meeting, almost directly after Bill's visit to the CIA, led me to believe you were assigned the task of solving the upload problem."

"That's brilliant. I was indeed tasked with identifying

the responsible party and ensuring the stolen information is retrieved or otherwise destroyed. Bill, Jacky, and Lucy now know as well. I would have preferred not to have to tell them, but Lucy believed I was involved in a sinister plot involving the Alzheimer's cure. She couldn't accept that someone would be willing to help them without wanting a reward of some kind, so there was no other recourse than to tell them who I work for."

"She's an astute lady."

"You must know the family better than anyone."

"I suppose I do."

"Tell me something about the history of the company."

"Alfred Morgan's father founded the company, selling elixirs, aspirin, and painkillers. He recognized the importance of insulin and penicillin when they were discovered, and he decided to mass-produce them. The company quickly expanded, and when he died, Alfred worked tirelessly to build Morgan Pharma into what it is today—probably the largest pharmaceutical company in the world.

"After the car crash that caused Alfred's untimely death, Jacky had to ask Bill for help with company matters that couldn't be addressed by her lawyers. She appointed him chairman of the board. They became close, and they married two years later.

"Bill, in effect, now heads the company, with Jacky assisting him. They take all major decisions together. Lucy has been involved with the company ever since she graduated from college. She likes to travel, and as a result, she's taken responsibility for the PR and marketing department."

"Has her socialite background influenced her work in any way?"

"No, she keeps her private life private. I know that for a fact because I fly her to wherever she wants to go. The only gray area in that respect is her attendance at parties in LA when she visits Bill and her mom. They live in Beverly Hills. I find it difficult to judge if her main reason for flying to LA is to visit Jacky and Bill or to attend parties when she's there."

"Thanks for telling me. Lucy is to accompany me to Moscow to attend a conference on Alzheimer's later this year. I want to present a paper about the medicine. While I'm there, I'll spread the word that I'm willing to work in Russia for a higher salary than I can earn in the US. Lucy and I will pretend to be in a relationship for which I need a greater income so as not to be dependent on her financially.

"The Russian pharmaceutical company responsible for the computer hack will need someone like me to help them interpret the data they stole. Since I helped to develop the cure when I was working on my PhD, I hope to be approached by them about working in their lab, which would allow me to sabotage whatever they're doing. I'll need to escape from Russia afterward. That's what I wanted to talk to you about."

"I'm one step ahead of you, Oliver. I think you'll want me to pick you up after the sabotage because the Russian Federal Security Service, the FSB, will be looking for you. You won't be able to leave the country using regular transportation."

"That's correct. If the pharmaceutical company is based in or around Moscow, I would travel to somewhere near the border with Belarus, where I was hoping you could collect me in a touch-and-go operation."

"Leave that to me. I'll research the possibilities."

"That's great. It's still early days, so there's more than enough time to finalize the arrangements."

"You're not putting Lucy in danger, are you?"

"I wouldn't dream of it."

"I'm very fond of Lucy, Oliver. She's a wonderful woman. I've flown her everywhere since she was seven. She confided in me on many occasions, especially when her father was still alive. He never spent time with her, and he often stopped her from doing things she wanted to. That changed when Jacky started seeing Bill. Lucy always referred to Bill as her big 'Teddy Bear' because, as you know, he's built like a wrestler. Did you know he used to be a weightlifter when he was in college?"

"No, I didn't, but his physique tells me he visits the gym regularly. He's certainly impressive."

"That's correct. And you'll have noticed that Lucy inherited her regular features—her beauty—from her mother?"

"Yes, I've noticed the strong resemblance."

"I need to return to the cockpit. Is there anything else you want to talk about?"

"No, not now, thanks."

Mitch returned to the cockpit while Oliver started making notes on his laptop about the paper he wanted to present in Moscow.

4.

EN ROUTE TO MOSCOW

Back in Boston, Oliver worked on the paper with Will Bryce. They decided to disclose that Morgan Pharma had made significant progress in developing a medication capable of preventing the buildup of beta-amyloid—linked to the plaques in the brain—and tau, the protein responsible for the collapse of the brain's cell transport system. However, they carefully avoided revealing the exact nature of the cure, instead focusing on how the medication worked to prevent these harmful accumulations.

Three weeks after submitting the paper, Oliver received word that it had been accepted. Not only that, but he was invited to present it as a keynote address at the opening of the session dedicated to new drug developments. With the details finalized, he could now plan his trip to Moscow—with Lucy. The opportunity gave him the perfect excuse to call her, something he found himself looking forward to.

"Hi, Lucy, it's Oliver. I just got word that our paper has been accepted for the conference I mentioned. That means we can start planning the trip—if you're still up for accompanying me to Moscow."

"I'm actually looking forward to it."

"That's great. We'll need to be at the Ritz-Carlton, where the conference is being held, by around three in the afternoon on November seventh, local time. I'd like us to make an entrance at the cocktail party, which starts at five. The conference itself runs for three days, and I'm scheduled to present our paper on the morning of the second day."

"Leave the logistics to me. I'll have our travel department take care of everything. I was also thinking of having one of our security officers from the Saint Petersburg office meet us when we arrive."

"That sounds like a cool plan."

"Just make sure you apply for a visa if you haven't already. I'll call you once everything is arranged."

"Thanks, Lucy. Talk soon."

***

The next day, Lucy called Oliver.

"Hi, Oliver. Everything's set. Mitch will fly us to Moscow. To arrive at the hotel by three in the afternoon on Sunday, November seventh, we'll need to leave Boston at eight in the evening on the sixth. I'll board at Teterboro, and we'll pick you up at the Boston Logan Private Jet Terminal around seven-thirty. I've booked the hotel for four nights."

"That sounds perfect."

"Also, the CEO of our Saint Petersburg office has arranged for a security officer and a chauffeured car for our entire stay. They'll be waiting for us at Domodedovo Airport when we land."

"You're a wizard, Lucy. Thanks a lot. I'll see you at Logan the week after next."

***

When Oliver arrived at Boston Logan Terminal V on the evening of November 6, he found Mitch Bannister waiting for him. Mitch stood up from the table he'd been sitting at, drinking a coffee, when he saw Oliver approach.

"We arrived a little early, Oliver, so I thought I'd wait for you here. I did some research on the best place to pick you up in Russia or Belarus. If it's something you still want me to do, I'll leave Dave in charge of the plane for a while to tell you what I've found out."

"That's great. I appreciate the time and effort you've put into this."

Oliver handed his suitcase to Dave, who stowed it in the baggage compartment. He then climbed the stairs and boarded the plane, carrying his backpack.

"Hi, Lucy," Oliver said as he entered the cabin and saw her seated in one of the comfortable seats offering a view of the cabin door.

"Hello, Oliver."

She stood up and extended her hand for him to shake.

Lucy had spent countless sleepless nights thinking about Oliver after he left Monaco. He intrigued her in a way none of her past boyfriends ever had. During those intense hours they had spent together, she had come to realize she had feelings for him—but it seemed clear he hadn't felt the same. She convinced herself that he might not be interested in her, perhaps because he believed the tabloid stories about her. That realization stung, and after it sank in, she lost interest in the usual weekend outings with her friends.

Determined to protect herself from rejection, Lucy resolved to keep her distance when she saw him again. She would act indifferent, detached—anything to hide what she truly felt. That was why she now offered him her hand when, deep down, all she really wanted was to pull him into a hug after six long weeks apart.

"Thanks again for organizing the travel arrangements and the hotel," he said.

"You're welcome."

"Shall I sit facing you, or on the other side of the aisle?"

"Whatever you wish."

"I'll sit facing you. That will make it easier for us to talk."

Annette came to say hello and to hand each of them a glass of champagne. She shared a look of understanding with Oliver.

"Would you like to eat something before going to sleep?"

"I'm fine, Annette," Lucy said. "I'll let you know when we want to turn in."

"I wouldn't mind a coffee and a glass of water after take-off," Oliver added.

They were in the air not much later. Nothing was said as they watched the lights of Boston recede as they gained height.

"You weren't featured in any of the society columns these last weeks," Oliver said suddenly. "Are you aware of that?"

Lucy was taken unawares by the question, and for a moment, she was unsure how to respond. She had decided before she wouldn't tell him about her resolve to no longer go to parties.

"I've been rather busy," she answered.

"What is a typical week for you?"

"When I'm in New York, I go to the gym with a small group of girlfriends every second morning. I spend every afternoon of those days, and the days in between, at the office. I'm ultimately responsible for much of the overall marketing and PR we as a pharmaceutical company need to do. I manage small teams in both New York and Los Angeles. It causes me to travel a lot. I try to keep my weekends free to relax and do other things."

"So, what have you been doing these last five weekends?"

"Why do you want to know?" she asked boldly.

"Just curious."

"I've decided not to tell you more about myself until you've told me what I want to know about you. If you choose not to, then tell me in more detail what our relationship needs to portray when we're in Moscow."

Oliver smiled. She suddenly realized he had already concluded she no longer wanted to see her socialite friends. She was angry with herself for being so transparent. *Or is he just sharp-witted?* she asked herself.

"You smiled at me like that when I picked you up at Nice Airport. Why would you now?" she asked him, taking another swallow of her champagne.

"I'm sorry. I didn't mean my smile to indicate anything but pleasure at presumably having established why you don't want to tell me what you've been doing these last few weekends."

"If you remain smug while I'm trying to turn this trip into a pleasurable outing, I'll order Mitch to turn the plane around."

"Dearest Lucy, I'm not being smug at all. I like interacting with you the way we are. It fascinates me—and you interest me. I think I told you that six weeks ago."

Lucy's annoyance gave way to confusion. Questions flooded her mind. He had called her *dearest Lucy* and admitted she interested him. He had said something similar once before. What did he really mean?

Her thoughts swirled in turmoil, leaving her momentarily speechless. She studied him intently, searching for clues in his expression as she struggled to find the right response.

"Okay, I believe you, but you need to explain to me in plain language why you like interacting with me in riddles half of the time…and why I interest you."

"I'm not aware of talking to you in riddles, but my interest in you comes from the open-hearted person you are. I haven't met anyone like you before. I suspect we share the same interests and worldview, although most people find me to be somewhat withdrawn and introverted."

"That's the first time you told me something about yourself not related to the computer hack. I don't find you to be withdrawn or introverted at all, by the way. Is your interest in me platonic or otherwise?"

"That's a really personal question, and one you shouldn't ask a guy who's only known you, all told, for what, less than ten hours?"

"I'm sorry, but I'm confused. One minute you say things one of my previous boyfriends would say, while the next minute you sound very distant and aloof, as if I'm trivial or insignificant."

"You have me baffled. I'm at a loss for words. But let me just say you're by no means trivial or insignificant to me. I can't think of anything I said that would make you believe that."

"It's not something you've said, but a feeling I get when you criticize me for being a popular and sociable person. As I said before, it caused me to feel bad about who I am—trivial and insignificant somehow."

"Yes, I can see why you might have thought that," he said, smiling.

His smile caused her to become angry with herself again. She knew she had to change the subject before she made a fool of herself.

"Tell me what our relationship needs to portray when we're in Moscow," she said again.

Oliver searched her face for a sign indicating her state of mind. She turned and looked the other way, feeling all too vulnerable.

"Sure, but please don't feel bad about our carefree banter

just now. It's one of the pleasures life offers when talking to someone like you."

Lucy's confusion peaked. He was again speaking in riddles, and, not knowing what he implied, she felt the urge to question him, but decided not to.

"Right, Moscow," he said, becoming serious. "As I indicated when talking to you, Jacky, and Bill six weeks ago, I need to be convincing when I tell people at the conference that I want to leave Morgan Pharma for a higher salary to be able to maintain my relationship with you. Your presence will cause them to believe me, particularly when they notice how much I love you. You, on the other hand, need to portray the person the tabloids have made you out to be.

"You're not in love with me, and your reason for being with me is nothing more than you like having male company to make you feel wanted. You should show off your extravagance by wearing the most expensive clothes you have with you, or by going shopping and showing me something expensive you've bought while I'm in the presence of others. I'll pretend to be annoyed because I can't keep up with your lifestyle."

"That's how I understood it when you briefly explained it in Monaco. So, I've booked two suites in the hotel. They're next to each other on the eleventh floor. That will help convince those who need to know that you're enjoying life literally at my expense. When I had the suites booked, I was wondering whether I should've booked just the one—to be more convincing we're in a relationship."

"That would indeed be more convincing. But, hey, we'll ask the hotel staff to open the communicating door between the suites. That should convince the Russians we're in a relationship in the same way knowledge of us sharing a single suite would. But if by chance you're questioned about why we aren't, you could explain that you wouldn't think of sharing a bed with someone. I believe you would probably have said that to some or all of your boyfriends because of not being in love with them?"

"I can't believe you're asking me that. I don't want to talk to you about my boyfriends. You're critical of them, so why should I tell you what I did or didn't do when I was dating them? Tell me something about your girlfriends for a change."

"Don't get angry. I only wanted to offer an explanation you could use if the Russians were to doubt we're in a relationship because of having booked two suites."

"I understand, but why ask me that very personal question?"

"I'm sorry. It wasn't my intention to pry into your private life. It was impertinent of me and it won't happen again."

"Apology accepted. I hope one day to be able to convince you that you know very little about me and that your conclusion about who I am is totally incorrect. Now, if you don't mind, I want to try to get some sleep."

Lucy no longer wanted to talk to him. Without a word, she stood up and walked to the front of the cabin, cold-shouldering him as she asked Annette to prepare the beds for the night. Retrieving a pair of loose-fitting leggings, a pajama top, and her toiletry kit from her overnight bag, she made her way to the bathroom.

When she slipped under the blankets, she turned onto her side, facing the plane's fuselage—anything to avoid the temptation of watching Oliver get ready for bed. She tried to sort through her thoughts, but the more she did, the more tangled they became. She wasn't just frustrated with him—she was annoyed with herself. Somehow, yet again, their conversation had left him knowing more about her, while he remained an enigma.

She replayed his words in her mind. He had said he suspected they shared the same interests and worldview. That had surprised her. She had assumed they were completely different. Then again, what did she really know about him? Not even whether he had a girlfriend.

Sleep eventually came, but it was restless.

***

Oliver, too, replayed their conversation, analyzing every word. He hadn't expected her to be drawn to him—not like this. He knew he was nothing like the men she had been attracted to in the past.

But the truth was, he had grown more than just fond of her. And that was a problem. He frowned, knowing he couldn't allow them to get too close. In hindsight, asking her to accompany him to Moscow might have been a mistake—even if her presence made his cover story more convincing and reduced the chances of those behind the hack seeing through it.

***

When he finally noticed that Lucy had fallen asleep—after more than half an hour of tossing and turning—Oliver got up, walked to the cockpit, and tapped Mitch on the shoulder.

"Shall we have that talk now, Mitch?"

Mitch followed Oliver to the rear of the cabin, where they sat down opposite each other.

"I've studied possible landing sites for a jet aircraft southwest of Moscow. I believe I've found the perfect place. It's Orsha Airport, formerly known as Balbasova Air Base, seven miles south-southwest of the city of Orsha in Belarus. The shortest route to the airfield is by way of the M1, which leads all the way from Moscow, through Smolensk, to the border. The road is then signposted as European Route E30.

"Thirty miles after crossing the border, the E30 passes

nine miles north of the runway. The road that intersects the E30 at that point is the P15. You need to head south along the P15 until it turns to head east. The road intersects another road there, enabling you to head farther south until you reach the runway.

"The airport is used by the occasional commercial flight. It doesn't have immigration and customs facilities. International travelers who wish to visit Orsha fly to Minsk and take the train from there. The airbase was previously home to the 402nd Heavy Bomber Aviation Regiment, flying Tupolev Tu-22M3 aircraft—the so-called Backfire. The regiment was disbanded in 1993. The airport has only three stands for commercial aircraft and thirty large revetments built for those bombers.

"The single runway is approximately ten thousand feet long. I could land there when the authorities least expect it, when it's dark, taxi to the end of the runway, pick you up, and take off before they know what's happening. If I were to fly from Helsinki to Damascus, I'd pass over Orsha while flying a great circle route. A hundred or so miles out from Orsha, I'd turn off my transponder, reduce my altitude to a minimum, douse the lights, land, and take off again to fly at low altitude for another hundred miles before climbing to my allotted altitude and switching the transponder on once more."

"You've really put your teeth into this, Mitch. I appreciate that."

"Yes, but there's a problem. I can't use this plane for that purpose. It's too well-known, and I don't want Morgan Pharma to be in trouble if I get caught or identified as having landed in Orsha without permission. I need Bill's approval to charter another plane—preferably a Gulfstream G650, which can fly faster than any other private jet. I'm prepared to contact Bill about that if you're serious about leaving Russia in this way."

"Yes, it sounds like the perfect escape. I'll make my way to the Belarusian border by car, cross it on foot, and walk or jog to the pickup point. Bill, Jacky, and Lucy are aware of my plan, and they agree it needs to be done. I believe they'll allow you to do whatever is necessary to make my escape possible. How much time do you need to charter the plane and be ready at Helsinki Airport?"

"It's difficult to say. It depends on the availability of a G650. I'll contact Bill on arrival in Moscow for permission to take the relevant steps."

"I'll call you on your cell phone to let you know when I can be at the designated location. At which end of the runway do you want me to wait for you? I need to know now because there won't be much of an opportunity to talk about such details once we're in Moscow."

"At the northeast end of the runway, away from the hangars and buildings at the other end."

Oliver thanked Mitch again, and they swapped cell phone numbers before Mitch returned to the cockpit.

***

Annette woke them up at 5 a.m. Eastern Standard Time. Oliver turned on his side to look at Lucy.

"Good morning. How did you sleep?"

"Not as well as I'd hoped," she replied. "And you?"

"Fine, thanks. I noticed you tossing and turning in your bed some of the time. Are you aware you do that?"

"Not consciously, but it must be during nights I don't sleep well."

"Is it because something is troubling you?"

"Yes..."

"Do you want to tell me about it? It might help if you did."

"In what way?"

"By simply sharing the problems causing you to worry

and not sleep well. I might be able to help you solve them."

"Thanks for the offer, but I can't. They're too personal. You might want to give me a bit of space this morning because it takes a while for the lethargy to disappear."

"Sure, but please tell me what worries you when you're ready."

Oliver stood, took one of Lucy's hands in his, and bent down to press a gentle kiss to her forehead. Then, without a word, he grabbed his backpack and walked to the bathroom.

Lucy stared after him, stunned. *He kissed me!* A voice in her head shouted the words, echoing through her thoughts. The grogginess she had woken up with vanished, replaced by a rush of exhilaration. *He must truly care about me*, the voice insisted.

And Oliver did care. He knew he was the reason she wasn't sleeping well, and the guilt gnawed at him. He wanted nothing more than to take her in his arms, apologize, and reassure her. But he couldn't. The consequences were too great.

As he stepped into the shower, the weight of reality settled heavily on him. The knowledge that he would never be able to hold her, kiss her the way he wanted, or make love to her consumed him. It was a truth he had no choice but to accept.

When he finished dressing, he caught his own reflection in the mirror. With a shake of his head, he silently challenged the man staring back at him—as if daring his reflection to defy the decision he had made. As if, deep down, he wished he could.

"I've tried not to make a mess of the bathroom, Lucy," he said as they bumped into each other when he emerged.

She smiled at him while she made her way to the bathroom.

Annette prepared their breakfast afterward. They ate in silence. Lucy desperately wanted to tell him she had developed feelings for him, while Oliver wanted to apologize for causing her distress. Neither of them was willing to do so.

Mitch left the cockpit before they finished their coffee to say they'd be landing at Domodedovo International Airport in half an hour.

"We'll be able to park close to the Business Aviation Center so we can walk to the terminal. It's largely used by people traveling to Moscow by private aircraft."

5.

THE COCKTAIL PARTY

Once passport and customs officials had cleared the aircraft, Mitch accompanied them to the terminal, carrying Lucy's baggage. When Oliver had loaded their bags onto a baggage cart, Mitch bid them farewell—he, Dave, and Annette had been booked into a hotel near the airport.

Dimitri, the security officer, was a sturdy-looking man with close-cropped hair and strong, chiseled features. He reminded Oliver of a nightclub bouncer he had encountered during a previous assignment—he could have easily passed for one if not for the suit and tie. Oliver was pleased to discover that Dimitri spoke flawless English.

Dimitri led them to a black Mercedes E-Class parked in the kiss-and-ride lot. Without a word, he efficiently loaded their baggage into the trunk.

Their chauffeur, Sergei, also spoke fluent English. Tall and lean, his pockmarked face and unruly dark hair—long in the front and falling over his forehead—gave him a rough, almost unkempt look. The thick sideburns extending to his jawline would have made him stand out in any crowd. Yet when he introduced himself with a friendly smile and gestured toward the car, any fleeting suspicion of Bratva connections vanished.

His crisp suit and tie only reinforced the impression of professionalism.

He pulled open the rear doors, allowing Oliver and Lucy to slide into the back seat.

The thirty-mile drive to the hotel stretched to an hour and a half due to relentless traffic. Dimitri, however, kept the conversation flowing, engaging them in steady, meaningful dialogue throughout the ride.

"I need to thank you, Miss Lassiter, for booking Sergei and me into the Ritz-Carlton as well. We don't often get to stay at such a hotel."

"That's the least I could do in exchange for keeping us safe," Lucy explained.

"But it's what we do when we need to look after Morgan Pharma staff when they visit Saint Petersburg or Moscow. We get paid for that."

"I know, but we want you to stay close to us wherever we go, twenty-four hours a day, every day."

"Do you carry a weapon, Dimitri?" Oliver asked.

Dimitri answered by opening his jacket to show Oliver his holster and the Glock 22 in it. Sergei then pointed to the glove compartment, which Dimitri opened. It also contained a Glock 22.

"Crime in Moscow is a serious problem, Dr. Corbyn. People driving an expensive car often keep a gun on their person or in the glove compartment."

"I know... Let's not mention the dangers of being wealthy in Moscow, please. It might frighten Miss Lassiter," Oliver replied in Russian.

"I didn't know you spoke Russian, Oliver," observed Lucy. "What was it you said?"

"Dimitri shouldn't be talking about crime in Moscow. I don't want you to also worry about that."

"Where did you learn to speak perfect Russian?" Dimitri asked him in English.

"I've been to Russia many times, and I have a knack for languages."

"Now I know something else about you, Oliver," Lucy said, smiling at him. "I'll uncover all of your secrets eventually."

"Don't ask me why I've visited Russia before, Dimitri. I don't want Miss Lassiter to know because it might also frighten her," Oliver added in Russian.

"What was that all about?"

"Nothing important."

Lucy asked herself if she should complain about not knowing what he said to Dimitri. She decided not to comment.

"I was told that you are here to call attention to the medication for curing Alzheimer's," Dimitri continued.

"That's correct," Lucy replied. "Dr. Corbyn will be presenting a paper about the medicine at the conference."

"Your presence here in Moscow will cause the media to want to take your photograph and write about you."

"I'm used to that, Dimitri. I usually try to avoid publicity as much as possible, but I hope it will now cause the media to write about the cure."

***

Upon arriving at the hotel, porters swiftly transferred their baggage onto carts. Sergei handed the car keys to the parking attendant, freeing himself and Dimitri to escort Lucy and Oliver to reception. There, the hotel manager personally greeted them and handed over the key cards to their rooms and suites.

With professional courtesy, the manager then led Lucy and Oliver to their suites, explaining the available amenities along the way. When Lucy noticed the connecting door between their suites was locked, she requested that it be opened. The hotel manager apologized for not anticipating their preference to have the adjoining suites function as one. Without delay, he called reception and instructed the desk clerk to bring the key.

A few minutes later, the clerk arrived, accompanied by a porter who placed their baggage on the baggage racks. Once everything was settled, the manager assured Lucy that she could reach out anytime should they need assistance. With that, he and his staff took their leave, leaving Lucy and Oliver to settle in.

"I've never been welcomed like that at hotels I've stayed at," Oliver told Lucy while they walked through the suites.

The suites featured a foyer, a combined sitting-dining room, a large bedroom with a king-size bed and vanity table, a walk-in closet, and a luxurious bathroom.

"Being wealthy has its perks, Oliver."

"Okay, point taken. It's nearly three-thirty, so we have little more than an hour and a half to prepare for our first acting session. We should arrive a little late—around five-fifteen. Most conference delegates will have arrived by then, so everyone will see our entrance. Dress in a way to make people notice you. Dare I add you'd be noticed even in a drab dress of sorts?"

Lucy smiled at him.

They each retreated to their respective suites.

Lucy decided to take a shower, hoping the warmth of the water would soothe her nerves. She didn't want to let Oliver down. While she had made grand entrances at countless parties and social events before, this time felt different—more significant. The pressure weighed on her.

Allowing herself the indulgence of a ten-minute shower, she then washed her long blonde hair, dried it, and curled it into soft waves.

For the occasion, she had bought a tailored blue pantsuit—sleek, sophisticated, and more professional than anything else she owned. Underneath the one-button blazer, she opted for a crisp white sleeveless top. From the jewelry case she had brought, she tried on several necklaces before settling on a delicate gold piece studded with diamonds, pairing it with a matching bracelet and earrings. High heels and a dark blue beret completed the ensemble. When she finally stepped back and assessed herself in the mirror, she was satisfied.

Next came makeup—blue eyeshadow to complement her eyes, dark mascara to enhance her lashes, and a bold red lipstick for the finishing touch. Just as she completed the last detail, Oliver called from the open connecting door.

"Are you ready?"

Meanwhile, Oliver had taken a quick shower and dressed in a dark suit over a white shirt, leaving the top two buttons undone. Before heading to Lucy's suite, he called Dimitri, asking him to meet them in the corridor outside their suites.

"Wow, Lucy, you look absolutely stunning," Oliver said when he saw her. "Many jealous women and numerous men won't be able to keep their eyes off you."

"You look smart yourself, Oliver. I haven't seen you wearing a suit before. It gives you a distinguished look."

"Are we going to hold hands, or are you going to hook your arm through mine when we make our entrance?" Oliver asked.

"I'll hook my arm through yours."

They met Dimitri near the elevator and rode it down to the second floor, where they were approached by a young man representing the conference committee. He asked if they were attending the cocktail party, and when they confirmed they were, he led them to the registration desk.

"This is Miss Lucy Lassiter, and I'm Oliver Corbyn," Oliver told one of the three women sitting behind the tables that had been arranged in the hallway of the large ballroom where the cocktail party was being held. "I preregistered us some weeks ago."

"We've been looking forward to seeing you here, Dr. Corbyn. Hello, Miss Lassiter. We have a bag here for each of you with a copy of the papers, your name badge, some folders, and some other materials you might find interesting."

Oliver accepted the bags and handed them to Dimitri.

The three of them walked to the open double ballroom doors. Lucy hooked her arm through Oliver's.

The noise of four hundred people talking was short of deafening, but by the time they had taken five steps into the ballroom, it had subsided. People looked at one another to determine why they had stopped talking. Everyone had fallen silent ten seconds later.

Ten or so people converged on them and began taking photographs. Oliver instinctively held his hand across the lower part of his face, while Lucy smiled from ear to ear.

"The inevitable paparazzi," she told Oliver. "It's something you'll have to get used to if we're going to be together more often."

Three athletic-looking men then decidedly pushed the paparazzi into the hallway.

An older man with white hair and a white beard walked up to them. The name on his badge indicated he was Dr. Mikhail Lenkov, chairman of the conference committee.

"Welcome to Moscow, Miss Lassiter, and you, Dr. Corbyn," he said. "This conference has been an annual event for more than twenty years, and it's the first time a member of a family that owns one of the largest pharmaceutical companies in the world honors us with a visit. We took the liberty of informing the press about your presence here, for which I need to apologize. We didn't realize it would result in a scene like the one we've just witnessed. Some of those who took your photograph have traveled halfway across the world to be here for that purpose."

"I'm here to spend time with my friend, Dr. Lenkov," Lucy replied. "The conference was a good excuse to escape the office for a while. That doesn't mean to say I don't appreciate the conference as such. I believe it's important to share the results of research on Alzheimer's."

"We are of the same mind, Miss Lassiter."

A waitress walked up to them, offering a tray with various drinks. Lucy chose a glass of champagne and Oliver orange juice.

"We were delighted to receive your paper, Dr. Corbyn. We were impressed when we read it. We understand it is your first?"

"Yes, except for my PhD thesis, which was classified and not released to the public."

"I'm assuming that the subject of your thesis was the development of medication to prevent or cure Alzheimer's disease?" Dr. Lenkov asked.

"Yes, it was."

"Have you worked for Morgan Pharma since?"

"I decided to travel for an extensive period afterward. I considered myself too young to embark on a professional career in the pharmaceutical industry or at a university. But my need for income to pay my way through life forced me to take up a position with Morgan Pharma when it was offered to me.

"It was the best move I could have made because I met Miss Lassiter there. I'm pleased to say she's now much more than a friend. I'm presently considering moving elsewhere, where the monetary reward is greater because of the life I now share with her."

Oliver kissed Lucy on the cheek. Lucy frowned when he did, in an attempt to show her disapproval.

Various men and women had closed in on where they were standing to listen to the conversation. Oliver noticed that Lenkov seemed to thrive on seeing more people approach them.

"Tell me, Dr. Corbyn, has Morgan Pharma really succeeded in developing medication that prevents the abnormal buildup of amyloid and tau proteins in the brain of those susceptible to Alzheimer's?"

The heads of those around them turned to Oliver when this question was asked.

"Unequivocally yes. Once we found how to avoid the buildup of amyloid-beta protein deposits in the hippocampus, the tau protein soon followed. We're now in the last phase of developing the cure."

"Will you be providing information on the medicine itself during your keynote address the day after tomorrow?" one of the bystanders asked.

"Enough for everyone here to realize that the release of the medicine is not far away, but not to the extent of allowing another pharmaceutical company to copy it," Oliver answered with a smile. "Now, please excuse us. We need to say hello to other people who are here."

Oliver placed his arm around Lucy's waist and led her away from the small crowd that had surrounded them.

"We need to expose ourselves to more people than the group we just left, Lucy. I hope you don't mind."

"Not at all, but let's first say hello to Alex Davidson, the CEO of our Saint Petersburg office."

Lucy had seen Alex standing some distance from where they had been talking to Lenkov. She led Oliver to him.

"Hi, Alex. I didn't know you were going to be here," Lucy said as she shook his hand.

"I wasn't planning to because, as you know, my office is concerned with retail and not with R&D, but when I learned you were going to be here, I decided to come. Are Dimitri and Sergei looking after you properly?"

"They are. I want you to meet Oliver Corbyn. He'll be

delivering the keynote address the day after next."

Oliver and Alex shook hands.

"So I've heard. I wasn't aware of who he was until I arrived here. People have been telling me that your paper on Alzheimer's is an exceptional document."

"I can't take the credit for that, Alex. I did little to expedite the development of the medicine after I left Harvard."

Oliver stopped talking when someone tapped him on the shoulder from behind.

"I apologize for interrupting your conversation, Dr. Corbyn, but we need to speak to you in private. Can you come with me for a few minutes, please?"

Oliver turned to find a woman with dark hair neatly pulled into a bun peering up at him over the top of her rimless glasses. She was striking in a distinctly Slavic way—her round face, high cheekbones, and full lips gave her a natural elegance.

She wore a white top that accentuated her curves and a black frock, her posture poised and assured. There was something about her demeanor—calm yet deliberate—that told him she wasn't here by chance. Whatever her business with him was, it was important.

"I'm sorry, sweetheart," Oliver said, turning to Lucy. "Will you be okay while I talk to this lady?"

"No, I prefer you to stay with me, but go if you must," Lucy said, frowning again.

"Thanks... I love you," Oliver said before placing a hand on her waist and kissing her on the lips.

Lucy was momentarily stunned by the kiss. It had caught her completely off guard. She knew Oliver was merely playing his part, and she should have expected some display of affection from him—but it still took her by surprise.

Meanwhile, Oliver turned and followed the woman to where two men stood in the corner of the room. With a composed demeanor, she introduced them to him.

"These are my colleagues, Alexei and Anatoly," she said, "and I'm Sasha. My colleagues don't speak English very well, so I'll talk to you on their behalf. Dr. Lenkov told us that you are considering leaving Morgan Pharma for a position elsewhere that offers you more money. Is that correct?"

"Yes… I'm willing to consider it. I prefer not to be reliant on Miss Lassiter's wealth to maintain my relationship with her."

"We are willing to pay you whatever you want for your availability—within limits, of course."

"What would you say if I told you that I'd consider working for a pharmaceutical company here in Russia in exchange for a monthly remuneration of one hundred thousand US dollars, to be paid into a US bank account at the end of each month?"

"Let me discuss your proposal with my colleagues." She turned to the two men. "Believe it or not, but he wants one hundred thousand US dollars every month. Shall I tell him it's too much?" she asked them in Russian.

"No, the director will want him, whatever the cost. We need him to help us interpret some of the files and to assist us in determining the precise composition of the medicine."

"So what should I tell him?"

"Tell him that we need time to consider his proposal and that we'll contact him after his lecture on Tuesday."

Oliver pretended not to have understood what Sasha had discussed with Anatoly.

"What did Anatoly say?"

"We need to discuss your proposal with our director. We'll contact you on Tuesday after your keynote address. Is that acceptable?"

"What company do you work for?"

"We work for RusPharma."

"Your laboratory is here in Moscow?"

"No, in Zelenograd."

"Okay... I need to return to Miss Lassiter. I'll speak to you on Tuesday."

Oliver returned to where Lucy was standing. He noticed that a group of younger men had gathered around her and that she wasn't happy about it.

"Excuse me, gentlemen," he said during a pause in what Lucy was telling them. "I need to speak with Miss Lassiter."

He pushed two of the men aside to be able to take Lucy by her arm and lead her away.

"Where's Dimitri? He should have protected you from those men while I was away."

"He's talking to Alex, but it's okay. They meant no harm. I felt uncomfortable because they were as close to me as you are now, that's all."

"We've achieved what we set out to do, Lucy. I'll tell you why when we're alone."

They remained at the cocktail party for another thirty minutes. Knowing they had achieved what they had come for, Oliver proposed they call it a day.

"Shall we leave now?" he asked her.

"Yes. I just need to say goodbye to Alex."

They walked to where Alex was talking to Dimitri.

"We're leaving now, Alex," Lucy said. "Give my regards to the staff at Saint Petersburg."

"Are you coming, Dimitri?" Oliver asked. "See you around, Alex."

***

"Do you want me to stay on guard outside in the corridor, Dr. Corbyn?" Dimitri asked him when they had returned to their suites.

"What do you want to do, Lucy? It's nearly six in the evening, but according to our biological clocks, it's only ten in the morning. To overcome jet lag as quickly as possible, we should consider it nearly time for dinner. We have the option of having room service bring us dinner, or we can go to one of the hotel restaurants. The O2 seafood restaurant on the roof is supposed to be excellent."

"What would you prefer?" she asked him.

"The seafood restaurant. It's early evening, and sleep won't catch us until well past midnight local time. We have at least five or six hours to kill before going to bed."

"Okay, but let me change into something more suitable first."

"Why don't you and Sergei have dinner with us?" Oliver suggested to Dimitri. "If you were to sit at a table near ours, you could keep an eye on us."

"Thank you, Dr. Corbyn. We would like that."

"And please call me Oliver."

Dimitri was visibly affected by this token of respect and friendliness. He called Sergei to inform him they had been invited to the seafood restaurant on the roof while Oliver called reception to request they make reservations for the four of them. Lucy, meanwhile, changed into a colorful flower-print dress, tied a belt around her waist to accentuate her figure, brushed her hair, and touched up her makeup. Her appearance made Oliver look at her much too long when she joined him. Her blush told him she'd noticed his gaze.

The three of them made their way to the restaurant, where Sergei was waiting for them. A hostess welcomed them and showed them to two tables near each other, as reception had ordered, and handed them each a menu. The head waiter, who had been informed who they were, wished them good evening when they had seated themselves and asked them what they wanted to drink. Lucy ordered a martini and Oliver a

Heineken. They were silent as they studied the menu. When they knew what they wanted, the headwaiter took their orders and collected their menus.

"There are people here who were also at the cocktail party, Lucy," Oliver said. "They know who we are, so we need to keep up appearances and play our respective roles while we're here. I'd hoped it wouldn't be necessary."

Lucy nodded. She secretly wished that their respective roles would cause him to kiss her again.

When they were served their drinks, Lucy held up her glass.

"What shall we drink to, Oliver?"

"To us...we make a great team."

"I'll drink to that."

"We've achieved what we set out to do by going to the cocktail party," Oliver began, while taking both of Lucy's hands in his. "The woman who asked to talk to me in private led me to two men. Dr. Lenkov had told them that I would consider leaving Morgan Pharma for a position elsewhere that offered more money. I confirmed that to be the case, explaining that I wanted to avoid leeching on your wealth while I maintain my relationship with you.

"When I proposed the remuneration I wanted, she conferred with her colleagues in Russian. She told the men that the amount I had mentioned was too high, and she asked them if she should tell me that. One of the men then said, and I quote, 'No, the director will want him, whatever the cost. We need him to help us interpret some of the files and to assist us in determining the precise composition of the medicine.' She then told me they needed time to consider my proposal and that they would talk to me again on Tuesday after my address. When I asked her the name of the company they worked for, she said RusPharma."

"Does the reference to the word 'files' by those men mean

they have the files that were on our server in Boston?"

"I believe so," Oliver replied, now withdrawing his hands from hers. "What do you know about RusPharma?"

"Not much, except that they have a reputation for producing medicines in tablet form no longer protected by patents. Their production facility is near Moscow somewhere."

"I thought it would be relatively difficult to establish contact with those ultimately responsible for the computer hack, so the result of going to the cocktail party is beyond what I'd imagined. We should celebrate in some way."

"In private, or here for everyone to see?"

"Here and now. I prefer not to impose on you in that way when we're alone."

"Okay, I think a celebration would need to start by you giving me a kiss."

Lucy leaned forward across the table, closing her eyes in anticipation. Oliver had no option but to oblige. He also leaned across the table and kissed her hard on the lips. He was saddened by the knowledge he'd never be able to hold and kiss her the way he really wanted to.

"I'm sorry if that kiss didn't meet your expectations, but it should be good enough to convince the conference attendees who are here that something is going on between us."

Lucy was flustered by the kiss. She had noticed his intent to kiss her with feeling, as she had. She decided to ask him what he thought of their kiss.

"Seriously, Oliver, how would you rate that kiss?" she said with a smile.

"When compared to the many kisses your boyfriends gave you, I think you would rate that as a peck."

"As a kiss intended for the people looking at us, it scores top marks," she said. "But what did you mean when you said you didn't want to impose on me in that way when we're alone? You're talking in riddles again."

"I'm sorry. I assumed you understood what I meant."

"No...I didn't. Why would you be imposing when you would want to celebrate having identified the company responsible for the computer hack?"

"That's simple. That discovery is of great importance to me, as I originally estimated my chance of doing so during the conference was only fifty percent. I can't imagine you being affected like that. You could have come here thinking this is a chore like so many you have on your plate. A celebration like the one I imagined would then be imposing on you."

Lucy looked at him, again wondering how to reply. She finally decided it was time to indicate in a roundabout way how she felt about him.

"You're wrong, Oliver. Don't you remember when we spoke on the phone about the logistics of traveling here that I was looking forward to coming here with you? You interest me as much as I interest you. I remember you telling me on two occasions that I interest you. So you wouldn't be imposing unless you were thinking of celebrating in terms of doing something I wouldn't feel comfortable with."

"I'd never do anything that would make you feel uncomfortable. Heaven forbid."

"That reminds me, Oliver, what did you mean when you said, and I quote, 'Heaven forbid, no, definitely not, you're out of my league,' when answering my question about whether you were hitting on me?"

"I remember saying that. I thought that what I implied at the time was obvious. You move in social circles that are not mine. I'm aware that the role I'm playing here in Moscow suggests I want to move into those circles with you, but I'd dread actually needing to, for reasons you're probably aware of."

Their appetizers arrived. They were quiet while they savored the food, each thinking about what the other had said. Lucy was acutely aware that her confession about her interest in him had not resulted in the desired effect of letting him know she had feelings for him—feelings she hadn't experienced before. She feared that all her efforts to tell him how she felt had failed.

"So, what are you going to do tomorrow?" Oliver asked her after they had finished their appetizers.

"I haven't thought about it. Are you going to attend the conference?"

"Yes, I have to, although most of the papers to be presented don't interest me all that much."

"You told me on the plane that I should perhaps buy something expensive and show it to you when you're in the presence of some of the conference delegates."

"Yes, I did, but there's no need for that sort of thing now that we've been contacted by the people responsible for the hack."

"But I wouldn't mind going to the stores anyway."

"Sure, as long as you take Dimitri and Sergei with you when you do."

"I will."

Their conversation faltered as the waiter arrived with their entrées. The shift was subtle but undeniable. They had reached a point where lighthearted banter no longer felt natural, and playful remarks about their relationship no longer fit. A quiet seriousness settled between them.

Lucy wanted to say it outright—that she had feelings for him. Meanwhile, Oliver wrestled with his own truth: that while he was undeniably drawn to her, he couldn't allow his emotions to deepen. Both hesitated, unwilling to voice what they truly felt.

After dinner, they parted ways and retired to their respective suites. Oliver told Lucy he needed to start preparing his presentation. The moment the words left his mouth, he saw the flicker of disappointment in her eyes. He suspected she had hoped he would suggest exploring one of Moscow's sights before calling it a night.

But they both knew that the carefree ease that had defined their relationship until now was slipping away. There was no going back.

6.

THE BRACELET

Breakfast the next morning was a buffet at the hotel's Café Russe restaurant, and the first ten minutes or so saw Lucy, Oliver, Dimitri, and Sergei helping themselves to the food and drinks laid out before queuing for coffee from the coffee machine. Despite Dimitri's efforts, both Lucy and Oliver refused to be drawn into a meaningful conversation. It was obvious to him that something had upset them.

"Look after Miss Lassiter today, Dimitri. Please keep her safe," Oliver said as they stood up from the breakfast table. "And please don't go overboard with what you want to buy today, Lucy," he added.

"Why shouldn't I?" she retorted. "I was hoping we would have had time to do things together, but it appears I'm left to my own devices. Shopping is a good option in that case."

"I'm terribly sorry if you feel neglected. I'll make it up to you as soon as I can. Now give me a kiss, please."

Lucy lifted her face to his, and Oliver kissed her, pulling her close. The intensity of his kiss caught her off guard, stirring something unexpected deep within her. For a moment, she smiled against his lips, surprised by the passion in his touch. A fleeting thought crossed her mind—this kiss wasn't just for the conference delegates watching them.

***

Oliver chose a seat at the back of the ballroom, now transformed into an auditorium. As he waited for the session to begin, he flipped through the book of research papers, skimming those that had his interest.

Dr. Lenkov's opening speech caught his attention. It was filled with bold claims about Russia's advancements in Alzheimer's research, which struck Oliver as odd. From everything he had studied, Russian pharmaceutical companies had made little progress in recent years. But what surprised him even more was Lenkov's assertion that a Russian company would complete a cure within the year.

The day's presentations focused on the diagnosis and treatment of Alzheimer's disease—most of which Oliver was already familiar with. By the afternoon, boredom crept in. Spotting a copy of *Izvestia* on a nearby empty chair, he picked it up and discreetly folded it to avoid drawing attention to the fact that he was reading a Russian newspaper.

On page three, he found a photograph of Lucy and himself at the cocktail party. The accompanying article detailed Lucy's background, emphasizing her social standing, and claimed she was at the conference to generate publicity for Morgan Pharma's Alzheimer's medication.

***

At five o'clock, after the final paper had been presented, Oliver made his way back to his suite. Just outside, he found Dimitri standing in the corridor.

"When did Miss Lassiter and you return from shopping?"

"About an hour ago. She said she wanted to take a nap. Do you mind if I return to my room? We walked for miles, and we must have visited ten stores and several malls."

"Sure, but I want to ask you something before you go. Let's go to my suite to talk."

Dimitri followed Oliver into his sitting-dining room. Oliver indicated he should sit and then tiptoed into Lucy's suite to check on her. He found her asleep on the bed. When he returned, he told Dimitri about the computer hack.

"We believe RusPharma stole the data. I've offered my services to them. They need someone like me to take the final steps in determining the composition of the medicine. I've already talked to the three RusPharma scientists who are attending the conference, and we'll probably come to an agreement tomorrow.

"I'll work at the RusPharma laboratory in Zelenograd for as long as is necessary to find a way to sabotage what they're doing. I then need to escape from Russia as quickly as possible because they'll immediately realize I'm to blame. I need someone to drive me from a location close to their laboratory to the border with Belarus by way of the M1. Would it be possible for you to do that?"

"When would I need to be in Zelenograd to pick you up?"

"I don't yet know. But it will be after dark. I'll call you the day before on your cell phone. It could be in a week, in a month, or in three months."

"Are you flexible regarding the pickup date? I might be on a job with others elsewhere I'd need to give priority to, to avoid getting into trouble with my boss."

"I understand. Would it help if I were to let you know a week in advance?"

"Yes, I could then notify Alex in time to not roster me in on that day because of a private matter."

"But our chance of reaching the Belarus border undetected

in the dark would be better if you were to drive the company car, the black Mercedes."

"I realize that. Leave it to me. I know what I need to do."

"Okay, I'm counting on you. Don't let me down."

They exchanged cell phone numbers before Dimitri left.

***

Oliver now attended to his PowerPoint slides, which formed the basis for his address the following morning. He was more than halfway through when he heard Lucy call him from the door between their suites. He walked to where she was standing. He noticed she had taken a shower and was now wearing leggings with a pink motif, a white T-shirt, and a long pink cardigan. Her hair was still damp.

"How was your day? Dimitri told me you walked for miles."

"I did something you didn't want me to do. I bought you a present."

She gave Oliver a small, gift-wrapped package. He looked at her, searching her face for a sign that would indicate what she was up to. She smiled.

The package contained a small, blue velvet box. He opened it to find a sterling silver bracelet studded with diamonds. He removed it from the box. It felt heavy and looked expensive.

"I can't accept this. It must have cost a fortune."

"At first, I thought about getting you a friendship ring," Lucy said. "I even found a beautiful men's ring at the Piaget store on Red Square. But knowing that friendship rings are traditionally given as a promise of devotion and commitment in a romantic relationship, I decided on the bracelet instead."

Oliver studied her for a moment before asking, "Because you can't promise devotion and commitment?"

The question slipped out before he could stop it. The

moment it did, he realized it would upset her.

"That hurts, Oliver. Why would you say that?"

"I'm sorry," he said quickly, regretting his words. "But if we were in a romantic relationship, that could still be a reason you didn't buy the ring. I shouldn't have asked."

Lucy's eyes filled with tears. The tension between them—stretching back more than six weeks—had finally worn her down. Without thinking, she clenched her fists and pounded his chest, overwhelmed by frustration, confusion, and heartbreak.

"Why, Oliver? Why?"

Then, as if exhausted by her own emotions, she wrapped her arms around him, pressing her face against his chest.

"I'm sorry, Lucy," he murmured, his voice pained. "I didn't mean for it to come out that way."

But it was too late. Lucy's shoulders began to shake as she cried in earnest. She covered her face with her hands and fled to her bedroom, not wanting him to see how much he had broken her.

Oliver stood frozen for a moment, overcome with emotion. He knew what had caused this. He didn't want them to become close. He also knew that if he went to comfort her, he would have to explain himself. And if he explained himself, he would have to admit the one thing he had been fighting against all this time—he loved her.

But the sound of her muffled sobs shattered his resolve.

He followed her into the bedroom and found her curled on the bed, her body trembling with quiet sobs. Gently, he lifted her and made her stand in front of him. She tried to push him away, but he held her arms, guiding them around his waist. Then, cupping her face in his hands, he tilted her chin up and kissed the tears from her cheeks.

Lucy's breath hitched. For a moment, she was too stunned to react. But then, as she searched his face, she realized—his kisses weren't just meant to console her. It was something more. A confession in itself.

With a sudden surge of emotion, she flung her arms around his neck and kissed him with all the passion she had kept bottled inside.

Their embrace lasted a long time. Each time their lips parted, their eyes met, searching, questioning—before they came together again, as if afraid to let go. Slowly, the weight of all the tension, all the longing, melted away.

Finally, they sat down on the bed. Oliver pulled her close, gazing into her tear-streaked but beautiful eyes.

"I'm sorry, Lucy," he said softly. "I never meant to hurt you."

"I love you, Oliver. I tried to forget you after you left Monaco, but I couldn't. The feelings I have for you are different from anything I've experienced before. You were right when you said I'd never been in love.

"I tried to let you know how I felt several times, although in a roundabout way. I was afraid to be more direct because I expected you to reject me. You kept me guessing about your feelings for me. Some of the things you said made me happy, but I interpreted others to mean you weren't interested in me beyond helping you with what you wanted to achieve here in Moscow."

"I know, but I have reasons for not becoming attached to you. I tried hard not to let you know how I felt. Even now, I realize that what I've done in letting you know I love you is foolish. I sometimes dropped my guard, like this morning after breakfast when I kissed you how I wanted to. I was also moved when I discovered you'd tossed and turned in your bed on the plane because of what I said. I asked you to tell me why, knowing that if you did, I'd have to tell you I care for you in a way you weren't aware of."

"Why didn't you want to become attached to me?"

"Because of the possible repercussions. Would you mind if I didn't tell you?"

"Yes, I would. We shouldn't now be keeping secrets like that."

"I agree, but let me think about it for a while, please."

Lucy was disappointed, but more than happy about his confession. She realized that whatever his reason for not wanting to become attached to her was, it had to be extraordinary. She resolved to do everything in her power to find out.

"Can I take you somewhere this evening to make up for neglecting you yesterday and today?"

"I want to be alone with you this evening, to get to know you. We have a lot to talk about."

"Sure... I'll call Dimitri and tell him we won't be joining him and Sergei for dinner."

***

Lucy brushed her hair and repaired her makeup while Oliver returned to his suite to make the call. He studied the room service menu and called out different appetizers and entrées for her to choose from.

"I want to order a bottle of wine, Lucy. White or red?"

"White, please," she replied.

Oliver ordered a bottle of Sauvignon Blanc with the food.

Two waiters arrived not long after to lay the table and set out the food. Oliver gave them a handsome tip and poured the wine.

Lucy smiled when she entered his sitting-dining room and saw the table laid out, ready to eat.

"None of my boyfriends would have done something as simple as organize dinner for two like you have."

"I keep asking myself how someone as intelligent and

levelheaded as you could have succumbed to the advances of worthless men."

"I asked myself the same question each time I broke up with them."

"Is it because you needed to feel wanted and loved?"

Lucy looked at Oliver intently before answering his question.

"It's more complicated than that," Lucy admitted. "My friends and I were always surrounded by men, no matter where we went. And we always talked about them—comparing, judging, trying to decide if any of them were good enough for one of us. But I can't remember a single time we ever discussed that 'butterflies in your stomach feeling,' as you call it, when one of us started seeing someone new."

She paused, swirling the wine in her glass before continuing.

"For me, it was about the novelty—being with someone new every so often, hearing that I was beautiful and desirable. That was my motivation. So whenever I ended a relationship, I was already looking for the next one."

After dinner, they moved to the couch, lingering over the last sips of wine. Lucy leaned into him, and Oliver instinctively wrapped his arm around her.

"Are you at peace with the world as much as I am?" he asked, his voice low and content.

"The anxieties I've been living with ever since meeting you have gone. I felt a strange sort of calmness come over me when we kissed. There was this little voice in my head constantly saying, 'He loves me.' It was the strangest thing."

"How did our kiss compare with the kisses your boyfriends gave you?"

"There's no comparison, Oliver. I didn't love them. I wasn't even aware of what love was. I began to feel what it was after we met. That feeling reached a crescendo when we were on the plane. It hurt me terribly, and I remember thinking it was better not to fall in love if love affected me like that."

Lucy's eyes filled with tears again when she explained this. She looked at him, no longer afraid of revealing she was once again emotional.

He felt deeply for her, for the forthright way in which she confessed to what her feelings for him had caused. He didn't know how to respond other than to kiss her again.

"Will you let me make love to you, Oliver? I can't help but want you."

"I've often thought about making love to you, Luce. I can still feel the heartache, knowing I couldn't allow that to happen."

Lucy stood, took his hand in hers, and led him to her bedroom. Without a word, she pulled back the blankets and gave him a gentle push, silently urging him to lie down. Kneeling beside him, she slipped off his shoes, unbuttoned his shirt, and loosened his belt. Her fingers moved with deliberate care as she unzipped his pants and slid them down his legs.

She then undressed herself, removing her shoes, cardigan, and T-shirt, followed by her bra and leggings.

Straddling him, she leaned down and began to kiss him—softly at first, then with lingering affection. She traced his face, his neck, his throat, and his torso with her lips, savoring the moment, letting desire build between them. When she finally lay beside him, her hand explored his body, slipping beneath the fabric of his shorts, discovering the warmth of him.

Oliver turned onto his side, pressing his body against hers, making it impossible for her hand to remain between them. Their noses brushed, breaths mingling.

"Let's just enjoy this," he whispered. "Your body against mine—nothing else. Can you do that?"

"I can't..."

She didn't resist when he eased her onto her back. He sat

up briefly, removing his shirt, then gently slid her panties down her legs, followed by his shorts. As he moved between her thighs, she wrapped her legs tightly around his waist, her body arching toward him, aching for more.

But he wasn't ready to give in just yet.

"Slow down, Luce," he murmured. "Let's make this last."

"I'll try," she breathed, loosening her grip.

He lay beside her again, his hands tracing slow, reverent paths over her skin. He kissed her breasts, his lips warm and patient, drawing soft gasps from her. She writhed beneath him, moaning as his touch traveled lower, mirroring the way she had explored him moments before.

When he sensed the urgency between them building to its peak, he shifted once more, settling between her legs. This time, she wrapped herself around him again, guiding him closer.

The moment they joined, Lucy gasped, her hips rising to meet him with desperate need. Their movements grew frenzied, all restraint unraveling as they lost themselves in the rhythm of their bodies. Together, they reached for the crest of pleasure, waves crashing higher and higher until, at last, they shattered—giving in completely, consumed by a release more powerful than either had ever known.

***

They lay in stillness, their bodies entwined, savoring the warmth of each other and the lingering aftershocks of pleasure. Neither spoke. There was no need. As their eyes met and their lips found each other again in a slow, tender kiss, they both understood—something had changed. In surrendering to each other completely, they had created something beyond desire, something deeper.

After a few quiet minutes, Oliver gently withdrew, settling

beside her. He pulled the blankets over them, cocooning them in warmth.

He knew the moment was coming. The conversation that would follow—the one he had been avoiding. But after everything that had just passed between them, he could no longer hold back.

So he exhaled, turned to her, and began to speak.

"Tell me something more about yourself, Luce. As I already told you, I was attracted to you from the moment I met you, and I quickly developed feelings for you. I've never encountered a woman like you before. You're beautiful and intelligent, and when you're not angry at me, you possess a sparkling personality. Am I correct in assuming it's been difficult to avoid being harassed by boys and men from an early age? I don't mean to pry, so don't tell me anything if you don't want to."

"You can ask me anything you want, dearest Oliver. I now have no qualms about telling you everything about myself. You should know, first, that I lost my virginity when I was in high school. There was this boy I liked, and I went to bed with him more than once in his room when his parents were away.

"In college, I was attracted to a guy, and we made love whenever we could until I discovered he was seeing someone else at the same time. That, and other things that happened, made me believe men were only interested in sex. It turned me off for a long time, until well after I started seeing this group of girls I'd met.

"As I said before, we always ended up in the company of men, and inevitably one of us would go home with one of them. It was obvious to me that those men were also only interested in sex. I rejected the advances I was constantly subjected to until one of those men sat down with me once for a serious conversation.

"We talked all evening and part of the night. I was drawn to him, and when he asked me to have a coffee in his apartment, I went with him. There he forced himself on me. Bondage was his thing, and he tried to tie my hands and feet. I told him I needed to go to the bathroom first, and he let me. I managed to escape.

"I've had many boyfriends since my college days, but I always ended the relationship when it needed to go a step further—into the bedroom."

"I'm sorry you had to live through all that. As I said once before, there are many men out there with honest intentions. You just don't meet them in the circles you move in. But returning to my question, how did you become so skilled in bed when you haven't had sex with your boyfriends after your college years—what, two or three years ago?"

"Three years... I don't know. What I did came naturally, although my girlfriends would always be talking about making love. Each of them who had been involved in a one-night stand or a more lasting relationship would tell us about it. We would all learn something from what we heard."

"I was amazed to find you were able to slow down when I asked you to. People who haven't made love for a long time usually lose the stamina they need to make the experience special."

"But you're forgetting that most women in my position have toys to play with."

"I didn't realize that."

"What about you? What can you tell me about your girlfriends?"

"There's not much to tell. I had two girlfriends in high school and a girlfriend at Harvard, the last of which led to a serious relationship. Her name is Alice. She moved in with me, but when she suggested we get married and have children, I hesitated. She understood that to mean I didn't love her, and she left. I couldn't fathom why she left without even wanting to talk about it. I concluded she wasn't in love with me. I saw her on campus not long afterward, arm in arm with another guy."

"You weren't in love with her?"

"Loving you like I do tells me I wasn't."

"So, that's it—just three?"

"No, I had relationships since then with women who worked for the criminal organizations I needed to infiltrate. That was to get them to vouch for me—to win their trust and to allow me into their inner circle, as it were. There were no feelings involved."

As they lay side by side, looking into each other's eyes, Lucy decided to raise the question that was foremost in her mind.

"Who are you, Oliver? You need to tell me. When we were on *Artemis*, you told me you were assigned to help us deal with the consequences of the computer hack by important people who want to see Morgan Pharma develop the Alzheimer's cure as soon as possible. You said you worked for the CIA. Are those facts related to why you didn't want to admit you loved me?"

"They are."

"Please tell me everything. I want us to be honest, transparent, and open. I can handle something that needs to be kept strictly secret, whatever it is. Trust me, please."

Oliver knew it was no longer possible to not tell her. It would destroy the meaning of what they now shared.

"After completing my PhD at Harvard, now more than two and a half years ago, I decided my life was dull and boring. I have no brothers or sisters. My parents died in a car crash, and my grandparents, who raised me, have passed. I experienced firsthand what it means to have Alzheimer's disease when I helped my grandfather look after my grandmother, who contracted the disease in its worst form some four years before her death. It was a major factor in deciding to study the disease for my PhD. Anyway, I applied for a position with the CIA. Because I wanted to work in the field and not behind a computer, they put me through a tough six-month program. I passed with flying colors.

"I was assigned several tasks afterward, mainly here in Russia, for which I needed to learn the language. That's the reason, by the way, for holding my hand across my face when the paparazzi took our photo yesterday. Or didn't you notice me doing that?"

"No, I didn't."

"If the criminals I was involved with were to recognize me from a photo in the newspaper, like the one in *Izvestia* today, you and I wouldn't be safe. There were occasions I had to kill Bratva criminals that were ordered to look for me and kill me while making my escape after having achieved what I needed to do."

"But wouldn't the simple fact of reading your name in the newspaper, or hearing it on some news program, be reason for them to look for you here? Your announcement tomorrow about the Alzheimer's cure is bound to end up on some TV program."

"My name wouldn't mean much to them because I was then using another name. I also wore a disguise. I don't think anyone would recognize me from the photos that were taken yesterday or from the photos that will be taken tomorrow. But to be certain, I need to partly cover my face like I did yesterday."

Lucy gave Oliver a puzzled look as she tried to understand the enormity of what he had said.

"Why did you tell me that the people who assigned you your present task don't want to be identified when they are the people who employ you—the CIA? And what are your exact reasons for not wanting to become attached to me?"

"Please be patient; I'll tell you in a minute. I've just realized that by letting you know all this, you might not love me anymore. Has what I told you lessened your feelings for me?"

"No, but it's totally changed the picture I'd made up of you in my mind."

"In what way?"

"Well... I imagined you to be a scientist with an extraordinary devotion to developing the Alzheimer's cure. A man with compassion for others and willing to undertake a dangerous mission to help my parents and me. I had made you into a hero."

"And now...am I still your hero?" Oliver asked her with a smile.

"Yes, perhaps more so. But you need to answer the two questions I just asked before I make up my mind," she said seriously.

It was obvious to Oliver that Lucy was troubled by what he'd told her. He still had his arm around her naked body, and he now drew her closer to him.

"Are you sure you want to hear more?"

"Yes, I want to know everything."

"Do you remember Bill telling you he visited the director of the CIA to discuss the computer hack?"

"Yes."

"I was at CIA headquarters that afternoon in the office of Ken Rivera, the director, reporting on my last assignment, when he told me about Bill's visit and, knowing I'd studied the possibility of developing a cure for Alzheimer's, informed me of the upload. The worldwide hack had apparently been the subject of a meeting at the White House during lunch. When Ken reported what Bill had told him, the president became extremely concerned. He called while I was talking to the director to ask what the CIA had decided about the problem. Ken told him he would take care of it, not yet knowing how to approach the issue. The president asked how, and Ken had me talk to him about what we would do.

"The president was aware, he said, that millions of people would be adversely affected if, for example, Russia were to launch the medicine first. His administration would then be considered ineffective for not having been able to prevent the information from being stolen. He asked me to report to him personally on my progress whenever I could, and he ordered me not to tell anyone about his involvement in what I needed to do."

"Perhaps you shouldn't have told me that. You broke a promise you made to the president."

"I know, but I'd have lost you if I hadn't. So, one of my reasons for wanting to avoid becoming attached to you is the promise I made to both the president and the director of the CIA to not tell anyone about myself and my assignments—something, in my judgment, you wouldn't have tolerated if we were to become close. What would you have said or done if I'd told you I couldn't or wouldn't tell you when you asked me who I was?"

"You're right; you would have made me unhappy again."

"So, am I still your hero?"

"More so than before," she said as she cuddled up to him.

The touch of their naked bodies aroused new desires. Lucy noticed his hardness and suggested they make love again.

This time it was Oliver who took the lead. He asked her to turn on her side away from him.

"Why?" she asked as she did.

"I'm not going to hurt you or tie you up, don't worry."

Oliver caressed her gently, his fingers weaving through her hair before his lips found her shoulder, her neck, and the curve of her back. He nibbled softly at her earlobe, eliciting a quiet gasp, then let his fingertips trace a slow, deliberate path down the front of her body—starting at her neck, lingering over her breasts, and gliding down to her stomach, where he paused, savoring the way she responded to his touch.

When she began to squirm, he retraced his path, this time focusing on her breasts, drawing lazy patterns over her skin. He waited for her to settle, then repeated the motion, lingering once more where she was most sensitive. By the third time, she was writhing beneath his touch, her moans soft but urgent.

When he moved to return to her breasts once more, she caught his hand, guiding him to where she needed him most.

Slowly, he entered her. The intensity of their shared arousal made it impossible to take his time. He matched her rhythm, their bodies moving together in perfect sync, both chasing the same inevitable release.

Afterward, he remained behind her, wrapping her in his arms, his body pressed close in the afterglow. Eventually, she turned to face him, her eyes searching his before she kissed him softly.

"I had no idea lovemaking could be like this," she whispered. "Don't ever leave me."

Oliver brushed a strand of hair from her face, his voice steady, certain. "I won't, sweetheart. Trust me."

"There's one other thing you need to tell me," Lucy said minutes later, when the wondrous feeling of their intimacy had lessened.

"What's that?"

"Why did those kids and the lifeguard want your autograph when we were at the pool in Monaco?"

"They recognized me."

"That's not an answer to my question."

"I know. Are you sure you want me to tell you?"

"Yes. I want to know everything about you."

"I became a strong swimmer during my years at Harvard, and I won numerous events at intercollegiate meets. I was chosen to represent the US at international events."

"But when I looked you up on the internet that first day when I collected you at Nice Airport, there was nothing there. The Oliver Corbyns listed didn't look like you at all."

"That's because Oliver Corbyn isn't my real name."

"What do you mean?"

"The CIA provides a new identity for some of its field agents every time they're sent on a new assignment. They provide a new passport, a new driver's license, a new Social Security number, a new credit card, and so forth. Oliver Corbyn was assigned to me specifically for the Morgan Pharma undertaking.

"You would have needed to look me up on the internet using my real name to find out more about me. The kids and the lifeguard at the pool knew me as the person who had won several international swim meets, and when they asked me for my autograph, I had to comply using my real name."

"I can't wrap my head around that. The things you're telling me are mind-blowing. So, what is your real name?"

"Are you sure you want to know? That information, if it were to become known in the wrong circles, would make it easier for those wanting to kill me."

"Yes, I want to know."

"It's Liam Richards."

Lucy was quiet as she let this sink in.

"That has a better ring to it than Oliver Corbyn," was her only comment.

"I know. But you need to keep calling me Oliver Corbyn for as long as my assignment lasts. The danger of using the wrong name at the wrong time becomes too great otherwise."

"I understand."

Lucy had no more questions. A peaceful silence settled between them as they gazed into each other's eyes, neither feeling the need to speak. After a few minutes, she closed hers, and before long, sleep claimed her.

Oliver watched her for a moment, knowing exhaustion had finally caught up with her. She hadn't been sleeping well for days—maybe even weeks—and the jet lag had only made it worse. Gently, he slipped his arm from around her and eased hers from around him, tucking the blankets around her before settling in beside her.

Moments later, he, too, drifted into sleep.

7.
HARSH REALITY

Oliver woke up early, aware he had yet to finish his PowerPoint presentation. He left the bed, collected his clothes from the floor, and headed to the shower. After dressing, he sat down to finish his presentation. He decided it represented what he wanted to say half an hour later. He then made two coffees and woke up Lucy.

"Wake up, Luce. You have forty-five minutes before we need to go down to breakfast."

Lucy smiled, remembering what had happened the previous evening. She sat up and pushed her pillows up against the headboard to drink the coffee Oliver offered her. He wished her good morning and kissed her.

"Do you have any regrets, Oliver, about what we said and did last night?"

"No regrets, sweetheart. You belong to me, and I belong to you from now on."

Oliver returned to his room to let Lucy shower and dress. She was ready at eight-fifteen, which allowed them to meet Dimitri and Sergei in time for breakfast. When they discussed their plans for the day, Lucy said she wanted to attend the conference when Oliver presented his paper. Oliver told them he needed to stay for the remaining presentations until RusPharma contacted him. He offered to take Lucy somewhere afterward.

***

By eight-forty-five, the three of them arrived at the auditorium. Lucy and Dimitri took seats in the front row while Oliver stepped onto the stage to test the microphone and laptop set up for his presentation. He inserted his flash drive, carefully reviewing the PowerPoint slides as they appeared on the large screen behind him, ensuring both text and images displayed correctly. Satisfied, he returned to his seat beside Lucy.

She leaned in, kissed his cheek, and whispered, "Good luck."

At exactly nine o'clock, the chairman of the morning session opened the proceedings. He introduced Oliver as one of several scientists at Morgan Pharma working on a cure for Alzheimer's disease. As Oliver stood to take the podium, two photographers stepped onto the stage, cameras in hand.

He had expected this—he had seen it happen the day before. Keeping his expression neutral, he raised the hand holding his clip-on microphone near his face, pretending to struggle with attaching it to his collar. It was a subtle but deliberate move, ensuring they wouldn't capture a clear photo of him.

Once they stepped away, he took a steady breath and addressed the assembled delegates.

"Thank you, Mr. Chairman. Good morning, everyone. Before I begin my address, I would like to clarify that my co-author, Dr. Will Bryce, who cannot be here today, has been on the Morgan Pharma staff for much longer than I have. He was largely responsible for the fact-finding research program Morgan Pharma implemented five years ago. That program led to the development of the medication I will present today, which, we hope, will soon be approved by the US Food and Drug Administration—the FDA.

"In my address this morning, I will describe this program in a different light than presented in the paper and provide a brief overview of other efforts to develop a cure, consistent with the nature of a keynote address. It will, I hope, elucidate what we have achieved in a way for everyone to grasp. The paper, which addresses several technical details, is there for you to study whenever you want to. Lastly, I will not be answering questions about the nature or composition of the cure. It should be obvious to everyone why I won't."

Oliver then proceeded to present his address. Lucy later said she now understood the details of what the staff at the Boston lab had achieved. The address was lucid and informative. Delegates from different countries asked questions afterward, but no one asked him about the medication itself.

***

During the coffee break, after the second paper had been presented, Oliver saw Sasha walking toward him.

"Look after Miss Lassiter, Dimitri," he said when he decided to meet her halfway.

"Good morning, Sasha. Have you talked to your director?"

"Good morning, Dr. Corbyn. Yes, I have."

"And what can you tell me?"

"We accept your proposal, but we would like to impose certain conditions on your employment."

"What conditions?"

"We want you to take up lodgings in the small hotel we have on the premises. You are not to leave the premises except on a Friday evening, when you might want to visit a restaurant, a movie theater, or some other attraction. One of us will accompany you when you do.

"The second condition we want to impose involves your cell phone. You need to hand that to us when you arrive. You might want to delete sensitive messages to your lady friend, for example, if you feel your privacy is being invaded. You will also not be provided with access to the internet.

"Finally, we want you to start tomorrow. We will pick you up here at the hotel at nine o'clock and drive you to our laboratory. I will wait for you in the lobby."

"Isn't that somewhat unusual and over the top, as we say? What's the reason for imposing such conditions?"

"Our director wants to rule out any possibility you're not who you say you are. We find it hard to believe that we can't find anything about you on the internet."

Oliver knew he needed to try to change these conditions in his favor before consenting to work for them.

"I think you should set a time limit on those conditions. A month, for example. I would then like to be able to leave the premises in the evening, and you would need to return my cell phone and allow me access to the internet."

It was clear that Sasha hadn't prepared for a discussion of the conditions her director wanted to impose.

"I must call the director to find out if he can agree to that."

Sasha took several steps away from him and proceeded to call her director. She told him about Oliver's counterproposal. Oliver listened carefully to what she was saying.

"Yes... I'll tell him. What do you want me to do when he refuses to accept?... I understand. *Dasvidaniya*."

She turned back to Oliver. "My director is willing to accept your proposal, but not before we've had the opportunity to assess your value to us over a period of two months."

"Let's compromise and agree to six weeks instead," Oliver countered.

"I'm allowed to accept that," she said, offering her hand to seal the agreement.

***

"It's done," Oliver told Lucy and Dimitri when he returned to where they were standing. "They've imposed harsh conditions. I start working for them tomorrow. They're picking me up at nine."

"What conditions?" Lucy asked him.

"I'll tell you later. You should now slap me. Sasha and her colleagues are watching, and they'll expect you to be angry with me for having decided to leave Morgan Pharma and work for them. Slap me as hard as you can. It's important."

"I don't want to, Oliver."

"You have to, sweetheart. Please take her back to her suite, Dimitri, as soon as her anger is apparent. I'll join you there as soon as I can."

She scowled and slapped him hard. She then turned to Dimitri and asked him to escort her back to her suite.

Oliver remained where he stood, nursing the side of his face. He waited until after the conference had reconvened and most of the people had entered the auditorium. He noticed that Sasha remained to watch him. Oliver decided to talk to her again.

"Miss Lassiter was outraged when I told her I would now be working for you. I hope it doesn't mean the end of our relationship. That would defeat the purpose of working for you. If I'm not in the lobby at nine tomorrow morning, you'll know I won't be able to honor what we've just agreed. Sorry."

Oliver turned and left without waiting for Sasha's response. He knew she would now be apprehensive about whether he would be in the hotel lobby the following morning.

***

Lucy clung to Oliver when he returned to her suite. Dimitri had prepared an ice pack, which Oliver held against the inflamed side of his face.

"Did I hit you too hard?"

"No, it was perfect, considering what's at stake. The way you slapped me suggests you've slapped others before. Were your boyfriends that much of a nuisance?" Oliver said with a twinkle in his eye.

"They were. Knowing what we now have together has made me realize that I threw away part of my life before meeting you."

"Don't be so critical of yourself, Luce. That part of your life has helped to shape you into who you are—impressive. There isn't a better word."

"You're making me blush. Now tell me what that Sasha woman said."

Oliver recounted his conversation with Sasha and the restrictions he faced.

"Does that mean we won't be able to talk to each other by phone during those six weeks?"

"Probably. Those six weeks will be difficult to get through for both of us."

Oliver noted her dismay. He decided she needed cheering up.

"What if we were to visit Gorky Park this afternoon? It offers enough things to see to make us forget we'll be saying goodbye to each other tomorrow."

"Sure. I'll change into something more appropriate."

"I'll order an early lunch to be brought up. Are you particular about what I order?"

"Not really. A salad, perhaps?"

Oliver turned to Dimitri. "It might be six weeks or more before I can call you about our rendezvous. Is that okay with you?"

"No problem, Oliver."

"Why don't you call Sergei and ask him to come here for lunch?"

***

Sergei drove them to the parking lot at the entrance of Gorky Park on Krymsky Val.

Lucy had never been there before. Despite the light dusting of snow, she was surprised to see preparations underway for the opening of the ice-skating rink. Around them, people cycled, skateboarded, rode Segways, rollerbladed, and played hockey, volleyball, and table tennis in the sports center. The park was alive with activity.

They explored Luna Park, braving the roller coaster, the eerie house of horrors, and the gravity-defying Fly Machine. Oliver couldn't help but smile, watching Lucy laugh and enjoy herself.

As they strolled through the park, they walked hand in hand, their fingers interlaced, with Lucy leaning into him more often than not. By the time they returned to the hotel, well after dark, they were debating where to have dinner.

Lucy suggested a restaurant she had spotted near the hotel, and the four of them decided to try it. It was late by the time they returned. Dimitri and Sergei bade them good night and headed to their rooms.

"Go to bed, Luce. I'll join you as soon as I've deleted sensitive information on my phone and my laptop. That could take up to an hour or so. I'll try not to wake you when I'm done."

"We'll see about that," she said with a smile before kissing him.

Oliver methodically deleted certain phone numbers and text messages from his cell phone, jotting down on paper the ones he would need later to facilitate his escape. Over time, he had developed a habit of embedding a specific combination of digits into critical numbers—an added layer of security in case he was subjected to a thorough search.

Next, he erased select files from his laptop, ensuring that

no sensitive information remained. Only when he was satisfied that both his phone and laptop were clean did he pick up the hotel landline to call Mitch Bannister. He knew landlines offered more security than cell phones.

The call woke Mitch.

"It'll be at least six weeks before I can tell you when to pick me up," Oliver said.

Mitch, though groggy, understood. "Got it."

"Have you told Bill what we discussed?"

"I have, and he's given me permission to buy or lease a Gulfstream G650. I've made inquiries, and I've found a G650 that we might purchase. When I'm back in the States, I need to check the aircraft's mechanical and cosmetic condition, its legal status, the FAA records, and the STC paperwork. That will take at least four weeks, so your six-week delay is more than welcome."

"That's great. I'll call you in six weeks. By the way, Lucy will want to leave tomorrow. She'll need time to pack. She should be at the airport around noon. I'll have her call you if she plans otherwise."

Once he was certain that everything was in place for his pickup by RusPharma personnel—aside from packing his baggage, which he planned to do in the morning—Oliver undressed and slipped into Lucy's bed. She was already asleep, which didn't surprise him, given how little rest she'd had in recent nights.

Lying on his side, he watched her for a moment before closing his eyes. He knew how lucky he was to have won her love, yet he had so little to offer in return. Uncertainty weighed on him. The road ahead would be difficult—was their love strong enough to withstand it?

***

Something stirred Oliver awake early the next morning. Careful not to disturb Lucy, he decided to let her sleep as long as possible. He showered, dressed, and quietly began packing his belongings.

When he finally woke her, handing her a cup of coffee, she sat up and took it with a sleepy smile—only for disappointment to flicker across her face as realization set in. She had missed her last chance to make love to him before he left.

"Why didn't you wake me up when you went to bed and again this morning when you took a shower?"

"Sorry, Luce, but you were fast asleep, and I know you've been sleeping poorly recently. I would've been selfish if I had."

"But I wanted to say goodbye to you in a way you'd remember."

"Nothing can destroy the memories I have of you, sweetheart. I'll cherish them forever."

Oliver finished packing while Lucy took a shower and dressed. Dimitri arrived at eight-thirty, as agreed.

"Miss Lassiter will want to leave the hotel at around ten this morning," Oliver told him. "Please ensure she gets to the airport before noon, unless she has other plans."

He turned to Lucy. "Now remember, Luce, you're still mad at me. So don't lavish any kisses on me when I leave to go to the lobby. I called Mitch yesterday to say you would probably want to leave Moscow later this morning. I told him you might be at the airport around noon. Does that sound about right?"

"Yes, I can manage that."

"I haven't thanked you for the bracelet," he continued while the elevator took them down to the Café Russe. "I'll treasure it forever because it was the item that brought us together."

He saw that Lucy was about to cry.

"Push the red button on the button-select panel, Dimitri, quickly!"

When the elevator car stopped between floors, Oliver cupped her face in his hands and kissed her. She clung to him, not wanting to let him go.

"Don't cry, Luce. It's okay. I'll see you again soon."

"I hope so, Oliver. Please be careful."

Lucy did her best to appear angry while they were having breakfast, but anyone watching would have noticed it was a half-hearted effort. She was on the verge of tears again when Oliver stood up to leave.

"Don't, Luce, please."

Lucy turned her head away from him. He shook the hands Dimitri and Sergei offered. He was gone before Lucy turned, wanting to watch him leave.

8.

RusPharma

Sasha was waiting for Oliver in the hotel lobby. He thought he saw her breathe a sigh of relief as he walked toward her.

"Good morning, Sasha. Were you worried I wouldn't show up this morning?"

"A little."

"Miss Lassiter and I talked about my move to RusPharma. She now understands what I want to achieve—specifically, to earn more money to allow me to remain financially independent while we're in a relationship. As long as I'm able to see her regularly, things should go well between us."

"I wouldn't have been too disappointed if you'd decided not to honor our agreement. I believe we're perfectly capable of developing the medicine without your assistance. My director thinks otherwise, however, and there's nothing I can do to change that."

"I hope to prove you wrong. I'm eager to discover the stage you've reached in your research."

Oliver recognized the vehicle parked in front of the hotel—a Bremach Taos, a Russian all-wheel-drive SUV. The driver loaded Oliver's baggage into the rear compartment before opening the back doors for them to get in.

They set off, heading northwest to intersect the Garden Ring at the Mayakovskaya Metro Station. From there, they continued along Leningradsky Avenue, a route Oliver knew well—it led to Sheremetyevo Airport and the M10 highway. As expected, they followed the M10 until reaching the exit for Zelenograd, where they turned left onto the road leading to the Polytechnic University.

They continued past the university, where the driver took the second exit at a three-way traffic circle, the road there narrowing to a single carriageway. They had entered an industrial complex. On their right, patches of grass and clusters of trees lined the road; on their left, a series of warehouses and factory buildings.

They pulled up at the gate of a site enclosed by a high wire fence that extended as far as Oliver could see. A sign on the guardhouse beside the gate displayed the address: Georgievsky Prospect 7. The guard on duty gave them a brief glance before waving them through.

Rather than stopping at the entrance of the large warehouse-like building in front of them, the driver continued along a narrow road running around its perimeter. Ahead, Oliver spotted three smaller, two-story brick buildings, their windows evenly spaced. The driver stopped at the entrance to the first one.

"This is our office building," Sasha explained as the driver unloaded their baggage.

Oliver followed Sasha inside. They were greeted by an elderly woman who introduced herself in halting English as Elena.

"She's the director's secretary," Sasha added.

Elena led them down a corridor lined with offices and meeting rooms. At the last door on the left, she knocked before pushing it open.

As they stepped inside, Oliver was met with an unexpected

sight—Dr. Lenkov, seated behind the desk, waiting for them.

"Hello, Dr. Lenkov. What are you doing here?"

"Welcome, Dr. Corbyn. I'm the director and part owner of RusPharma."

"I had no idea. Why could I not have spoken with you about my employment instead of Sasha?"

"Sasha is perfectly capable of doing what she does on my behalf. Besides, I didn't want you to know of my involvement with RusPharma if we hadn't come to an agreement."

"And shouldn't you be at the conference?"

"No, I wanted to be here when you arrived. I'll resume my presence at the conference this afternoon. I need to say a few words during the closing ceremony. Sit down. We need to talk before Sasha shows you our small hotel and the laboratory. Can I offer you coffee, perhaps?"

"Yes, please."

Dr. Lenkov ordered Elena to bring him, Sasha, and Oliver coffee.

"I assume that the conditions concerning your employment here are clear?" Lenkov asked.

"Perfectly," Oliver replied. "They are somewhat unusual, but I can understand why you'd feel the need to ensure I know on which side my bread is buttered, as we say."

"I haven't heard that figure of speech before, but it describes the situation you are in perfectly. Let me reiterate what the agreement between us entails."

Lenkov explained the conditions they would impose during the first six weeks of his employment, as agreed with Sasha.

"I agree with those conditions, but I want to be able to call Miss Lassiter every few days to allow me to maintain my relationship with her. If I don't, she's likely to find someone else to be with. She wasn't exactly happy when I told her I would be working for RusPharma from now on, but she understands the importance I place on not leeching off her wealth and thus on earning a higher salary."

"I'm not prepared to say yes to your request now. Let's see how we get along first. Now, do you have something you want to give to me?"

Oliver pulled a face to indicate how unhappy he was. He handed Lenkov his cell phone and a slip of paper on which he had written the particulars of the bank account the CIA had opened in the name of his assumed identity. Lenkov then addressed Sasha in Russian.

"You are now to show him the hotel and the laboratory. Ask the guard at the hotel to check him and his baggage for anything unusual he might have brought with him."

He switched back to English when addressing Oliver.

"Finish your coffee. Sasha will show you your room in the hotel, the laboratory, and your office. I will speak to you again later."

Sasha left the building through the back door and walked to the nearest of the remaining two buildings. Oliver followed, carrying his baggage.

"This is the hotel I was telling you about," Sasha explained. "It has ten rooms. The director had the hotel built several years ago to allow visitors who needed to be here for more than a day to stay on site."

As Oliver stepped into the building, he found himself in a short corridor with two offices—one on the left, one on the right. Behind a desk in the left office sat a uniformed guard, dressed identically to the one stationed at the front gate.

Sasha entered the guard's office while Oliver remained in the corridor. He overheard her informing the guard that the director had ordered a search of his belongings. The guard scowled, clearly irritated by the disturbance.

Sasha turned to Oliver. "Please allow him to check your baggage," she said.

Oliver complied, setting his suitcase on the desk and opening it. The guard rifled through his clothes and personal items without care, leaving them in a disorganized heap. When he reached the bottom, he gave a cursory glance at the papers Oliver had placed there before gesturing for his backpack.

This time, his inspection was more thorough. He powered up the laptop to confirm it was legitimate, then examined the laptop and phone chargers as well as Oliver's toiletry bag.

Finally, he motioned for Oliver to raise his arms. Oliver stood patiently as the guard frisked him.

Satisfied, the guard grunted and waved them through.

At the end of the corridor, Sasha pushed open a door, revealing a cafeteria that spanned the entire width and length of the remaining first-floor space. A small, functional kitchen stood at one end while rows of tables and chairs provided seating for about twenty-five people. Two elderly women worked in the kitchen, moving methodically through their tasks.

"The cafeteria is mainly used by staff for lunch," Sasha explained. "But those staying in the hotel also have breakfast and dinner here."

She then led Oliver back into the corridor, guiding him toward a staircase on the left.

On the second floor, a corridor stretched the length of the building. Five doors on either side led to a total of ten rooms. Sasha stopped at the first door on the right and opened it.

"This is your room, Dr. Corbyn."

Oliver placed his baggage on the bed, took a brief look around, inspected the bathroom, then walked to the window. From there, he could see the building where he had met with Lenkov, as well as the large factory-like structure behind it.

Sasha led him back downstairs and outside, guiding him toward the entrance of the third building.

"This is our laboratory," she said.

The entrance consisted of an air lock, which led into a

dressing area where staff changed into sterile attire. Inside a large cabinet, neatly organized drawers held the necessary clothing: white coveralls secured at the wrists, ankles, and neck with elastic, disposable shoe covers, nitrile gloves, and disposable head covers.

Sasha selected fresh garments for both of them and handed Oliver his set. He put them on, as did she. Once they were fully suited, she opened the door to the lab.

Inside, the space was well organized and equipped with modern technology—most of which, Oliver guessed, had been sourced from the US or Europe. He scanned the room, taking in the centrifuges, microscopes, freezers, hot plates, incubators, coolers, stirrers, and water baths. A dozen researchers worked at the various benches, including Alexei and Anatoly, who acknowledged him with a brief nod.

As Sasha guided him through the lab, Oliver carefully observed the ongoing work. He quickly noticed that some of the tasks being performed had little relevance to producing a medication for Alzheimer's. If left to their own devices, they still had a long way to go.

After the tour, they returned to the dressing room and removed their sterile clothing. Sasha then led him up a staircase to the second floor, entering through another door in the air lock.

This level housed a series of offices—nine on either side of the corridor. Each office was identical, furnished with a desk and chair positioned opposite the door, a cabinet in the corner, and two guest chairs in front of the desk. Two computer monitors sat side by side on the desk, with the computer tower placed on the floor.

"Every one of our scientists, after working in the laboratory, retreats to his or her office on this floor to write up the results of their research," Sasha said. "There are sixteen of us, including me. I'll introduce you to each of my colleagues properly during lunch. Your office is the last on the right."

"Where do you do your pharmaceutical manufacturing? I've been told you do a lot of that."

"We do that in the large building you saw when we arrived."

"I'd like to visit that too at some stage," he said.

"Don't worry, you will. You'll need to help us set up the production line for the medicine there. You might now want to settle in, both in your room and in your office," Sasha continued. "I'll collect you for lunch."

Following Sasha's suggestion, Oliver returned to the hotel and unpacked, neatly arranging his clothes in the wardrobe. He tested the bed and found it firm enough that he would likely sleep well. A quick check of the door revealed something unexpected—it couldn't be locked from either the inside or the outside.

Picking up his laptop and charger, he made his way back to the office assigned to him. He powered up the desktop computer and browsed through its files. Most were in Russian, containing reports on the work Sasha and her colleagues had conducted. He decided to review them later.

One folder caught his attention: "Morgan Pharma."

When he opened it, he found the files that had been stolen from the server in Boston. He hadn't expected to locate them so easily. Playing along, he decided he would act surprised when they eventually revealed their existence to him.

***

At twelve-thirty, Sasha came to collect Oliver for lunch.

As they entered the cafeteria, she introduced him to her colleagues. Most spoke little to no English, which made Oliver wonder how they were supposed to study the Morgan Pharma files. So far, only Lenkov and Sasha had demonstrated fluency in reading, writing, and speaking English. The realization hit him—his presence here was more essential than he had initially thought. No wonder they had approached him so quickly at the cocktail party once they learned he was open to working in Russia.

Lunch consisted of *kotleti*—pan-fried meat patties. He shared a table with Sasha, quietly processing everything he had just learned.

"What do you want to do first?"

"I want to speak with all of your people about what they are presently engaged in," Oliver replied. "When I was in the laboratory before lunch, I noticed some of them performing tasks that have no bearing on the development of the medication. I want to point that out to them and explain what processes they could be doing instead."

"I'll need to discuss that with the director because he provides each of us with a list of what needs to be accomplished every week. Your proposal would interfere with what he wants us to do."

"Okay. I'll study the files on the computer in my office while you talk to Dr. Lenkov."

"Most are in Russian," she added.

"That shouldn't be a problem if they contain descriptions of chemical compositions and reactions and mathematical formulations."

"By the way, Dr. Corbyn, you'll find files on your computer we've been able to obtain from Morgan Pharma."

Oliver feigned surprise. "That's impossible. How?"

"I don't know. The director didn't tell us. We think someone at Morgan Pharma sold them to him."

Oliver feigned even greater surprise and shook his head. "That's hard to believe."

Sasha looked at him without saying anything. Oliver was unable to decide whether she was aware of the computer hack.

"So, what have you been able to learn from those files?" Oliver continued.

"Only the director and I have studied them. My other colleagues are presently learning English to be able to also study them. I find the contents of the most important documents to be very difficult to understand. They refer to chemical processes we know little about."

"But this morning you told me you were confident in being able to develop the medicine without assistance."

"I am, but that would take more time than we have if we want to be the first to introduce the medicine."

"You'll find that those files become easier to understand after I teach you and your colleagues the processes I referred to earlier. When you speak to Dr. Lenkov, you should point that out to him."

After lunch, Sasha left to speak with Lenkov. Later, she informed Oliver that the director had approved his plan. He had already decided to teach them a mix of relevant and irrelevant chemical processes, ensuring they remained uncertain about what was truly necessary.

***

Oliver established a routine at RusPharma, starting each day with a thirty-minute run along the inside of the perimeter fence at seven in the morning. He had brought his running shoes, knowing it would be the only way to stay fit. His daily run also gave him a chance to observe the site in detail. Afterward, he spent fifteen minutes stretching and exercising before showering and dressing for breakfast at eight.

During the day, he worked diligently—preparing lessons when he wasn't explaining chemical methods to Sasha. He often stayed late in the laboratory, earning their respect over time as they warmed up to him.

For the first three weeks, Oliver never left the premises. He repeatedly asked Sasha to arrange permission for him to call Lucy, but each time Lenkov refused. He longed to hear her voice but avoided pressing the issue. Even if permission were granted, he worried the call would be monitored, and the risk of saying something that could jeopardize the assignment kept him from pushing further.

The monotony of his work soon became suffocating. Evenings were the worst. With the staff gone by six, he was left alone to reheat the dinner prepared for him and eat in silence. The hotel rooms had no television, no internet—nothing to distract him. He regretted not bringing books or anything to occupy his mind. Inevitably, his thoughts drifted to Lucy as he lay on the bed, staring at the ceiling.

***

By the end of the third week, Oliver had finished teaching Sasha's colleagues new chemical processes. The task had taken longer than expected due to Sasha having to interpret everything for them. Now, he knew they were expecting him to explain the Morgan Pharma documents. To avoid revealing anything critical, he started with the most inconsequential, hoping he could stall long enough to escape before having to address the more important ones.

To help with his explanations, Oliver asked Sasha for a whiteboard. She arranged for one to be delivered and mounted on the wall of his office. Both she and Lenkov attended his first session. While Lenkov listened selectively, often walking out before the explanations were complete, Sasha remained engaged, taking meticulous notes. Before long, Oliver discovered she was translating everything into Russian for her colleagues.

During the fourth week, Oliver told Sasha he wanted to go out for dinner on Friday night. He asked her to accompany him so they could talk about something other than work.

She hesitated for a moment, then smiled. He couldn't recall if she'd ever smiled at him before.

That Friday night, the same driver who had picked them up at the Ritz-Carlton drove them to a nearby restaurant. The food was mediocre, but at least it was different from what he'd been eating for weeks. Surprisingly, Sasha turned out to be better company than he had expected.

Over dinner, she shared her story—why she had chosen to study pharmacy, how she had ended up at RusPharma, and her frustrations with the way Lenkov stifled initiative. She admitted she wanted to work abroad one day, but for now, she stayed because she knew that if their team succeeded in developing a cure for Alzheimer's, their names would become well-known. That recognition, she believed, would be her stepping stone to leaving Russia.

As Oliver listened, he realized something else—Sasha now respected him too.

***

By the sixth week, Oliver had begun formulating his sabotage plan.

His plan was simple—set fire to the laboratory after everyone had left and unleash a virus on the connected computers. The virus, stored on his laptop, would spread across the entire local system, wiping out crucial data.

The real challenge, however, was Lenkov's computer. If it wasn't connected to the network and also held the stolen Morgan Pharma files, it would need to be either destroyed or infected separately. Oliver decided to bring it up with Sasha during their next outing.

That Friday, she once again agreed to have dinner with him, and they were driven to the same restaurant. This time, Sasha seemed more animated than usual, engaging him in lively conversation. Oliver couldn't shake the feeling she was hitting on him.

At one point, she subtly steered the discussion toward their working relationship.

"Do you like working with me?" she asked, her tone light but curious.

Sensing an opportunity, Oliver played along, feigning interest in a way he knew she would notice.

Then she brought up Lucy.

"Do you think she's waiting for you?"

Oliver hesitated before answering. "She probably has another boyfriend by now."

Sasha studied him for a moment, then reached across the table and placed a comforting hand on his arm when she saw the sadness in his expression.

Oliver took it as the right moment. "You need to tell me, Sasha, how you acquired the Morgan Pharma files. It troubles me greatly to learn that perhaps you and Dr. Lenkov used illegal means to obtain them."

It caused a lull in their conversation for the first time.

"I don't know what to say, Oliver. I think they were obtained illegally, but I'm not certain. The director was proud to announce he had acquired them. Questions we raised about how he came to possess them were not answered. All he did was smile at us."

"Does he study the files in detail?"

"He does. I've seen him make notes when studying the files at his desk. And he eagerly reads my notes on your explanations on the whiteboard."

Oliver had heard enough. He now knew he needed to destroy the computer in Lenkov's office as well.

He already held keys to the laboratory, allowing him to

work after hours if needed, but he had no access to the building where Lenkov's office was located. That meant he would have to force the back door. The risk of being caught was minimal—the guard stationed at the hotel always left with the other staff members at the end of the day, and the one at the front gate was too far away to see or hear anything.

When the driver dropped him off at the hotel before taking Sasha home, Oliver turned to her, offering a polite yet deliberate gesture—a kiss on the cheek.

"Thanks for tonight. I enjoyed your company," he said.

Sasha blushed and smiled, clearly pleased.

Oliver had seen that reaction before. He knew he had won her over—just as he had won the trust of women in every organization he had ever needed to infiltrate.

***

Oliver's cell phone was returned to him after he had been present for precisely six weeks. That Wednesday evening, on December 22, he called Mitch Bannister.

"Hi, Mitch, are you alone? Can you talk?"

"Sure."

"Is Thursday next week at two in the morning a possibility? Just say yes or no, please."

"Yes."

"Okay. I'll call next Monday to confirm."

Oliver then called Dimitri.

"Hi, Dimitri. Is next Tuesday at eight in the evening a possibility?"

"Let me look into that, please."

"Okay. I'll call again the day after tomorrow."

Oliver thought about calling Lucy, but with his escape imminent, it felt too risky—no matter how short. If his calls were being monitored, contacting Dimitri and Mitch was already pushing his luck.

Still, guilt gnawed at him. He had the chance to hear her voice, yet he was deliberately staying silent. He felt especially guilty for not insisting on calling her on her birthday, December 10. Did she miss him as much as he missed her? Was she even still waiting for him?

Pushing those thoughts aside, he focused on the plan.

***

On Christmas Eve, Oliver called Dimitri again. A surge of adrenaline coursed through him when Dimitri confirmed he could pick him up on Tuesday, December 28, at eight in the evening.

Next, he called Mitch. "I'll be at the agreed location on Thursday, December thirtieth, at two in the morning," he said, keeping it brief.

If everything went according to plan, he would be gone before he had to reveal anything truly critical. By the time of his escape, he would have covered almost every Morgan Pharma document on his list. The next phase—detailing the exact method for producing the medication and revealing its chemical composition—was where he had to draw the line.

He needed to leave before he reached that point.

***

Oliver continued instructing Sasha in his office over the following days, including December 25—after all, Christmas in Russia was celebrated on January 7.

That morning, Sasha hesitated before asking, "Do you want to take the day off?"

He noticed the eagerness in her voice, the unspoken hope he would say no.

"Let's keep working," he replied. He wasn't sure how he would have spent the day alone anyway.

9.
ESCAPE FROM ZELENOGRAD

Oliver released the virus onto the computer in his office at precisely 7:15 p.m. on Tuesday, December 28—after everyone had left the premises. He knew that once the network came online, the virus would spread to every connected machine.

Back in his room, he changed into all black: a T-shirt, pants, North Face parka, sneakers, and a balaclava—one he had crafted from an old sweater during his solitary nights. He packed his laptop and everything he couldn't afford to leave behind into his backpack, abandoning the rest of his belongings.

With the backpack slung over his shoulder, Oliver returned to the laboratory. He grabbed a container of white gasoline—fuel used by Sasha and her colleagues for a specific burner—and doused the lab cabinets, ensuring the liquid seeped into the compartments where flammable and explosive chemicals were stored. Then he struck a match and flicked it onto the gasoline.

He hurried to the back door of the office building. Using his elbow, he shattered the small window, reached inside, and turned the key in the lock. As expected, Lenkov's office was also locked, but since the door opened inward, a well-placed kick shattered the lock, sending it swinging open. Oliver emptied the remaining gasoline onto Lenkov's desk, computer, and desk drawers—pausing when he spotted several drives inside. He soaked those as well before igniting the liquid.

As he exited the building, a thunderous chain of explosions tore through the laboratory.

Oliver sprinted toward the front gate. As he rounded the medicine-production building, he spotted the guard emerging from his post, a cell phone pressed to his ear. Without hesitation, Oliver stepped out of his path, his dark clothing allowing him to vanish into the night.

He kept running, his pace unrelenting. The parking lot opposite the university, where he had asked Dimitri to park, was three hundred yards away. When he reached it, relief washed over him—there it was, the black Mercedes.

Throwing open the back door, Oliver leaped inside, ripping off his balaclava as he did.

"Drive, Sergei, before they discover us!"

"Hello to you too, Oliver," Dimitri said from the passenger seat.

"Sorry, Dimitri, I'm a little tense. I set the lab on fire. Firefighting services and the authorities will be here soon, and they might close off the whole area. We need to hurry."

"Do you still want us to drive you to the Belarus border via the M1?"

"Yes... I've arranged for a pickup in Belarus."

"It's about a six-hour drive by way of the intersection with the MKAD Ring and the Mozhayskoye Highway, where the M1 starts. The road is signposted as the M1 and sometimes as the E30."

"I know. I've driven along the M1 myself. How did you get Alex to allow both of you to pick me up with the company car?"

"Miss Lassiter arranged it."

"What do you mean?"

"When we were driving her to the airport after you left, she asked me if you and I had talked about picking you up. I didn't want to lie about it, so I said we had. She wanted to know all the details. She subsequently contacted Alex and asked him to allow us to pick you up."

Oliver smiled to himself. Lucy was smart for having suspected he needed to be picked up somewhere and that he would have talked to Dimitri about it.

"Did you tell Miss Lassiter where I asked you to take me?"

"I did. It caused her considerable worry because I wasn't able to tell her what you were going to do once you reached the border."

Oliver settled into the back seat, shifting slightly to find a comfortable position. He closed his eyes, willing himself to sleep—knowing rest would be scarce once they reached the border. The warmth of the car, the steady hum of the engine, and the rhythmic whisper of tires against the asphalt lulled him into an uneasy slumber.

When he woke, the car was no longer moving. Blinking away the haze of sleep, he realized Sergei had pulled into a gas station. Through the window, he saw him stepping out, the cold night air briefly swirling into the car as the door opened and shut. A moment later, Oliver spotted him inside the station, picking up food and drinks before heading to the pump to refuel.

For now, the road was still.

But for how long?

"We're making good progress, Oliver," Dimitri said. "We should be at the border in three hours."

"You need to let me out of the car about half a mile before the border, Dimitri. You should then turn around and go home."

"But how are you going to cross into Belarus? The border crossing is guarded by the Federal Border Guard Service—the FPS."

"I'll figure something out when I'm there. But we can't risk crossing the border in this car. They might have orders to check every car intending to leave Russia on discovering the fire and the explosion were willfully caused. Even if I were to cross without being detected, and you were to cross intending to pick me up some distance past the border, they would find out who you are and that this car is owned by Morgan Pharma. We want to avoid that at all costs."

"I hadn't given that much thought. You're right. We need to return to Saint Petersburg without being stopped to explain who we are."

Little was said for the remainder of the drive. When Sergei estimated they were about half a mile from the border crossing—where the dual carriageway narrowed into a divided highway—he pulled over to the side of the road.

Oliver shook hands with both men, gratitude evident in his expression. "I hope we cross paths again someday," he said as he stepped out of the car.

Sergei nodded, then turned the vehicle around. Oliver watched as the car accelerated into the distance, its taillights fading into the night. Once they disappeared, he turned and continued on foot toward the border.

He knew that, at this point, the Russia-Belarus border ran down the middle of the highway for half a mile. Buildings lined both sides, offering services and rest facilities while a queue of trucks waited for inspection. Skirting the tree line along the roadside, he moved carefully. Where the cover thinned, he increased his distance from the road. As long as no one got too close, he was invisible in the darkness.

After crossing the border undetected, Oliver pressed on. The remaining forty miles to the runway had to be covered on foot. He started jogging.

***

After having covered approximately half the distance, the silhouette of a lone shed materialized in the farmland to Oliver's left, standing out against the overcast night sky. Fifty yards from the road, it offered the shelter he needed.

With sunrise only an hour away, he took the opportunity to rest. He lay down on the rough wooden planks of the shed floor, trying to make himself as comfortable as possible. But the cold gnawed at him, and every joint ached from the exertion. Sleep eluded him—until the sun had begun to rise.

***

Oliver woke after only two hours. His body was stiff, his muscles sore from the distance he had covered. But staying hidden during daylight hours was necessary. Dressed as he was, any passerby would find his appearance suspicious.

The day dragged on. He tried to sleep again, but rest wouldn't come. When darkness finally fell, he resumed his journey. With nine hours left until the pickup, he no longer needed to hurry. He alternated between jogging for fifteen minutes and walking briskly for another fifteen.

Three hours later, he reached the intersection with the P15. Mitch had instructed him to follow the road south until he found a bend where a secondary road branched off—his final route to the airfield.

It took him another two hours to find the runway. He approached its northeastern end and searched for cover, knowing he still had four more hours before extraction. A cluster of low shrubs about a hundred yards from the tarmac provided a sufficient hiding spot. He settled in, exhaustion weighing heavily on him.

His escape from Zelenograd, from the moment he had

set the RusPharma laboratory ablaze, had stretched to twenty-six hours. Now, he needed to stay alert for just four more—if Mitch had managed to secure the Gulfstream and make it to Helsinki Airport in time for their flight to Damascus.

Fighting exhaustion, Oliver checked his phone, just as he had done countless times since crossing the border. No signal.

At 2:05 a.m., with no sign of Mitch, he considered making his way to the far end of the ten-thousand-foot runway, where construction sites might offer a better chance of connecting to a network. Then a sound cut through the silence.

A jet engine.

Oliver stood, heart pounding, as the familiar hum grew louder. Moments later, bright white landing lights flicked on, illuminating the aircraft as it descended onto the runway. It touched down smoothly, then immediately dimmed its lights, taxiing at high speed toward his position.

Oliver sprinted forward, closing the distance between himself and the plane. But as he ran, a flash of movement caught his eye. At the opposite end of the runway, headlights blazed to life. Vehicles. Moving fast.

His pulse hammered as the realization set in: They weren't alone.

The Gulfstream executed a rapid U-turn just as Oliver reached it. The cabin door swung open, and a familiar face appeared in the doorway.

Dave.

"Hurry!" Dave shouted, reaching out as Oliver leaped onto the boarding stairs. He grabbed the handrails, using them to pull himself up against the force of the turning aircraft.

As soon as Oliver was inside, Dave slammed the door shut and yelled toward the cockpit, "We've got him!"

The jet's engines roared to full power, propelling them forward—straight toward the oncoming vehicles.

"Sit down and fasten your seatbelts, you two, quickly!" Mitch shouted as the plane hurtled toward an imminent fate.

The distance between the jet and the vehicles quickly reduced. Just when it looked as if a collision was unavoidable, the vehicles swerved to the side of the runway. The jet took to the air a few seconds later. Dave had returned to his seat in the cockpit. Oliver remained in the seat he had jumped into to catch his breath.

"Thanks, both of you," Oliver said when he judged it was safe to talk to Mitch and Dave in the cockpit. "I hadn't allowed for something like that to happen, assuming everyone would be asleep when you landed."

"Nor did I," Mitch replied. "They must now monitor their radar displays around the clock—probably as a result of the tension between Russia and the NATO countries. I believed I was flying low enough not to be detected by radar. It was a close call. You might want to return to your seat, Oliver, and fasten your seatbelt again, just in case we need to take evasive action along the remainder of the route out of Belarusian airspace."

Oliver was hungry and, after eating and drinking what was available, did as Mitch suggested, glad to be able to sit in a comfortable seat once again. Drowsiness soon overwhelmed him. The stress had left his body.

***

Oliver woke up when Mitch tapped him on the shoulder. He noticed they had landed.

"Sorry to wake you, Oliver, but we need to talk. Your clothes are filthy and torn. Are you in a rush to get to the States?"

"No, not really. Why, what's wrong?"

"There's nothing wrong, but you can't leave the plane looking like you do. That will lead to all sorts of questions about who you are, both here in Damascus and back home. Have you got an extra set of clothes in that backpack of yours?"

"No. I thought I wouldn't need to change my clothes."

"Dave and I have to get some sleep before we fly to LA. If our logbooks show we flew the plane from Helsinki to LA via Damascus without a rest along the way, we'll get into trouble. We're thinking of booking a hotel near the airport. I'd prefer you stay on board to avoid questions being asked about having a passenger on arrival when we didn't when leaving Helsinki. I'll loan you a shirt and pants."

"I'll take a shower and change into those clothes, Mitch. I'll stay here."

"No problem. You probably have good reasons to do so. As soon as Dave has overseen the refueling, we'll leave and return in about eight hours."

"Sure. Thanks again for picking me up. I owe you one. Why are we flying to LA instead of to Boston, New York, or DC, by the way?"

"Bill's orders. He wants to talk to you. He told me I could fly you to wherever you wanted to go afterward."

When Dave returned, Mitch handed Oliver a shirt and a pair of pants. He and Dave left, taking their baggage with them. Oliver took a shower, changed his clothes, and rearranged the seating on the G650 to make a bed.

***

Oliver woke up when Mitch and Dave returned. He looked at his watch. It was two-thirty in the afternoon, Moscow time, on December 31.

"You might be interested to know there was a major fire at the RusPharma site," Mitch said. "I made a point of looking up the local news in Moscow."

"Thanks, Mitch. I was aware of that."

10.

LOS ANGELES

The Gulfstream touched down at Van Nuys Airport at 7:10 p.m. local time on Friday, New Year's Eve. As soon as the plane taxied to the Jet Aviation terminal, passport and customs officers boarded to complete their inspections.

Mitch turned to Oliver. "No need to wait for us," he said. "We've got another fifteen minutes of paperwork to handle. Lucy's probably waiting for you."

Oliver nodded, shaking hands with both Mitch and Dave. "Thanks again—for everything."

With that, he stepped off the plane and entered the terminal.

The moment he walked through the doors, he spotted her.

She was running toward him, her colorful dress flowing with every step. Her long, light blonde hair curled in soft waves, cascading over her shoulders. The bright red of her lips matched the bold streaks in her dress, a striking contrast against the color of her skin.

Then, in an instant, she was in his arms.

She leaped, wrapping her arms around his neck and her legs around his waist, pressing her lips to his in a deep, desperate kiss.

The world around them faded—until the sound of applause brought it rushing back.

People in the terminal had stopped to watch, breaking into cheers and claps.

Oliver smiled against her lips. "Didn't realize we had an audience."

Lucy pulled back just enough to look at him, her blue eyes shining. "Let them watch," she whispered before kissing him again.

"Wow, a welcome like that would make any man want to go away somewhere just to be able to return," Oliver said after their embrace.

"I was worried you wouldn't return at all."

"Why would you think that?"

"The Russians might have wanted to harm you or take you prisoner if they were to discover what you intended to do."

"I'm okay, sweetheart, apart from needing another set of clothes."

"What happened to your clothes?" she asked while they were walking toward the red Audi R8 convertible parked nearby.

"You don't want to know," he replied.

"But I do. I want to know everything. What you did at RusPharma, and now everything about your clothes."

Oliver smiled and kissed her on the cheek when they reached the car. He placed his backpack behind one of the front seats, opened the door for her to get behind the wheel, and then climbed into the passenger seat.

"I'll tell you everything you want to know later. Mitch told me that Bill wants to talk to me."

"We all want to talk to you. We heard there was a major fire at the RusPharma facility. We assumed you had something to do with that."

"Thanks for talking to Alex about allowing Dimitri and Sergei to pick me up, by the way."

"I was angry with you, Oliver, when I found out you'd talked to Dimitri about driving you to the Belarus border and again when I found out you'd talked to Mitch about picking you up."

"I wanted to avoid alarming you, Luce. I figured you might be worried all the time I was away if you knew the details of what I had to do. This is a nice car. Is it yours?"

"Are you changing the subject?"

"I guess I am."

"But why?"

"It's complicated. Would you mind if we talked about this later?"

"Because you don't know what to say just now?"

"I do, but I'd rather tell you under different circumstances."

"Are you talking to me in riddles again? What circumstances are you referring to?"

"When the joy of seeing you again has become manageable. It's not manageable just now, and I don't want to lose the happy feeling I have by talking about what happened in Russia."

Lucy studied his face, searching for any sign of hesitation, any hint that his reluctance to talk about Russia was anything but genuine. But what she saw convinced her—his silence wasn't evasion; it was the weight of the moment.

Relief washed over her. More than that, she was moved by how deeply their reunion had affected him. Seven weeks apart had been long, but seeing the emotion in his eyes, she realized just how much he had missed her.

And she had missed him just as much.

"I thought you lived in New York, Luce. I wasn't happy when Mitch told me he had to fly me to LA until I saw you running toward me."

"When Bill told me he wanted to talk to you immediately after you returned, I asked Mitch to fly me to LA before he had to fly to Helsinki. The seven weeks you were away were hard on me."

"I'm sorry. I was alone in my room at the RusPharma site virtually every evening, without TV, internet, or books to read. All I could do was think of you. I relived every moment we spent together a hundred times. I'd have given anything to have been able to talk to you while I was there. I asked the director to allow me to call you every few days, but he refused, even when I said, on December tenth, it was your birthday."

"That puts my mind at ease, knowing you missed me as much as I missed you. What are the implications of that for our future together?"

"I've thought about that too, sweetheart. I don't know the answer to that question. Let's enjoy the moments we can be together, okay?"

Lucy didn't answer him, and Oliver realized she would want a serious discussion about her question soon.

Lucy had taken Interstate 405 south from the airport. She took the off-ramp to head east on Sunset Boulevard and then headed north on Benedict Canyon Road, finally reaching the cul-de-sac called Hilary Lane in Beverly Hills, where she parked the car in the designated parking space of the last house. She led him inside, and, placing his backpack in the hallway, he followed her to the sundeck at the rear of the house, where Jacky and Bill were enjoying a glass of wine.

"Welcome, Oliver," Bill said, standing up to shake his hand. Jacky, likewise, stood up to welcome him.

"Can I get you two something to drink?" Bill asked.

"I wouldn't mind a beer," Oliver replied.

"Let me get the drinks," Lucy offered.

"Please excuse the way I'm dressed," Oliver said. "The shirt and pants I'm wearing were loaned to me by Mitch. I escaped from Russia wearing black clothing because I wanted to be inconspicuous during the night. My clothes were torn and dirty by the time Mitch picked me up. I had to leave almost everything behind."

"Tell us what happened. All we know is that the RusPharma lab burned to the ground two days ago."

"I'll spare you the details, but the short of it is quickly told."

Lucy joined them and placed the drinks on the table. She had prepared herself a martini. She moved her chair up against Oliver's. He placed his arm around her shoulders. She smiled at him.

"When I arrived at RusPharma, I discovered they had a long way to go to develop the medicine without outside help. Their chemical processes were archaic. I spent the first three weeks or so teaching them new ones, some important for the production of the medicine and some not.

"I found the Boston files on the computer they gave me to use. They wouldn't tell me how they came to have them. I spent the next three weeks as a college professor would, explaining what some of those files meant.

"They returned my cell phone to me at the beginning of the seventh week. I called Dimitri and Mitch and arranged when and where I wanted to be picked up. Early in the evening, a few days later, after everyone had left, I set the lab and an office building on fire and escaped. Dimitri and Sergei drove me to the Belarus border. I jogged the forty miles to Orsha Airfield, where Mitch picked me up very early in the morning."

"Was it really that simple?" Jacky asked. "Or have you left things out to make it sound simple?"

"It was hard, Jacky, mainly because of being alone every evening with nothing to do. I'm glad it's done. I need to thank both of you for allowing Mitch to do what I asked him."

"We needed a second plane anyway, Oliver," Bill said.

"So, was it necessary to do what you did? Would they have been able to develop the medication on their own?" Jacky asked.

"I believe they might have been able to if they seriously studied those files, which they hadn't when I arrived, but it would take them a long time. They needed someone like me if they wanted to introduce the cure before Morgan Pharma can. There was no alternative but to go there and destroy their lab and the files, as I did. They would otherwise have continued with what they were doing."

"Would you do it all again if necessary?" Bill asked.

"Yes, if necessary."

"How can we reward you for what you did?"

"Don't worry about it, Bill. I've already been rewarded."

"What do you mean?"

"During the days Lucy and I were together, I discovered who she really is."

"Yes, I noticed you two look cozy. Does that mean what I think it does?" Jacky asked.

"Are you going to answer that question, Luce, or shall I?"

"I love him, Mother, in a way I didn't know existed. I want to be with him all the time."

"Bill and I guessed as much from what you told us on returning from Moscow, and from no longer wanting to be associated with your previous friends. Isn't that a reason, Oliver, for needing to tell us a little more about yourself? To us, you're still very much a mystery, and we're very particular about someone who has an interest in Lucy like you have."

"Did you also ask Lucy's boyfriends to tell you more about themselves?"

"Don't get angry, Oliver. The fact is that Bill and I knew that none of Lucy's boyfriends would go the distance when we saw how she acted around them."

"I'm not angry for you asking me to tell you something about myself. I told Lucy everything about myself. Do you mind if we left it at that?"

"Lucy would have wanted to know everything about you to find out if you loved her, but Bill and I need to know your intentions. As you know, Lucy will inherit Morgan Pharma one day, which will make her one of the wealthiest people in the world."

"I've come to know Lucy as a levelheaded and intelligent woman. She would already have noticed if I had devious intentions. You're not giving her due credit. But let me put you both at ease. I told Lucy, and Lucy told you, I work for the CIA. But what you don't know is that I'm a field agent and take orders directly from the director and someone else in an important position. This last person—I had to promise never to mention his name—ordered me to do everything in my power to ensure Morgan Pharma was first to introduce the Alzheimer's cure. Morgan Pharma has friends in high places.

"You also need to know that I have no designs on Lucy's wealth. I hope to always be able to provide for myself. I only want her to love me, like I love her, for the rest of my days. I'll stand by her and support her in every way I can."

Jacky and Bill were stirred by Oliver's genuineness.

"I apologize for acting as though I have doubts about you, Oliver. Please accept my apology," Bill said.

"And mine," Jacky added.

Lucy was happy to hear Oliver confess his love for her in the way he had. She left her chair to sit on his lap and, putting her arms around him, kissed him.

"I'm yours to have and hold forever," she whispered. "You mustn't tell anyone what Oliver just said," Lucy commented, turning to look at her parents. "You'll be making his work much more dangerous if people were to know who he is and what he does."

Jacky and Bill nodded, and Oliver concluded his secret was safe with all three of them.

"Can we talk about something else now, please?" Lucy asked.

"Before we start, I just want to say—I'm not comfortable in these clothes. I need to hit some stores and pick up some clothes and shoes. Also, if it works for you, I'd love to go for a swim in your pool while I'm here. I haven't been able to swim in seven weeks."

"Let me take you to the store to buy you clothes," Lucy proposed.

"But it's nearly nine in the evening on New Year's Eve, and the stores you'd want to visit are closed," Jacky commented.

"Not necessarily. Let me make a phone call."

Lucy left and returned a few minutes later.

"A friend of mine owns a well-known men's clothing brand. She lives near here. She's willing to open the Beverly Hills store exclusively for us."

***

Lucy drove Oliver to her friend's boutique, where he picked out a complete casual outfit, several shirts, T-shirts, and shorts. He also selected a suit, a swimsuit, and—upon discovering the store carried shoes—a pair of sneakers along with a stylish pair to match the suit. Before returning, they stopped by a nearby twenty-four-hour store to pick up a suitcase.

Back at the Lassiter home, they were greeted with the news that the cook was preparing a late dinner. With just enough time for a swim, Oliver didn't need to be told twice.

***

Dinner was a semiformal affair in the elegant dining room. Oliver, ravenous after the meager offerings on the plane, welcomed the meal. He and Lucy sat side by side, while Jacky and Bill took the seats opposite them. The arrangement allowed Lucy to brush against him playfully under the table, her touch light but mischievous.

Laughter and conversation flowed easily, spirits lifted further by the wine. As midnight approached, they raised their glasses and wished each other a happy New Year.

When Lucy announced she was ready for bed, Jacky smiled and turned to her. "Why don't you show Oliver the guest suite?"

"No, Mother, I want Oliver to sleep with me. We have a lot to catch up on."

"I understand, dear. Sorry."

Oliver followed Lucy into her bedroom, taking in his surroundings with quiet amusement. The room had changed little since her teenage years—posters of boy bands still adorned the walls, remnants of a time when life was simpler. It reminded him of the bedroom where he and his first girlfriend had shared their most intimate firsts, a memory that felt both distant and strangely familiar.

When the door clicked shut behind them, Oliver turned to Lucy, and she was already in his arms. Their kiss was deep, unhurried, and filled with the longing of weeks spent apart. As her hands reached for his shirt, he gently stopped her.

"I need a shower first, Luce," he murmured against her lips. "Before we do anything. May I use your bathroom? I promise I won't take long."

Lucy smiled playfully, already unbuttoning her dress. "Of course. You'll find towels under the vanity."

Fifteen minutes later, Oliver slipped beneath the blankets, his skin still warm from the shower. The bed was smaller than the one they had shared in Moscow, forcing them closer—something he didn't mind at all.

He turned to Lucy. She lay on her back, eyes closed, her breathing even. As he studied her for a moment, something told him she wasn't really asleep—just waiting, teasing. A slow smile crept onto his lips.

He leaned in, brushing his lips lightly against hers before trailing soft kisses over her closed eyelids, along the curve of her cheek, down to the sensitive hollow beneath her ear. He moved slowly, deliberately, savoring every subtle shift in her breathing.

Lucy remained still, as though determined to keep up the illusion. But when his lips traced lower, beneath the hem of her pajama top, he felt her muscles tighten ever so slightly.

He smiled against her skin.

Continuing his gentle exploration, he kissed her in places that made her breath hitch, places that tested her resolve to keep pretending. He noticed the way her fingers curled against the sheets and how her breathing deepened, uneven and shaky.

But it wasn't until he kissed the most sensitive part of her body that her restraint crumbled. A soft gasp escaped her lips, her fingers tangling into his hair, holding him in place as if afraid he might stop. She shuddered beneath him, her quiet whimpers breaking into something more primal, more urgent.

Only when her trembling ceased did Oliver pull the blankets back over them, drawing her into his arms. As her breathing steadied, she finally opened her eyes.

She smiled, her fingers tracing the line of his jaw. "You knew, didn't you?" she whispered.

Oliver smirked. "Knew what?"

She laughed softly, curling against him. "That I wasn't really asleep."

Oliver smiled, not wanting to answer the implied question.

"You've just fulfilled a fantasy I've had since I was a teenager: being awakened in my bed by a man I love who is making love to me," she said. "It's one of those fantasies girls have about the person they're head over heels in love with—like I am with you."

"But you were only pretending to be asleep."

"I was."

"I tried to let you keep believing that I didn't know you were faking by doing things that allowed you to keep relatively still until the end. But I'm willing to make the whole of your fantasy come true by making love to you while you're truly asleep. I won't tell you when. It'll be a surprise."

"I hope that's not an empty promise, Oliver."

"I wouldn't break a promise like that. What makes you think I would?"

"I'll tell you later, after I've made love to you."

Lucy slipped off his T-shirt and shorts, shedding her pajama top and panties in turn. Pressing herself against him, she reveled in the warmth of their bare skin, the way their bodies fitted together so seamlessly—as if they had been made for each other.

Her hands explored him slowly, tracing the contours of his back, the firm lines of his chest. When her fingers found him, she caressed him in slow, delicate strokes, her lips moving against his in a kiss that sent heat surging through him.

He groaned softly, knowing his restraint wouldn't last long if she continued.

She needed to slow down.

Gently, he caught her wrist and brought her hand away.

"I want to please you," he whispered against her lips.

Lucy sighed in protest. "No, it's my turn."

He smiled, taking her hand in his and guiding it lower, pressing both of their fingers against her most sensitive place. He moved in a way he knew she'd like, teaching her with his touch. For a moment, she let him lead. Then, as he withdrew his hand, she made her choice—teasing him once more, pushing him right to the edge.

Oliver knew he couldn't wait any longer.

Sliding his hands down her thighs, he pressed them further apart and moved between them. Lucy instinctively wrapped her legs around his waist, pulling him closer, silently telling him what she wanted.

Slowly, he entered her.

The pleasure built between them, deep and consuming, their bodies moving in perfect rhythm. When the moment came, it was powerful—more intense than anything they had shared before, even in Moscow.

Afterward, they lay together, breathing slowing, their bodies still tangled. Minutes passed before either of them spoke.

Then Lucy looked at him, her voice soft but filled with meaning.

She asked the question he had been dreading.

"I assume you'll need to leave soon to report back to the CIA. Will you be ordered to take on a new assignment that will require you to be away for a long time again?"

"That's happened each time so far."

"Where does that leave us? When I referred to an empty promise earlier, it was because I assumed we wouldn't be able to see each other very often...perhaps as little as two days every month or so."

"I honestly don't know. I knew you'd ask me that question eventually. I wouldn't blame you if you wanted to break off our relationship. I can't ask you to wait for me each time."

"I'll pretend I didn't hear you say that, Oliver. What if Bill appointed you CEO of the Boston office and lab to oversee the medication taking shape and to lead the effort to get it through the FDA and onto the market? It would be an extension of your present assignment to do everything possible to allow Morgan Pharma to be first to introduce the Alzheimer's cure."

"I joined the CIA to avoid the life of having to go to the office every day. I did that for years while at Harvard, and I began to hate it after a while."

"Isn't your desire to be with me greater than your need to continue with what you're doing?"

"You can't ask me that question, Luce. It's not fair. I shouldn't have to choose between you and the work I do."

Oliver noticed that Lucy was about to cry. He racked his brain for a solution.

"What if you were to return with me to see what assignment, if any, I'm given, and talk about this again? I could also try, when not abroad on an assignment, to fit in a day for us somehow."

Lucy didn't reply. She turned her back to him so he couldn't look into her eyes. He knew they'd be filled with tears. They eventually fell asleep without saying anything else.

***

Lucy and Oliver spent the weekend wrapped in each other's world, living as if time didn't exist beyond the present moment. They laughed, explored, and cherished every second together, never revisiting the unresolved issue of Oliver's long absences. For now, the weight of that conversation remained unspoken, hovering just beneath the surface.

On Saturday morning, Oliver woke first. Watching Lucy sleep, peaceful and unaware, he decided to surprise her with breakfast in bed.

Slipping quietly out of the bedroom, he made his way to the kitchen, where he ran into Jacky. When he mentioned his plan, she smiled and immediately offered to help. Together, they arranged a tray with fresh pastries, fruit, and coffee.

Before he left, Jacky plucked a single red rose from the garden and placed it delicately on the tray.

Back in the bedroom, Oliver leaned over Lucy, waking her with slow, lingering kisses.

When she opened her eyes and saw him, she stretched lazily, a smile curving her lips. "You'll have to kiss me again," she murmured, pulling him closer. "I wasn't fully awake for the first one."

Chuckling, he obliged before setting the tray on her lap. She adjusted her pillows against the headboard, sitting up with an appreciative glance at the beautifully arranged breakfast.

After they ate, they found their way to the shower, where they made love under the warm cascade of water.

Later, when Oliver mentioned he had visited Los Angeles many times but never played tourist, Lucy decided to change that.

They strolled along Venice Beach, weaving through crowds of street performers, artists, and fortune tellers. The boardwalk was alive with color and energy—an endless display of eccentricity. They wandered into odd little shops, admired the quirky houses, and eventually kicked off their shoes to walk along the sand, hand in hand.

By the time they reached Santa Monica Pier, the sun was high, casting a golden glow over the ocean. Lucy leaned into Oliver as they walked, her fingers interlaced with his, the warmth of her body pressed against his side.

Hunger eventually pulled them away from the shoreline. They found a food truck—Tocky's Pita—near the pier and grabbed a simple lunch before heading to Palisades Park. There, they found a bench overlooking the ocean, the rhythmic noise of waves offering a soothing contrast to the bustling boardwalk.

As they ate, a silence settled between them—not uncomfortable but charged with unspoken thoughts.

It was here, in this moment of calm, that Oliver finally gave voice to the question that had been lingering in his mind since Moscow.

"I'm curious, Luce. What caused you to develop feelings for me?"

Lucy looked at him and smiled. "Why would you want to know that when you know my love for you is pure and everlasting?"

"But tell me what brought you to love me. Whenever I see you asleep next to me, I can't help but be amazed you would want to love me. I'm meaningless in your world. I hope it's more than just physical attraction."

Lucy suddenly realized he was serious. She felt a sense of panic as she thought he might want to end their relationship. She edged closer to him, placing the tub of salad she was halfway through finishing on the bench to look into his eyes.

"You're serious, aren't you? Very serious."

"I am, Luce. Why would you fall in love with the likes of me?"

"Isn't it enough to know I have?"

"Please, Luce, tell me."

Lucy was afraid of what their conversation might lead to. She wiped a tear from her eye, not caring he saw how emotional she'd become.

"I've thought about it a hundred times, dearest Oliver. It's a question I needed to answer for myself when things between us had become worrisome enough to cause me lack of sleep and continual anxiety. The spark that kindled into a flame later was simply your appearance at Nice Airport when I picked you up.

"I remember being struck by your unruly hair and the fact it's blond, while your eyebrows and eyelashes are dark. Your captivating smile when you saw me standing there waiting for you made my heart skip a beat. I'd broken up with my last boyfriend the week before, and I was ready to become involved with another man. I didn't know then you'd affect me in a way the fifteen or so boyfriends I've had never did."

"Would you agree with me that the beginning of your love for me was physical attraction?"

"Yes, but the conversation we had during our drive to Monaco, and the following day when we walked to the Olympic pool, added another dimension to that spark. You made me see things for the first time, and I became spellbound by your logic and empathy.

"When you took hold of my hands on board *Artemis* to explain you were employed by the CIA, and when I saw the compassion on your face for me, I knew I wanted you. I'd never met anyone like you. You became everything I wanted, and I wanted you so badly it hurt. I don't know how to qualify my wanting you, Oliver, but it wasn't just physical attraction."

Lucy wiped another tear from her eye when she finished explaining the genesis of her love for him. Oliver was moved by how much she loved him.

"I apologize, Luce, for asking the question. I shouldn't have. I understand, deep inside, how much you love me, but occasionally, I can't help but think I'm simply your next boyfriend. You're precious to me, and I wouldn't be able to continue to function as a normal human being if you were to break up with me like you have with all your boyfriends."

"I was afraid you were going to break up with me when you asked me why I loved you."

"I promise you here and now, Luce, I will never cause us to end what we have together."

Oliver rose from the bench and gently took her arm, urging her to stand. He pulled her close, wrapping her in his arms. The warmth of his embrace and the depth of his emotional response filled her with a happiness unlike anything she had ever known.

"I had to write an essay once in high school for my English teacher," Oliver continued. "He gave each of us a slip of paper that listed the subject. Mine was love, which got quite a laugh from the other students in my class.

"I researched the topic seriously, and I remember writing that nothing has intrigued humanity more than the fabric of love. That it is the subject that dominates literature, music, and films to this day. I discovered that conjecture about the subject had made place for scientific analysis, and I quoted psychologist Robert Sternberg, who'd developed a theory of love based on its three properties: intimacy, passion, and commitment.

"I remember writing that intimacy refers to feelings of attachment, closeness, connectedness, and bondedness; that passion refers to drives connected to both limerence and sexual attraction; and that commitment refers to the quality of being dedicated to the other. I wrote that true love is all of that."

"I agree, Oliver. The strongest feelings I have for you occur when we're close together, like when you held me just now. I see our lovemaking as something that is a result of that, while my dedication to you is boundless. You're not meaningless in my world, Oliver—you *are* my world."

They were quiet while they finished their lunch, thinking about what had just happened.

"Would you mind telling me what caused you to love me, Oliver?"

Lucy smiled when she asked him this, and Oliver realized her question had not originated from doubt about his love for her, unlike his, which had originated from the occasional thought that he was just her next boyfriend.

"If I had to use your analogy, I'd say the spark that ignited my feelings was the picture I still have in my mind of you waiting for me in the arrivals area at Nice Airport. I'd never seen a more beautiful woman, and you were waiting for me!

"That was pure physical attraction, I know, but I found out not much later that you're intelligent, forthright, and sincere. I loved our discussions. My feelings for you quickly developed, and as you know now, I had great difficulty in not letting you know.

"I should have told you I loved you when I knew I did, during the flight to Moscow, in response to your subtle remarks that you had feelings for me. But the way we finally bonded surpasses any other way of bonding. I never wear the bracelet you bought me for fear of losing it. I will always cherish it."

Lucy was happy to hear Oliver's confession. She stood up to sit on his lap, placed her arms around his neck, and kissed him.

They lingered on that bench in Palisades Park long after finishing their meal. The world around them faded into a tranquil blur—the gentle rustle of palm trees overhead, the rhythmic noise of waves against the shore, and the golden light stretching across the Pacific. Despite the occasional passerby, it felt as if they were the only two people existing.

Neither of them spoke much. They didn't need to.

As the sun dipped below the horizon, painting the sky in hues of amber and violet, they finally rose and made their way back.

***

They slept in on Sunday morning, just as Jacky and Bill often did. By the time they emerged for breakfast, all four of them sat around the table in their dressing gowns, sipping coffee and indulging in a slow, easy morning.

Afterward, Oliver swam laps in the pool, the cool water a refreshing contrast to the warmth of the Los Angeles sun.

Then, early in the afternoon, Lucy whisked him away for a tour of Universal Studios, where they lost themselves in the magic of Hollywood. Later, they made their way to Griffith Park and the observatory, standing side by side as they gazed out at the sprawling city below.

Lucy had arranged dinner at a small, tucked-away restaurant in downtown Los Angeles that evening. She was certain they wouldn't be recognized, and she was right. They had taken every precaution—dark sunglasses, subtle clothing, Lucy's floppy straw hat, Oliver's baseball cap.

For a few more hours, they were just two people in love, enjoying each other's company without the weight of reality pressing down on them.

Later that night, in the quiet intimacy of Lucy's bedroom, they made love once more, cherishing every moment as if it might be their last.

***

The next morning, Mitch, Dave, and Annette flew them to Washington Dulles Airport, where Oliver would return to his apartment in Arlington, Virginia. Afterward, the jet continued to Teterboro Airport in New Jersey, where Lucy would return to her apartment overlooking Central Park in Manhattan.

Jacky and Bill had seen them off at Van Nuys Airport, and Oliver had thanked them warmly for their hospitality. But now, as the Gulfstream cruised through the sky, the mood on board was markedly different.

The weight of reality had settled in.

The time they had spent together had only deepened their bond, making their impending separation all the more difficult. Oliver found himself thinking—*really thinking*—about what it would take to be with Lucy permanently. The only real answer was to resign from the CIA.

But could he do it?

Every time he tried to convince himself there was another way, he hit the same dead end.

Lucy, too, wrestled with the problem. She knew Oliver couldn't be confined to a nine-to-five life, that his work defined him in ways she couldn't change. If he ever left the agency, it would have to be for something just as compelling, just as meaningful. But what?

Neither of them had an answer.

They sat across from each other, hands occasionally reaching across the space between them, but words failed. Nothing meaningful was said. Lucy felt the sting of unshed tears, knowing that once he was assigned a new alias, he would disappear from her world again. He wouldn't be able to call, and she wouldn't be able to reach him—unless it was safe.

Oliver dreaded the moment they would have to say goodbye.

When the Gulfstream touched down at Washington Dulles and taxied to the Jet Center, a heavy silence filled the cabin.

Without a word, Oliver reached for Lucy, lifting her from her seat and pulling her into his arms. She clung to him tightly, her body trembling as she fought to hold back tears. But she couldn't. The moment cracked her open, and she wept against his shoulder, her fingers gripping his shirt as if she could keep him from slipping away.

"I love you," Oliver whispered, his voice raw.

Gently, he pried her arms from around him, his touch lingering for a second longer than necessary.

Then he turned away.

He walked off the aircraft, collected his baggage, and headed toward the terminal without looking back.

But Lucy remained at the cabin door, watching him go—a silent, heartbroken figure against the backdrop of the fading day.

11.

LUCY LASSITER

After returning home, Lucy struggled to find a new balance in her life.

During the weeks Oliver had spent at RusPharma, she had gradually withdrawn from her usual routines, even skipping her gym sessions with her girlfriends. The days they had shared in Moscow had left her spellbound, but their weekend in Los Angeles had awakened something else—an agonizing uncertainty about their future.

She couldn't just work, sleep, and spend her days waiting for Oliver to return from each assignment. That wasn't a life. She needed something more.

Her first step was to rejoin her friends at the gym, trying to slip back into her old routine. But it didn't take long for them to notice she had changed. The late-night parties, the glamorous social scene, the endless chatter about eligible men—none of it interested her anymore.

She no longer gossiped. She had nothing to say when her friends giggled about their latest flings.

The distance between them grew, unspoken but undeniable.

Before long, they stopped inviting her altogether.

Zoey, Lucy's closest friend, explained, "The girls think you're a spoilsport because you no longer want to have fun and go to parties. What's changed?"

"I've met my soulmate, Zoey. He's changed who I am."

"Why haven't you introduced him to us? We obviously want to meet him."

"He would hate to go to the parties we go to. He works hard, and he's away a lot."

"How has he changed you?"

"By showing me that my desire to truly love someone—and be loved in return—can't be fulfilled by someone from the circle of friends we've always been part of. He convinced me that the sort of man I was looking for wouldn't be interested in me."

"I don't understand."

"He wouldn't be interested in me if I were the shallow person the tabloids have made me out to be."

Zoey thought about this before replying. "You could be right. But how did you get to meet him if it wasn't through the parties we go to?"

"He needed to speak to my parents when we were in Monaco on our summer vacation. They asked me to pick him up at the airport. I was fascinated by him from the start."

"Does he work for your parents?"

"He did for a while."

"He's not a salaried worker, is he?"

"What's wrong with working hard and earning a salary?" Lucy asked.

"Well, nothing, I suppose, but that in itself distinguishes him from most of the men we go out with."

"Whether a man is rich or poor has never affected my thoughts about what a man needs to be like for me to love him, apart from being able to support himself. The only thing I'd wish for in that regard is that he's important in some way in what he does in life."

Zoey was impressed by what Lucy shared with her. When Lucy suggested they go to the gym on days their other friends didn't, Zoey readily agreed. She enjoyed the idea of spending time with Lucy without the distractions of their usual social circle—and, if she was honest, she was eager to meet the man who had captured her friend's heart.

But as the weeks passed, Oliver remained absent.

Zoey's curiosity only grew. She pressed Lucy for details, and though Lucy hesitated at first, she eventually revealed his name—Oliver. She didn't want to seem secretive, knowing it would only lead to awkward questions she couldn't, or wouldn't, answer.

Meanwhile, Lucy immersed herself in work. Her hours stretched longer, her schedule more demanding. She began traveling more frequently, visiting Morgan Pharma offices around the world. Jacky and Bill took note of her deepening commitment, and in recognition of her dedication, they gave her unrestricted access to the company's Gulfstream whenever she needed it.

Eight weeks passed without a word from Oliver.

At first, Lucy tried to push the worry aside, telling herself he was simply caught up in his assignment. But as the silence stretched on, unease crept in. What if something had happened to him?

Unable to shake her concern, she reached out to Mitch. By the weekend, she was on a flight to Los Angeles, determined to speak with Jacky and Bill.

She had devised a plan—a way to find out where Oliver was and what he was doing.

But for it to work, she needed Bill's cooperation.

"I'm worried something has happened to Oliver," she told her parents when she arrived. "Oliver told me he'd call me when he could, but he hasn't. I can't call him because the CIA provides him with a new identity with each new assignment. That includes changing his name and passport, as well as his cell phone, credit card, bank account, and driver's license. You need to help me, Bill, to find out where Oliver is and what he's doing."

"I suppose you want me to contact the director of the CIA like I did when we were concerned about the computer hack?"

"Yes; schedule an appointment for both of us to visit him."

"If I do and tell him why, he might just say he can't talk to us about Oliver and not agree to the appointment."

"So don't tell him why you want to speak to him. Just say it's important."

"Do it, Bill," Jacky interrupted.

"The chance he'll tell us what we wish to know is small, but okay, I'll call him first thing on Monday."

***

Bill set up a meeting at CIA headquarters for the following Tuesday at ten in the morning. Mitch flew them to Dulles on Monday and drove them to Langley the following morning.

They identified themselves at the main entrance to CIA headquarters the following morning. The driver was told where to park, and an escort was assigned to take them to the office of the director, Kenneth Rivera. He stood up when they entered.

"Good morning, Bill. It's a pleasure to see you again."

"Likewise, Ken. I want you to meet my stepdaughter, Lucy."

"Welcome, Lucy. Sit down, please," the director said, gesturing to comfortable armchairs arranged around a small coffee table.

"What can I do for you?" the director asked when the coffee was brought to them.

"I won't beat around the bush, Ken. We would appreciate knowing where Oliver Corbyn is and, more importantly, if he's safe."

The director was clearly startled when Bill explained why they wanted to speak with him.

"How did you find out he's with us?"

"He told me," Lucy said.

"He wasn't supposed to do that."

"I know, but I couldn't understand why he'd want to go undercover to infiltrate the company that stole the information on the Alzheimer's cure and to sabotage what they were doing. I made life difficult for him by saying that I thought he had ulterior motives for doing so. He then confessed to working for you. We fell in love when we were in Russia together to attend the conference on Alzheimer's disease."

"When we trained him, he was instructed not to become romantically involved because of the possibility it would compromise his identity."

"His identity is perfectly safe with us," Lucy countered.

The director looked at both Lucy and Bill as if to determine what to say next. "So your reason for wanting to know where he is isn't associated with the Alzheimer's assignment, as we call it, which he completed nearly nine weeks ago?"

"That's correct. I'm worried something has happened to him. He promised to call me now and then, but he hasn't," Lucy continued.

"Have you considered he may be somewhere he can't call you? That would be the case, for example, if he doesn't have access to a mobile network. Besides, he might have been forced to relinquish his cell phone, just like he was at the RusPharma laboratory."

"Are you offering those possibilities because you don't know, or simply as some measure of consolation?"

The director took his time to answer once again. "As much

as I'd like to, I can't say more than I already have. He's on a secret mission, and anything I tell you about it could jeopardize its outcome and cause him to be in more danger than he already is. Besides, your reputation as someone who socializes with people who I'd consider to be a risk in any undertaking precedes you, Lucy, if you don't mind me saying so. In my view, it would be dangerous to tell you anything that's confidential."

"She's changed, Ken. Oliver made her realize things she hadn't before. Believe me when I say that."

"May I ask if you or others have heard from Oliver at all?" Lucy asked.

"No, we haven't, and we don't expect to, knowing how he operates. He'll come in when he's ready to file his report and to receive instructions on his next assignment."

"Would you be willing to provide us with information if you were to discover something has happened to him?" Lucy asked. "He has no next of kin. He's an only child. His parents died in a car crash, and his grandparents, who raised him, have passed."

"Yes, I am, insofar as that something was to end his career with the CIA."

"You mean if he was killed or seriously injured?"

"That's correct."

"Okay, Ken, thanks for making time available for us," Bill said as he stood up, ready to leave.

They shook hands on parting.

***

"I'm terribly disappointed," Lucy said when they had seated themselves in the car for the drive to Dulles. "I had high hopes of hearing that Oliver had been in touch. We're no wiser than before we left LA."

"I'm sorry, Lucy. I had a suspicion he wouldn't tell us very much. I can understand why."

Lucy was more than just disappointed—she was beginning to feel the weight of uncertainty pressing down on her. The only small comfort was that Oliver hadn't yet reported back to the CIA. It meant he was still engaged in whatever mission had taken him away nine weeks ago.

If something had happened to him, she told herself, the CIA would be the first to know.

But that reassurance did little to ease the ache of not hearing from him.

The days following her meeting with the CIA director stretched into weeks.

Lucy's once-bright spirit dimmed, her usual spark fading. The absence of news had taken its toll, and those around her noticed. Even Zoey, who had always been able to lift her mood, found it impossible to pull her out of the sadness that had settled over her.

She buried herself in work, filling every moment with meetings, calls, and reports. But no matter how hard she tried to stay distracted, her thoughts always drifted back to Oliver the second her mind had room to wander.

***

After another three weeks of silence, Lucy had to travel to Saint Petersburg for a meeting with Alex Davidson about marketing strategies.

Mitch piloted the Gulfstream, flying her across the Atlantic. When she arrived at Pulkovo Airport, Dimitri and Sergei were there to greet her, just as they always had.

She settled into the back of the car as Dimitri and Sergei drove her through the city.

But something was different this time.

Dimitri stole occasional glances at her in the rearview

mirror, his expression tightening with concern. He could see it—the sadness that clung to her, the heaviness in her eyes. She wasn't the same woman who had once lit up Moscow with her laughter and warmth. He had seen firsthand how deeply she and Oliver had fallen for each other. He had watched their love grow. And now, looking at her, he knew something was wrong.

Something had happened.

And he needed to know what.

"Have you seen Oliver recently, Miss Lassiter?" he asked.

"Not for twelve weeks, Dimitri. I don't know where he is. He promised to call me from time to time, but he hasn't. I can't call him because he has a different cell phone, and I don't know his number."

Dimitri didn't pursue the issue. He felt sorry for her, and he wished he could do something to make her feel better.

"Do you want to go somewhere this evening, Miss Lassiter? Sergei and I would be happy to escort you."

"Thanks, Dimitri, but I'm tired. I think I'll turn in early. Can you both join me for breakfast at eight tomorrow? I want to speak to Alex afterward."

Lucy checked into the Four Seasons Hotel on Admiralteyskiy Prospekt—her usual choice. She had booked three adjoining rooms, as she always did when traveling alone to Saint Petersburg. Security was a constant concern, especially given the frequent kidnappings of unescorted wealthy individuals in Moscow and Saint Petersburg. Having Dimitri nearby gave her peace of mind. As usual, she ensured the connecting doors remained closed but unlocked, a precaution they had followed every time.

Normally, she would have dinner with Dimitri and Sergei after checking in, taking a shower, and changing into something comfortable. But tonight, exhaustion pressed down on her. Instead, she opted for a simple meal delivered to her room. She ate quickly, then settled in with the papers she had brought to prepare for her meeting with Alex.

By the time she turned off the lights and slipped beneath the blankets, she already knew—sleep would not come easily. It hadn't for weeks.

The following morning, Lucy joined Sergei and Dimitri for breakfast.

Her sullen mood cast a shadow over the table, and soon it seeped into them as well. The conversation was sparse, weighed down by the unspoken worry hanging between them.

After breakfast, she returned to her room to collect the papers she needed for her meeting. When she reappeared, Dimitri led her outside, where the black Mercedes waited at the hotel entrance, freshly retrieved by a parking attendant.

Sergei stood by the open back door, ready to help her inside.

That was when it happened.

A large Russian-model SUV screeched to a halt behind the Mercedes, its tires skidding violently against the pavement.

Before anyone could react, two men sprang out.

One lunged for Lucy, seizing her arm in a crushing grip and yanking her toward the waiting vehicle. The other raised a gun, waving it threateningly at bystanders, warning them to stay back.

For a split second, Lucy froze. Then instinct kicked in.

She twisted, struggling against her attacker, her purse and briefcase slipping from her hands as she fought to break free. Her heart pounded as she clawed at his grip, nails digging into his skin.

"Let me go!" she screamed, her voice cutting through the morning air.

A few feet away, Dimitri and Sergei were already moving.

They weren't about to let her be taken.

"Help me! Dimitri, help me!"

Dimitri ignored the gun aimed at him, his hand already reaching for the Glock 22 in his holster.

The gunman reacted instantly.

A shot rang out.

Dimitri staggered, his body crumpling to the pavement.

Lucy froze. The sound of the gunshot echoed in her ears, her breath catching as she watched Dimitri collapse. The fight drained from her in an instant—resisting was futile now.

By the time Sergei managed to reach for his own weapon in the glove compartment, it was too late. Lucy had already been dragged into the SUV, and the gunman had slipped back into his seat beside the driver. The vehicle sped off, weaving into the traffic on Admiralteyskiy Prospekt. Firing into the crowded street wasn't an option.

***

Chaos erupted outside the entrance to the hotel.

Bystanders rushed toward Dimitri's motionless form, some kneeling beside him, others shouting for someone to call emergency services. The hotel concierge, visibly shaken, fumbled for his phone and called 112.

Sergei, on his knees, ripped open Dimitri's shirt to expose the wound. Blood soaked his chest, pooling beneath him. Grabbing the first aid kit from the trunk of the Mercedes, he pressed a thick gauze pad against the wound, applying pressure to stem the bleeding.

"Hold on," he muttered under his breath, his hands firm and steady despite the adrenaline surging through him.

Ten agonizing minutes later, the ambulance arrived. The paramedics worked quickly, assessing Dimitri's condition.

"We think the bullet missed vital organs," one of them said after a quick examination. "He should pull through."

Sergei exhaled a breath he hadn't realized he was holding.

He retrieved Lucy's purse and briefcase from where they had fallen, then climbed into the Mercedes and followed the ambulance to the hospital.

Once there, after being directed to a waiting room, Sergei pulled out his phone and called Alex Davidson.

The moment Alex picked up, Sergei got straight to the point.

"Lucy's been kidnapped. Dimitri's been shot. I'm at the hospital."

There was silence on the other end. Then Alex, voice controlled but tight, said, "I'm on my way."

When Alex arrived, the doctors had already completed surgery to remove the bullet. The news was reassuring—the bullet had narrowly missed anything life-threatening. Dimitri would recover.

But Lucy was still missing.

Wasting no time, Alex drove back to the hotel. He spoke with witnesses, gathering details about the kidnapping and shooting. Then, knowing there was no choice but to inform her family, he called Bill Lassiter.

It was 11:15 p.m. in LA when Bill picked up.

"Lucy's been taken," Alex said without preamble. "She was abducted as she was about to get into the car for the drive to the office."

On the other end of the line, silence stretched for a long moment. Then, movement. Voices. Urgent whispers.

"We're coming," Bill said firmly.

He and Jacky packed immediately, preparing for a prolonged stay in Saint Petersburg. The Lassiter jet sitting on the tarmac at Van Nuys airport was readied for departure. With Mitch, Dave, and Annette now assigned to the Gulfstream and at a hotel near Pulkovo Airport waiting to fly Lucy back to New York, the second crew responsible for the Lassiter jet flew them to Saint Petersburg.

The police arrived at the hotel more than forty-five minutes after the attack.

They took notes, asked a few perfunctory questions, then left.

To any interested onlooker, one thing was clear.

They didn't care.

***

Late that afternoon, a note arrived at the Morgan Pharma office.

It was written in Russian.

"We will release Miss Lassiter when Oliver Corbyn is in our custody. The exchange is to be made in Alexander Garden, opposite Saint Isaac's Cathedral, on Monday, March 28, between ten and eleven in the morning. Oliver Corbyn is to be there alone."

The message was chilling in its simplicity.

When Bill and Jacky arrived in Saint Petersburg the next day, the note was handed to them. Alex had it translated. Bill read it twice, his grip tightening on the paper, his expression darkening.

They had feared something like this.

But the real problem wasn't just the demand—it was finding Oliver.

He had been gone for weeks. No calls. No messages. No way to reach him.

And now, Lucy's life depended on a man who might not even know she was in danger.

"We need to call the director of the CIA. He knows where Oliver is," Jacky proposed.

Bill agreed, and he called Ken Rivera that afternoon.

"Ken, we need to contact Oliver. Lucy was kidnapped in Saint Petersburg yesterday. Our office received a note stating they will release Lucy when Oliver is in their custody. Jacky and I are here in Saint Petersburg, but apart from having found out the details of what's happened, there is little we can do. You or I need to contact Oliver to ask him to come here."

"Have the kidnappers informed you why they want Oliver?"

"No, but we believe it's related to the Alzheimer's cure. Oliver is aware of its composition and the method of production."

"Have they issued instructions for the exchange?"

"Yes, next week on Monday between ten and eleven o'clock here in Saint Petersburg."

"We'll try to contact Oliver, Bill, but I need to warn you we might not be able to because of where he is. I'll call you as soon as we know more."

The director of the CIA returned Bill's call the following day.

"I'm sorry, Bill. We haven't been able to contact Oliver. We called him several times and we've left a message on his voicemail. There's nothing further we can do."

"What is liable to happen if Oliver doesn't turn up in time?" Bill asked Ken.

"If RusPharma is desperate to have Oliver working for them again, they'll probably extend the date by which the exchange is to be made. I don't think Lucy's life is in imminent danger."

"Okay, Ken. I greatly appreciate your help. I'll call you when there are further developments."

***

Bill and Jacky were beside themselves with worry over Lucy's safety.

On the morning of March 28, Bill went to Saint Isaac's

Cathedral at the appointed time. The sun was shining, and Alexander Garden was filled with people—tourists, locals, families enjoying the crisp spring air. He scanned the crowd, searching for any sign of Lucy's captors, but saw nothing out of the ordinary. No one lingered suspiciously; no one appeared to be watching him.

An hour passed.

Frustrated and empty-handed, Bill returned to the hotel.

Later, he called the CIA director to update him. The director wasn't surprised by the lack of suspicious movement at the exchange location. When Bill raised the idea of involving the local police, the director dismissed it outright.

"They've been bribed to look the other way," he said grimly. "It's happened before in cases involving US citizens. You won't get any help from them."

Bill clenched his jaw, his frustration mounting. They were on their own.

Three days later, another note arrived at the Morgan Pharma office.

"We are prepared to extend our offer to release Miss Lassiter by two weeks. The exchange is to be made as specified before—on Monday, Wednesday, or Friday during those two weeks, between ten and eleven in the morning. Oliver Corbyn is to be there alone."

It was clear—the kidnappers weren't backing down.

There was nothing more Bill or Jacky could do. They had exhausted their options.

Reluctantly, they decided to stay in Saint Petersburg for one more week, hoping for a breakthrough. But when no new developments surfaced, they had no choice but to return to Los Angeles, where urgent business matters awaited them.

Before leaving, they met with Alex, who assured them he would contact them immediately if there was anything to report.

On the same day Bill and Jacky flew back to LA, Dimitri was discharged from the hospital. The bullet wound had healed, and after three more days of rest, he resumed his work at Morgan Pharma.

But despite his recovery, one thing remained unchanged—Lucy was still missing, and time was running out.

12.
THE ASSIGNMENT

After saying goodbye to Lucy at Dulles International Airport, Oliver took a taxi to his apartment in Arlington. He scheduled an appointment to see the director of the CIA, Ken Rivera, the following morning.

One of the assistants to the director told Oliver, on arrival, he could go straight through to the director's office because he was eager to see him. He handed Ken Rivera his brief report on what had transpired in Russia during the seven weeks he was there.

"Congratulations, Liam, on having destroyed the RusPharma laboratory," the director said while he remained seated behind his desk. "We added two and two together and concluded RusPharma had stolen the Alzheimer's files when we discovered their facility had been destroyed by fire. I'll read your report, label it top secret, and have it filed away, as always."

"Thanks, Ken. What's my next assignment?"

"The president will fill you in on the details. All I know is that I'm to provide you with the identity of a person who used to live in one of the so-called closed cities and towns in Russia, which are presently being redeveloped.

"Our data analysts found details of a person from the closed town of Voskhod in Moscow Oblast. He died in a car crash in Austria eleven months ago. He has a grandmother living in Voskhod. You are to make her believe you are her grandson, so you can move in with her while you're there. As far as we know, she doesn't know her grandson is deceased.

"You need to visit our chief of disguise this afternoon to make you look like him. This is his photograph."

Oliver looked at the photograph. He realized he would need to undergo a significant makeover to have someone believe he was the person whose identity he had to adopt.

"What you must know, Liam, is that Voskhod has been a closed town since it was founded in 1965. After the formation of the Russian Federation in 1991, some of those closed towns and cities opened up to a certain extent, sometimes allowing non-Russians to visit them, but others didn't. All those towns and cities were in some way related to the development of nuclear weapons, to the Russian space program, or to the development of some other strategic device—nerve gas such as Sarin, for example.

"For a while, Voskhod was one of those towns that allowed visitors to enter and leave. Then, about six months ago, a new, high barbed-wire fence was built around its perimeter, and people other than returning residents and those with a special permit are no longer allowed to enter. The president is probably going to ask you to enter the town to find out what's going on.

"Only about two thousand people live there. It's the smallest of all the closed towns and cities. The town is not connected to the internet and is not serviced by a cell phone network."

"That doesn't sound too complicated, Ken. Have you had someone prepare the documents I'll need for this assignment?"

"I have. You'll find everything you need in this folder except for the Russian and US passports and the Russian driver's license. Have your photo taken after the makeover to allow the documents people to finalize them."

Oliver opened the folder the director handed him and looked through its contents. It contained a Russian birth certificate, a Russian credit card, and details of a Russian bank account. He was also given a Russian smartphone.

"So my new name is Oleg Balabanov," Oliver said.

"Yes, your grandmother is Daria Balabanov."

"I'll set you up for a meeting with the president at the White House for tomorrow morning at nine. He's keen to see you. You might now want to visit the data analyst responsible for Moscow Oblast to check on the layout of the town and other information he might be able to give you."

They shook hands when Oliver stood up to leave. The director wished him good luck.

Oliver visited the data analyst the director had referred to. He knew who he was because of previous briefings on specific sites in Moscow Oblast.

***

"Hi, Liam. You caused quite a stir at the RusPharma facility. When one of our satellites detected the blaze, and when we found out the site was occupied by a pharmaceutical company, we figured you were involved."

"Yeah, the director told me you had correctly guessed at my involvement. What can you tell me about Voskhod?"

"The closed town in Moscow Oblast? There are several places in Russia with that name."

"Yeah, the closed town."

"All I can tell you is that the town has received considerable interest from the governor of Moscow Oblast and his ministers. It has led to a lot of new construction. Entrance is now tightly controlled by the Federal Security Service, the FSB, and a new barbed-wire fence has been built around it. We recently prepared a map showing what we know about the layout of the town and the functions of the various buildings. I believe the town is being prepared to serve as a hub for research and development activities in some specific field or fields."

"What evidence do you have for that?" Oliver asked.

"A significant number of laboratory items have recently been sourced from outside Russia and transported to the town. We're trying to figure out what all that equipment is used for. It would have to be for more than a single laboratory because of the nature of the equipment."

Oliver studied the map the data analyst had handed him. "Can I keep this?"

"Yeah, but don't lose it. We don't want the Russkies to know we're onto them."

Oliver visited the cafeteria for lunch and then made his way to the office of the chief of disguise, with whom one of the assistants to the director had made an appointment for Oliver's makeover.

The makeover consisted primarily of dyeing his hair, eyebrows, and eyelashes black and applying a beard and mustache in the same color. He needed to be clean-shaven to apply the facial hair. A special silicone glue was used to attach the hairpieces, allowing Oliver to keep them in place for several days. He was told to remove them to shave, and to wash them every three or four days. He was given solvent to remove any remaining glue on his face and a tube of glue so he could reapply the beard and mustache. Oliver was also provided with hair dye to touch up his roots if the assignment lasted more than two or three weeks, and a small bottle of vinegar to remove the dye from his hair at the end of the assignment.

When Oliver looked in the mirror after the transition, he knew no one would recognize him as himself, Oliver Corbyn, or one of his other identities.

Oliver had his photo taken after the makeover. He was given the US and Russian passports and the Russian driver's license an hour later. He noticed his US passport contained a visa for Belarus. Oliver smiled to himself when he realized they had assumed he would once more escape from Russia via Belarus. The Russian passport contained a valid D long-stay Schengen visa that would have allowed Oleg Balabanov to stay for a year in Austria or any other Schengen country.

***

Oliver didn't possess a car, so he took a taxi the following morning to his meeting with the president. When he arrived at the entrance to the White House on Pennsylvania Avenue, the Secret Service agents on duty asked him for proof of his identity when he told them he had an appointment with the president at nine that morning. But because the photo in his true US passport was vividly different from how he now looked, he was denied entry. He had to call the White House chief of staff for assistance. It took ten minutes and the involvement of the president himself to convince the Secret Service agents to allow him to enter.

The president welcomed Oliver warmly.

"Hello, Liam, I'm glad to see you again safe and sound. I'm amazed at what the CIA can do to alter someone's appearance. I should think of adopting a disguise like yours sometimes to become anonymous. There are meetings I'd love to attend as someone other than the president to hear what people say behind my back. I can think of other advantages of a disguise, but I won't expand on that—you might get the wrong impression about me," he said, smiling.

"Your secrets are safe with me, Mr. President. I could give you some pointers on what you could achieve when wearing a disguise."

"Thanks for the offer, Liam, but this job of mine is too serious to consider such things. Congratulations, by the way, on bringing the Alzheimer assignment to a successful close. I hate to think of the consequences if you hadn't been able to.

"I now have an equally important assignment for you. I've already alerted the director of the CIA about preparing you for what I want you to do. That's the reason for the disguise you're wearing. We're concerned, Liam, about the reinstatement of a number of closed towns and cities in Russia. We believed for some years that our agreements with Russia would lead to the dismantling of nuclear weapons and a general easing out of service, or ban, of other weapons, such as nerve gas. But, as you know, tension with Russia has increased since the annexation of Crimea as a state within the Russian Federation in 2014 and the preparations to invade Ukraine.

"We need to find out why they've reinstated those closed towns and cities. Our satellites show in virtually every case that a major renovation of buildings and facilities is being carried out. It's been difficult—in most cases impossible—for our operatives to enter those sites. Discussions with the CIA and the military about what we should be doing have been unproductive. The secretary of defense, in particular, refuses to take a proactive stand on the issue. I, on the other hand, want to know what's going on and now take measures to avoid serious consequences later.

"Since previous residents of those towns and cities are allowed to enter, it's been suggested we should send someone to one of these sites, disguised as a previous resident. If we were to find that those towns and cities are again being used for the development of weapons, I'll address that in the upcoming NATO summit and, hopefully, with my Russian counterpart when I get to meet him to discuss the Ukrainian issue. Your findings will form the basis of my discussion with him on that subject.

"In providing you with your present identity, the CIA has indirectly forced the issue of which closed city or town you need to investigate. Voskhod is where you come from. Entry into the town should be no more than a formality in your case. It's one of the smallest closed towns.

"Apart from finding out what the Russians are doing, I want you to sabotage their plans if they are detrimental to the US—for example, if they're developing new weapons. You need to plant evidence that Chechen terrorists are responsible for the sabotage to avoid further deterioration of relations with the Kremlin."

"I understand, Mr. President. The director of the CIA assumed my task would be to find out what's going on in Voskhod, but he didn't mention destroying whatever it is they're doing."

"No one knows, Liam, just you and me—and that's to remain that way, okay?"

"I understand," Oliver replied.

"All I can do is wish you well. Report back to me on your return, please."

"I will."

***

Oliver left the Oval Office and hailed a taxi on Pennsylvania Avenue to return to his apartment. He booked an economy ticket on a flight from Dulles to Vienna with Austrian Airlines leaving late that afternoon, using the particulars in his fake US passport, and the next flight with Aeroflot from Vienna to Moscow, using his Russian passport. He didn't want the authorities in Moscow to find out he had flown to Vienna from the US. That would raise questions he didn't want to be confronted with. He knew that a flight from Vienna to Moscow wouldn't be cause for alarm, considering the evidence contained in his Russian passport that he had flown to Vienna nearly a year ago.

To avoid his fake US passport from being stamped on arriving in Vienna, he planned to remain in the transit area while waiting for the flight to Moscow. The CIA had the foresight to provide an imprint of the stamp used by Austrian immigration in his Russian passport, listing the presumed date Oleg Balabanov had flown there.

Oliver was tired when he finally arrived at Domodedovo International Airport in Moscow, after having slept very little for nearly forty hours. He decided to check into a cheap hotel nearby to sleep and to attend to his facial appearance, heeding the advice of the chief of disguise at CIA headquarters to remove the beard and mustache after three days and to reapply them after a shave, wash, and the removal of any remaining glue from his face.

After checking out of the hotel in the morning of the second day after arriving in Moscow, he visited a secondhand car dealer and purchased a six-year-old Zhiguli with his Russian credit card. He then drove to Voskhod via the A107 and the M9, taking two and a half hours to cover the ninety miles.

13.

VOSKHOD

Snow fell late that winter. When Oliver escaped from Russia on December 30, the snow that had fallen wasn't much of a deterrent for driving on the main roads in and around Moscow. On his return eight days later, while driving to Voskhod, the situation hadn't changed significantly. It was only after leaving the M9 that he encountered snow that required him to drive carefully.

Oliver arrived at the entrance to Voskhod before dark. He joined the queue that had formed to complete entrance formalities. He showed his Russian passport to the FSB officer who had walked to his side of the car and told him he had been away for nearly a year and that he had returned to visit his grandmother. The officer returned to the guardhouse, taking his passport with him. Oliver saw him access a computer. He returned the passport to him a minute later and waved him on.

Oliver had memorized the map of Voskhod he had been given by the CIA data analyst. He knew every street and every building of any importance. The CIA had numbered each building, and he knew Daria Balabanov lived on the second floor of building number six. It was a three-story building that provided simple lodgings for residents in fifty apartments. He found it without difficulty.

He parked his car on a snow-covered area devoid of vegetation in front of the building, retrieved the bags with his belongings from the trunk, donned his North Face parka because it was cold, locked the car, and walked to the front door of the building. It wasn't locked. He entered a hallway that was badly in need of a coat of paint. Various notices had been hung on one of the walls. He knew it was probably important to read them, but he was anxious to meet Daria Balabanov to find out if he could make her believe he was her grandson. The outcome of his mission hinged largely on being able to blend in with the people who lived in the town. He would read the notices tomorrow, he decided.

After climbing the stairs to the second floor, he found himself in a long corridor. Ten doors on either side provided access to as many apartments. As he walked along the corridor, he noticed some doors had names on them, which he assumed were the surnames of the occupants. He found the name Balabanov on the door of the fourth apartment on the right. He knocked with apprehension.

He heard movement in the apartment. The door opened a little later and an older woman confronted him. Oliver judged her to be about seventy. Her gray hair was tied behind her head in a bun, and her wrinkled face revealed years of hardship. She wore a long, drab gray dress, a black cardigan, black stockings, and worn-down sandals.

"Hello, *Babushka*," he said.

The woman stiffened. She was clearly startled by his appearance.

"Oleg?" she asked.

He embraced her and kissed her on the cheek as if she were his real grandmother. She released herself from his embrace far too quickly for her to be convinced he was her long-lost grandson, he thought. He sensed her animosity.

She looked intently at him. "Why have you returned? You said you would never come back when we argued."

Oliver realized she had accepted he was her grandson, but he was somewhat surprised to hear her question.

"I came to realize we shouldn't have argued. I want to make things right again."

"I thought I would never hear you say that. Do you want to come in?"

"Yes, please, we have a lot to talk about."

She led him inside, out of the small hallway. He looked around and noticed that a door on each side of the hallway led to where he assumed the bedrooms to be. The hallway led to a small living room with a minimalistic kitchen on one side. The apartment was tiny and, like other parts of the building, in need of a coat of paint.

Oliver deposited his baggage in a corner of the living room, and when she sat down, he did too.

"You hurt me terribly when you called me an old hag before you left. I had reconciled myself to never seeing you again. You had no right to say what you did after all the years I looked after you, providing you with everything I could."

Tears appeared in her eyes. Oliver was moved by her statement. He stood up and embraced her again.

"Please forgive me, Babushka," he said.

"You've changed. Everything about you is different from what I remember," she said.

Oliver realized he needed to come up with a plausible story to settle her doubts about his identity.

"I traveled to Austria when I left, found a job, and a place to live. But in living by myself, I came to respect what you did for me all those years you looked after me. I came to realize you had placed my welfare ahead of yours all the time. Those feelings became stronger as time went on. When I lost my job,

I decided to return and apologize."

"Have you returned because you lost your job and you now need me to support you again?" she asked him.

"No, Babushka, I'll support you while I'm here. I managed to save some money while I was in Austria."

Oliver was satisfied she had accepted his explanation when she tried to smile.

"The color of your eyes is different from what I remember, and your voice is different," she said suddenly.

"It must be the poor light in the room, and I'm still feeling the effects of the flu I had before I came here. Can I help you make dinner?"

"All I have is some soup, Oleg. I didn't have the money to buy anything else this week."

"Let me take you to the grocery store—if it's still open," he offered.

Daria Balabanov looked at the clock on the mantelpiece and said, "It closes in half an hour."

"That should leave us enough time to buy groceries," Oliver replied.

She nodded, stood up from her chair, chose a shopping bag from a cabinet in the kitchen, and put on a coat hanging from a small coat rack affixed to the wall of the hallway. They left the apartment and walked to the grocery store together.

"You're taller than I remember," she said during their walk.

"That's because of the thick soles on the shoes I'm wearing. And you've probably become shorter. People shrink as they get older."

"How much money are you prepared to spend on groceries, Oleg?" she asked him when they entered the store.

"Don't worry about the money, Babushka—just choose everything you need."

She did what he said without checking the cost of the

items she wanted like she usually would to avoid choosing more than she could pay for. Oliver knew the old age pension in Russia was barely two hundred US dollars a month, and a substantial part of that would have been needed for the rent of the apartment.

Oliver paid for the groceries, and they left with the bag filled to the brim, which he needed to carry because of its weight. When she smiled at him as they left the store, he realized she had accepted he was her grandson, and she was happy he'd returned.

Oliver helped her prepare dinner, which she considered unusual. She didn't question him about it, however. After dinner, she said she needed to prepare his room because she had used it for repairing old clothes for people who were less fortunate than she was. He followed her to the room and helped her move an old sewing machine and some clothes to the living room.

The room was tiny. Besides the bed, it contained a small table, a chair, and a washbasin. Like so many older apartments in Russia, Daria's apartment didn't have a shower or a bath—or hot water.

After they had again seated themselves in the living room, Oliver started asking questions to find out what was going on in the town.

"Things have changed since I was here last. It's much more difficult to enter the town. I noticed a new fence has been built, and there's a lot of construction work going on."

"It started about six months ago," she said. "The authorities informed us that the town is to be returned to full closed status like it was before because several large companies want to base their research here.

"The town is to be modernized. The construction work will provide employment for everyone. The people I know who couldn't find work before are now all employed by the company that's responsible for the construction work you see around you. You should be able to find work there if you want to."

"I'll go there tomorrow to find out if they want to employ me. Is the construction company asking for people with experience?" Oliver asked her.

"I don't know, but if Mikhail can find a job with the construction company, you should also be able to. You remember Mikhail, don't you?"

"Yes, I do."

Oliver continued to ask Daria about developments in the town, but she had little information about the companies moving their research departments there or their expected arrival dates. As their conversation lost momentum, Oliver suggested they turn in for the night.

Daria agreed, and they wished each other good night.

Lying in bed later, Oliver felt a sense of satisfaction. Daria Balabanov had accepted him as her grandson. He realized it wasn't just his appearance that had convinced her—it was his genuine sympathy for her struggles. He had won her over by caring. He would ease the hardships of her life, knowing how little she had to survive on with her meager pension.

The next day, Oliver secured a job with the construction company. During his interview, he was asked about his experience in construction. He admitted he had none. In response, he was offered a general laborer position, assisting carpenters, electricians, bricklayers, and plumbers as needed. The company had secured the contract under the condition that all work be completed by a strict deadline. That meant working seven days a week.

Oliver agreed.

He quickly settled into a rigid routine: wake up at seven, change into the overalls provided by the company, help Daria prepare breakfast, make sandwiches for lunch, and then walk to the administration office to receive his daily assignment.

Work hours ran from 8 a.m. to 6 p.m., with floodlights installed at each building site to compensate for the winter darkness—sunrise wasn't until 8:45 a.m., and sunset came early at 4:30 p.m.

After work, he would wash up in the small basin in his room, tend to his beard and mustache, change into casual clothes, and help Daria prepare dinner. Most evenings, they would walk to the local stores for supplies, with Oliver quietly covering all expenses.

***

During his first week, Oliver made a discovery. One of the four buildings nearing completion was a hotel—intended to house the scientists who would be working in the other three buildings. Yet the purpose of these three buildings remained unclear. The architectural drawings he studied at the administration office offered no clues as to who they were being built for. What was clear, however, was their design. Each building was rectangular, lacking architectural embellishments. They were three stories tall, with the top two floors designated as offices. The first floor was a vast open space, labeled only as a laboratory. They were fitted with pressurized air locks at the entrance; each air lock led to dressing rooms—one for men, another for women. The restrooms were accessible from both the dressing rooms and the laboratory.

It was clear to Oliver that these were high-security research facilities. But what exactly was being developed here?

Two days into the job, Oliver befriended Mikhail, a fellow laborer who lived two doors down from Daria. Mikhail immediately recognized him as Oleg Balabanov and treated him like an old friend. Oliver quickly realized that "Oleg" and Mikhail had known each other before, adding another layer of complexity to his cover.

Mikhail was a heavy drinker and spent most evenings at

the only bar in Voskhod. After repeatedly asking Oliver to join him, Oliver eventually relented. The night ended with him having to half-carry Mikhail home.

As he checked the progress of the three mystery buildings, Oliver estimated it would take three to four more months before they were operational. A construction schedule posted in the administration office confirmed his suspicions.

The realization troubled him deeply. Lucy would be waiting for him after what was supposed to be just a few weeks' absence. When he had taken this assignment, he had assumed it would be a straightforward task—assess why Voskhod had been reinstated as a closed town. Even the additional directive—to sabotage any activities detrimental to US interests—had seemed manageable.

Now, it was clear this wasn't a two-week operation. It would require months.

Oliver considered contacting Lucy, just to let her know he was alive. But there was no safe way to do it. To make a call, he would have to leave Voskhod, travel to a location where he could access a cell network, and risk exposing himself in the process. The CIA had instructed him and others during training sessions not to use personal devices while undercover in hostile environments—assuming all calls were digitally monitored, just as the CIA monitored both domestic and foreign "targets."

His laptop was also out of the question. He hadn't brought it for fear the FSB would search his baggage and check the files it contained. And given Voskhod's isolation, it was unlikely there were internet cafés nearby.

That left him with one option: He would need to leave Voskhod for two days, drive to the Morgan Pharma office in Saint Petersburg, and call Lucy from there.

But taking two days off after working for only a few weeks would be suspicious. Workers were only allowed one day off per month, and his position depended on maintaining access to the construction site. If he compromised his cover, he would lose the only way to gather intelligence. The situation frustrated him to no end. During his six months of CIA field training, he had earned a reputation for always finding solutions, no matter the challenge. Yet here he was—stuck, without a way forward. And deep down, he knew why. This was the consequence of breaking one of the agency's most ironclad rules—never become romantically involved while undercover. For a fleeting moment, he thought, *Maybe I was a fool to ignore that rule.*

But then, Lucy's face appeared in his mind. Her laugh. Her touch. Her love. And just like that, he dismissed the thought. Because no matter what the CIA rule book said, *Lucy was worth it.*

***

Time moved slowly in Voskhod.

Oliver remained diligent, earning the respect of the tradesmen he worked with. His cover was solid. But every time he stepped into the administration office for his daily assignments, his eyes swept the room, searching—subtly, carefully—for anything that might reveal the purpose of the three mystery buildings.

In the tenth week, Oliver and Mikhail were carrying furniture into the hotel, hauling desks, chairs, bed frames, and mattresses up the stairs. It was grueling work, but they had a rhythm.

Then three cars pulled up outside.

This wasn't unusual—officials had visited the construction site before, checking progress. But this time, something made Oliver pause. He thought he saw familiar faces. He couldn't be sure. Not yet.

Inside the large reception area, Oliver turned to Mikhail.

"I need a break," he said.

Mikhail raised an eyebrow. Oliver—the one who never complained—was asking for a rest? That was usually his excuse. But he shrugged and dropped his end of the desk.

Oliver rested his hands on the desktop, making it look like he was catching his breath.

But in reality, he was watching. The visitors had stepped inside. One of the construction engineers was explaining the layout of the building, gesturing toward the hallway and stairwell.

Then Oliver's stomach tightened. The visitors were none other than Dr. Lenkov, Sasha, Alexei, Anatoly, and five other RusPharma scientists.

Oliver listened. The construction engineer spoke, but Oliver focused on Lenkov's words.

"RusPharma will occupy one of the three buildings. Our scientists will stay at the hotel Monday through Friday. An advance party will arrive next week to begin fitting out the lab and offices."

The pieces fell into place. The Oleg Balabanov identity that had forced the CIA's hand in choosing Voskhod for his mission had unknowingly placed him at the center of something much bigger. RusPharma had chosen Voskhod as the site of their new laboratory.

It was pure coincidence. Or was it? Oliver thought fast. Was Lenkov still interested in the Alzheimer's drug? Without the Morgan Pharma files, without outside assistance, the research would take years—maybe decades. If that was the case, then maybe destroying their lab a second time wasn't necessary.

***

The following week, when Oliver and Mikhail again visited the bar, something was different. The moment he stepped inside, Oliver froze. There, sitting alone at a corner table, sipping a cocktail, was Sasha. She looked different. Gone was the rigid, clinical demeanor of the RusPharma scientist. Her hair was down, her posture relaxed, and her outfit casual. For a moment, Oliver wondered if he was mistaken. But no—it was her.

Mikhail noticed his reaction. Oliver turned to him.

"I'm going to talk to her."

Mikhail smirked knowingly. "Good luck," he chuckled, raising his glass.

Oliver ignored the implication.

His interest in Sasha had nothing to do with attraction. It had everything to do with what she knew—and what she might be willing to say.

Oliver walked over to Sasha's table.

"Hello, may I join you?" Oliver asked in Russian.

"Why would you want to?" she replied.

"I noticed you sitting here all by yourself, and while the friend I'm with is more interested in getting drunk than in a conversation, I'm alone as well. From what I can see, we're the only two lonely souls in this establishment. Because we have that in common, I was wondering if you might be interested in talking to me."

"That's a very roundabout way of saying you want to sleep with me tonight," she said.

"Far from it. I sensed you were lonely, and I thought you might like some company, that's all. I'm Oleg, by the way," he said as he offered her his hand.

"All right, take a seat. I'm Sasha."

"I haven't seen you here before, Sasha. What do you do in Voskhod?"

"I'm a member of an advance party to assist in organizing the laboratory in one of the three buildings that are nearing completion. What do you do?"

"I'm employed by the construction company. My friend over there, drinking too much vodka, and I do various jobs.

Can I get you another drink?"

"A cosmo, please."

Oliver went to the bar to order the cosmo and a Baltika Number 3 lager for himself. He returned to where Sasha was sitting with their drinks.

"So, who do you work for?" he asked when he had resumed his seat opposite her.

"A pharmaceutical company called RusPharma."

"Let me guess what your task is," Oliver said with a smile.

"Your smile reminds me of someone, but I can't think of whom—I should probably stop drinking."

"I think you're a secretary to the boss. What do you call the boss of a pharmaceutical company?" Oliver said, ignoring the remark about his smile.

"We call him the director."

"And are you his secretary?"

"No, I'm a chemist; but the boss, as you call him, gets me to do things for him a secretary could also do."

"The way you said that makes me believe you're rather unhappy with your job."

"Yes, I suppose I am."

"Why don't you look for another job?"

"Because I want to work at the forefront of some major discovery, to make a name for myself. My job at RusPharma allows for that if we're successful in what we're doing."

"So, what major discovery are you likely to make?"

"Medication to cure Alzheimer's disease."

"Wow, that would indeed be a major discovery," Oliver replied. "So why are you unhappy?"

"It's rather personal."

"May I make a guess?"

"Go ahead."

"I think you have feelings for a man, but that man has no

feelings for you."

"It's much more complicated than that," she returned.

"Why don't you tell me? It often helps to talk to someone about problems like that."

"That's a kind offer—if you're sincere. But you're a stranger, although I feel a sense of familiarity with you when we talk like we've been doing."

"Are you going to be in Voskhod long?" Oliver asked to steer the conversation away from her last comment.

"I'll be here indefinitely, every Monday to Friday. I'll return to Moscow on weekends."

"Are you staying in the new hotel?"

"Yes. Where are you staying?"

"I live with my grandmother. I've lived here all my life except for a year when I worked in Austria."

"You're fortunate to have lived outside of Russia for a year. I would also like to. I have dreams of living and working in America. I hope to be able to achieve that after we've developed the medication I mentioned."

Oliver noticed that Mikhail was causing an argument.

"I'm sorry, Sasha, but my friend is causing a problem. I should take him home to avoid it turning into something worse."

"That's a pity, Oleg. Just when the conversation was becoming interesting."

"I'm not going anywhere, Sasha. I'll see you around."

***

Oliver made a point of talking to Sasha whenever he went to the bar with Mikhail. She usually sat at a table by herself. He sensed she was looking forward to resuming their discussions every time. These would sometimes last for hours until, eventually, Mikhail became drunk and violent, requiring Oliver to take him home.

After another two weeks had passed, Oliver decided they were familiar enough with each other to start asking her questions about RusPharma.

"Hi, Sasha, you're looking worried again," he said when he'd ordered a lager and sat down opposite her.

Oliver noticed she had done her best to look pretty that evening. She had used makeup, which she hadn't before. She had braided her hair into a long ponytail. She wore a tight-fitting sweater and a short frock that most women would have worn in the summer—not in April. She was unquestionably trying to make an impression.

"Am I?" she asked.

"Yes, definitely. What's wrong?"

"I'm sorry, it wasn't my intention to look worried. I want to avoid burdening you with my problems."

"So you admit to having problems?"

"Yes. Doesn't everybody?"

"I suppose we all do, in one form or another. But I've found it helps to talk about them. You might remember that I offered to listen to your reasons for being unhappy once before."

"But it's complicated—as I said before."

"That can't be the reason for not wanting to talk about it, can it?"

"No, I suppose not."

She hesitated but then decided to tell him. "My director wants to develop the medication I told you about before anyone else. He tells me it will earn the company trillions of rubles. To develop the medicine quickly, we need outside assistance.

"We thought we'd found the right person last November. He was working for an American pharmaceutical company at the time. When we approached him, he agreed to join us if we paid him one hundred thousand American dollars every month. I was suspicious of him initially, but he worked hard and gained our respect and trust. I even developed feelings for him, but he was romantically involved with an American woman.

"Then, after about seven weeks, he set fire to our laboratory and a nearby office and disappeared. We concluded that Morgan Pharma, the American company he was working for when we approached him, must have been afraid of us introducing the medicine first and ordered him to destroy our laboratory."

"Unbelievable, Sasha. Are you unhappy because you fell in love with this man to find out later he was an imposter?"

"I didn't fall in love with him. I had feelings for him, and it might have become more if he wasn't someone who wanted to sabotage what we were doing."

"So you're not unhappy and worried because of being heartbroken?"

"No, because of what happened afterward."

"There's more?"

"My director is part owner of RusPharma, but the main shareholders are men holding high positions in the Kremlin. They decided not to give up the development of the medicine. They offered my company the possibility of building a new laboratory here in Voskhod. But as I said before, we need outside assistance if we want to be the first to introduce the medicine. My director decided to force the man who had assisted us before to return to us.

"So they kidnapped the American woman he's presumably in love with when she visited the Morgan Pharma office in Saint Petersburg ten days ago. They delivered a note to their office explaining she would be released when he takes her place as our prisoner.

"Now you know what makes me both unhappy and worried. I've come to realize the owners of the company I work for are criminals."

A jolt of shock surged through him, sending goosebumps racing across his skin. His hair stood on end, his pulse hammering in his ears. His fists clenched instinctively. He forced himself to hide them beneath the table, out of Sasha's sight. The overwhelming urge to stand up and run—to storm out and start planning Lucy's rescue immediately—nearly overpowered him.

But he couldn't. Not yet. He needed to stay in control. Oliver fought to keep his expression neutral, forcing down the surge of panic threatening to consume him. He had to look unaffected. Sasha mustn't suspect a thing. He needed every bit of information she could give him—who had taken Lucy, where she was being held, how much time he had. So he swallowed his agony, burying it deep. And with a calmness he didn't feel, he looked at Sasha and spoke.

"Has the person to take her place come forward?"

"Apparently not because he was to be taken here to start assisting us immediately, and he's not here."

"What's to prevent him from escaping once he's here?"

"I don't know. I suspect he'll be escorted by the FSB everywhere he goes."

"Who told you about the kidnapping?"

"The director told me. We had an argument before we moved here. I told him we would be happy to work as a team in developing the medicine without any outside help. I agreed it would take several years, but once it was available, we could sell it at a price that Morgan Pharma couldn't or wouldn't. We would still earn an unimaginable profit.

"He didn't agree, and he insisted we accept the plan he had devised. I questioned him about those plans, and he told me what I just told you."

"So you're unhappy and worried because you've realized your superiors are ordinary criminals?"

"It's not that simple because in destroying our laboratory in Zelenograd, Morgan Pharma is just as evil as my superiors are. We seem to have been caught up in a terrible battle with them, and it's difficult for me to accept what my superiors are doing is wrong."

"But you can't just kidnap people to reach your ambition. That's a step short of murdering someone."

"Yes, I realize that."

"I really feel for you, Sasha," he said as he covered her hand with his. "As I see it, you have two options. The first is to quit your job and look somewhere else for work you'd want to do. The other is to continue what you're doing to try to change the direction your director is heading in."

"I've already done everything possible to change the director's plans."

"What would happen if you confronted him as a team, with all of you threatening to leave RusPharma if things don't change?"

"I've thought of that as well. Unfortunately, some of my colleagues have a lot of sympathy for how the director is handling this crisis. They're very upset about the destruction of the Zelenograd laboratory because working there allowed them to go home to their families every evening, whereas they need to stay in the hotel here except for weekends."

"It sounds as if you've done everything in your power to change things. I have a lot of respect for you," Oliver said in an attempt to end their conversation.

"Thanks, Oleg. Do you want to come to my room for a coffee?"

"Some other time, Sasha, when Mikhail isn't with me. I feel responsible for him. If I don't take him home in time, he'll keep on drinking and cause problems. I should take him home now."

Oliver said goodbye to her. He realized he'd been abrupt and hadn't allowed their conversation to end naturally, but he knew he needed to come up with a plan to rescue Lucy, and he was in a hurry.

14.

A RISKY UNDERTAKING

After dropping Mikhail off at his apartment, Oliver returned home. Normally, he would chat with Daria before turning in—unless he came home late, in which case she was already in bed. Tonight, however, he simply told her he was tired. She nodded, offering him a warm smile before pressing a gentle kiss to his cheek. She didn't say it aloud, but Oliver knew—his presence had given her a new lease on life.

Stretching out on his bed, Oliver stared at the ceiling, his mind racing. He needed a plan. The first phase was straightforward enough. He would request two days off. Leave Voskhod in his car and drive to Saint Petersburg. Check into a cheap hotel on the outskirts of the city. Erase his cover—remove the beard and mustache, wash out the dye from his hair, eyebrows, and eyelashes, and shave. Change into casual clothes and head to Morgan Pharma, where Alex Davidson could advise him on how to get Lucy released.

The second phase, however, was more complicated. Once he was taken prisoner and driven to the RusPharma laboratory, Dimitri and Sergei would have to return his car to Voskhod, parking it outside the fence where others also left their vehicles. He would need to find a way to escape—to outside the town—so he could return as Oleg Balabanov in his car without raising suspicion.

His escape had to be flawless—he couldn't afford to jeopardize his mission. And that was the problem. No matter how he ran through the scenario, he struggled to envision a plausible escape. He needed to get back to Voskhod quickly—not just for his cover, but because abandoning the mission wasn't an option.

Oliver slept badly that night. Lucy was all he could think about. For the first time, he truly regretted involving her in the Alzheimer's assignment. He had asked her to accompany him to Moscow, thinking it would be a straightforward operation. But if she hadn't come, would they have bonded the way they had? Would he have fallen in love with her so deeply? These thoughts saddened him. A part of him felt selfish—had he brought her along because she intrigued him, even before their relationship began? Would she have been safe if he hadn't?

By morning, the answer to his escape problem came to him. He would tape the fake beard and mustache to his stomach, along with a small flask of glue. Wear the construction worker's overalls beneath a shirt and pants. Once his captors returned him to Voskhod, he would bide his time, pretending to settle into his new role at the laboratory. At the end of the workday, he would reapply his disguise in the restroom—glue on the beard and mustache. Remove the outer clothes, leaving only the construction overalls. Put on his ushanka, the Russian trooper hat with ear flaps he had bought to better blend in with the citizens of Voskhod and to obscure the color of his hair if that became necessary. Walk out of the building with other construction workers, blending in. Retrieve his car and queue up to re-enter Voskhod.

It was risky, but it was the best of all the plans he considered.

The following morning—Sunday, April 10—during breakfast with Daria, he told her, casually, that he wanted to take two days off to visit Moscow. Later, at the administration office, he made the same request. To his relief, the response was unconcerned—he had been employed for nearly thirteen weeks and was actually entitled to three days off. It was easier than he expected. He also informed Mikhail, who merely grunted in acknowledgment, momentarily too focused on his work to ask questions.

Returning to his room, Oliver packed the essentials he needed into the smaller of the two bags he had taken with him from Washington. Everything was set. Now it was time to act.

***

The drive to Saint Petersburg took seven hours. By the time he arrived, fatigue was setting in, but he couldn't afford to relax—not yet. He found a suitable hotel, one that was cheap, discreet, and forgettable, paying in advance for the room to avoid needing to visit reception the next morning.

Once in his room, he ordered *Borscht*, the classic beetroot soup with sour cream, as a starter and *Pelmeni*, traditional Russian-style meat dumplings, as his main course. When room service delivered the food, he insisted on paying immediately, minimizing further interaction with reception and room service.

After finishing his meal, he set to work. In the bathroom, he poured a quarter of the contents of the bottle with vinegar the CIA had provided into the vanity, adding water. He leaned over and scrubbed his hair, eyebrows, and eyelashes for fifteen minutes, removing the dye. Once satisfied with the result, he peeled off the beard and mustache, using a solvent from his kit to wipe away any remaining glue residue. By the time he looked at himself in the mirror, Oleg Balabanov was gone.

Oliver skipped breakfast the next morning. He showered, shaved, and mentally prepared for what was to come. Next came his disguise preparations. He taped the beard and mustache to his stomach, securing them in place. He hid a small vial—one he had taken from Daria's kitchen—on a lower part of his body, where a frisk for weapons wouldn't easily detect it. It was filled with glue from the larger CIA container. He put on his construction worker overalls over his shorts. He slipped his Russian passport and driver's license into one of its pockets. He layered a clean shirt and pants over the overalls to conceal them. He tucked his ushanka into the largest pocket of his North Face parka. Once everything was set, Oliver packed his belongings in his bag, placed it in the trunk of the Zhiguli, and drove to the Morgan Pharma office.

When he arrived, he went straight to the reception desk and calmly announced he was Oliver Corbyn and that he needed to speak with Alex Davidson. The receptionists froze. The name alone was enough to send a ripple of relief through the office. Lucy Lassiter had been kidnapped. Anyone connected to her would have feared her fate was now imminent. Murmurs spread as calls were made, and within minutes, Oliver was ushered upstairs. A door opened on the second floor, and inside, behind a sleek, polished desk, sat Alex Davidson. The moment Alex looked up, his eyes widened in shock—then relief. He stood up immediately, stepping forward.

"Oliver," he said, his voice warm but serious. "It's good to see you. You're just in time to rescue Lucy. I assume you've heard she's been kidnapped?"

"I heard about it the evening before last. I believe she was kidnapped two weeks ago?"

"Yes, and the kidnappers have left us with just three more opportunities for you to take her place."

"When and where, Alex?"

"Today, Wednesday, and Friday, between ten and eleven in the morning, in Alexander Garden opposite Saint Isaac's Cathedral."

"Can Dimitri and Sergei take me there?"

"Of course. You have no idea about the stress the kidnapping caused Bill and Jacky. They were here for nearly two weeks, but after not finding a single possibility to facilitate her release, they returned to LA heartbroken. Bill calls me every day to find out if there are any developments. They will be unbelievably happy to have Lucy returned to them."

"I have three requests, Alex."

"You can ask me anything, Oliver."

"It's an urgent matter. I'd like Dimitri and Sergei to drive the car I arrived in to a town called Voskhod, in Moscow Oblast—to park it there in a spot I'll identify to them. That needs to be done today, immediately after Dimitri and Sergei drop me off at Alexander Garden and return here with Lucy. Don't ask me why, please."

"Consider it done, Oliver. I'll ask Dimitri to come here in a minute so you can explain what you want him and Sergei to do."

"The second request concerns Lucy's safety. She's in danger of being kidnapped again if I were to escape before she's left the country. She should return to the States as soon as she can, preferably today if possible. You might want to call Bill immediately to organize for their plane to pick her up. The FSB might try to kidnap her again, for example, when she's on the way to the airport. You and one or two others should accompany her when she leaves here. Please be alert."

"I understand. What's the third thing you want me to do?"

"I need another parka. The one I'm wearing is associated with the person I'm impersonating in Voskhod—not with Oliver Corbyn. It's too late to buy one. Can someone here loan or sell me one—or a coat of some sort with deep pockets to put my ushanka in?"

"You can have my coat, if it's suitable."

After Oliver had ascertained that the pockets in Alex's coat were large enough to fit his ushanka, he put it on.

"There's one more thing, Alex, if you don't mind," Oliver continued. "I want to return here when my assignment is completed, one way or another. I would then like Dimitri and Sergei to drive me to Helsinki to allow me to catch a plane back to the States."

"When will you return?"

"I don't know just yet, but when I do, I need to escape from Russia as quickly as possible."

"I understand. Let me get Dimitri for you."

***

Dimitri was enormously pleased to see Oliver again.

"I apologize for not being able to prevent Miss Lassiter's kidnapping, Oliver. The men responsible surprised us. They shot me while I was reaching for my gun."

"I didn't know, Dimitri. Are you okay?"

Dimitri nodded.

"I want you and Sergei to do something for me," Oliver continued. "I drove here in a Zhiguli. It's parked outside. Here are the keys. I want you to drive it to the closed town of Voskhod, in Moscow Oblast, and park it fifty yards to the right of the entrance to the town, where some other cars are parked.

"Don't go near the entrance. If you do, you'll be questioned and perhaps apprehended. You should arrive after dark and be as inconspicuous as possible. Leave the keys on the ground, just inside of the left front wheel.

"Have Sergei follow you in the Mercedes so you can return here as quickly as possible to protect Lucy if she hasn't already been taken to the airport by Alex. I'm going to try to escape as soon as possible from the people who want me to take Lucy's place, and if I'm successful, those men will probably want to abduct her again if she's still in Russia."

Satisfied that everything was in place, Oliver turned to Alex and shook his hand.

"Look after Lucy," he said, his voice firm but filled with emotion.

Alex gave him a solemn nod. "I will."

Before leaving, he placed his North Face parka in the trunk of the Zhiguli, where he had earlier put the bag containing everything he had brought with him from Voskhod. He then joined Dimitri and Sergei for the drive to Alexander Garden. It took just ten minutes.

They parked along Admiralteyskiy Prospekt, near Saint Isaac's Cathedral. Oliver stepped out, saying a final goodbye to Dimitri and Sergei before walking fifty yards into the park.

There he waited. Minutes passed. A cold unease settled in his chest. *What if they don't let her go? What if this was all a trap—to hold both of us captive?*

Then—movement. From the direction of the Neva River, he saw her. She walked toward him, flanked by two men in plain, unmarked clothing. His breath caught. She looked thin, exhausted. Her eyes searched for him, wild with emotion, and even at a distance, he could see she was barely holding herself together.

The men stopped twenty yards away, scanning the area. One of them broke off and approached. Oliver stood still, suppressing every instinct that screamed at him to react. The man frisked him, patting down his arms, torso, and legs—checking for weapons. Satisfied, he motioned for his partner to bring Lucy forward.

When she was close enough, she broke free and ran the last few steps, throwing herself into Oliver's arms.

She sobbed, shaking against him. He held her tight.

"Chin up, Luce," he whispered. "You need to get back to the States as soon as you can. You're not safe here. I'm so sorry for everything."

Her grip tightened. "What about you, Oliver? What's going to happen to you?"

He forced a small smile. "They need me. They'll think twice about hurting me."

The men yanked her away, shoving her toward the road. She resisted, her tear-streaked face turning back to him. "I love you," she said, her voice breaking.

Oliver swallowed hard. "Go, Luce. Dimitri is waiting for you in the car. I love you too. I'll get us out of this. Trust me."

He heard her sob as she turned and walked toward the waiting Mercedes. His chest ached watching her leave. If there had been another way—if he could have been with her permanently from now on—he would have given up everything.

But this wasn't over yet.

Not even close.

The Mercedes pulled away, taking Lucy with it.

One of the men motioned for Oliver to follow.

They walked toward Admiralteyskiy Prospekt, where a large black SUV waited.

The driver opened the rear side door. Oliver climbed in beside one of his captors, while the other took the front passenger seat. Oliver checked the route the driver was taking, and when they turned onto the M10 highway, he knew they were on the way to Voskhod. He exhaled slowly, closing his eyes.

So far, so good.

Everything had gone according to plan. But the hardest part was still ahead. His escape once they reached Voskhod was by far the riskiest phase. A thousand things could go wrong. If he failed, they would discover his true identity. He would be sentenced to a penal colony and never see Lucy again. He would also be unable to complete his assignment. It was essential he arrived before the laboratory emptied for the night. Timing was everything. He had one shot. And it had to be perfect.

***

The drive to Voskhod took six hours. The driver was in a hurry, he noticed. When they took up a position in the queue to enter the town, it was four-forty-five. The driver showed the FSB officer who had walked to the car a pass and a document. It was already dark, and the officer used his flashlight to read the document.

"Who is the prisoner?" the officer asked, shining his flashlight on the remaining men in the car.

When he was told who it was, he aimed the flashlight at Oliver's face long enough for the officer to be able to recognize him if he were to see him again. They then drove into the town to stop at the entrance to the RusPharma laboratory. Oliver was relieved to find he was where he wanted to be with enough time on hand to carry out his plan. He was pulled out of the car in a heavy-handed manner by the man who had been sitting next to the driver.

"I'll see you at midnight," the man told his partner, who had remained sitting in the back seat.

Oliver understood this to mean they were going to guard him in turn.

The man who had pulled him from the SUV now led him into the laboratory. The many pieces of equipment that had arrived—which Oliver and Mikhail had carried inside—were still in disarray, and little had been done to resolve this.

There were exclamations of surprise when he entered the laboratory. Sasha was first to react. She walked up to him and slapped him in the face.

"You should be locked up and the key thrown away instead of being brought here to work with us again. We trusted you, and you abused that trust," she said in English.

"I'm sorry, Sasha, but before you accuse me of any wrongdoing, you should know that the computer files we were working with before I left Zelenograd were stolen by Lenkov from Morgan Pharma. I'm aware you've asked him to explain how he obtained them and that he wouldn't tell you, but he might just confirm what I've said when you tell him you and your colleagues now know he stole those files."

Sasha's colleagues who were present had also walked to where Sasha, the FSB officer, and Oliver were standing. One of them, a big, burly man, punched him in the stomach. The punch came as a surprise, not allowing Oliver to flex his stomach muscles in time. It winded him badly.

"I wouldn't work with him anymore, Sasha," the burly man said in Russian.

"I wish we had that option, Ivan, but the director wants us to. There's no alternative."

Oliver pretended not to understand what had been said. He decided to offer a token of cooperation by telling them how the laboratory needed to be organized.

"Is this your new laboratory?" he asked Sasha.

"Yes, and as you can see, we're struggling to find the most efficient way to position the equipment."

"Let me help you," Oliver said.

He took Sasha's arm and left the group that surrounded them. He proceeded to tell her where the benches, machines, and equipment needed to be positioned. He helped the construction workers who had been seconded to Sasha's team to move the equipment.

Every item had been positioned an hour later. When someone shouted it was time to call it a day, the construction workers left the laboratory to go to the dressing rooms.

"I need to go to the restroom, Sasha," Oliver said. "Will you ask the officer for permission?"

The FSB officer nodded when Sasha told him that Oliver needed to use the restroom.

Oliver hurried inside, exhaling a quiet breath of relief when the agent chose not to follow him.

He moved quickly. He shrugged off his coat, first retrieving the ushanka from its pocket. Stripped off his shirt and pants, revealing the overalls underneath. Rolled up the clothing into the coat, creating a compact bundle. Applied glue to the beard and mustache—working by touch alone, as he had no mirror. Finally, he donned the ushanka, which he pulled low over his forehead, obscuring as much of his hair, eyebrows, and eyelashes as possible.

His transformation was complete. Now, he just had to get out.

Oliver exited the restroom and entered the adjacent men's dressing room.

Keeping his bundle of clothes tucked under his arm, he moved to the windows. When no one was looking, he unlatched one, pushing it open slightly.

Then he slipped into the air lock alongside two other construction workers in identical overalls.

He barely suppressed a curse when he almost collided with Sasha and the FSB officer.

They were waiting for him in the air lock rather than outside, as he had thought. Oliver kept his pace steady, giving them nothing more than a brief glance before continuing forward. If Sasha thought he was Oleg Balabanov, she wouldn't call out, he thought. She would be too focused on watching who else exited the dressing rooms. She didn't.

That's when he knew his disguise had worked. There were no shouts, no alarms, no rushing footsteps behind him.

Outside, Oliver ran. He hugged the cover afforded by the

trees, moving as fast as he could without drawing attention. At the town entrance, he waited, staying out of sight until both FSB guards inside the checkpoint booth were distracted—checking the identities of drivers in the queued-up cars. The second their focus shifted, Oliver slipped past them, heading straight for his Zhiguli. The keys were exactly where he had asked Dimitri to leave them. The car was still warm. He knew what that meant—Dimitri and Sergei had arrived only minutes ago, likely having just parked it before leaving for Saint Petersburg in the Mercedes.

Oliver slid into the driver's seat, started the engine, and merged into the queue to re-enter the town.

At the checkpoint, he handed over his passport. The officer scanned it, glanced at him, then walked to the guardhouse.

Stay calm.

After a pause, the officer returned his passport without raising questions.

Then Oliver saw it—his FSB escort from earlier was sprinting toward them, shouting.

"Stop anyone trying to leave!"

The alarm had been raised. They had discovered his escape. But he was already inside.

Oliver drove the Zhiguli back to Daria's apartment, parking in his usual spot.

***

The moment he stepped inside, she greeted him warmly, wrapping her arms around him.

"I thought you weren't coming back," she said, her voice laced with worry. "That you lied about going to Moscow just to avoid saying goodbye."

Oliver smiled softly, shaking his head. "How could you think that, Babushka? I left most of my things here. You should have known I'd return."

She sighed, cupping his face briefly before stepping back. "I'm sorry, Oleg. I was afraid I wouldn't see you again. Let me make you a nice dinner."

"I'd love that. But first, I need to wash up and change."

She nodded. "Give me your dirty clothes when you're done. I'll wash them for you."

In his room, Oliver got to work immediately. He dyed his hair, eyebrows, and eyelashes, carefully following the CIA's instructions. He then removed the beard and mustache, only to reapply them with greater precision. When he checked his reflection from the small mirror above the washbasin, he knew Oleg Balabanov was back.

Only then did he feel the tension drain from his body. The stress, the uncertainty, the constant pressure—all of it momentarily faded. He had done it. For now, his cover was safe.

After changing into a fresh shirt and pants, he gathered his dirty clothes and brought them to Daria, joining her in the kitchen. He was home. At least for now.

***

After drinking a cup of coffee with Daria after dinner, he asked Mikhail if he wanted to go to the bar with him. Oliver hoped to see Sasha there to hear how his disappearance had affected them and, if possible, something about their plans. He particularly wanted to know if they were going to attempt to kidnap Lucy again now that he'd escaped.

He was disappointed to not see her in the bar. She was usually there well before they arrived. Oliver saw Sasha walk in later. She looked flustered, he thought. He ordered a cosmo for her and a beer for himself and joined her when she had seated herself.

"You look flustered if not upset, Sasha. Are you okay?"

"You'll never guess what happened today," she said. "Do you remember me telling you that the owners of my company had kidnapped the American woman who the person who destroyed our previous laboratory was in love with?"

"Yes."

"He showed up at the location where the exchange was to take place this morning. The woman was released, and he was taken prisoner instead and driven here. We met him at the laboratory late this afternoon. He helped us to position the equipment in the best possible way, and when he went to the restroom, he escaped through a window in the men's dressing room."

"That's unbelievable. Do you think he's left town?"

"No, I think we were in time to warn the officers at the entrance to stop anyone from leaving, so he should still be here. When FSB reinforcements arrive tomorrow, they'll carry out a systematic search."

"What are you going to do if you can't find him?"

"It's not my decision to make. I'd prefer for him not to be involved with us anymore. I believe we can develop the medicine without his help, as I said before."

Oliver decided she had not been informed of what Lenkov now wanted to do.

"What I don't understand is why he helped you organize the laboratory before he escaped. If he wanted to stop you developing the medicine, it wouldn't have been in his interest to get the laboratory up and running."

"I don't know. But I believe he's not as evil as we think he is. When I confronted him with what he did in Zelenograd, he told me the computer files we had been working on together were stolen by my director. If that's true, he would indeed have had a reason for destroying our laboratory. And after we kidnapped the woman he loves, he'd be justified in hurting us in some way. Now that he's here, he might just be planning to do that."

Oliver was surprised at the accuracy of Sasha's analysis. He decided not to debate her conclusion with her.

"I need to take Mikhail home now," he said when he noticed Mikhail starting to shout at the bartender. "I'll see you around, Sasha."

15.

CLOSURE

Oliver arrived at work the next morning as he did every other day, knowing he would attract less attention among his construction colleagues than if he stayed in the apartment with Daria. That morning, four FSB officers conducted a thorough search of the town, inspecting every apartment and every section of the grounds within the barbed-wire enclosure. Longtime employees of the construction company had to identify themselves but were not questioned. By the time Oliver returned home that afternoon, he overheard people saying that the FSB had concluded the escaped prisoner had fled the town after all.

Despite this, Oliver remained uneasy. He still didn't know the purpose of two nearly completed buildings, and his mission was clear: sabotage all three laboratories if they were being used for weapon development or any project harmful to US interests. His plan was already in place—he was ready to act.

Noticing that no one monitored the inventory of explosives in the construction company's storeroom, Oliver began stealing small amounts, smuggling them home, and hiding them beneath the floorboards in his room. Over time, he had accumulated fifteen sets of explosives and detonators. He had also studied the construction drawings and knew exactly where to position the charges for maximum destruction.

Four weeks after Lucy's release, Oliver was in the administration office when he was assigned to move newly arrived equipment into the laboratories of the second and third buildings. He received technical drawings detailing where each piece should be placed and bolted to the floor.

The plans for Building Two bore the logo of JSC GREC Makeyev, a renowned Russian developer of intercontinental ballistic missile systems. Studying the schematics and the chemicals that had arrived alongside the equipment, Oliver concluded that the laboratory was intended for research on a new type of ballistic missile fuel.

The setup for Building Three's laboratory had been designed by the Kalashnikov Group, infamous for the AK-47 assault rifle. The delivered equipment included components for assembling a large-caliber remote-controlled weapon. While Oliver wasn't as familiar with this technology as he was with the chemicals in Building Two, the implications were clear—he had to destroy all three buildings.

***

It took a week to install the equipment in the two laboratories. Oliver decided to wait two more days before planting the explosives, giving himself time to observe any changes in security. By then, the first scientists assigned to the laboratories in Buildings Two and Three had arrived. Like Sasha and her colleagues, they were housed in the hotel.

At 2 a.m., Oliver put his plan into motion. Dressed entirely in black—T-shirt, pants, North Face parka, sneakers, and the balaclava he had worn during his escape from Russia earlier—he emptied his large bag and packed the explosives and detonators in it.

He slipped out of the apartment and made his way toward the target buildings. He knew they were neither locked nor patrolled at night. In Voskhod, a closed town, security relied on strict entry controls rather than internal surveillance. As long as no outsiders were present, officials saw no need for constant monitoring.

Moving swiftly, Oliver planted the explosives at the designated points and set the detonators for 4 a.m. Before heading back, he stopped at the hotel, pulled out a can of red spray paint—another stolen item from the construction company's storeroom—and scrawled "Freedom for Chechnya" in large Russian letters across its walls.

He returned to the apartment, undressed, and concealed his clothes beneath the floorboards.

The explosions were massive. Since he couldn't synchronize the detonators to a precise second, fifteen thunderous blasts erupted in rapid succession, shaking the ground. The force jolted Daria awake. Moments later, she appeared at his door in an old dressing gown, eyes wide with alarm.

"Oleg, wake up," she said.

"I heard it, Babushka. We should go outside to see what happened."

They stepped outside and joined about twenty neighbors gathered at the corner of their building, all staring in stunned silence at the construction site. Of the four buildings that had stood there, only one remained intact. The other three had imploded, their upper floors collapsing onto the rubble of what had once been the ground level. Fires raged in several areas where ruptured gas lines spewed flames into the night.

People were converging on the site, but there was little they could do. Among them were the scientists who had been asleep in the hotel, now standing in disbelief. Oliver knew the town lacked emergency services—there were no fire crews or police to secure the area, only the chaotic crowd of onlookers. Eventually, someone shut off the gas main, and as the fires sputtered out, most people drifted back to their residences. Daria and Oliver did the same.

***

The next morning, Oliver went to work as if nothing had happened. He joined fifty or so colleagues at the entrance to the builder's administration office, waiting for instructions. Instead, they were told there was nothing for them to do—the site would be leveled by bulldozers and the rubble hauled away by truck to an undisclosed location. No one mentioned what would come next. With no work remaining, everyone was laid off, and their outstanding wages were paid. Oliver and Mikhail walked back to their apartments, agreeing to meet later for a drink at the bar.

Once again, the FSB dispatched agents to investigate, conducting searches just as they had before. High-ranking businessmen and government officials arrived, surveyed the destruction in silence, and left.

Late that afternoon, Oliver and Mikhail went to the bar. It was busier than usual—many former construction workers had nowhere else to be, and some of the displaced scientists had also gathered there for a drink. Among them, Oliver spotted Sasha sitting with Alexei and Anatoly. When she glanced up and saw him, he gave her a small wave but chose not to join them, instead taking a seat with Mikhail in a quiet corner.

They were about to leave for dinner when Sasha approached their table. Without hesitation, she pulled out the only available chair and sat down beside Oliver.

"We've been ordered to take two weeks off to allow the director to decide what he wants to do," she said. "There's not much we can do without a laboratory. We might need to look for employment elsewhere. I leave tomorrow, so I won't see you again."

"We've also been laid off. I'll also need to look for work somewhere else."

She stood up and offered her hand for him to shake. He stood up, shook her hand, and kissed her on the cheek. She looked at him. He saw her hesitate before turning around to leave.

After breakfast the following morning, Oliver told Daria he'd be leaving to find work in Moscow. She wasn't as disappointed as he'd thought she would be.

Daria looked at him intently. "I want you to know that I found out you're not Oleg," she said.

Oliver looked at her, speechless.

"I knew almost immediately after you arrived. Your behavior, kindness, and consideration are so unlike Oleg. The color of your eyes, your voice, and your physique gave you away. But your secret is safe with me. I suspect you're the person the authorities are looking for and that you caused the explosions."

"I'm surprised you didn't tell me before."

"I didn't want you to leave, which you might have if I had told you earlier. These last eighteen weeks have been the most carefree of my life. I want you to know that," she continued.

"Dearest Daria, I will always cherish our time together. I'll send you money every month so you don't need to worry about how to pay for your next meal. When people ask you where the money is coming from, you need to tell them that your grandson Oleg has found work elsewhere, okay?"

Oliver packed his belongings into his two bags. As he turned to Daria, he embraced her and said goodbye.

Without another word, he left the apartment, loaded his bags into the trunk of the Zhiguli, and drove toward the town's entrance. When he reached the checkpoint, he handed his passport to the FSB officer, explaining he was leaving to find work elsewhere after being laid off by the construction company. The officer barely glanced at him before waving him through.

He drove straight to Saint Petersburg, checking into the same hotel he had stayed at before. That evening, he had dinner in the hotel restaurant, then retired early—he hadn't had a proper night's sleep in days.

***

The next morning, Oliver made the final leg of his journey to the Morgan Pharma office. Upon arrival, he approached reception and asked to see Alex Davidson. A few minutes later, Alex came downstairs, expecting to meet someone named Oleg Balabanov.

Oliver took him by the arm and guided him to a quiet corner, ensuring they wouldn't be overheard. Then, in a low voice, he said, "I'm Oliver Corbyn."

"I don't understand," Alex said.

"I entered Russia as Oleg Balabanov, with a Russian passport, and I need to maintain my disguise when leaving the country. The people who kidnapped Lucy might still be watching this office to see if Oliver Corbyn returns. You should know I escaped captivity after I took Lucy's place, to assume this disguise again to enable me to finish my assignment. You will have been told that I work for the CIA?"

"Yes. What can I do to help you leave the country?"

"I need your help with several issues. I bought a six-year-old Zhiguli when I arrived in Moscow. I'd like Dimitri to sell it and to send the proceeds to Daria Balabanov in Voskhod, Moscow Oblast. I also want to send her the equivalent of five hundred US dollars in rubles every month. Can you organize that for me without letting her know the money was sent by Morgan Pharma?"

"Sure, if you give me her address and bank particulars."

"She doesn't have a bank account. You'll have to send her a money order each time. I'll arrange for reimbursement."

Oliver handed him the piece of paper on which he'd written her name and address.

"I want to take a flight to Washington Dulles from Helsinki," he continued. "I would be questioned if not apprehended if I were to travel to the US from here. Is it possible for Sergei to drive me to Helsinki? It will take about nine hours to drive there and back."

"I'll ask my secretary to check the availability of a flight, and I'll ask Dimitri and Sergei to drive you there. Should she book the flight?"

"Yes, please. Use the name and particulars of my fake US passport," Oliver said while handing him the passport.

16.

LETTING GO

Oliver returned from his assignment eighteen weeks after bidding Lucy farewell at Washington Dulles. Dimitri and Sergei had driven him to Helsinki, where he caught a Finnair flight to London Heathrow before transferring to a British Airways flight bound for Washington Dulles, arriving at five in the afternoon that same day.

The call with Lucy, made from his Russian cell phone as soon as he crossed the border en route to Helsinki, hadn't gone as he'd hoped. They exchanged details about what had happened after he had taken her place as prisoner, but something felt off. Lucy sounded distant—detached, even.

Sensing her mood, Oliver tried to lift her spirits, saying the things he knew she usually loved to hear, but nothing seemed to land. His words felt hollow against the weight of her silence. When he finally asked if something was wrong, she deflected, changing the subject.

A strained pause followed. Then, without much of an explanation, she simply said goodbye and ended the call.

Now, standing at the baggage carousel, Oliver retrieved his two bags and made his way through customs. As he stepped into the arrivals area, his eyes immediately found Lucy among the crowd waiting for passengers. Her colorful outfit made her impossible to miss. Yet she hadn't spotted him—unsurprising, given his disguise.

Oliver took a steadying breath and walked toward her, approaching from behind.

"Dearest Lucy, you need to stop picking me up all the time," he whispered in her ear.

She turned to look at him. "Oliver?"

By way of an answer, he kissed her on the lips and hooked his arm through hers. She kept looking at his face.

"I hadn't realized you'd be wearing a disguise."

"I'm on my way to my apartment. Are you coming with me to watch as I transform myself into the person you love?"

"Yes... I'm not going to let you out of my sight until we've had a serious talk."

"Should I take that to mean I'm in trouble?" he said with a smile.

"You shouldn't make fun of what I just said."

"I'm not, Luce, but I can't be serious just now. I want to avoid ruining the happy feeling that came over me when I saw you."

She smiled at him and wrapped her arm around his waist. He placed his arm around her. She led him to the exit, where Mitch was waiting with her baggage. He had hired a car with a chauffeur from the Dulles Limousine Service to take them wherever they wanted to go. Mitch shook Oliver's hand after Oliver revealed who he was.

"Let me know when you want me to pick you up, Lucy. Bill asked me to fly to LA tomorrow. I should be back the day after."

After saying goodbye to Mitch, the chauffeur of the car Mitch had arranged placed their baggage in the trunk.

"1800 North Lynn Street, Arlington," Oliver told the

chauffeur before closing the glass partition separating them from him.

"I apologize for my long absence, Luce. The assignment I was on had me go to a place in Russia without cell or internet service. I wanted to let you know that the assignment would take three to four months instead of two to three weeks as I'd hoped, but there was no way I could. I'm sorry."

"I've been worried sick because of not knowing where you were, what you were doing, whether you were in danger, and when you'd return."

"I know, Luce. I was completely isolated. I would have needed to abort my assignment to get a message to you. It took some ten days for the news of your kidnapping to reach me and then only because of exceptional circumstances."

Lucy didn't reply, and Oliver realized his absence had affected her much more than he assumed. They fell silent, with Lucy not wanting to preempt the discussion she wanted to have with him later and Oliver wishing to change the subject but not knowing how without seeming to trivialize the impact of his long absence.

***

Lucy was surprised by the luxury Oliver's apartment offered when she inspected it. It was a two-bedroom, two-bathroom unit. She concluded that Oliver earned a decent salary to be able to afford it.

"Make yourself comfortable, Luce. I need to wash my hair, remove the hair from my face, take a shower, and shave."

"Let me give you a hand washing your hair. A mixture of vinegar and warm water is very effective in removing the dye."

"I know. The CIA chief of disguise taught me everything I needed to know. I have some vinegar left."

Oliver stripped to the waist and prepared the vinegar-water mixture in the basin of the bathroom vanity. He bent down to allow Lucy to wash his hair. When she had, and after waiting ten minutes before rinsing, he looked in the mirror and noticed that all traces of the dye had disappeared.

"You forgot something," he said.

"I've decided not to give you a kiss until after you've removed all that hair from your face."

"There's that, too, but I was really referring to something else."

She looked at him quizzically, refusing to ask him what he meant.

"You forgot to wash my eyebrows and eyelashes. You'll need a wash cloth or the corner of a towel."

Lucy dipped the corner of a towel in the vinegar-water mixture, faced him, and began to rub his eyebrows and eyelashes. Oliver held her close.

"I think you wanted to hold me like you are when you asked me to remove the dye from your eyebrows and eyelashes."

"Was it that obvious?"

"It was."

"Can you blame me when the most beautiful woman in the world is in my bathroom with me?"

"Stop it, or I'll poke you in the eye. Now, please remove all that hair from your face."

"I hadn't realized that a beard and a mustache would be such a barrier when wanting a kiss."

Oliver peeled the beard and the mustache from his face. He used the solvent he was given to remove the remaining glue before showering, shaving, and dressing in a clean shirt and jeans.

"So, how do I look?" Oliver said when he returned to the living room.

"That's a lot better. I'll have to get used to you being clean-shaven," she replied.

"I want that kiss now."

Lucy embraced and kissed him with passion. It brought back memories of when she'd done that before to both of them. She released him, knowing if she didn't, they would end up in the bedroom. Oliver looked at her and recognized her demeanor for what it meant. She was definitely not happy with him, and he knew why.

"What do you want to do about dinner, Luce? We could go to a nearby restaurant, or we can eat in."

"Let's stay here. We need to talk."

"I suspected you'd say that. Okay, pick whatever suits your fancy from this menu."

Oliver handed her the menu of a nearby restaurant that offered takeout and delivery.

After they'd both chosen their meals, he called the restaurant and ordered. He locked away the false passports he had used and other Russian documents and retrieved their US equivalents.

They discussed trivial things during dinner, avoiding the topic Lucy wanted to talk about. Oliver knew what it was, and he thought hard about how he would answer the question she was bound to confront him with.

"Let's sit on the couch while we finish the wine, Luce. I'll pour you a coffee in a bit."

Lucy did as he suggested.

"So, what do you want to talk about?" he asked.

"About us."

"Before you continue, I need to say it's time to call me by my real name. Do you remember what it is?"

"Of course I do."

"Oliver Corbyn was the name I needed to adopt for the Alzheimer's assignment. My name for this last assignment was Oleg Balabanov. Please call me Liam."

"You'll have to be patient with me, Liam. Over the past eight months, my life has been centered around a man named Oliver Corbyn. It's going to be difficult to call you something else."

"Keep calling me Oliver in that case. I really don't mind. It might, in fact, be better if you did."

"In what way?"

"Because, as you found out, the name Oliver Corbyn won't mean much to anyone who wants to find out stuff about me. What I do for a living, who I work for, and so on. Besides, everyone around you calls me Oliver—Bill, Jacky, Mitch, Dave, Dimitri, Sergei, Alex, and others. Let's leave it at that, okay?"

"Sure."

"Let me get you a coffee before we talk about us."

Oliver returned five minutes later with two cups of freshly brewed coffee.

"I insist we sit at the table, Oliver," Lucy said firmly. "I want to look into your eyes while we talk—without the temptation to cuddle up to you."

A sense of unease settled over him. "You're scaring me, Luce. Are you planning to let me go?"

She hesitated. "It might come to that."

His stomach clenched. "Then please, tell me what's wrong."

Lucy exhaled slowly, as if steadying herself. "It's simple. I can't handle your long absences. I love you, but when you're away, I worry to the point of feeling miserable—grumpy, sick. I sleep badly, and I become unbearable to be around."

She looked away for a moment, blinking back tears. "Something has to change. If we can't find a solution, we need to let each other go. It'll be painful for both of us, but maybe, in time, we'll be glad we did."

Oliver felt the blood drain from his face. He had expected another plea for him to leave the CIA, but he had underestimated just how much his absence had affected her. The thought of losing her terrified him. For once, he was at a loss for words. He stood and began pacing the room.

"My last assignment took much longer than expected. I thought I'd be back in half the time."

"I can't handle nine weeks, Oliver. Not even four," she said softly. "I'm sorry."

Her voice wavered, and she quickly wiped at her eyes.

Oliver wrestled with the implications of leaving his job. He would be letting Director Rivera down. He had completed five successful assignments, each one pushing him to his limits, each one fulfilling in its own way. He dreaded the idea of sitting behind a desk, trapped in the monotony of a nine-to-five routine. But as Lucy's words echoed in his mind, a painful realization settled over him.

She was right. If she were to let him go, in time, she would move on. She would rebuild her life—without him. And suddenly, he knew the answer.

"I hadn't realized my absence hurt you this much," he admitted. "I missed you too. But I found comfort in knowing I'd see you again, in imagining the moments we'd share once I returned."

He hesitated then added, "But I can't walk away from this, sweetheart. The people I work for count on me. I've touched the lives of many people during my assignments, and that gives me purpose. It motivates me to keep going. Besides, I can't see myself sitting behind a desk."

"Oliver, please!" she cried, her voice breaking.

He froze, his determination crumbling as he watched her unravel before him, doubt gnawing at his heart.

"Let's talk about this," Oliver urged, desperation seeping into his words. But Lucy only stared at him, wide-eyed and trembling.

Slowly, she shook her head, a silent refusal more devastating than any scream.

When he reached out to her, she recoiled, tears now streaming down her face. Without another word, she fled the room, leaving him standing in the wreckage of what they once were.

17.

HEARTBROKEN

Lucy locked herself in the guest bedroom, refusing to discuss her ultimatum. When she finally emerged the next morning, her bags were packed—she was ready to leave.

She stood in the living room, avoiding his gaze. "Please call me a taxi to Dulles," she said, her voice flat, drained of emotion.

Oliver's chest tightened. "Please, Luce, don't do this," he pleaded.

He could see she'd been crying. Her eyes were red-rimmed, her face drawn. He searched for any flicker of hesitation, any sign she might reconsider, but there was none. She had made up her mind.

Defeated, he called for a taxi, then carried her bags to the entrance of his apartment building. They stood in silence until the car arrived. Oliver placed her baggage in the trunk while she slipped into the back seat without a word.

She didn't look at him. She didn't say goodbye. The taxi pulled away, leaving him standing there, watching her disappear.

***

When Oliver first called to say he was flying home, Lucy had felt an immense weight lift from her shoulders. But as time passed, anxiety crept in. She thought long and hard about confronting him with her ultimatum, knowing she was taking a significant risk. There was a very real chance he would refuse to change, and that terrified her.

If he chose his work over their relationship, didn't that mean she loved him more than he loved her? The thought unsettled her.

Even after his arrival, she hadn't been entirely sure whether she would go through with it. But as she stood in his apartment, watching his reaction, she knew she had to. His shock was obvious—he had never truly considered the possibility of leaving the CIA for her. He had never thought he might lose her.

When Lucy returned to her apartment that afternoon, the weight of what had happened crashed over her. She barely made it to her bedroom before she broke down completely. She threw herself onto the bed, sobbing uncontrollably.

The night before, there had been no doubt in her mind about what she needed to do. But now, in the stark light of day, the harsh reality of her decision settled in.

She wept until there were no more tears left.

**

When Zoey came to collect Lucy the following morning to go to the gym, she found her still in bed. She had let herself in.

"Wake up, sleepyhead," Zoey said as she opened the curtains.

"I don't want to go to the gym today, Zoey."

"Why not?"

"I broke up with Oliver."

"When did that happen?"

"The evening before last."

Zoey sat down on the bed. "But you told me he's your soulmate. It's hard to believe. Is he involved with another woman?"

"No, nothing like that. I just can't deal with his long absences. I picked him up at the airport two days ago after not having spent time with him for eighteen weeks. We went to his apartment. I told him I worry when he's away to the point of feeling downcast, grumpy, and sick and that I sleep badly. I said things needed to change, and if they didn't, we had to let each other go. I told him that letting go would be hard on both of us, but perhaps after a year or so, we'll be glad we did."

"What was his reply?"

"He said he couldn't stop what he was doing."

"What did you do when he told you that?"

"I left the room and barricaded myself in the guest room. He pleaded with me to reconsider and not leave. I left the following morning and caught the shuttle to LaGuardia."

"You'll come to regret what you've done if Oliver is really the man you described to me. Shouldn't you have tried harder to resolve the issue somehow?"

"That thought occurred to me yesterday when I went to bed. I was too shocked when the tone in which he said he couldn't quit his job allowed for little chance of seeing things my way. It caused me to not try to come to some sort of compromise."

"Call him and ask him to meet you to talk about it again. You'll lose him if you don't."

"I can't, Zoey. It's the nature of the work he does. When he's abroad, he has little influence on the duration of the assignment he's sent on. It really boils down to him having to find other work to enable us to see each other more frequently. A compromise would be next to impossible."

"Okay, if you feel you can't, I should start cheering you up.

Get up, take a shower, and get dressed. I'll think of something for us to do today to take Oliver off your mind."

***

Lucy did as Zoey suggested. They went out to lunch together and to dinner that evening. They avoided talking about Oliver all day. Zoey wanted to take her to a party after dinner.

"Come with me to the party Pamela's organized," she said.

"I haven't been to a party since I met Oliver eight months ago. I don't know if I should."

"But if you've broken up with him, there's no reason why you shouldn't. Besides, it will help you forget him."

That argument, and the thought that it would spite him, made Lucy decide to accompany Zoey to Pamela's penthouse.

It was a wild party—the kind Lucy would have avoided had she known what she was walking into. She tried to remain inconspicuous among the tangled bodies of couples making out around her. Sitting in a corner with a drink in hand, she kept to herself, hoping the night would pass quickly.

But then, one of her ex-boyfriends pulled her to her feet, grinning as he leaned in to kiss her. She barely had time to react before a camera flashed.

Days later, the tabloids had a field day. "Lucy Lassiter Returns to the Social Scene!" The headline was everywhere, accompanied by the damning photo.

When Lucy stumbled back to her apartment in the early hours of the morning, she collapsed onto her couch, her mind spinning—not from alcohol, but from regret. She replayed memories of Oliver, the happiness they had shared, and the love she had walked away from.

Doubt crept in, suffocating her.

Tears streamed down her face until exhaustion finally pulled her into sleep.

***

Over the following weeks, Lucy continued going to parties with Zoey. She discovered alcohol numbed the misery that clung to her like a second skin. Soon, drinking wasn't just an escape—it became a habit. She started early in the day and kept going, chasing oblivion from morning until night.

When she and Zoey went out, she no longer just sipped her drinks. She downed shots, desperate to drown out the pain. Work at Morgan Pharma became an afterthought. More often than not, she simply didn't show up. Nights blurred into mornings, and mornings into afternoons. She would stumble home at dawn, sleep until noon, then do it all over again.

Jacky and Bill came to see her, their faces tight with worry.

"Lucy, you have to pull yourself together," Jacky pleaded. "This isn't the way to forget him."

"You're drinking too much," Bill added. "You're only making things worse."

But Lucy barely heard them. Forgetting Oliver was all that mattered.

A month after the breakup, she took her self-destruction a step further.

Party drugs had always been around—passed from hand to hand—little pills of reckless abandon. She had never joined in. But now, she watched the way others' faces lit up after taking them, how they laughed and danced with euphoric abandon, untethered from reality.

She wanted that feeling. So she took the first pill. And then another.

And for a little while, it worked. The memories faded. The heartbreak dulled. She could exist without the weight of him pressing on her chest.

But the reprieve never lasted.

The moment the high faded, the memories of Oliver came

rushing back, sharper than ever. And every time, she cried.

So she took another pill. And another.

Because forgetting—even for a few fleeting hours—was the only thing that kept her breathing.

18.

WORK HARD TO FORGET

Oliver didn't sleep the night Lucy locked herself in the guest room. He lay awake, his mind churning, searching for a way to undo the damage her ultimatum had caused. But the more he thought, the more hopeless it seemed.

She had been unwavering—resolute when she confronted him, firm when she refused to discuss it further. Her mind was made up. There was no room for negotiation.

He was devastated.

Trying to forget her felt like an impossible task. He loved her—every part of her. The way she laughed, the way she challenged him, the way she made him feel alive. Losing her left a hollow ache in his chest that nothing could fill.

He had no choice but to move forward. And since he couldn't have her, he would throw himself into the only thing that remained—his work.

Maybe, in time, the constant knots in his stomach would ease. Maybe the sharp sting of her absence would dull.

With that resolution, he forced himself to focus. He sat down at his desk and wrote a short report on his last assignment. When he finished, he printed it, slipped it into a folder, and hailed a taxi to CIA headquarters.

By the time he arrived, it was three in the afternoon. He walked straight to the director's office, but since he hadn't scheduled an appointment, he was asked to wait.

The minutes dragged unbearably. Sitting still only made it worse—his mind kept drifting back to Lucy, replaying their moments together. The silence. The finality. The way she wouldn't even look at him before leaving.

When he was finally told Ken Rivera was available, he exhaled in relief. At least now, for a little while, he could focus on something else.

"Congratulations once again, Liam, on having successfully carried out your assignment. Our data analysts informed us there were a series of explosions in Voskhod. We immediately knew you were responsible. What were the buildings you destroyed used for?"

"One of them was to be used by the Kalashnikov Group to develop a large-caliber remote-controlled assault weapon. Another was for Makeyev to develop a new type of fuel for intercontinental ballistic missiles. The third was to be a new lab for RusPharma. I wouldn't have discovered the new RusPharma facility if your people hadn't decided I needed to adopt the disguise of someone that had lived in Voskhod. We were lucky in that regard. I decided it needed to be destroyed as well. Here's my report. It's all there."

"Thanks, Liam. I'll read it and have it filed away, as always."

"What's my next assignment, Ken?"

***

Oliver returned to his apartment after his meeting with Ken Rivera. His new assignment required him to travel to Russia once again, but as he tried to focus on planning his next steps, thoughts of Lucy crept in, relentless and unshakable. The ache of her absence gnawed at him, leaving him hollow.

For a fleeting moment, he considered going to New York—seeing her, trying to find some way to bridge the gap between them. But he dismissed the idea almost as quickly as it surfaced. There was nothing he could offer her that would change their reality. His job wouldn't change. His purpose wouldn't change. And she had made it clear that neither could she.

Hoping to shake the exhaustion pressing down on him, he went to bed early, but sleep, once again, eluded him.

***

Eleven weeks later, after completing his assignment, Oliver returned and instinctively searched the tabloids for any mention of Lucy. He wasn't prepared for what he found.

The headlines painted a picture of a woman he barely recognized. Lucy Lassiter was back in the social scene, drinking heavily, partying endlessly—nothing like the woman he had known. He read between the lines, concluding she was neglecting her responsibilities at Morgan Pharma.

For a moment, he again entertained the thought of going to New York, confronting her, making her see reason. Once before, she had listened when he explained the pitfalls of a reckless lifestyle. But this time, he suspected it wasn't about the parties or the attention.

This was about him.

She was doing this because he had refused to give in to her. And if that was the case, she wouldn't stop—if only to spite him.

One detail, however, unsettled him more than anything else: Lucy was frequently intoxicated in public. That meant she was vulnerable. She knew too much about him—his true identity, his missions, the nature of his work. A single careless slip among her so-called friends could put his entire existence at risk.

He had no choice.

Within days, he relocated to a new apartment, ensuring no loose ends could tie him to his old address.

***

Oliver reported back to Ken Rivera three days later.

Rivera briefed him on his next mission—a politically charged operation that had come directly from the president. The CIA was to extract a high-profile Russian opposition leader imprisoned in the penal colony in Solikamsk, managed by the Federal Penitentiary Service, the FSIN.

It was a lifetime sentence handed down in a sham trial. Everyone knew it.

Oliver understood the stakes immediately. The mission was straightforward in theory, but in execution, it would be the most dangerous operation he had undertaken.

Back in his apartment, he mapped out a plan. He would once again assume the identity of Oleg Balabanov, traveling to Solikamsk via Helsinki before covering the remaining distance by car. Once at the penal colony, he would apply for a job.

His gamble worked. Due to a severe shortage of non-FSIN personnel, he was hired immediately—assigned to janitorial duties.

For twelve weeks, he observed, planned, and waited. When he was finally reassigned to the section where the opposition leader was held prisoner, he had already devised a detailed escape plan.

But he never got the chance to execute it.

Before he could act, news spread that the opposition leader was dead. The whispers were immediate—the FSB had ordered the FSIN to poison him. The mission was over before it had even begun. Thirteen weeks after leaving the US, Oliver returned to his apartment. But his mind was elsewhere.

He had thought of little else during the assignment besides Lucy. The possibility of reconciliation had taken root in his mind, growing stronger with each passing day. If there was even the slightest chance that she still wanted him, he was ready to take it.

But as he scanned the latest news, his heart sank.

A long article in *The Washington Post* detailed Lucy's engagement—to Prince Alexander Alexandrovich, a prominent member of the Russian Nobility Association in America and grandson of the last pretender to the Russian throne.

Oliver sat frozen, rereading the words, trying to process them. Then, his eyes drifted to a smaller article on the same page.

Bill Lassiter had been kidnapped in Saint Petersburg while visiting the Morgan Pharma office.

The air left Oliver's lungs.

Lucy was engaged.

Her stepfather had been taken.

And Oliver had never felt more lost.

19.

THE RUSSIAN PRESIDENT

Four men sat in the lavishly furnished office of the Russian president at his private residence on the Novo-Ogaryovo estate, nestled in the Odintsovsky District of Moscow Oblast. This was no official meeting—there was no record of it in government schedules, no aides taking notes. It had the air of a private gathering, a discreet exchange among men of influence.

Seated behind his grand mahogany desk, the president observed his guests: Dr. Mikhail Lenkov, Prince Alexander Alexandrovich, and Andrei Balakin.

Prince Alexandrovich, grandson of the last pretender to the Russian throne, was officially a US citizen, but his deep and enduring ties to the Kremlin ensured he remained a trusted insider. Andrei Balakin, as governor of Moscow Oblast, wielded considerable political power in the region.

The three men sat in a row of plush armchairs, facing the president. A maid had entered earlier, serving coffee and pastries before quietly exiting, closing the door behind her.

The room settled into a thick silence. Then the president leaned forward slightly and addressed his guests.

"I've asked you to come here to discuss a matter that has

upset me greatly. As you know, I acquired a forty-five percent stake in RusPharma more than a year ago when I was informed that you, Lenkov, told the press that a medication to cure Alzheimer's disease was to become available soon. In our discussion at the time, you informed me that RusPharma would earn trillions of rubles if you were the first to introduce the medicine.

"You said you'd acquired the information to produce the medicine from Morgan Pharma by paying REvil to hack their computers on which that information was stored. I believed the information you thus acquired would have led to the introduction of the medicine by now. Yet, more than a year later, you are no closer to doing that than before you acquired that information.

"I've been told that your laboratories in Zelenograd and Voskhod have been destroyed. The laboratory in Zelenograd by someone who was working for you at the time, and the one in Voskhod by Chechen terrorists. You need to explain to us, as shareholders, why you haven't delivered on your promise."

It was obvious to those present that the president was indeed upset. Most people would not have guessed he was seventy years old, but when sitting no more than six feet from him, the wrinkles on his face were telling. As always, he was well-groomed, immaculately dressed, and his thinning hair neatly combed. As he waited for Dr. Lenkov to reply, he loosened his tie and undid the top button of his shirt.

"It's complicated, Mr. President. Allow me to explain. The point is that the information REvil obtained revealed we needed assistance in taking the last steps, which involve determining the precise chemical composition of the medicine. Morgan Pharma was in the process of determining that when the hack took place. We considered contracting REvil again to perform another hack later to obtain that information, but by then, Morgan Pharma had taken steps to secure their computer network.

"Then, in November of last year, during the annual conference on Alzheimer's disease held in Moscow, an American scientist who had worked on the Alzheimer's program at Morgan Pharma informed me he was considering leaving his employer to work elsewhere for more money. His name is Oliver Corbyn.

"The reason he wanted more money was rather strange. His girlfriend was none other than Lucy Lassiter. Her parents own Morgan Pharma. Corbyn told me he wanted a higher income to avoid being reliant on Miss Lassiter's wealth. I told my people to contact him, and we came to an agreement. He started work in our laboratory in Zelenograd three days later.

"I was told Miss Lassiter slapped him when he told her, and it seemed they ended their relationship at that point. Seven weeks after he began working for us, he set fire to the laboratory and disappeared. We concluded that Morgan Pharma had discovered the hack and the subsequent upload of the information to REvil's IP address, and the offer by Corbyn to assist us was no more than a front to be able to sabotage what we were doing for having stolen the information."

"That sounds as if the CIA was involved," the prince commented.

"I doubt whether that's the case. Corbyn holds a PhD from Harvard, where he studied the possibility of developing a cure for Alzheimer's. He, in fact, identified the critical path out of the conundrum that had slowed down Morgan Pharma."

"What about the explosion that destroyed the lab in Voskhod?" the president asked.

"Allow me to backtrack before I get to that," Lenkov replied. "As you know, Andrei here offered us the use of one of the new laboratories being built in Voskhod after our lab in Zelenograd was destroyed. It had originally been intended for another company. Was that because of your twenty-five percent stake in RusPharma, Andrei?"

"It was, although that shouldn't become known outside this office."

"That was kind of you, but it didn't solve the problem of still needing someone to help us define the medicine. We were busy preparing the laboratory when explosions destroyed all three buildings containing laboratories. The graffiti on the wall of the hotel nearby suggested that Chechen terrorists were responsible."

"Is it possible this Corbyn person might have also been involved in destroying those laboratories?" the president asked.

"That possibility was raised by the FSB later because we had Miss Lassiter abducted when she visited Saint Petersburg to force Corbyn to return to us. Corbyn was taken to Voskhod when he turned up to get her released. He escaped a day later. The laboratories were destroyed some five weeks later. We simply don't know."

A heavy silence settled over the room as the four men processed what Lenkov had just told them. Each was deep in thought, weighing the implications.

It was clear that Lenkov was embarrassed. He had likely spent hours agonizing over how to present the matter to the president when he was summoned. Now, sitting under the weight of their scrutiny, he looked distinctly uncomfortable.

His usually sharp appearance was gone. His white hair and beard were unkempt, as though he hadn't bothered to groom himself. His suit hung loosely on his thin frame, as if he had recently lost weight or simply stopped caring about his appearance.

"So now you know why we haven't been able to develop the medicine," Lenkov continued, as if to draw a conclusion from what he'd told them. "We are presently without a laboratory and without data on the medicine now that the files we stole from Morgan Pharma have been destroyed. We either need someone familiar with the work Morgan Pharma did or to steal the data from Morgan Pharma a second time. We wouldn't need outside assistance in that case because that data would now be complete enough to take the medicine into production."

"You've been very quiet, Alexander," the president said. "Any ideas on how we can still reach our goal?"

"Let me first fill you in on this man, Corbyn, and on Lucy Lassiter," he replied. "As you know, I live in New York, and the tabloids, which you probably don't get to read, followed those two for a while. They've been in a romantic relationship since the conference in Moscow Lenkov told us about.

"Miss Lassiter is a well-known socialite. She frequents parties the upper class organizes since she started working for Morgan Pharma, except for about a month before the Moscow conference and seven months after. It's been suggested that Corbyn didn't want her to attend those parties. She started to attend them again with her girlfriends about two months ago. The tabloids have concluded she's no longer in a relationship with him."

"Get to the point, Alexander," the president interrupted.

"The point is we've not been smart enough. Our problem needs to be tackled in a more subtle way. Shall I explain what I think needs to be done?"

"Go ahead," the president replied.

"It wouldn't be difficult for me to get introduced to Miss Lassiter's group of friends. I believe that if I court her and give her the attention she craves, she'll eventually accept me as her new romantic partner. She has a reputation for entering into relationships quickly. She's rarely seen without some man nearby, but none of her relationships last because the men disappoint her in one way or another. I believe she has to feel wanted, and I think I can fulfill the role of someone who can give her what she wants. She would be quite a catch, by the way."

"What will that do for our cause?" the governor asked.

"It's simple. Once I've won her trust, the FSB should kidnap Bill Lassiter. I believe he'll need to travel to their office in Saint Petersburg at some point. He's the chairman of the board of directors. Miss Lassiter would then take his place as acting chairperson, but if she were to be ill, she would perhaps ask me to take her place if we'd become close. I would need to ask her to marry me, for example. I believe I can make that happen."

"And then what, Alexander?"

"Once I'm controlling the company, I'll arrange temporary work visas for the best RusPharma scientists to work at the Morgan Pharma Boston laboratory until we've secured the necessary information for producing the medicine. Only Corbyn can connect those scientists to the computer hack and the theft of the information more than a year ago, but he's no longer a threat to our cause because he's no longer associated with Miss Lassiter."

"That would be brilliant if you can pull it off," the president said. "What about Lassiter's wife? Won't she assume the chairmanship of the board after her husband has gone missing?"

"I don't think she will. She's played a lesser role in the company since she married him. But if she were to become chairwoman because of Miss Lassiter's illness, we'll send her a note saying we'll hurt her husband unless she steps aside."

"For your plan to succeed, Miss Lassiter must be incapacitated when her stepfather is kidnapped. How are you going to make that happen?"

"Come on, Lenkov, you're a pharmaceutical scientist. You shouldn't ask me that question. I'll give her something to drink each day. She's addicted to alcohol and frequently hungover, for which she would need something to make her feel better.

"Once I have full control of Morgan Pharma, I'll dispose

of her if she becomes difficult to handle because of realizing what I've done regarding the Alzheimer's medicine, or else allow her to become my playmate if she's tame and accepts me and my leadership of the company."

Silence settled over the office once more after the prince had outlined his plan. He sat back, a satisfied smile stretching across his face as he studied his fellow investors.

Though small in stature, Prince Alexandrovich exuded confidence. He was widely regarded as handsome, his pencil-thin mustache and neatly brushed-back black hair giving him the air of a classic aristocrat. Every detail of his appearance was thoughtfully chosen—the expensive suit, the perfectly knotted tie—all reinforcing the regal image he carried so effortlessly. At that moment, he looked every bit the nobleman accustomed to getting what he wanted.

"I always knew you were a good strategist, Alexander. When all this is over, and we've all become much richer, I want you to become one of my advisors," the president said.

"Thank you for your trust in me, Mr. President, but I prefer to keep living in New York. The Americans respect me. Because I'm an aristocrat, the people here consider me to belong to the past. They look down on me. But Americans love me. I regularly receive invitations to events and functions just for being what I am. Women sometimes literally throw themselves at me.

"What I've just proposed must remain secret. I'm a prominent member of the Russian Nobility Association in America—an association that is recognized as having no sympathy for your autocratic rule of Russia. I would need to resign from all of my positions on the boards of various American companies and my membership in the association if it were to become known I have ties with you, Mr. President."

20.

LUCY'S NEW BOYFRIEND

It was early August, and Manhattan was oppressively hot and humid. Zoey had a new boyfriend, Jonathan, and this time it was her turn to plan an outing for their group of friends. Eager to help, Jonathan took charge of organizing the event. Given the stifling weather, he decided to host a rooftop party at his apartment building, complete with catering, a DJ, and a few of his own friends on the guest list.

As usual, Lucy sought a quiet spot, away from the crowd, where she could drink in solitude—at least until she could push thoughts of the man who had once been the love of her life out of her mind. But before she could fully retreat into herself, Jonathan approached and introduced her to one of his friends.

"I'd like you to meet Prince Alexander Alexandrovich, Lucy. Alexander, this is Lucy Lassiter."

"Hello, Lucy. I've heard a lot about you."

Lucy was taken aback by this interruption of her train of thought. She held out her hand for him to shake, but he kissed her hand instead.

"Hi, Alexander. What have you heard?"

Lucy thought he was handsome. He reminded her of Clark Gable.

"I was told you're a prominent member of this group of friends and that your mother has a majority shareholding in Morgan Pharma, one of the largest biomedical companies in the world. I also heard you're unhappy after breaking up with a man called Oliver Corbyn."

"Who told you about the breakup?"

"Zoey told Jonathan, and he told me. Jonathan and I are friends."

"Zoey shouldn't have told Jonathan. It's a private matter."

"But the society columns have already hinted at the breakup because you weren't going to parties while you were seeing him, and you are now—for some three months already. Besides, your habit of sitting alone at parties for a while before joining in the fun tells me you're very unhappy about the breakup."

"I'm not going to respond to that. You shouldn't be prying into my private life. Are you really a prince?"

"Yes, I'm the grandson of the heir to the throne of Russia."

"So what do you do for a living, if anything?"

"I hold a degree in business management, and I sit on the board of several companies here in New York."

"Why haven't we come across each other before? You obviously go to parties like I have for years."

"I'm not a party person, Lucy. I came here this evening because of repeated invitations and because I had nothing else to do."

"Am I correct in assuming you don't have a girlfriend because you're here by yourself?"

"Yes, and I assume you're currently without a boyfriend?"

"Correct."

"Do you want to be here, Lucy, or would you like to go somewhere else?"

"With you?"

"Yes, I was thinking of going to Little Italy to drink an espresso and talk."

"I was thinking of drowning my sorrows, but your suggestion is a better one. I'll go with you."

They left without saying goodbye and caught a taxi to Mulberry Street. They resumed their conversation in a coffee shop.

"What causes your sorrow, Lucy? Is it something you want to talk about?"

Lucy thought hard about his question. His sympathy for her made her decide to tell him.

"I fell in love with Oliver when we attended the Alzheimer's conference in Moscow in November of last year. I ended the relationship eleven weeks ago. You probably know all about it if Zoey told Jonathan, and he told you. I ended it because he was away for months at a time, and I only got to see him for one or two days in between. I couldn't handle that."

"You must still love him to be sad all the time and to need alcohol to forget him."

"Let's not talk about him, please. I'm doing my best to forget him."

***

They discussed the work each of them did, their hobbies, places they had been to, and more. When Lucy said she wanted to go home, Alexander proposed escorting her.

"I'll take you home," he said.

"You don't need to. I'll catch a cab."

"I'll share one with you. We can drop you off first."

Lucy agreed.

"I'd like to see you again, Lucy," Alexander said when the cab arrived at her apartment building.

"Sure. I'd like to see you again too."

"What if I were to pick you up here at seven for dinner the day after tomorrow?"

"I'd like that."

Alexander left after kissing her hand again. Lucy remained standing on the sidewalk for a minute as the taxi drove away.

***

Lucy and Alexander went out for lunch or dinner every couple of days. She felt at ease with him—conversation flowed naturally, and to her surprise, he even made her laugh several times, something she hadn't done in a long while.

Three weeks in, after a dinner at a chic restaurant, Alexander casually suggested they go back to his apartment for coffee. Lucy hesitated for a moment—but then agreed.

***

"Make yourself comfortable, Lucy, while I attend to the coffee."

She walked through his apartment. Everything told her a man had decorated it. The ambiance was cold and masculine. It disappointed her because she somehow expected it to be warm and cozy.

When Alexander returned, she sat down in one of the big leather armchairs. He gave her the coffee he'd poured and sat opposite her on the couch.

"I have to own up to something, Lucy. We've spent a lot of time together these last three weeks, and I've become very fond of you. I don't know if the feeling is mutual, but your readiness to spend time with me as often as you have tells me it is. I want to take our relationship one step further, if you're willing."

Lucy was perplexed. She had never considered the possibility of a romantic relationship with him. His companionship had simply been a welcome distraction, helping her think about Oliver less than she did when she was alone. That was the real reason she had agreed to see him whenever he suggested going out.

Still, she understood why he might have assumed she was ready for something more.

"I'm not sure I'm ready, Alexander. My thoughts are still focused on Oliver. You need to give me more time."

"Okay, I understand. Please know I want to be there for you when you need a shoulder to cry on."

"I appreciate that."

After that conversation, their relationship took on a different dynamic. The prince became more assertive—he would regularly put his arm around Lucy's waist, kiss her, and take charge of their plans, frequently deciding where to go and what to do without consulting her. At first, she found it unusual, but over time, she grew accustomed to it and saw no harm in his behavior.

They also started attending parties more frequently, usually at his suggestion. This struck Lucy as odd—when they first met, he had told her he never went to such events. Yet now, he encouraged her to go and urged her to drink excessively. More often than not, she ended up too intoxicated to make it home alone. In the past, Zoey would have taken care of her, but now, it was always him.

The first time he brought her home, she drunkenly gave him the code to her apartment's electronic door lock so he could help her inside. Once there, he began to undress her under the guise of helping her into bed. His hands "accidentally" lingered in places that stirred memories—memories of how happy she had once been when Oliver made love to her. Even in her intoxicated state, she always sensed his intentions and managed to stop him before he went any further.

After that first night, he showed up the next day with a small silver flask, telling her that a tablespoon of the liquid was an excellent hangover cure. Grateful, she followed his instructions every time she overindulged.

As their partying increased, so did Lucy's drinking. Soon, she started feeling unwell—constant stomachaches, headaches, and nausea plagued her. After a week of persistent illness, she called her physician, but after examining her, he found no clear diagnosis and simply advised her to take aspirin when needed. She dismissed her symptoms as emotional distress; after all, she had suffered similar ailments in the weeks following her breakup with Oliver.

But her condition only worsened. Now, she spent entire days in bed, too weak to do much of anything. On those days, the prince would show up unannounced, bringing flowers or chocolates. He would sit on the edge of her bed, talking as he poured himself a drink—then, inevitably, he would offer her one as well. By then, Lucy had become severely dependent on alcohol. And before he left, he always made sure she took a tablespoon of the "medicine" he had given her.

***

One Saturday afternoon, Lucy's parents came to visit. They found her still in bed, looking frail and sickly. Mitch had flown them in from LA that morning. They hadn't seen her in over a month. Nothing could have prepared them for the state she was in.

"We want you to come with us when we leave, Lucy," Jacky said. "We need to find out what's ailing you. Our physician is sure to find out, even if yours can't."

"There's no need for that, Mother. I just need to get over the breakup with Oliver. Immediately after we let each other go, I felt the same as I do now. All I need is time."

"But you're not giving that process much of a chance if you keep drinking."

"I drink because alcohol helps me to forget him."

Jacky and Bill kept pleading with her to return with them when suddenly, the prince walked into the bedroom. He had let himself in. He introduced himself to Jacky and Bill and presented Lucy with a bouquet of flowers.

"How nice to meet you, Mr. and Mrs. Lassiter. I assume you're as concerned about your daughter as I am. Lucy and I have become close. You don't need to worry about her as much as you do. I have everything under control. I've given her medicine to help her with her alcohol problem, and I'll call in professional help if she doesn't get better soon."

Jacky and Bill were amazed to see the concern the prince had for their daughter. They left later, convinced she was in good hands.

***

Not long after Lucy started feeling a little better, the prince took her to another party. But that night, something happened that would deeply unsettle her in the days that followed.

Once again, she had overindulged, too drunk to make it to the restroom on her own. The prince lifted her in his arms, intending to ask one of her girlfriends to help her. Seeing how close the two had become, Zoey and the others started teasing them, joking that they should get married.

Playing along, the prince turned to Lucy with a smile and asked her to marry him.

Her response was vague—she was too intoxicated to fully grasp what he had said. But to those watching, it looked like she had nodded in agreement. Someone snapped a photo, and before the night was over, people were already throwing out potential wedding dates. The next day, the media caught wind of it, and suddenly, their supposed engagement was making headlines.

***

The following week, Lucy was lying in bed watching CNN when a news report sent a shockwave through her. Bill Lassiter had been kidnapped in Saint Petersburg.

For the first time in a long while, she was sufficiently sober to take in the news. The weight of everything suddenly crashed down on her. The breakup with Oliver. Her spiraling alcohol addiction. Her mysterious illness. And now, this.

Tears streamed down her face as she clenched her fists and pounded them into the pillows. "Why?" she cried over and over again. A dark thought crept into her mind: *I don't want to do this anymore.* She lay there, numb, unable to find the strength to get up. That afternoon, she reached for a bottle and started drinking again.

***

The prince arrived the next day to find Lucy still in bed, already slightly drunk and visibly unwell. Without preamble, he handed her a document.

"Sign this, Lucy," he said. "It allows me to take over as chairman of the board at Morgan Pharma. Now that Bill is... unavailable, that position falls to you. But you need to focus on getting better first. This document ensures I'll handle things in your place until you're ready. You might remember, I'm on the board of several companies here in New York. I know exactly what to do to take care of Morgan Pharma."

Lucy sat up slowly, staring at him as if trying to process his words. But instead of questioning him, she simply took the pen and signed the document without reading it. Then, exhausted, she collapsed back onto the bed, shutting her eyes.

The prince picked up the small silver flask—the so-called medicine he had been giving her—then left the apartment, closing the door behind him.

From that point on, he returned each day, either early in the morning or late at night, always administering another dose.

Lucy was now bedridden.

21.

COUNTERMOVE

When Oliver finished reading the *Washington Post* article about Lucy's engagement to Prince Alexandrovich and Bill Lassiter's abduction, a storm of emotions overtook him. But it was the mention of Lucy's mysterious illness that truly alarmed him—more than anything had in a long time.

His fists clenched as he thought about how his connection to the Lassiter family had set everything in motion. Guilt and frustration gnawed at him.

He turned to the window, staring blankly at the cityscape, his thoughts a chaotic mess. Minutes passed before he could pull himself together. Doing nothing briefly crossed his mind—but he dismissed the idea the moment it surfaced.

Slowly, a plan began to take shape. It wasn't fully formed, but he knew one thing for certain: What he was about to do would change everything. This was his watershed moment.

First, he needed to speak with the CIA director and formally step away from any future assignments.

Wasting no time, Oliver finished writing his final mission report in just over two hours, then hailed a taxi to Langley. Upon arriving at headquarters, he barely had time to announce himself before one of the director's assistants approached him.

"The director needs to see you urgently," she said.

"I came to hand you my report, Ken," Oliver said as he sat down in the chair in front of the director's desk.

"Thanks, Liam," the director replied as he flicked through the pages of the report Oliver had handed him. "I'm sorry the assignment turned out the way it did."

"So am I. I would've been able to extract the target by obtaining permission to work in the section he was imprisoned in a week before he was murdered. I consider it an error in judgment on my part for not having tried to enter that section earlier."

"There's nothing to feel guilty about, Liam. We didn't know the FSB intended to murder him after he'd been incarcerated for all those months."

"I have a request, Ken. I want to leave the CIA."

The director was stunned. He looked at Oliver intently before he replied.

"I prefer not to let you go, Liam. You're one of my best field agents. Do you need some time off?"

"I need the rest of my life to do what I have to do."

"Take all the time you need, but don't resign."

"I must, Ken."

"Should I ask why?"

"It's complicated. It concerns the Lassiter family. I need to fix the terrible situation Bill, Jacky, and Lucy are in. Lucy is important to me. She left me nearly six months ago when she said she wanted me home more often, and I said I couldn't. As I see it, her behavior these last six months is a consequence of our breaking up. I need to be there for her from now on—if she'll still have me. That would prohibit me from working for you."

"That's why I'm glad you came in today. You should know that the Russkies now control Morgan Pharma. I don't know if you've heard, but Lucy is engaged to Prince Alexandrovich, and they're soon to be married. We have a file on him. We know he has strong ties with the Kremlin, which is unusual for a Russian aristocrat.

"Lucy has resigned her position on the board in favor of the prince. The board is pleased with him, and they recently appointed him CEO of the Morgan Pharma office and laboratory in Boston. He's caused several scientists there to leave, and he's organized Russian scientists to take their place. I was alarmed when I was told Russians are now controlling the Boston lab—and so is the president. You should be too because of their ability to now access the data on the Alzheimer's cure.

"Then there's the kidnapping of the only member of the family who might be able to stop what's going on. Is what I just said new to you?"

"Much of what you said is. I rarely access the internet or use my cell phone when I'm in Russia, so I haven't been able to follow the news."

"You need to do everything possible to prevent the Russkies from taking control of Morgan Pharma. We've never encountered such a deceptive plan by a foreign entity aimed at taking control of a US company. We'll be skinned alive if that becomes known. You don't have much time. Once Lucy marries the prince, it'll be impossible to stop what's going on."

"I'll do what is necessary, Ken. Trust me."

"I do, Liam. And let me just say I understand your reason for wanting to leave. I'm aware that during the past three years, you've taken, all told, no more than ten days off. I hope you and Lucy can get together again. If so, you should take up a position with Morgan Pharma to see the Alzheimer's medication become available to everyone who would benefit from it. See it as the last assignment I'll give you. Let me know if you need our help, regardless of what it is."

"Thanks, Ken. I appreciate your understanding."

***

Oliver left Ken Rivera's office in a daze. The information Ken had just given him, combined with what he already knew about Lucy, painted a clear and unsettling picture of what the Russians were doing.

Prince Alexandrovich had likely given Lucy the attention she desperately needed—attention she would have been vulnerable to after their breakup. Oliver knew her well enough to understand that. Add to that her intoxicated state at the parties they both attended, and it wouldn't have been difficult for the prince to win her over. And now, with her mysterious illness weakening her further, handing over her position as chairperson of the board after Bill's abduction would have been almost effortless.

The pieces fit too well.

Back at his apartment, Oliver called Mitch. Over time, Mitch had become more than just an acquaintance—he was someone Oliver trusted. And right now, he needed an ally.

"Hi, Mitch, this is Oliver. Where are you?... Can we meet in the Dulles arrivals area in, say, two hours?... Great! We need to do something to stop the Russians from taking control of Morgan Pharma... What do you mean they already have?... The prince has been given the authority to commandeer the Gulfstream?... Ignore him, please, and come as fast as you can. I have a plan I want to talk to you about."

***

Oliver outlined his plan when they met in the arrivals area at Dulles Airport after Mitch had flown the Gulfstream there from Teterboro.

"As you know, Lucy and I broke up six months ago in May. It had an enormous effect on her. As you undoubtedly know, she started partying again, but this time drinking heavily and perhaps also taking party drugs. I believe she was unable to withstand the charms of the prince when he gave her the attention she needed. But I can't believe she agreed to marry him. She wouldn't be herself if she did. We must take her out of the party scene."

"What do you mean?"

"It's simple. We need to take her from her apartment and fly her to somewhere we can heal her of her alcohol addiction and her illness."

"Where will we take her?"

"To my apartment. No one knows where I live."

"Okay, I'm in. Something needs to be done."

"Great, but we have to do something else first. We must involve Jacky. The media would be very critical of the situation if they were to find out that two men had taken Lucy from her apartment, so we have to fly to LA first to pick up Jacky."

"I agree. Dave will have to know what we're doing."

"Can we trust him?"

"Implicitly."

"So when can we fly to LA?"

"I have to obtain a slot to know for sure, but I suspect in about an hour."

Both men felt relieved to be doing something.

It was four-thirty in the afternoon when they left the Jet Center at Dulles. Like Oliver, Mitch felt the urgency of what they needed to do. They arrived at Van Nuys Airport a few minutes past six in the evening local time. Mitch asked Dave to have the plane refueled while he and Oliver caught a taxi to Beverly Hills.

***

Jacky was eating her dinner when the maid let them in. She was surprised to see them.

"Sorry to disturb you, Jacky, but we need to talk," Oliver said.

"Nice to see you again, Oliver. You too, Mitch."

Jacky was surprisingly calm, considering Bill's abduction and Lucy's predicament.

"We're worried about Lucy. We have to help her."

"You're to blame, Oliver, for Lucy's situation. We were aware she had broken up with you, but when Bill and I visited her in New York three weeks ago, she told us in detail what happened—that she had broken up with you because she couldn't deal with the long periods you were away.

"She loves you deeply. The breakup has caused her to revert to her previous life. But it's worse than before because she's developed a bad drinking habit. I suspect she's into drugs this time as well.

"We pleaded with her to return with us, but she wouldn't. When we were there, her prince walked in and introduced himself. He is the slickest and smoothest man I've ever encountered. She fell for him. You know why?"

"I think I do, Jacky."

"She needed to feel wanted again."

"I'm terribly sorry, Jacky. I'm here to set things right."

"Tell me how you propose to do that."

"I want to take her to my apartment, where she won't be found. I'll treat her drinking habit and her drug habit if she has one. I know what I need to do. But we want you to be involved. She needs her mother. I plan to find Bill when she's regained her health."

"I knew you were a good man when I first met you, Oliver," she said with tears in her eyes. "Tell me what I need to do."

"I want you to come with us. Pack for a long stay away and bring your passport."

***

Jacky was ready to leave forty-five minutes later. The driver and bodyguard, permanently stationed at the Lassiter home, drove them to Van Nuys Airport, and by nine that evening, they were back in the air.

Mitch knew that he and Dave had been flying for far too long—pushing past exhaustion. But right now, nothing mattered more than what they were doing.

On the plane, Oliver adjusted the seats into a bed for Jacky. She drifted into a restless sleep not long after, but he remained awake. His thoughts were relentless, immune to fatigue, refusing to let him rest.

After landing at LaGuardia, Mitch managed to rent a limousine and drove Jacky and Oliver straight to Lucy's apartment building on Park Avenue. He pulled up directly across from the main entrance. As they stepped out, the doorman on duty opened one of the large glass French doors for them.

The doorman recognized Jacky immediately—he had been working the last time she and Bill visited Lucy.

"Hi, Ben, we're here to pick up my daughter. She's not feeling well."

"Hello, Mrs. Lassiter. I thought as much because she doesn't look well, and she behaves strangely sometimes."

"So I've heard, Ben."

They took one of the elevators to the sixty-fourth floor. When they pressed the button on the electronic front door lock, it prompted for an access code. Jacky entered the code and opened the door. She led the way to the master bedroom, where they found Lucy asleep.

"Would you pack the clothes and other things Lucy needs into a suitcase, Jacky? Please don't forget to take her purse, phone, tablet, and passport," Oliver said.

Oliver was startled to see Lucy when he walked up to the

bed. Her face looked pale and drawn. He realized she'd been through hell. He decided to wake her up.

"Hi, Luce, it's me—Oliver."

He repeated this several times. She didn't react at first, but after a while, she turned her head in the direction of his voice without opening her eyes.

"Let me sleep, Oliver. I'm tired."

Then, as if she suddenly realized who had been talking to her, her eyes sprung open.

"Oliver?"

"I'm here, Luce."

"What are you doing here?"

"I'm here with your mother and Mitch to take you away."

Lucy tried to sit up. Oliver had to help her.

"What do you mean?"

"I'm taking you to where I live."

She looked at him inquisitively, as if to decide what he meant. "To your apartment, where we let each other go?"

"I live somewhere else now, Luce."

"Do you still love me?" she asked.

"I haven't stopped loving you. Do you still love me?"

"I haven't stopped loving you either, Oliver."

"Then come with me, please."

"I will, but you need to help me. I'm no longer steady on my feet."

She tried to turn back the blankets to get out of bed, but failed. He was suddenly overwhelmed with emotion and not able to halt the tears appearing in his eyes. He took her in his arms, kissed her, and sat her down on the bed.

"Your mom is packing the things you need."

Lucy looked at him as if he needed to explain that again.

"I need help dressing up, Oliver. I want to look pretty for you."

"You're beautiful to me as you are, Luce. You don't need to

get dressed. I'll carry you."

Jacky entered the bedroom. She started to cry when she saw her daughter.

"Has Bill returned, Mother?" Lucy asked. "I've heard he's been kidnapped like I was."

"Not yet, Lucy. Oliver promised to look for him when you feel better."

Lucy nodded.

"Let Lucy wear this coat, Oliver. It's cold outside."

Oliver helped her into a coat over her pajamas and wrapped a blanket around her for warmth. When they were ready to leave, he lifted her gently from the bed. As he did, she instinctively put her arms around his neck, pressing soft, lingering kisses against his skin.

She looked up at him, her gaze unfocused and distant. A dullness in her eyes made his stomach tighten—she seemed drugged.

Mitch picked up the two suitcases Jacky had packed, and together they left the apartment, closing the door behind them.

Back in the lobby, Ben, the doorman, held open one of the large glass doors, allowing them to step outside. The night air was cool against Oliver's skin as he carried Lucy across the sidewalk to the waiting car. He eased her into the back seat, then slid in beside her, wrapping an arm around her shoulders. She let out a soft sigh, closed her eyes, and leaned into him. Before long, she was asleep.

Mitch drove them straight to LaGuardia.

Once on board the Gulfstream, Oliver carried Lucy inside and laid her down on the bed he had set up for Jacky the night before. She didn't stir. He took a seat across the aisle and watched her, struggling to contain the emotions threatening to overtake him.

The flight to Dulles lasted an hour. Upon landing, Mitch

arranged for a limousine and chauffeur. Oliver carried Lucy to the waiting vehicle and gave the driver an address—455 South Maple Avenue, Falls Church. His apartment. He had chosen it for its privacy, the gym, and the large outdoor pool, but this morning, none of that mattered.

When they arrived, Oliver carried Lucy inside, straight to his bedroom. He carefully removed the blanket and coat, then tucked her under the covers.

Grabbing a chair, he placed it beside the bed and sat down.

He wasn't going anywhere.

This was his vigil now.

22.

WITHDRAWAL

Lucy had been oblivious to everything around her since falling asleep in the limousine on the way to LaGuardia.

When lunchtime approached, Oliver decided she needed to eat. He called her name several times, gently shaking her shoulder. But she didn't stir.

His stomach tightened.

She should have woken up by now.

The unshakable heaviness of her sleep confirmed what he had already feared—she had been seriously drugged.

Without hesitation, he reached for his phone and called Ken Rivera. When the director's assistant answered, Oliver stated his name and the urgency of the call.

Then came the hold music.

Seconds stretched into minutes. His patience wore thin. Every passing moment felt like a delay he couldn't afford.

"Ken, it's Liam. I need to ask you for a favor. Can you organize a doctor to come to my apartment, someone who won't ask questions? Lucy's been drugged. I can't get her to wake up."

Oliver was surprised when the director mentioned that they had several medical professionals on site, including a doctor who specialized in drugs and substance abuse.

The doctor arrived an hour later. Without hesitation, he grabbed Lucy by the shoulders and shook her forcefully, jolting her awake.

Oliver winced at the roughness of it.

Lucy's eyes fluttered open, but her gaze was unfocused. Confusion clouded her face—she had no idea where she was or what was happening.

"She's been drugged," the doctor said after his examination. "I can't be sure with what without the results of urine tests, but everything points to scopolamine—also known as Devil's Breath. It would have been mixed with something else to eliminate its bitter taste. In high doses, the drug can cause a zombie-like state, in which she would lose both her memory and her free will.

"The drug leads to dangerous side effects, such as a fast heart rate, confusion, hallucinations, seizures, and even coma. It can cause death in a matter of weeks if you take it often and in high doses."

"But she didn't seem to be as affected this morning at seven as she is now. Is there an explanation for that?"

"It takes approximately four to eight hours for the drug to reach peak effectiveness. Its effect then slowly declines, but is still noticeable after twenty-four hours. She would have taken the drug early this morning if she was reasonably alert when you first saw her."

"What should we do?" Oliver asked.

"Assuming she's no longer in danger of someone administering the drug, you need to prevent her from drinking alcohol. She's going to develop serious alcohol withdrawal symptoms when you do. These symptoms will begin between twelve and twenty-four hours after the last intake of alcohol and reach a peak between twenty-four and seventy-two hours. She'll feel a lot better on day seven if all goes well. The symptoms are lethargy, insomnia, anxiety, agitation, nausea, vomiting, trembling, a fast heart rate, a mild fever, and sweating.

"But in connection with the drug she's taken—or was forced to take—she could also suffer from seizures, hallucinations, and disorientation. Someone needs to watch her closely. You should call 911 if she has a seizure."

"Do you agree to Lucy taking a benzodiazepine-type of medication to help alleviate the symptoms?"

"Yes, alcohol withdrawal is most often treated with diazepam, which reduces anxiety and the likelihood of seizures because it relieves muscle spasms. When administered orally, she should take ten milligrams three or four times during the first twenty-four hours and five milligrams three or four times daily thereafter. It's also a sedative that will help her sleep.

"She's likely to be vitamin deficient if she hasn't eaten properly. I would recommend you have her drink a multivitamin supplement.

"Finally, she should drink a lot of water, especially after sweating or vomiting."

"Can you provide the diazepam? We don't want anyone to find out she's here."

"Sure... I, or someone else, will bring you that as soon as possible, probably later this afternoon. Call me anytime, or 911, if there are complications."

***

"I'm going to watch her day and night for as long as is necessary," Oliver said after the doctor left. "You should make yourself at home in the guest room, Jacky. The couch is what remains, Mitch, if you want to stay."

"No, Dave and I will move into a hotel at the airport to remain close to the aircraft in case Lucy's prince has people looking for it. I'm not going to answer his or anyone else's calls, apart from yours, from now on."

"May I ask you for a favor before you go?"

"Anything…"

"Could you take Jacky to the store to buy groceries for a week? I always eat out or order in because I'm away most of the time. There's no food or drink here, apart from a few bottles of wine. The doctor recommended sports drinks containing electrolytes. We'll need as many as eighteen cans, perhaps."

Mitch said goodbye after he and Jacky returned with a heavy load of groceries, which Jacky placed in the kitchen cabinets and the fridge.

"Thanks for everything, Mitch. As soon as Lucy feels well enough to travel, we need to start looking for Bill. I'll keep you updated on her progress."

***

Lucy had fallen asleep again after the doctor examined her. It was nearly six o'clock when she woke up. Oliver saw her open her eyes.

"Oliver," she called out.

"I'm here, Luce."

"Could you get me a drink, please?"

"Sure…water, coffee, or a sports drink?"

"No, a martini, please."

"I can't give you that, Luce. The doctor who examined you this afternoon told us you must stop drinking alcohol. You're sick, and you won't get better otherwise."

Lucy closed her eyes. She seemed to ponder what he'd said.

"Oliver, I need to pee," she said after a few minutes.

"I'll get your mother to help you go to the bathroom."

"I don't mind you taking me."

Oliver was surprised by her statement. He decided to consult Jacky.

"Jacky," he said softly when he entered the living room, where she had settled into an armchair to read the newspaper she had bought while shopping with Mitch. "Lucy wants to go to the bathroom. I told her I would get you to help her, but she said she wouldn't mind if I took her. What should I do?"

"That's the ultimate proof she's given herself to you, Oliver. A girl wouldn't agree to that otherwise."

"So you approve?"

"Of course I do."

Oliver returned to the bedroom, pulled back the blankets, and carefully helped Lucy to her feet. She swayed unsteadily, her body weak, forcing him to support her as they made their way to the bathroom.

Once there, he gently guided her down onto the toilet, pulling down her pajama bottoms and panties for her. She blinked up at him, a hint of confusion in her eyes.

Afterward, Oliver stepped back, watching as she attempted to pull up her clothes on her own. When her fingers fumbled weakly, he stepped in and did it for her.

He then helped her back to bed, adjusting the pillows and easing her into a seated position.

"The doctor left medication for you to take, Luce."

Oliver handed Lucy a diazepam tablet along with a glass of water. "Take this," he urged gently.

She obeyed, swallowing the pill before he encouraged her to drink all the water. She finished it without protest.

Next, he gave her a chewable multivitamin. She chewed slowly, then swallowed.

When he helped her lie back down, she turned onto her side, her gaze settling on him.

"Alexander always gives me what I want," she said. "Why don't you?"

"What is it you want, sweetheart?"

"A drink, of course."

"I can't give you alcohol, Luce. It will worsen your condition. Alexander is stupid for giving you alcohol when it was obvious you were sick. Did he also give you drugs to take?"

Lucy looked at him in the same quizzical way she had before. "I don't think so. He did give me something to drink, something that made me forget you."

She closed her eyes.

As Oliver sat watching her, he considered what the doctor had said—if her first request for a martini came between twelve and twenty-four hours after her last drink, then she must have had her final drink late the previous night or very early that morning. Most likely, at the same time she had taken the drug.

An hour later, Lucy's eyes fluttered open. She had slept on and off.

"I really want that drink," she said. "My mother will give it to me. Will you ask her to come here?"

Oliver obliged and asked Jacky to come to the bedroom.

"Lucy wants to ask you something, Jacky."

"Will you get me a martini, Mother? Oliver refuses."

"The doctor told us not to give you alcohol, Lucy. The condition you're in is the result of excessive drinking these last months. I'm sorry."

Lucy didn't react to what her mother told her. She turned her head away from them.

"I've prepared a simple dish containing a mix of quinoa, turkey, and broccoli for dinner, Oliver. I was hoping you'd try to get Lucy to eat some of it."

Jacky gave him a plate of food and two forks.

"Would you like something to eat, Luce? You haven't had anything to eat all day," Oliver asked her.

"I'm not hungry."

"Have a taste, Luce. It's good."

She took two bites but refused to eat more. She did drink the contents of half a can of sports drink that Oliver offered her in a glass. She closed her eyes and fell asleep not long after but woke up again after about an hour.

"I need that drink, Oliver," she said as soon as she opened her eyes.

"You know I can't give it to you, Luce."

"Why are you so stubborn?" she retorted, now becoming angry with him.

***

As the evening wore on, Lucy's requests for a drink turned into demands. She argued relentlessly, insisting that Oliver give her what she wanted.

He watched her, torn between heartbreak and resolve. How could this incredible woman—the one he loved so deeply—become so aggressive? But he knew the answer. It wasn't *her* speaking; it was the alcohol. Her craving had taken hold, overpowering reason, twisting her every thought.

Yet no matter how much she fought him, his love for her remained unchanged.

"I'm going to bed now, Oliver. Call me if I need to do anything for you," Jacky said when she decided to retire.

"I will, Jacky. Thanks for your help."

Oliver was thankful when Lucy closed her eyes after Jacky had said good night. She seemed to sleep for about half an hour, but then opened her eyes again to repeat the argument she had made before about bringing her a drink.

Oliver helped her to sit upright and had her take the next diazepam tablet, the remainder of the sports drink, and another multivitamin tablet. When he made her lie down again, she turned on her other side, away from him.

***

Lucy's demands for a drink continued throughout the night.

By five in the morning, Oliver noticed her body had begun to tremble. Alarmed, he sat her up again, gave her another dose of medication, and made her drink a full glass of water. Then, carefully, he tucked her in, pulling the blankets up to her chin in an attempt to warm her.

But the shivering only worsened in the hours that followed. She thrashed restlessly, unable to find comfort. Oliver knew her withdrawal symptoms were reaching their peak.

Desperate to soothe her, he undressed and slipped under the blankets, wrapping his arms around her trembling body. He held her close, hoping his warmth might calm her.

It didn't.

The shivering intensified; her body wracked with tremors.

An hour later, she started hitting him with clenched fists.

"I hate you, Oliver. How can you not give me a drink when I need it so badly?"

"I'm so sorry, Luce. I wish I could give you something that would help you get through this, but there's nothing."

Lucy started to cry. She buried her face against his chest. "I'm sorry, Oliver. This is all my fault."

"It isn't, Luce. It's all my fault for not recognizing your needs on the day you left me. I was selfish when I said I wouldn't stop what I was doing when you asked me to. If I had, all of this wouldn't have happened."

Lucy's only response was to briefly wrap an arm around him. She was too weak to do anything more.

***

Neither of them slept. The hours dragged by at an agonizing pace, each minute stretching longer than the last. Oliver had never experienced time moving so slowly.

At eleven in the morning, he left the bed to give Lucy her next dose of medication. She sipped from a can of sports drink, managing to finish half of it.

When she quietly told him she needed to use the bathroom, he helped her to her feet and guided her to the toilet. Once again, he had to pull down her pajama bottoms and panties. She didn't resist, showing no shame or hesitation—just exhaustion.

Afterward, he helped her back to bed and slipped under the blankets beside her.

By some small miracle, they both fell asleep.

Lucy stirred at two in the afternoon. Her movement roused Oliver, pulling him from much-needed rest.

"I'm going to make us a very late breakfast, Luce. What do you want?"

"I'm not hungry."

Oliver went to the kitchen, poured coffee, and prepared a big helping of scrambled eggs on toast.

"When I looked in on Lucy this morning, I saw you two in bed together, and I decided not to disturb you," Jacky said.

"After she started to shiver, I joined her in bed to try to stop it, but to no avail. We must have finally fallen asleep at around eleven, after I made her take her medication."

When Oliver returned to the bedroom, he noted Lucy had managed to sit upright and turn down the blankets.

"It's hot in here," she said.

Oliver noticed the sheen of sweat on Lucy's skin. He pressed a hand to her forehead—she was running a fever.

The next phase, he thought. Her body was fighting back, moving through withdrawal. That gave him some comfort, but he knew her struggle wasn't over yet.

Lucy tried to eat some of the scrambled eggs, but after only a few spoonfuls, she suddenly tensed.

"I need to throw up," she said weakly.

Oliver reacted instinctively, doing what his mother had done for him as a child. He scooped Lucy into his arms, carried her to the bathroom, and set her down on her knees in front of the toilet—just in time.

Her body convulsed as she emptied her stomach. When the nausea passed, he brought her a glass of water. She took a few sips, then grimaced.

"Bad taste," she muttered.

"Brush your teeth," he suggested. But when she struggled to squeeze toothpaste onto her brush, he took it from her and did it himself.

Afterward, he helped her back to bed. This time, he noticed something different—she seemed a little steadier on her feet. The last traces of whatever drug the prince had been giving her were finally wearing off.

***

By late evening on the second day, Lucy's violent shivering had eased, but her craving for alcohol hadn't.

She no longer fought him over it. Instead, she pleaded.

Oliver stayed firm. Eventually, when it became clear he wouldn't give in, she stopped talking to him altogether.

Her fever persisted, but it never climbed above 102 degrees, for which he was grateful. He took her temperature every three hours and made sure she drank as much fluid as she could tolerate.

Neither of them slept until six in the morning, when Lucy finally drifted off for two hours.

The next morning, Jacky made a hearty breakfast—bacon, ham, and eggs. Oliver helped Lucy sit up and fed her a generous portion. This time, it didn't make her nauseous. She also managed to drink most of her coffee. After taking her medication, she admitted she was exhausted and fell asleep soon after.

Oliver wasn't surprised. She hadn't truly rested in days.

At eleven, he gently woke her for more medication and a glass of water, then helped her to the bathroom. She went back to sleep afterward and didn't stir until well past five, when he roused her again for her medicine and a can of sports drink.

That evening, Jacky prepared fried chicken with broccoli and mashed potatoes. Oliver patiently fed Lucy spoonfuls until she shook her head, signaling she'd had enough. After taking her medication and drinking as much as she could, she said she wanted to sleep again.

At first, this worried him—she had already slept most of the day. He watched her closely, searching for any sign of something unusual. But as he observed her, his tension eased. The shivering had stopped. Her temperature had dropped to 99.5. There were no signs of twitching or weakness in her limbs.

She wasn't slipping away—her body was healing. And sleep was precisely what she needed.

***

Lucy woke late on the morning of day four.

When she saw Oliver watching her from his chair, she reached out her hand.

He took it, squeezing gently.

Then, for the first time, she smiled.

The sight of it made his chest tighten, his throat burn. He wanted to cry.

Later that day, Jacky prepared an early dinner since they had skipped lunch. Lucy ate everything.

"I was hungry," she said simply.

And Oliver knew, at last, she was coming back to him.

"I need to go to the bathroom, Oliver. I'll take my medication afterward. Will you then join me in bed?"

Oliver did as she wanted, wrapping his arms around her as they held each other close. He watched as her breathing slowed, her body relaxing into sleep.

That evening and the following night passed more easily than before. They both drifted in and out of sleep, finding moments of rest between wakefulness.

At six in the morning, when they were both awake, Oliver got up. He helped Lucy take her medication and made sure she drank a full glass of water.

"How do you feel, Luce?"

"I have a terrible headache, but I feel better in a way I can't define just now."

"Let me get you something for your headache," Oliver said, knowing he kept aspirin in the kitchen.

From that moment on, Lucy's recovery accelerated.

If someone had told Oliver she would be relatively alert just five days after her last drink, he wouldn't have believed them. Yet here she was—more aware, steadier on her feet. It was now clear to him that her previous lack of coordination had been caused by the drug, not alcohol withdrawal.

The realization fueled his rage.

When the opportunity came, he vowed he would kill the prince.

**

For six long days, Oliver remained by Lucy's side, caring for her without pause. But now, she was getting stronger. She had started getting out of bed on her own, no longer needing help to go to the bathroom. She even joined him and Jacky for meals in the kitchen.

Color had returned to her face, and he swore she was beginning to put on weight.

On the morning of the seventh day, during a late breakfast, Lucy made an announcement.

"I want to take a shower, wash my hair, and get dressed," she said. "I don't want to go back to bed."

Oliver could have shouted for joy.

While she showered, he went into the kitchen, opened a cabinet, and pulled out the bottles of wine he had stored there. Without hesitation, he dumped the contents down the sink. He wouldn't let her touch another drop—not if he could help it. He knew that if she saw the bottles, she might be tempted. He wasn't willing to take that risk.

For the first time since bringing Lucy to his apartment, Oliver let himself breathe.

The weight pressing down on him for days—crushing, relentless—lifted all at once, leaving behind a bone-deep exhaustion he had never felt before.

Jacky, who had quietly observed everything, took it all in. She had watched Oliver care for her daughter with unwavering patience and devotion, and she knew Lucy's recovery had been possible largely because of him.

Now, as she studied him, she saw something new.

He was exhausted.

And he needed rest just as much as Lucy had.

"You should get some sleep, Oliver," she said. "I'll look after Lucy, and if she has a relapse, I'll wake you up."

"I appreciate the suggestion, Jacky, but I'd intended to start looking for Bill now. The three of us need to travel to Russia. I have an idea about how to find him."

"As much as I want that to happen as quickly as possible, you're in no shape to do so. I insist you go to bed and sleep."

Oliver let himself be persuaded by Jacky's insistence, and before Lucy even stepped out of the shower, he was fast asleep.

***

Oliver woke to the sensation of Lucy slipping under the blankets beside him. He glanced at his watch—9:00 p.m.

"Do you mind me keeping you company tonight?" she asked.

"Of course not, Luce. You have no idea how I feel about your recovery. I initially thought I'd lost you. I did my best not to show my anxiety when I discovered the condition you were in when we brought you here."

"I know, Oliver. I love you more than ever before."

"And I love you more than I did before. I didn't think that was possible."

"Please make love to me, Oliver, like you did when we were in Moscow and in LA."

"Do you really think we should? You need more than seven days to become strong again."

"I know, but let me relish the feeling of your body against mine, the feeling of your kisses everywhere, and the ecstasy of you being inside me. You have no idea how I've longed for that since the last time we made love so long ago."

"For just a minute after reading about your engagement to the prince, I believed I'd lost you. And the thought of you making love to him made me want to die. But I quickly discounted that possibility because of the love we shared. I just couldn't believe you would forget me that quickly."

"How could you even think about Alexander and me like that? He came on to me many times, but I don't love him, and while I let myself become involved in parties, as I had previously, I'd vowed not to become romantically involved with the men I met in the hope that you and I would somehow resolve our differences."

"Did you really? But what about your engagement to him?"

"That was a bad mistake. I don't exactly know how my girlfriends and I came to talk about one of us becoming engaged to him. He's handsome and attentive. Zoey, my closest girlfriend, considered him quite a catch. I had too much to drink, and I think at one stage, someone said we should get married.

"Someone took a photograph of him and me together and announced we were engaged. I let it happen. I believe someone even mentioned a wedding date, and I was told the newspapers published the photo and announced we were to be married."

"My world collapsed after you left me. I lost myself in my work. It was the only remedy I could think of after our disagreement. I wanted to look you up a hundred times to talk to you about how we could reconcile our differences, but I figured you wouldn't want to just to spite me for not having agreed to your wish for me to no longer be away as much as I was."

"Say no more, Oliver. Please make love to me, and make me deliriously happy."

Oliver made love to her—not just because she asked him to, but because he longed for her in a way he never had before.

He pulled off his T-shirt and slipped her pajama top over her head, wanting to feel the warmth of her bare skin against his. They lay on their sides, facing each other, their bodies close.

He kissed her eyelids tenderly, rubbed his nose against hers, and let his lips linger on the curve of her neck, whispering softly—words meant only for her. Then, teasingly, he brushed his lips against hers, light as a breath.

Lucy closed her eyes and searched for his mouth, finding it with a deep, urgent kiss.

Slowly, Oliver eased her onto her back, trailing his fingers down her body, slipping beneath the waistband of her panties. His touch sent shivers through her, making her squirm beneath him.

She wanted to match his intensity. Her hands explored his chest, then slid lower, slipping into his shorts. But before she could go further, he gently stopped her.

He knew why she was doing it. And he couldn't let her.

"Let me do the work, Luce. Enjoy what I'm doing."

His words troubled her—she wanted him to experience the same pleasure she did.

Oliver pulled back the blankets and removed her panties, then slipped off his shorts. Lowering himself, he trailed soft, lingering kisses across her stomach.

She cupped his face in her hands, guiding him exactly where she wanted him. The response was immediate, instinctive. When she started to lift her hips against his mouth, he knew she was close.

But just as her hands tightened against him, silently pleading for more, he pulled away. Gently resisting her attempts to keep him there, he moved over her, knowing she would welcome him.

She did.

Wrapping her legs around his waist, she held him close, giving herself to him completely. The moment he entered her, she met him with a deep, urgent thrust, her body pressing into his with all the strength she had.

Oliver quickly found the rhythm she needed, matching her movements as desire consumed them both.

When ecstasy finally took hold, she moaned his name, her voice breaking into incoherent whispers. At that moment, nothing else existed—only him. The man who had been elusive for so long. The man she could no longer live without.

As they reached their peak together, something shifted between them. It was more than just pleasure—it was a return, a reunion of souls that had been tested, broken apart, and somehow found their way back.

Their whispered confessions of love—despite everything

that had happened—added a depth they had never reached before. A new sense of devotion, of unbreakable connection, flooded through them, overwhelming and absolute.

Long after, they remained wrapped in each other's arms, holding on as if neither ever wanted to let go.

23.

THE SEARCH FOR BILL LASSITER

Throughout the past week, Oliver had kept Mitch updated on Lucy's condition as they nursed her back to health. On the morning of the eighth day—Wednesday, November 15—he finally made the call Mitch had been waiting for.

"She's strong enough to travel," Oliver said. He then asked Mitch to fly them to Helsinki that evening, ensuring they would arrive the following afternoon, local time.

While Jacky and Lucy packed, Oliver disappeared into the bathroom to assume a familiar disguise—the same one he had used for his mission in Voskhod. He dyed his hair, eyebrows, and eyelashes black, then carefully applied the false beard and mustache.

When he stepped out, both women looked up in surprise.

Lucy's expression changed instantly.

She remembered this disguise all too well. It was what he had worn the day of their disagreement—exactly six months ago.

And that troubled her.

"Is that disguise necessary, Oliver? You wore that on that fateful day six months ago when we let each other go."

"I knew you'd say that, Luce. I apologize, but it's necessary. Oliver Corbyn is a wanted man in Russia, and there isn't enough time to have the CIA organize another identity for me."

"I'm sorry. I understand. But the twinges in my stomach when you appeared just now made me briefly relive what I felt after our disagreement. I never want to experience that again."

"I hope to never have to wear this disguise again after we've rescued Bill, sweetheart."

***

They arrived at the Jet Center at Dulles Airport at 9 p.m., where Mitch was already waiting. His eyes immediately landed on Oliver's disguise—he recognized it at once.

Without a word, he led them to the Gulfstream, where Dave stowed their baggage in the baggage compartment. Once on board, Annette greeted them and offered a selection of juices. At Mitch's instruction, alcohol was not an option.

They settled into the plush seats. Oliver sat across from Lucy, while Jacky took a seat across the aisle.

An hour into the flight, Mitch joined them. At Oliver's request, he would be part of the discussion about the plan to find Bill.

"Okay, let me fill you in on my plan to find Bill. We'll be arriving at approximately two-thirty in the afternoon local time. Is that correct, Mitch?"

"Yes, give or take fifteen minutes, depending on how busy the airport is. Helsinki is seven hours ahead of us."

"We'll be checking into Hotel Kämp, which is twelve miles south of the airport. I've taken the liberty of involving the

Morgan Pharma Saint Petersburg office in what we need to do. I called Alex Davidson about freeing up Dimitri and Sergei for the days we'll be there. We need Dimitri to protect us in case we get involved with unsavory people, and we need Sergei to drive us to where we need to go. I told Alex why. He said he would help us where he could in our search for Bill.

"The reason for flying to Helsinki is to prevent the Russian authorities, specifically the FSB, linking our presence in the country to Bill's rescue—if we can find him. Besides, there wasn't enough time to obtain visas to enter Russia for those of us who haven't got one. I've assumed that neither Jacky nor Lucy presently possess a visa for Russia—right?"

Jacky confirmed that to be the case.

"I have a valid three-year multi-entry visa," Lucy replied.

"What about you, Oliver?" Mitch said. "You told me that your disguise is that of a Russian national. You'll need a visa to enter Finland."

"Yes, let me tell you about my disguise. It's that of a man called Oleg Balabanov. He's a Russian national who died in Austria in a car crash. I needed to impersonate him during one of my previous assignments. I have a Russian passport in his name, which allows me to travel to Russia without a problem, and also a US passport in his name. I'll use the latter to enter Finland and return to the US. As you know, US nationals don't need visas to enter Finland and other Schengen countries.

"I've assumed that Dave and Annette will be making their own hotel arrangements and that you, Mitch, will come with us. Dimitri and Sergei will be picking us up at the airport to drive us to the hotel. Dimitri, Sergei, Lucy, and I will leave the following morning at around nine. We'll cross the border into Russia well north of the normal route, where the FPS, the Federal Border Guard Service, only occasionally check for vehicles crossing the border. As I said, it's essential the FPS, which is part of the FSB, is unaware of our presence in Russia.

"We'll be checking into a cheap hotel just outside of Saint Petersburg, where the chance of remaining unobserved is considerably greater than if we were to check into a five-star hotel. The only baggage we need to take with us is what we need for one night at that hotel. I've stayed there before. I'll check in on behalf of all four of us using my Russian identity. By the way, you must always call me Oleg when we're near others. The FSB is still looking for Oliver Corbyn. No one should mention that name while we're in Russia.

"We'll leave the hotel the following morning. Our success in finding Bill depends on our ability to locate the house where the Bratva in Saint Petersburg lock up the people they kidnap. I suspect the FSB will have had Bill kidnapped by them. Contrary to what you might believe, the FSB and the Bratva often cooperate. The FSB doesn't want to be seen as having kidnapped an American citizen. If the Bratva is involved, that's where they will have taken you, Luce. To enable them to repeatably use the same hideout, they place a bag over the heads of those abducted during the drive there and back. Were you able to see anything about the route they took or the house you were taken to?"

"No. Apart from the bag on my head, I was beside myself, realizing that Dimitri had possibly died in the shooting. I hadn't considered needing to try to establish where we were going."

"That's okay, sweetheart. I think I know where to look. If Bill is there, we'll find him.

"My first assignment for the CIA was to investigate the kidnapping and possible rescue of the daughter of a US senator while she was visiting Saint Petersburg as a tourist. We rescued her while she was being driven to the place where the ransom was to be paid. We caused a roadblock and pulled her out of the car before the two men with her realized what was happening. She told me afterward that she was blindfolded but nevertheless managed to see that the house to which she was taken was green and that it possessed tinted windows. Of greater importance is the room she was kept in. It had a small ventilation window up near the ceiling, through which she could see three church steeples, close together, with a pink color. That's rather unusual, and I concluded that they would have to be the steeples of the Chesme Russian Orthodox Church. Do you remember seeing those, Luce?"

"I did, but I thought that all steeples in Russia were painted some color."

"Correct, but three steeples close together painted pink is relatively rare. So, assuming we'll find the house, I'll enter and rescue Bill. We'll then drive back to the border crossing we used before and continue on to Helsinki. It'll be late by the time we return. We should stay one more night at Hotel Kämp before returning to the States. Any comments or questions?"

"How do you propose to enter the building to take Bill from there once we've located it?"

"I don't know just yet, Luce. Knocking on the door and, once inside, incapacitating the person who opened it often works best. It depends on what we find when we're there."

"In what way do you want me to contribute to your plan, Oliver?" Mitch asked.

"By looking after Jacky while Lucy and I are away. I think nothing will happen in Helsinki, but I'd like you to be near Jacky all the same. I'd like for your room to be next to hers and for the communicating door to be open. If you agree, Jacky, I'll arrange that with reception when we get there."

"Why did you want me to accompany you on this trip if there's nothing I can contribute?" Jacky asked.

"There are several reasons. The most important of which is to not leave you behind in my apartment all alone. Prince Alexandrovich and his buddies in the Kremlin might try to find you if they decide to kidnap you after they discover that

Bill is no longer in their clutches. Besides, I'd assumed you'd want to see Bill again at the first opportunity, which would be in Helsinki if we're successful."

"Does Alexander have friends in the Kremlin?" Lucy asked.

"We know a lot about him, Luce. He lives in New York, but he frequently travels to Moscow, where he visits the Kremlin. He has access to its most important occupant. He's been engaged in a subtle plan to take control of Morgan Pharma. The first steps were to win your trust and take your position on the board. He then secured the trust of the board, which appointed him CEO of the office and laboratory in Boston. He caused several scientists at the lab to resign and organized Russian scientists to take their place. He managed to obtain temporary work visas for them.

"Bill's abduction was to allow you to take his place as chairperson of the board, and your illness, which he caused by having you take a dangerous drug, was to allow him to take your place. Bill's abduction was also intended to obtain a measure of leverage over you, Jacky, should you have wanted to involve yourself with the board.

"The worst of his crimes, as far as I'm concerned, was his intention to dispose of you, Luce, once he was chairman of the board. The drug he made you take regularly, combined with your alcohol intake, would have killed you within a few weeks. He had no further use for you once you allowed him to take your place on the board. I'm going to make him pay for what he did."

"How do you know all that?" Jacky asked.

"The people I work for have kept a close watch on him for years. They're very concerned about Morgan Pharma coming under Russian control. We urgently need to rescue Bill, as there's little you and Lucy can do to prevent the worst-case scenario from occurring as long as they have him. They'll threaten to kill him if you or Lucy try to do something to thwart their plans."

Lucy remained silent as Oliver laid out the situation at Morgan Pharma.

But when the full weight of it hit her—when she realized how the prince had used her to secure his position as chairman of the board and CEO of the Boston office and lab—she could no longer hold back.

A sharp breath escaped her, and she buried her face in her hands.

"Don't cry, Luce," Oliver said as he stood up to put an arm around her.

"It's all my fault," she said, looking up at him with tears in her eyes.

"It's not," he insisted. "It's all my fault. I should've tried harder to reconcile our differences. I had no idea how much my absences affected you. I'll make it up to you. I won't ever leave you again."

"You shouldn't promise me that," Lucy said, looking up at him again after wiping the tears from her eyes. "I know who you work for when you're on an assignment. You told me, remember?"

"But I am promising you that. I've already informed Director Rivera I wouldn't be available for further assignments unless you weren't willing to take me back."

Lucy couldn't believe what she was hearing.

When she realized how much she still loved him, she had decided she would accept his long absences if he chose to continue working for the CIA.

But now...this?

Overcome with emotion, she stood up, threw her arms around his neck, and kissed him. Fresh tears welled in her eyes.

"I don't know what to say," she said after they released each other. "You don't know how happy you've made me."

"Well, I'm glad that's out of the way," Jacky said as she watched Lucy and Oliver overcome the problem that had caused their separation.

"Sorry, Jacky. My reluctance to no longer be away as often as I have stood between us until now. I wanted to tell her about my decision to resign from the CIA another time, but after seeing how Lucy reacted to what I explained about the prince, I had to do it now."

"I understand, Oliver. I'm happy for both of you. I now know I needn't worry about Lucy anymore."

Mitch returned to the cockpit once there was nothing more to discuss. Meanwhile, Jacky asked Annette to prepare the beds for the night.

Lucy and Oliver moved to the couch, where they could sit together for a while and talk before heading to bed themselves.

***

Mitch landed the Gulfstream at Helsinki-Vantaa Airport at 2:45 p.m. local time.

Dimitri was already waiting. He led them to where Sergei had parked the Mercedes, but knowing the car wouldn't fit all six of them, he had arranged for a taxi to follow them to the hotel.

At Hotel Kämp, Oliver booked adjoining rooms for Mitch and Jacky and requested that the connecting door between them be opened.

That evening, they had a late dinner together at the hotel brasserie before retiring for the night.

***

The next morning, an early breakfast was delivered to their rooms. As planned, Dimitri arrived at 8:30 a.m. to collect them.

Before setting off, Oliver explained the plan for the day and the following one—primarily for Dimitri and Sergei's benefit.

Lucy was struggling more than usual with jet lag that morning, and Oliver suspected it was due to her still-incomplete recovery from her ordeal. As they left the hotel, he let her curl up in the back seat, resting her head on his lap.

Oliver knew the shortest and fastest route from Helsinki to Saint Petersburg was via the E18, which became the A181 in Russia—a 240-mile journey that typically took about five hours by car. But Dimitri had mentioned an alternative route, and Oliver was curious.

Sergei stayed on the E18 until Hamina, where he turned onto Highway 26 and then Highway 6 to Lappeenranta. From there, he chose the 390 toward Vainikkala.

At Vainikkala, he took a side road running parallel to the railway line and followed it for about a mile before Dimitri asked him to stop.

"We're now no more than half a mile from the border," Dimitri said.

The road ahead narrowed into a dirt path.

"Drive slow," Dimitri instructed.

Sergei nodded and eased forward, stopping again about 150 yards short of the border crossing.

"Stay here, all of you. I'm going to walk to the border to see if the crossing is manned."

Dimitri returned fifteen minutes later.

"There's no one there. We're in luck."

Sergei drove slowly across the border, passing the guardhouse on the Russian side without incident.

The dirt road soon transitioned into a secondary paved road, which led them toward the Buslovskaya train station. From there, they followed the route through Luzhayka and Seleznyovo, eventually rejoining the E18, now signposted as the A181.

The detour had taken them four hours.

At the first service station they encountered, they stopped

for a restroom break, ate a quick sandwich, and refueled the Mercedes.

By late afternoon, they arrived at their destination—the Time-Out Hotel in Sestroretsk, a quiet town twenty miles northwest of central Saint Petersburg.

Booking the rooms was easy. Oliver secured single rooms for Dimitri and Sergei and a double room for himself and Lucy for one night. He paid with his Russian credit card, and to his relief, the receptionist didn't ask for the names of his companions.

Keeping a low profile was essential, so they ordered dinner from room service instead of dining in the hotel restaurant. The long drive had exhausted them all, and after eating, they retreated to their respective rooms for the night.

***

"I want to say a few words about what we need to do today," Oliver said when they had left the hotel and seated themselves in the car the following morning. "We'll drive to the Chesme Russian Orthodox church on Ulitsa Lensoveta. We then need to systematically search the region around it for the house painted green with darkened windows. Many houses in Russia are painted green due to the greater availability and lower cost of green paint, but the combination with darkened windows isn't common. When we've located the house, we need to drive past it and park farther down the street, away from anyone who might be watching from inside."

***

It took all of five minutes to find the first house painted green after Sergei had driven them to the church. They found another two houses painted green soon after, but none with darkened windows. They found the house they were looking for a minute later. Sergei parked the car a hundred yards away.

"That has to be the house," Oliver said. "None of the others have tinted windows. The Bratva will have adopted those windows to disallow people from looking in while not hindering them from looking out. Have you got a scrap of paper in the car, Dimitri?"

Dimitri rummaged around in the glove box and retrieved a folded blank sheet of paper, which he handed to Oliver.

"And give me your Glock 22, Sergei, just in case."

Sergei obliged, reaching into the glove compartment and producing the gun. Oliver took it without a word. He checked the magazine—fully loaded. Satisfied, he slid the weapon into the waistband of his trousers at the small of his back, tugging his sweater down to conceal it.

"I'm going to talk my way into the house. Once inside, I'll do what I need to, find Bill, and come back here. It shouldn't take more than half an hour."

Meanwhile, Lucy's concern had grown with each passing moment. The reality of what was unfolding before her eyes was sinking in.

She knew Oliver had to go inside and search for Bill. But when he asked for the gun, the weight of the situation hit her differently.

This wasn't just a plan anymore—it was real, and it was dangerous.

As Oliver reached for the back door of the car, she grabbed onto him, holding him, unwilling to let go.

"Please be careful, Oliver," she said.

"I will, Luce."

As Oliver approached the house, he glanced down at the sheet of paper in his hand, then at the surrounding houses, before looking back at the paper again. To any observer, he would appear to be just another man searching for a specific address.

When he reached the front door, he knocked—loud and persistent, the kind of knock that signaled urgency. He needed them to believe his presence was important.

After a brief pause, the door swung open.

A sturdy-looking man stood in the doorway.

"What do you want?"

"I'm from the gas company. I have to check for leaks. Our measurements show there's a leak somewhere along this street. It's important to do that as quickly as possible because of the likelihood of a fire or an explosion if it's not found soon."

"Okay, come in."

"Can you show me where the gas line enters the house?"

Once Oliver stepped inside, the man shut the front door behind him.

They stood in a narrow hallway. Without a word, the man led him to a hatch in the floor nearby and pulled it open, revealing the gas, water, electricity, and telephone utility lines running into the house from the street.

Oliver crouched down, his eyes scanning the setup. He reached for the gas line, wrapping his hand around the point where it connected to the thick rubber hose that supplied the gas appliances.

"I believe there's a leak at the connection," Oliver said. "You should check to see if I'm right."

Oliver stepped aside, giving the man room to bend down. The moment he did, Oliver struck—seizing him from behind. His right hand clamped tightly over the man's mouth and nose, cutting off his air and silencing any cry for help. As the man flailed, Oliver's left hand shot forward, intercepting his opponent's left arm before it could assist in breaking the hold.

The man struggled violently, clawing at Oliver's grip, but he was no match. After three minutes, his movements weakened, then ceased altogether.

When Oliver checked for a pulse, there was none.

Moving quickly, he searched the man's pockets for keys or anything important, then shoved his lifeless body through the open hatch beneath the floor. It was a tight fit, taking longer than Oliver had anticipated, but it was necessary—if the others came looking for him, the body needed to be out of sight.

Once the hatch was securely closed, Oliver turned his attention to the rest of the house.

He opened the door at the end of the hallway and stepped into a corridor. Doors lined both sides, and at the far end, a staircase led to the second floor.

Then—a sound.

From the last door on the right, which was slightly ajar, the noise of a radio or television filtered into the corridor. Oliver peered inside.

A man sat in an armchair, his back to the door, watching TV with a beer in hand. On the coffee table, he noticed two other beers.

Three men, Oliver deduced.

Suddenly, a toilet flushed.

Oliver moved fast, positioning himself outside the door from which the sound had come. The second the door swung open, he grabbed the Bratva thug and clamped his hand over the man's nose and mouth, silencing him before he could react.

The man fought hard, using both hands to pry Oliver's grip away. He was strong—too strong—and, as before, Oliver had to use his left hand to restrain the thug's left arm, weakening his defense.

Seconds stretched.

Oliver could feel his strength waning, but just as his grip was about to fail, the man went limp in his arms.

Gasping for breath, Oliver barely had time to recover before moving to the living room.

Oliver moved in silently, slipping behind the third criminal like a shadow. In one swift motion, he clamped a hand over the man's nose and mouth and squeezed.

This time, there was no struggle. No flailing. Just a faint, pitiful shudder—and then stillness.

The man slumped forward when Oliver released his hold. He deduced that his last victim was drunk.

Oliver quickly searched the bodies, finding a bunch of keys in the jacket of the man who had been watching TV. He suspected that one of them would unlock the door where Bill was being held.

Moving swiftly, he checked the rooms on the first floor—nothing. He climbed the stairs, stopping at a locked door directly opposite the landing. His heart pounded as he tried one key after another. Finally, the lock clicked. He pushed the door open and exhaled in relief. Bill Lassiter sat in the corner on a thin mattress, his expression exhausted but alert. The room was bare, containing nothing but a toilet and a sink.

Oliver met his eyes. "Can you come with me, please, Bill?"

"Who are you?" Bill asked.

"I'm Oliver. I'm wearing a disguise."

"How did you find me?"

"I'll let Lucy tell you. She's outside in the car waiting for you."

"I don't understand. The last time we saw her, she was bedridden because of a strange illness."

"We managed to nurse her back to health, Bill."

Oliver assisted Bill when he noticed he was unsteady on his feet.

"I've been locked in this room for a long time, Oliver. It will take a few minutes to regain my former abilities."

Oliver helped him down the stairs. When Bill saw two of his captors on the floor, he asked if they were dead.

"They won't trouble us anymore."

"Can you help me look for my briefcase? It contained my phone and tablet. They took that from me before they locked me up."

It took barely a minute for Oliver to find Bill's briefcase and check its contents.

With that secured, he moved to the front door, opening it just enough to scan the street.

No one in sight.

Without hesitation, they slipped out. Oliver shut the door behind them and gripped Bill's arm, steadying him as they made their way to the Mercedes. As they reached the car, Lucy was already there, holding the rear door open. Bill climbed in first, then Lucy, followed by Oliver. The moment they were inside, Lucy threw her arms around her stepfather. He clung to her. Neither of them could hold back their tears.

"Drive, Sergei," Oliver said. "As fast as traffic allows, please. The sooner we reach Helsinki, the better."

Lucy and Bill had much to say to each other, their quiet conversation filled with emotion.

Oliver, meanwhile, closed his eyes, letting the tension drain from his body. The confrontation with the three Bratva criminals had left him on edge, but now, with Bill safe, the weight of the morning's stress slowly faded.

The return drive to Helsinki was uneventful.

By the time they arrived at Hotel Kämp at 10 p.m., exhaustion had settled over them—but it didn't dull the impact of the emotional reunion between Bill and Jacky. It stirred them all.

24.

OLIVER'S PLAN

Oliver ordered a late dinner from the room service menu for everyone. Jacky and Mitch had chosen to wait rather than ordering their meals earlier in the evening. Meanwhile, Lucy had updated Bill on the situation at Morgan Pharma, leaving him deeply concerned. Sensing Bill's anxiety, Oliver decided to share his plan to regain control of the company. He brought up the matter shortly after Dimitri and Sergei had retired to their rooms.

"Is this a good time to discuss how to rid Morgan Pharma of its Russian influence, or would you prefer to go to bed and discuss it tomorrow?"

"It's already late," Lucy said. "Bill hasn't slept well during his captivity, and it might be better to do that tomorrow."

"You're right, Luce. Sorry, Bill."

"After what Lucy told me, I won't be able to sleep," Bill said. "Let's discuss what we should do to regain control now."

"Are you happy with that, Luce?"

"Sure."

"I first want to point out that it's important for both of you to return with Lucy and me to my apartment in Falls Church. Too many people know where you live. The single bodyguard you have at home won't be able to prevent the abduction of either of you should the Russians want to regain control—control they've lost now that Bill has escaped.

"Besides, we need to visit both New York and Boston. So, I want you to stay at my apartment until all this is over. Apart from the CIA, no one knows where I live, and you'll be much safer there.

"Mitch and Dave, meanwhile, must safeguard the Gulfstream because the prince has secured permission from the board to use it. The situation is not different from when we were nursing Lucy back to health and when you and Dave were safeguarding the plane. Are you happy with that, Mitch?"

"Sure. If the prince really wanted to find where the plane was, it wouldn't be difficult to locate it if it was parked on the tarmac at Dulles. That's why we now park it in the hangar of the Jet Center."

"Can you all agree with what I've proposed so far?"

"Let me reply to that, Oliver," Bill said. "First, however, I want to thank you for all you've done for us. The most important of which, as far as Jacky and I are concerned, is rescuing Lucy and nursing her back to health. I couldn't think of anything else but her plight while I was held captive."

"I was the cause of her predicament," Oliver replied. "Please consider what I did in that light."

"I know, although Lucy sees that differently. I nevertheless want to thank you for your relentless help to us as a family. I agree we shouldn't return to LA and that we should stay somewhere on the East Coast for now. But we prefer not to impose on your hospitality. Wouldn't a hotel be just as safe?"

"I don't think so. You two are well-known, and if you're recognized at a hotel, it might lead to publicity we can do without just now...and you wouldn't be imposing."

"Okay, you've convinced me. Do you agree, Jacky?"

"Yes. During my stay with Oliver, he was the perfect host.

I still feel guilty about not being able to help him much in looking after Lucy."

"That's settled then," Oliver said. "The first thing we need to do after the weekend is for you, Bill, to regain control of the board. Am I correct in assuming that when the prince was chairman, he had full control of the company?"

"Yes... Morgan Pharma is a public company listed on the New York Stock Exchange. We, as a family, own fifty-one percent of the shares. The shareholders appoint the members of the board, but because of our majority holding, we effectively determine who is actually appointed.

"We further determine strategic objectives, appoint the CEO and CFO, and ensure that adequate financial resources are available to secure our objectives. We also set annual budgets, report back to the shareholders, and set the salaries, compensation, and benefits of senior management. During the weeks when the prince was chairman, he was acting on behalf of the family. In other words, he was indeed in full control. We met him just once. That was in Lucy's apartment when we were there to plead with her to return with us to LA. He introduced himself after letting himself in. I can understand why Lucy fell for him. He hadn't yet secured Lucy's position on the board at the time. Neither Jacky nor I saw the danger he represented. He seemed genuinely concerned for Lucy's welfare. After we left the apartment, we both started having doubts about the situation. We should have returned with our physician to properly examine her."

"As I see it, we urgently need to undo what he did when he was in charge," Oliver continued. "A meeting of the board is necessary if we want to do that as quickly as possible. It's likely the prince won't be present. Knowing how things work in Russia, he'll already have been informed of your escape. I wouldn't be surprised to learn he's on his way to Moscow as we speak. From what Director Rivera and Lucy told me, I believe he's clever enough to realize that the game he's been playing has come to an end. He possibly knows that if he remains in the US, he'll be charged with attempted murder and fraudulent misrepresentation in dealing with the board.

"The CIA believes the prince's introduction into Lucy's circle of friends was intended to win her trust, take advantage of her addiction, and secure the chairmanship of the board long enough to obtain the information on the Alzheimer's cure that, by now, is complete enough to take into production."

"Is there proof of that?" Lucy asked.

"Not proof in the sense of what a jury would require to convict him, but there are sufficient telling indications. He had the board appoint him CEO of the Morgan Pharma office and lab in Boston, for example. He caused several scientists there to leave and arranged for Russian scientists to take their place. The Russians have controlled the Boston lab since he became CEO. The information they need to produce the medication in Russia has probably already been stolen."

"I was struck by the subtlety and cunning of the plan by which they achieved that, if they have, when Lucy told me about it," Bill remarked.

"It could only have been thought up by Russians," Oliver said. "I've found them to be extremely cunning and devious at times. It's just as well they often let themselves down by the inferior way they put a brilliant plan into effect. I need to be present at the board meeting that you, Jacky, and Lucy have to attend. I must apprehend the prince if he turns up after all. But the situation in Boston must also be addressed as quickly as possible to prevent further damage.

"The plan I've come up with to achieve both tasks is to have two of my colleagues present at the board meeting in New York and at the Boston lab. I think we need to assume that one or more board members were bribed or coerced by the prince to allow him to carry out his plans. We must therefore ensure there's no contact between those members and the Russians at the laboratory during or directly after the meeting. They might otherwise want to inform them to steal the information they need and disappear, if the information hasn't already been stolen. It's important to take steps to avoid such a possibility, even though you might think it's a far-fetched idea.

"My CIA colleagues at the lab are to arrest the Russian scientists when they arrive for work. After you've informed the board of what's going on and we've obtained a detailed picture of what happened at meetings while you were away, we'll travel to Boston. So, what do you think?"

"You've thought of everything," Lucy said.

"I hope so, Luce."

"I like your plan," Bill said. "But some board members might not appreciate the treatment your CIA colleagues will subject them to. The majority of those members are powerful individuals in their own right."

"Is it possible to arrange the board meeting for ten a.m. on Monday?"

"It is if I call them personally to inform them that an emergency requires we convene a meeting. Most of the members are based on the East Coast, so we should be able to secure a quorum."

"Great. We could be in Boston at around two to visit the lab. Right, Mitch?"

"That's a tight schedule, but as long as you're done with the meeting by eleven-thirty, we could make it work."

***

They retired to their rooms. Oliver was looking forward to a good night's sleep. He embraced Lucy before they slipped under the covers. They held each other close.

"We have to agree to something, Oliver," Lucy said as she looked into his eyes.

"That look tells me it's something important."

"It is."

"Did I do something you don't agree with?"

"Yes, more than once."

"I'm sorry. Nothing comes to mind. I love you unconditionally with every fiber of my being. If I upset you in some way, you must tell me about it."

"I want you to stop taking the blame for everything that has happened to me, to Bill, and to Morgan Pharma. I've heard you repeatedly say it's your fault for not trying harder to reconcile our differences. It's just not true. I made it impossible for you to do so. I barricaded myself in the guest bedroom after we talked and then ran away to join my socialite friends and started drinking, mainly to spite you and to forget you. And, worst of all, I let myself be used by someone as devious as the prince. It's all my fault, not yours."

Tears appeared in Lucy's eyes.

"You're wrong, Luce. Jacky was right when she told me I was the reason for your condition before we took you from your apartment. When she and Bill visited you, you informed them that you had broken up with me because you were unable to deal with the long periods I was away. She also said that you loved me in a way she had rarely seen a woman love a man. She's right. I knew you loved me deeply, and I should've chosen for you and not for myself."

"I need to see everything that has happened differently," Lucy protested. "I'm aware that you see your decision to not consider my needs on that fateful day when I left you as wrong. But I should have been strong and fought for us. I didn't, and I allowed myself to fall in with the wrong people again and become addicted to alcohol. I feel very guilty about that, and each time I hear you say everything is your fault, that feeling of guilt consumes me."

"Please, Luce, don't feel that way. Jacky made me realize that in disappointing you in the way I did, your lapse was inevitable."

"I beg to differ, Oliver. I can't help myself."

Lucy began to cry, and Oliver realized that this conversation—one in which they acknowledged their mistakes—was long overdue. It was necessary, a release that finally freed them from their guilt.

"Let it all out, sweetheart. Don't hold back," Oliver murmured, gently kissing away the tears pooling in her eyes.

She clung to him, her grip desperate. He scooped her up, turned back the blankets, and laid her down without breaking their embrace. Pulling the covers over them, he held her close, offering the comfort she needed.

"I need you to forgive me," Oliver said, "for everything I caused."

"I forgave you when I came to my senses in your apartment when you nursed me back to life."

"Please say it, sweetheart."

"I forgive you. Now, please forgive me for not fighting for us when it counted."

"I forgive you, Luce."

She was happy to find he was as uneasy as she was by what happened on the day they let each other go. Oliver was happy she had forgiven him for having chosen for himself instead of for her when it mattered.

25.

AN UNEXPECTED ALLY

Mitch flew them to Dulles on Saturday. They had set an alarm early enough to finish packing, have breakfast, and drive to Helsinki Airport for their 10 a.m. departure. Jacky handled the checkout for all of them.

At the airport, they took a moment to thank Dimitri and Sergei for their help and unwavering support. Oliver embraced them both, deeply grateful for everything they had done.

Their flight landed at Dulles at 12:45 p.m.

"I'll see you all Monday morning," Mitch said once they had cleared airport formalities. "I'll have a car pick you up at seven-thirty."

Forty minutes later, they arrived at Oliver's apartment. While Jacky and Bill unpacked and settled in, Oliver excused himself. Knowing exactly what he needed to do, Lucy followed him to the bathroom to help remove his disguise and wash his hair.

Meanwhile, Bill got to work. He called the board members, emphasizing the urgency of the meeting he wanted them to attend. Oliver, in turn, contacted the CIA director's office, knowing he needed to call Ken Rivera at home since it was a Saturday. After explaining the gravity of the situation, an assistant provided him with the director's home number. When Oliver reached him, Ken Rivera listened carefully and quickly agreed to send two agents to the board meeting in New York and two more to the Boston lab first thing on Monday.

***

Sunday was a day of rest, reflection, and preparation. Jacky and Bill slept in, spent time discussing their situation, and took the opportunity to unwind. In the afternoon, they went shopping for clothes for Bill, as Jacky had packed only a limited selection, and he needed a proper suit for the meetings the next day.

The following morning, the drive to the Jet Center at Dulles took just over thirty minutes. Mitch secured a take-off slot shortly after they arrived, and by 9:15 a.m., they had landed at LaGuardia. They reached Morgan Pharma headquarters with fifteen minutes to spare.

Oliver quickly briefed his CIA colleagues, who had already arrived, on their roles.

The board members were caught off guard when they walked into the boardroom to find not only all three members of the Lassiter family but also three unfamiliar men. Bill welcomed them as they took their seats around the table, ready to begin.

"Welcome, everyone. I'm happy you could all come at such short notice. Please accept my apology for not having prepared an agenda. As you know, I was abducted by the Russian mafia three weeks ago. I was rescued by the CIA last Friday. What we as a family have endured at the hands of the Russians these last months is beyond belief. But before I explain, I want to introduce CIA Special Agent Corbyn to you. He has something to say."

Oliver, who had remained standing along with his colleagues, stepped forward. "Good morning. We have reason to believe that not everyone here has the best interests of Morgan Pharma at heart. Those I'm referring to may wish to inform certain parties elsewhere about the nature of the discussions that are to take place here this morning. To prevent that, my colleagues will now go around the table to collect your cell phones, tablets, and laptops. These will be returned to you at the end of the day. We require you to remain here until then. I apologize if this interferes with your afternoon plans, but I hope you'll accept it as a minor inconvenience when you hear what Bill has to say."

The CIA agents walked around the table and collected the board members' electronics and attached a sticky note to each item with the owner's name. Keith Dunbar, a prominent member of the board, refused to cooperate.

"You can't do this, Bill. We have rights. You need to have a warrant, which I don't think you have," he protested.

"Show him the warrant, Oliver," Bill said.

The warrant—prepared by Ken Rivera's assistants after his conversation with Oliver—charged unnamed members of the Morgan Pharma board with conspiracy to steal trade secrets from a US company. One of the agents collecting phones and computers held the document. Pausing his task, he handed it to Oliver, who then presented it to Dunbar. Upon reading it, Dunbar dropped his opposition.

"So, let me explain the situation we're in," Bill said. "After I was kidnapped while visiting our Saint Petersburg office, Prince Alexandrovich, who had won the trust of my stepdaughter, convinced her that he should take up the role of chairman of this board in her place. She allowed that to happen because she was ill at the time. It's been suggested in the press that her drinking habit was the cause of her illness, and while that played a role, it was the daily doses of a lethal drug the prince had her take that affected her most. It would have killed her in a matter of weeks. When the CIA became suspicious of what was happening, they rescued my stepdaughter and had her nursed back to health.

"The CIA has been monitoring the prince's career for a long time. He frequently visits the Kremlin. When this board appointed him CEO of our Boston office and laboratory, where he dismissed several of our scientists to replace them with Russian counterparts, the CIA concluded that the prince was the central figure in a plot to steal the details of the Alzheimer's cure, which, as you know, is soon to be evaluated by the FDA."

The members of the board, who had been listening attentively to what Bill was saying, expressed their surprise.

"May I address the board, Bill?" Oliver asked.

"Certainly."

"We'd hoped the prince would be present this morning. If he were, we would have arrested him for the attempted murder of Miss Lassiter and conspiracy to steal information about the Alzheimer's cure. We realized, however, that the news of Bill's rescue from his captors on Friday would have reached him that same day. He will now have fled to Russia, assuming we would have discovered he had Miss Lassiter take lethal drugs and that Bill's kidnapping was orchestrated by him."

"What we need to know," Bill continued, "is what happened at the board meetings at which he was chairman. Things you might now consider odd, given that the prince is a fraud." Bill looked around the room. "Who wants to address that?"

Katherine Osborne, the board member who was sitting next to Lucy and who had been having an animated conversation with her before the meeting, answered.

"His appointment as CEO of the Boston facility was a controversial issue we had to vote on. It was suggested he would be eligible to take up the vacant position of CEO of Morgan

Pharma as a whole, considering his experience in managing New York corporations. But that wasn't his ambition, he said. He wanted to be closer to the scientific aspects of the work we do. The vote we took was close and led to his appointment as CEO of the Boston office and laboratory.

"There was one other matter that raised concern among some of us. The prince proposed a joint venture with a Russian pharmaceutical company for the production of medication no longer protected by patents. He explained that those medicines could be produced at a lower cost in Russia than in the US.

"The discussion of his proposal led to a decision to look at its details. The prince then tabled a document outlining those details. Some of us were pleased with the proposal when he admitted that such medicines could be retailed under the Morgan Pharma label. He wanted an upfront payment of a hundred million dollars. He needed that, he said, to update the production plant in Russia.

"We took a vote on the proposal, which again resulted in a narrow margin in his favor. We instructed the CFO to transfer that amount in two installments to the company involved."

"Why didn't you delay a decision of that nature to allow us to take a look at the proposal?" Bill asked her.

"When some of us proposed to postpone a decision to a future board meeting, we were overruled by those who sided with the prince."

"The Russian company involved wouldn't be RusPharma, by chance?" Oliver asked.

"It is," she replied.

Bill and Oliver exchanged a look.

"You've all been tricked. The joint venture is nothing but a ruse to get you to pay that amount into an account managed by the prince," Oliver said. "May I suggest that you call for a coffee break while you check with the CFO to see if one or both installments have been paid?"

Bill agreed. He called for a short recess, asked his secretary to organize coffee for everyone, and made his way to the CFO's office. Oliver, meanwhile, led Lucy to a corner of the room where they couldn't be overheard.

"I need you to do something for me, Luce. Ask the woman sitting next to you who voted in favor of the prince becoming CEO of the Boston facility and in favor of the joint venture."

Lucy returned to her seat to drink her coffee and talk to Kathryn Osborne. She told Oliver a few minutes later that three members in particular had seemed to form a team with the prince, the most outspoken of whom was Keith Dunbar.

"Both installments have been paid," Bill said when he reconvened the meeting. "The second only as recently as late last Friday, after the prince called the CFO to let him know he was traveling to Russia to implement the work required for updating the designated production facility."

Several board members now apologized for their gullibility in accepting the prince's proposals without many questions. Oliver recognized that for the prince to have deceived not only Lucy but also these seasoned professionals, he must have been exceptionally cunning and manipulative.

With their primary objective achieved, Bill concluded the meeting, assuring everyone that a regular board session would be scheduled soon to address other business matters.

"Thank you once again for coming to this extraordinary meeting of the board. I was informed just now that three of you appeared to have been unduly influenced by the prince. I'm referring to you, Keith Dunbar; you, Barry McKenzie; and you, Ellen Wright. I'm suspending your membership of the board pending the investigation the CIA will want to carry out.

"If the investigation reveals the prince paid you or offered you some reward for supporting him by voting in his favor on the various issues that were raised, your membership of this board will be revoked. The three of you must remain here until after business hours. Your phones and tablets will be returned to you then.

"Everyone else is free to leave, but if anything of what transpired here this morning is leaked, either accidentally or intentionally, the CIA will want to know who is responsible. It's imperative no one knows of the control the Russians had, and to some extent still have, of the company until this whole affair has been resolved."

With no other pressing matters to deal with, Bill concluded the meeting. Bill, Jacky, Lucy, and Oliver left, leaving the board members behind in disarray, discussing what had taken place.

***

Mitch had arranged for a company limousine and chauffeur to drive them to LaGuardia. They had lunch during the flight to Boston Logan. On arrival at Terminal V, another limousine and chauffeur were waiting to take them to the laboratory.

"Let me handle things at the lab, Bill," Oliver said. "I'm on familiar ground, and I know most of the staff who work there."

When they arrived at the lab, they were met by Will Bryce, the chief pharmaceutical scientist. He led them to a meeting room where they could talk in private.

"It's a pleasure to meet you again, Mr. and Mrs. Lassiter," he said. "During all the years I've worked here, I've only occasionally met you face to face. Your contacts with both the office and the laboratory here were always with our CEO, who retired more than ten months ago."

"I'm sorry that didn't occur more often," Bill replied. "Please call me Bill. My wife's name is Jacky. Lucy has visited you many times before, and we've been kept up to date on your progress by both her and Oliver. We should have made a point of visiting you more often to hear of your progress firsthand. The Alzheimer's cure is by far the most important product Morgan Pharma has developed. Oliver told me that your contribution to the investigation was crucial."

"He's too modest. His involvement, at the time, proved to be more important than ours."

"Let me explain why we're here," Oliver said. "Bill was kidnapped while visiting the Saint Petersburg office, and in his absence, Prince Alexandrovich was appointed chairman of the board. That position was Lucy's to take in Bill's absence, but she was seriously ill at the time. The prince was able to win Lucy's trust, and she appointed him acting chairman of the board in her absence. As you know, the board appointed him CEO of this facility. The information we have is that he caused some of your people to leave so he could fill their vacancies with Russian scientists. Can you tell us what happened?"

"He caused trouble from the moment he informed us he was the new CEO. He took issue with some of our administration and reporting practices, and a few of our chemists and pharmaceutical scientists debated issues with him. He dismissed them all. I tried to stop what was happening, but to no avail. He then surprised us when he introduced seven Russian scientists who he had obtained temporary work visas for to take the place of those he dismissed. He allowed them unlimited access to our data and computer files, including the results of our Alzheimer's research."

"The CIA dispatched two agents here this morning to prevent those Russian scientists from leaving after they arrived," Oliver explained. "We believe the prince traveled to Moscow last Friday or Saturday to avoid his arrest for attempted murder. He caused Lucy's illness by giving her daily doses of a dangerous drug that would have killed her if we hadn't intervened. He might have warned his scientists to also return to

Russia, taking the information on the Alzheimer's medication with them. The two agents who are here were told to prevent that."

"That's what they told me when they introduced themselves early this morning. They're holding the Russians in a meeting room nearby. They've confiscated their cell phones, tablets, and laptops. I'll take you to them."

Will led them to a large conference room. Oliver shook hands with each of the agents. He wasn't surprised to see who the Russian scientists were. Every one of them had been, or still were, RusPharma employees.

"Hello, Sasha," Oliver said, offering his hand for her to shake after he had walked to where she was sitting.

Sasha was more than surprised to see him. She shook his hand but said nothing. Oliver nodded when Alexei and Anatoly also revealed surprise at seeing him.

"These men and women are, or were, employees of RusPharma, the company that stole the Alzheimer's data on July second of last year during the computer hack," Oliver explained afterward. "I want to interrogate Sasha in private. You can all stay to watch, but perhaps you, Jacky and Bill, might want Will to take you to where you can have a coffee while Lucy and I concern ourselves with the Russians."

This proposal was accepted. Oliver and Lucy returned to the room where the Russians were being held, where Oliver spoke to the CIA agents in a low voice about what he wanted to do.

"I want to confront Sasha to find out if the data on the main server here has been downloaded to take with them when they return to Russia. Please bring her to us in the small meeting room in about fifteen minutes."

Oliver took Lucy's hands in his when they sat down at the table.

"I want to propose something, Luce. Please hear me out.

Since we left the board meeting, I've been thinking of a way to destroy the data on the Alzheimer's cure they might already possess and retrieve the hundred million. It requires us to return to Russia. Is that something you're willing to do?"

"Only if we do everything together while we're there—everything!"

"Of course. I promised never to leave you again, remember?"

"In that case, tell me what you want to do."

"My plan is to make the prince and anyone associated with him believe we appreciate him for what he's done in standing by you while you were ill, for what he's done in leading Morgan Pharma through a difficult period while Bill was unable to, and for his initiative to embark on a joint venture. You need to send him a text to that effect."

"I already have. I tried to call him, but when I couldn't reach him, I sent him a long text thanking him for looking after me when I was ill, and for taking on the position of chairman of the board of directors when I couldn't. I informed him that I'd recovered from my illness sufficiently and that I would now take my rightful place as chairperson. Last but not least, I informed him that I never intended to become engaged to him, and I apologized for perhaps having given him and others the impression that I wanted to. I explained I had too much to drink that evening and that I didn't know what I had agreed to when questions were put to me about the engagement."

"When did you send that text?"

"On the day in your apartment when I had sufficiently recovered from my alcohol problem. I particularly wanted to thank him for everything he had done, and to clarify that the whole marriage thing came about because of having drunk too much alcohol. I didn't know then what I now know about him."

"Perfect. That text will help in making him believe you're truly unaware of his devious plan to gain control of Morgan Pharma long enough to steal the data on the Alzheimer's cure. Did he reply?"

"He never did—I don't know why."

"You should now send him another text about the possibility of extending the existing joint venture to include the production of the Alzheimer's medication and that you're prepared to pay for setting up the production line for that purpose. You should add that you estimate the associated cost to be about two hundred and fifty million US dollars, or some such figure. The idea of producing the medication legally, and the additional funding, should be enough bait for him to want to talk to you when you propose to travel to Moscow to discuss the details."

"How will that result in destroying the files they might have and the return of the hundred million?"

"Once the prince believes what you've proposed, he'll agree to sign an agreement. If we can get him to do that in his office, I'll force him to return the money he stole. I'll then gain access to the RusPharma computer system and delete the information if it has indeed been stolen. What do you think?"

"I don't know, Oliver. It's a very risky undertaking. After forcing the prince to return the hundred million, we'll become the focus of the FSB. Escape from Russia will be difficult if not impossible. Besides, you're already wanted by the FSB for having destroyed the RusPharma laboratory in Zelenograd. They'll arrest you when we get there."

"I won't let the prince live after he's transferred the money. He would have killed you if he had been given another one or two weeks, remember? I'll hide his body afterward to give us time to return to the US. And I wouldn't travel with you to Russia as Oliver Corbyn. I'll go as someone else. We'll need to speak to Ken Rivera about that."

Lucy remained apprehensive, but she realized that something needed to be done to prevent the prince and his associates from producing the Alzheimer's medication if the information required was already in their possession.

"Let me think about it some more before we decide," she said.

"The plan requires us to treat the Russian scientists in a friendly manner, as they may contact the prince or his associates as soon as they can after their cell phones and tablets are returned to them. Are you comfortable taking on a guileful role like that?"

"Is that the reason you informed me of your plan now?"

"Yes…and I wanted to bounce it off you first before approaching Jacky and Bill about it. They might disapprove because of the danger involved, and it would help if you and I agreed on this."

"What would you do if I disagreed?"

"I would honor my promise to never leave you again. Besides, I wouldn't be able to convince the Russkies of the proposal. Only you or Bill could."

"I agree to take on a guileful role, as you call it, but we need to discuss your proposal in detail before deciding."

At that point, one of the CIA agents entered the room with Sasha. Oliver pointed to the chairs on the other side of the table, and she sat down. It was obvious to both Lucy and Oliver that she was nervous.

"So we meet again, Sasha," Oliver began. "While the Lassiter family wasn't particularly impressed by the prince's behavior in dismissing chemists and pharmaceutical scientists who have been on the staff of this laboratory for years, they nevertheless appreciate you and your colleagues filling the vacancies. Although you may feel hostile toward me for having destroyed your laboratory, you should be aware that Dr. Lenkov stole the data you were using in the first place.

You might remember me telling you that when I was taken to Voskhod by the FSB.

"The Lassiter family also appreciates the prince's efforts in helping Morgan Pharma through some tough weeks while Mr. Lassiter was indisposed and Miss Lassiter was ill. He proposed a joint venture between RusPharma and Morgan Pharma, which the board of directors approved. As a matter of fact, the Lassiter family is considering expanding the joint venture to include the production of the Alzheimer's medication in Russia at a lower cost than it can be produced in the US. The family is prepared to contribute funds to the setting up or renovation of the production facility.

"It's important in that respect to know if the prince or anyone else who has traveled to Russia from here has downloaded the files on the main server to take with them. Do you know if anyone did?"

"I was present when Dr. Lenkov, who visited us here for a week, asked Andrei to download the files just before he left to return to Moscow," Sasha replied.

Lucy and Oliver exchanged a meaningful look.

"Mr. Lassiter will want you and your colleagues to return to wherever you are based these days to reinstate the scientists the prince dismissed. I'm aware that most of your colleagues have families they would have missed while being here. I assume all of you want to return home?"

"Everyone wants to return except me."

"Why don't you?"

"It's always been my ambition to work and live in America, free of persecution and free from what you call the Big Brother control over people's lives, such as exists in Russia when you work for a research company. I'm single with no strings attached, as you say in English. Apart from obtaining a permanent work visa, nothing prevents me from seeking employment as a research chemist in a company like Morgan Pharma."

Oliver knew of her ambition because she had told him about it before.

"You would need to align your sympathies with Morgan Pharma to work here. That might be difficult for you, considering everything that's happened."

"While that may have been the situation some time ago, it's no longer the case," Sasha said.

"What's changed?"

"It's what I now know about RusPharma. I was present in Dr. Lenkov's office when he received a phone call from one of the other owners of RusPharma. I learned that my colleagues and I are part of a plot to steal the information on the Alzheimer's cure that is now complete enough to be taken into production. Prince Alexandrovich is involved. I learned he is now in charge of Morgan Pharma because of his relationship with Miss Lassiter. He secured temporary work visas for seven of us, and we traveled here to familiarize ourselves with the work carried out in developing the medicine. So, I was surprised to hear you tell me just now that you appreciate the role taken by the prince."

"Does that imply you no longer want to work for RusPharma?"

"Yes, I was skeptical about some of the things Dr. Lenkov did, such as how he obtained the Morgan Pharma data on the Alzheimer's cure a year ago, but I only realized how evil he is after I witnessed that phone conversation."

"Do you want to ask Sasha anything, Lucy?"

Lucy indicated that she did.

"Are you aware that my stepfather was kidnapped while visiting our Saint Petersburg office? And if you are, do you know who could have been responsible?"

"When I heard about it, I assumed it was to allow Prince Alexandrovich to take control of Morgan Pharma. The kidnapping itself was probably carried out by the FSB, although they could have worked with the Bratva for that purpose. It's common knowledge that they frequently kidnap wealthy individuals for ransom." Sasha turned to Oliver. "May I ask you some questions?" she asked.

"Of course."

"Why were we detained when we arrived this morning?"

"That's simple. We wanted to ensure that you or one of your colleagues wouldn't download the Alzheimer's files today if that hadn't already been the case."

"I understand. Were you responsible for destroying our laboratory in Voskhod like you destroyed our laboratory in Zelenograd?"

Oliver pondered the question a fraction too long for Sasha not to notice.

"You needn't answer that question, Oliver. I'm now certain you are."

"Let's postpone a talk about Voskhod until another time. The question we now need to answer is whether you can be trusted. I'm inclined to say yes, but the people I work for will require that we take precautions. I'm prepared to try to place you in the custody of the FBI. You'd live at an FBI safe house in the suburbs of Boston and be driven to the lab and back every day until all this is over.

"To keep an eye on you, someone from here will be working with you in the same office. Will Bryce, the chief pharmaceutical scientist, will be your superior, and he'll offer you remuneration in line with your education and experience.

"Meanwhile, I'll request that your temporary work visa be exchanged for a permanent one. The staff here can assist you in seeking suitable lodgings in due course. Is that acceptable?"

"That's far beyond what I had hoped to achieve, Oliver. I'm grateful to you both. I won't let you down."

"You mustn't tell your colleagues of what we've just agreed to," Oliver added. "We don't want the prince and his associates to know what we've discussed. We want them to think we're interested in extending the joint venture, as I said. You might want to inform your colleagues accordingly before they leave."

"I understand. You needn't worry. When am I to be taken to the safe house you mentioned?"

"I need to make a phone call to arrange that. I would prefer you to be taken there later today. You should know that many FBI safe houses are actually witness protection facilities and that they are manned by housekeepers, often a husband and wife. They'll ensure that you're comfortable and well. We'll also be arranging for your colleagues to return to Moscow as soon as possible, in accordance with their wishes. They'll receive their phones and tablets when they leave here. You, on the other hand, won't be handed back your cell, tablet, or laptop until later. Okay?"

"Yes...thanks."

"In return, I want you to tell me the location of the RusPharma production facility where the prince and Dr. Lenkov want to produce the Alzheimer's cure."

"In Zelenograd. I don't think I or anyone else showed you the facility when you were there. It's a large facility and Dr. Lenkov would by now have started the work required to manufacture the medicine there."

"Can you also tell me where the prince lives and where he has his office when he's in Russia?"

"I don't know. I suspect he has an apartment and an office in Moscow."

***

Oliver and Lucy hadn't anticipated Sasha's surprising candor. The conversation had caught them off guard—they never expected one of the Russians to be so openly critical of her superiors, let alone so eager to defect and join Morgan Pharma.

Oliver relayed the discussion to Will, vouching for Sasha's skills and requesting that he bring her on board. He then asked Lucy to update Jacky and Bill while he contacted Director Rivera to arrange an FBI safe house and handle the necessary paperwork for Sasha to remain in the US.

Once everything was set in motion, Oliver rejoined Lucy, Jacky, and Bill.

"My mother and Bill aren't exactly happy about your plan," Lucy said when Oliver entered the room.

"I didn't think they would be. What are your main concerns?" he asked them.

"What will happen if the prince doesn't believe or accept your offer to produce the medicine in Russia because they intend to do that anyway? They might want to kidnap or kill you both," Bill said.

"I believe he'll give Lucy the benefit of the doubt. The offer of a quarter of a billion dollars will sway him enough to at least want to meet with her to discuss the proposal. He'll be considering ways to add that to the hundred million he's already appropriated under false pretenses. Lucy's presence is to convince him we know nothing of his intention to kill her. She needs to show him gratitude for his help when she needed it during her addiction."

"Why shouldn't I accompany you instead of Lucy?" Bill continued.

"Because, with respect, Bill, you wouldn't be able to achieve what Lucy can. She knows the prince intimately, and if we can make him believe she's thankful for him having looked after her when she was ill, it will be easier to reach our objective. But that's not the only reason I want Lucy to come with me. I promised to never leave her again, and I aim to keep that promise. However, I understand your concern for her safety, and I therefore propose that Dimitri and Sergei be present when we confront the prince and Lenkov.

"Before we decide, we need to look at the plan in more detail," Oliver said. "As I see it, Lucy needs to text the prince to see if he's willing to meet with us. She needs to do that as soon as possible if you were to agree. If he's willing to meet us, Lucy should tell him we'll be in Moscow three days later.

"I'll need to visit the CIA to have a new identity prepared for me. I was thinking of becoming an expert on joint ventures. It would be logical for Lucy to arrange for someone with that expertise to accompany her. We'll need a joint venture contract to take with us for the prince and Lucy to sign. That's for you or one of your lawyers to draw up, Bill. We then need to make travel arrangements. I suggest we take the Lassiter jet, not the Gulfstream, to give the visit greater visibility.

"That's when Alex needs to be contacted about making Dimitri and Sergei available in time to be at the airport to pick us up. We'll need to book into different hotel rooms, Luce, sorry. Perhaps in adjoining rooms, like the last time we were in Moscow.

"During the first meeting with the prince, Lucy needs to insist on inspecting the production facility where the Alzheimer's medication is to be produced, primarily to determine the cost of upgrading it. That should lead to a third meeting, hopefully at his office, to sign the joint venture agreement and to transfer the first installment of the two hundred and fifty million, or some other amount he's agreed to, into his bank account. I'll confront him there and do what's necessary.

"I'll then break into the production facility. I haven't considered that part of the plan in detail, but it will be based on downloading files from a hard drive that will replace all other files on their computer system with bogus files. So, what do you think?"

"I believe Lucy must decide whether we should embark on Oliver's plan," Bill said, turning to his wife.

"I agree," Jacky replied.

All eyes were now on Lucy. She pondered the question for a while.

"All I can do is believe in Oliver's confidence in the outcome of his plan," she finally said. "The Alzheimer's medication is important enough to accept the risk that comes with it."

"I hope everything proceeds as you think it will, Oliver," Jacky said.

"But please understand that my priority at all times is to avoid Lucy getting hurt," Oliver asserted. "If it looks like she might, I'll abort the mission or take measures to prevent it."

26.
PREPARATIONS

Lucy sent the text to the prince that evening after returning to Oliver's apartment. She received his reply the next morning. Lucy read it out loud.

'Dear Lucy, you have no idea how happy I am to learn you've recovered from your illness. I was distressed when I noticed your condition deteriorating from one day to the next. I was happy to have been able to guide Morgan Pharma through a difficult period while both you and your stepfather were indisposed. The joint venture I arranged with the board required me to travel to Moscow to assist in preparing the production facility. I was surprised to learn that your parents want to extend the joint venture to include the production of the Alzheimer's medicine. The associated cost would indeed be less than if it were to be produced in the US. But we would need to discuss under what name the medicine is to be retailed in that case. If we were to adopt the Morgan Pharma brand, we would not receive enough recognition for our role in producing the medicine. Our shareholders will want a compromise. I am looking forward to meeting you to discuss your proposal. Let me know when you can be in Moscow.'

"If I hadn't known better," Oliver said, "I would have

thought his answer to your text was sincere, Luce."

"He's a smooth talker as well. I believed everything he told me."

"We should now finalize our travel plans. If we aim for a meeting with the prince on Friday morning, we'll need to fly to Moscow tomorrow evening to arrive on Thursday afternoon. Can you ask Mitch to fly us to Sheremetyevo Airport instead of Domodedovo? It's closer to Zelenograd, where the RusPharma production facility is." He turned to Bill. "Should I call Alex about needing Dimitri and Sergei?"

"Let me do that," Bill replied.

Lucy sent the prince a text informing him of her availability on Friday at ten in the morning and that she would let him know where after she checked into her hotel.

Oliver's apartment became a hive of activity as Bill, Lucy, and Oliver all made calls to set their plans in motion. Lucy contacted the Morgan Pharma travel department to ask them to book two rooms and two adjoining suites in the Ritz-Carlton in Moscow for five nights, starting Thursday night. Bill called the head of the Morgan Pharma legal department to have them prepare a draft of a joint venture agreement with an as-yet-unknown entity in Russia for the production of the Alzheimer's cure. He also called Alex Davidson and asked him to make Dimitri and Sergei available starting at three o'clock on Thursday afternoon at Sheremetyevo Airport.

Oliver called Will Bryce to request that his IT department prepare a hard drive containing software for the production of aspirin or a similar medicine, using the same file names as those downloaded by Lenkov. Oliver asked him to have the drive delivered to Boston Logan Terminal V at 9 p.m. the following day for him to pick up. He then called Ken Rivera and requested fifteen minutes of his time to discuss an important matter.

***

Ken Rivera had his assistants clear his schedule for the meeting. Oliver had asked Lucy to accompany him. After greeting them, Ken asked Oliver to update him on the situation at Morgan Pharma. Oliver did in detail, not leaving anything out.

"I'm worried, Liam, about the information on the Alzheimer's medication now being in the hands of the Russians. The White House is not going to like it. What can we do to retrieve or destroy that information?"

"You know me, Ken. I wouldn't be here if I didn't have a plan. Lucy sent a text to the prince yesterday, thanking him for looking after the company while Bill couldn't and while she was ill. She proposed to extend the joint venture the board of directors had agreed on to include the production of the Alzheimer's cure to save on costs. The prince took the bait, and he's invited her to a meeting in Moscow to discuss her proposal. We'll be flying to Moscow late tomorrow, for which I need a new identity. I was thinking of becoming a lawyer with expertise in joint ventures. Would it be possible for you to organize that between now and our departure?"

Ken immediately instructed one of his assistants to coordinate a hurried search for a suitable identity.

"So, what do you plan to do once you've arrived in Moscow?" Ken asked.

"We hope to be convincing enough for the prince to invite us to his office to sign the agreement and pay the first installment. I'll eliminate him there and use his computer to return the hundred million he stole. I assume that by then, we'll have been shown the production facility, to which I'll return afterward to download a set of bogus files onto their computers and permanently delete all previous files."

"There's a lot you're not telling me, Liam, as always. But I have faith in you and your ability to do what is required. Is

Lucy aware she's the reason you want to leave?"

"She is. I tried hard not to fall in love with her during my early months as Oliver Corbyn. She's special. I couldn't stop her from getting under my skin. Believe me, I tried. It became increasingly difficult to pretend I didn't have feelings for her. I admit to having failed to navigate around the main obstacle I was warned about during my training as a field agent: becoming romantically involved and having to stop working for the CIA because of no longer wanting to be away on assignments all the time. I thought that wouldn't happen to me."

"I appreciate you telling me, Liam. You're a lucky lady, Lucy, to have snagged Liam."

"I know, Ken," Lucy said while squeezing Oliver's arm. "May I call you Ken?"

"Of course."

"May I also ask you a question?"

"Shoot."

"Is everyone that needs to know aware of Oliver's resignation?"

Ken looked at Oliver when Lucy posed the question.

"She knows everything, Ken. I told her about the president's involvement."

"No one is ever to know, Lucy. Please maintain strict secrecy. There would be a lot to answer for if the media found out the president had ordered some of the missions Liam has been on, which includes everything he did for Morgan Pharma, by the way. I haven't yet informed the president. I will in due course."

With nothing more to discuss, Oliver stood up to leave.

"I'll ask one of my assistants to call you tomorrow as soon as we've found a suitable identity for you. I'll have a US and a Russian passport ready for you after you've had your photograph taken following the makeover."

***

Lucy and Oliver decided to retire early that evening. Not because they felt especially tired, but because they wanted to be alone. Lucy had indicated she wanted to talk.

"Make love to me, Oliver," she said after they had undressed and prepared for bed.

"I thought you wanted to talk."

"I do, but I need you to hold me first, to hold me close, to make me feel wanted again. It's something I can't do without. That feeling consumes me from time to time when I think of you. I've tried to figure out why, and I think it's a reaction to having missed you so terribly all those months you were away. It flares up again every time you've been busy with something that doesn't involve me, even when I'm with you like today."

Oliver slipped Lucy's pajama top off her shoulders and eased her panties down. She stepped out of them, helping him remove his T-shirt and shorts in the process. Standing beside the bed, they took a moment to truly see each other. They had been naked together before, but never like this—never with such unguarded intensity.

Oliver drank in the soft curves of her body while Lucy admired the strength and masculinity in his.

"You're beautiful, Luce," he murmured, wrapping his arms around her from behind.

Lucy melted into him, tilting her head to meet his lips. His fingers tangled in her hair as he brushed it aside, pressing slow, lingering kisses to her shoulder and the nape of her neck. When she turned to face him, he teased her with fleeting kisses, his hands exploring every inch of her.

She traced the contours of his shoulders and chest, savoring the solid strength beneath her fingertips. Their mouths met again, deepening the connection between them. A quiet moment passed before she pressed herself fully against him, marveling at how perfectly their bodies aligned.

Oliver lifted her effortlessly and carried her to the bed, where they made slow, sensual love.

***

Afterward, they lay intertwined, wrapped in the afterglow of their intimacy. Oliver pulled the blankets over them, his fingers softly tracing the delicate features of her face. Lucy closed her eyes under his touch as he kissed her lips, her nose, her eyelids.

"I love you, Lucy Lassiter," he whispered.

She smiled, opening her eyes to meet his. "I love you too, Oliver."

***

"What did you want to talk about?" Oliver said when the spell that held them had waned.

"I don't know if we should talk about it now. You've made me happy beyond anything I thought possible. There's not a trace of selfishness in you, not even when we make love."

"But I want you to tell me if something is troubling you, Luce...please."

"I know you do, but what I want to say might sound critical, even if I don't mean it to be."

"There's no reason to hold back. I want us to be open and truthful. I prefer not to second-guess what you need me to do to make you happy. Please tell me what's troubling you."

"What I want to say follows on from our confessions during our last night in Helsinki. You made me happy beyond expectation with your promise to never leave me again. But that promise, combined with what you said about doing everything together from now on, has made me feel uncomfortable as well—as if I've forced you to tend to my every need.

"That feeling hit me this afternoon while we were talking to Ken. I'd also felt it earlier when we were talking to Jacky and Bill. I prefer not to be waited on hand and foot. I want you to be there for me when it matters, and not to the extent that, I think, you're implying. It wouldn't be fair of me to accept you in that role."

Oliver immediately understood her concern.

"I fully understand the reason you would want to bring that up, sweetheart, but please let me look after you in the way I want to. My desire to do that stems from needing to come to terms with my conscience for nearly having caused your death."

"Please don't say that. It makes me sad."

"I realize that. I might have the solution to your concern. Would you be happy to accept the way I want to care for you if that care meant something to both of us? That would prevent me from smothering you with unnecessary attention, which would lead to the feeling you described. I can agree with you about needing space at times."

"It's not the space, as in pushing you away. It's more about being your equal instead of someone you need to pamper. Can you give me an example of both kinds of attentiveness?"

"Sure. The first kind is one that requires us to do things together to achieve the goals we both want to reach but wouldn't be able to achieve on our own. Our visits to Russia fall into that category, for example, and every kiss, cuddle, and embrace, and our lovemaking as well. Doing things for you that you would want to do yourself and, indeed, pampering you if that were to take the form of how you and I would pamper a child are examples of the wrong kind. But I want you to accept manly courteousness like standing up from a table for you when you want to sit down and holding open a door for you."

"Agreed. I'll object nicely each time you do something that

makes me feel small or otherwise too dependent on you."

Lucy nestled closer to him, whispering once more that she loved him. Oliver, however, felt a lingering restraint, bound by the agreement they had made. She had begun to break down his unwavering resolve to protect her at all costs—especially after he had nearly caused her death. But he also understood that she needed to stand as his equal, to count in the same way he did. As sleep gradually overtook him, he accepted her need for balance between them.

Lucy closed her eyes first, and, moments later, so did he.

***

The next morning, Lucy and Oliver allowed themselves the rare luxury of sleeping in. They knew it would be their last peaceful morning together until after their return from Russia.

Meanwhile, Jacky and Bill had already organized breakfast and were waiting for them.

"I should receive the draft of the joint venture agreement today," Bill told Lucy during breakfast. "You should print it out to avoid the prince needing to read it on your tablet."

Lucy turned to Oliver. "I want to go with you to see Ken when he calls."

***

At three that afternoon, one of the CIA director's assistants called Oliver on his cell. A suitable identity had been found, she said, and asked him to come in right away.

"This photo is what our data analysts came up with about an hour ago," Ken Rivera explained. "His name is Edson Perez. We discovered him by cross-referencing endless obituaries with a long list of lawyers. His specialty was acquisitions and joint ventures. He lived a solitary life and was killed during a robbery that went sour five months ago at his home in Reston.

"We scoured the internet to find out more about the killing, but apart from a small item in a local newspaper, there's nothing to be found. The fact he's deceased will be very difficult for the prince and others to discover unless they search the internet intensively. His parents are Spanish. They migrated to the US before he was born and settled in Baltimore."

"But he doesn't even remotely look like Oliver," Lucy commented. "This man must be about thirty-five, seven years or so older than Oliver, and everything about him is different. His hair is dark brown, not blond; he wears glasses; and he has a goatee. He has dark brown eyes, and Oliver has distinctive blue eyes. It's impossible to make Oliver look like that."

"Wait before you pass judgment on our ability to transform someone into someone else, Lucy. Our chief of disguise is a magician. You should go there now, Liam. Have your photo taken after the makeover so we can finalize your passports. One of my assistants will print everything that's available on this man for you to read during the flight."

Oliver led Lucy to the office of the chief of disguise, where she watched as he was transformed into Edson Perez. His hair was trimmed and dyed deep brown, seamlessly blending with his naturally darker eyebrows and eyelashes.

From hundreds of options, a meticulously crafted goatee in the same shade was selected and affixed to his freshly shaved face with silicone glue. Colored contact lenses altered the hue of his eyes, and a pair of plain-lensed glasses completed the disguise.

Standing before the mirror, Oliver compared his reflection to the photo of Edson Perez. The resemblance was striking. He felt confident that no one would suspect he wasn't the man he needed to become.

Once the transformation was complete, Oliver had his photo taken. One of Ken's assistants asked them to wait while his passports were finalized. Before they left, another assistant handed Oliver a folder containing everything he needed to fully assume his new identity.

***

Lucy and Oliver returned to the apartment in time for dinner. They carefully packed everything they would need for Moscow into two suitcases and two overnight bags.

When the car and chauffeur Mitch had arranged arrived to collect them, they exchanged emotional farewells with Jacky and Bill. The moment weighed heavily on them all. Lucy and Oliver were deeply affected, and Oliver, in particular, felt the depth of his bond with Jacky and Bill—strengthened by everything they had been through together.

Bill led Oliver aside while Jacky was talking to Lucy.

"Please prevent harm from coming to Lucy at all costs, Oliver. The loss of a hundred million dollars is a small price to pay to see her return safely."

"How do you view, in comparison, not being the first to produce the Alzheimer's cure, Bill?"

"That would also not compare to losing Lucy, as I'm sure you'd agree."

"I do wholeheartedly. I promise to do everything possible to return Lucy to you safe and sound. Please trust me."

"You'll have noticed during these past weeks that Jacky and I trust you—like a son, Oliver."

"I know. Are you aware that we won't be able to call you while we're in Russia because of the possibility our calls are monitored?"

"I am," Bill replied.

27.

RETURN TO MOSCOW

Mitch touched down at Boston Logan at eight-forty-five that evening. He accompanied Oliver to Terminal V to pick up the hard drive.

To Oliver's surprise, Will Bryce was waiting for them. Will, in turn, was caught off guard by Oliver's disguise, his expression shifting with recognition and intrigue.

"I thought you'd send someone from the IT department," Oliver said.

"Knowing the importance of the hard drive, I wanted to hand it to you personally."

"I owe you one. Thanks a million."

Lucy and Oliver settled in for the nine-hour flight to Sheremetyevo. Once they reached cruising altitude, Annette approached to take their drink orders. At Mitch's request, she refrained from offering them champagne as she normally would.

"I remember you telling me you were on birth control when we were in Palisades Park in LA on New Year's Day. Are you still on birth control? We don't want little Lucies and little Olivers running around just yet, do we?" Oliver teased.

"It sounds as if you'd want them at some stage," she answered.

"Yes, but only if you agree."

"Do you consider marriage a prerequisite to having children?" Lucy continued, smiling.

"Yes...definitely."

"So shouldn't we be talking about marriage first?"

"Are you trying to preempt the plan I have about when and where to ask you to marry me?"

"No, you started this conversation about having children, which prompted me to ask you about the necessity of marriage first."

"We shouldn't be having this conversation until after we've solved all of our problems," Oliver said, becoming serious.

"You're right."

Lucy left her seat to sit on Oliver's lap.

"I love you, Oliver. I want the whole world to know. I've had an urge to shout it out a hundred times. You've made my life so much more interesting and intriguing. Even now, while we're on this dangerous undertaking, I wouldn't want to be elsewhere without you."

"I love you too, Luce. There aren't enough words to say how much."

They kissed, with Lucy carefully maneuvering her lips to avoid the glued-on hair of his disguise.

A little later, Annette transformed their seats into beds, one on either side of the aisle. They took turns using the bathroom, and after sharing a final good-night kiss, they lay down to sleep.

Fifteen minutes later, Oliver noticed that Lucy had drifted off. He rolled onto his back, staring at the ceiling without focusing on anything in particular. Once again, he let the phases of his plan unfold in his mind—something he had done countless times since first committing to this course of action. Yet, every time, he reached the same roadblock—the one problem he still hadn't been able to solve.

***

Annette woke them at 5:30 a.m. Eastern Standard Time—1:30 p.m. Moscow Standard Time—with one hour left in the flight.

After landing, Mitch followed the airport marshaller's instructions, taxiing to the private aviation terminal. Immigration and customs officials boarded the aircraft to check their passports, baggage, and the passenger manifest.

Once cleared, Mitch escorted them into the terminal, where Dimitri was waiting. Oliver briefly explained the reason for his disguise before they set off.

The twenty-mile drive to the Ritz-Carlton took over an hour due to heavy traffic. When they finally arrived, the hotel manager greeted them with the same level of attention as on their previous visit. This time, however, the door connecting their suites wasn't locked.

"What do you want to do about dinner, Luce? Stay in or go out? There's no need to remain unobserved. We're free to do whatever takes your fancy."

"Why not book a table at the O2 restaurant?" she called from the bathroom as she fixed her hair and makeup. "That's where I first kissed you, remember? I had to lean across the table to do it."

"I remember, sweetheart. We need to talk to Dimitri and Sergei about why we're here. We didn't get around to doing that during the drive from the airport. I'll book a table for four."

Oliver made a reservation for 7 p.m. and called Dimitri to invite him and Sergei to join them for dinner.

When Lucy emerged after getting ready, Oliver thought she looked absolutely ravishing. Her hair, curled into soft waves, cascaded freely around her shoulders. She had accentuated her eyes with mascara and eyeshadow, making her light blue gaze even more striking. Dark red lipstick, perfectly matching her skirt, added a bold touch. She completed the look with a white sweater, black pantyhose, and red high heels, striking the perfect balance between elegance and casual sophistication.

It was clear she had dressed with their restaurant destination in mind.

"You'll be the center of attention wherever you go this evening," Oliver said.

"Do you approve?"

"Very much so. Let me change my clothes to match your outfit, so I don't look improper next to you."

Oliver took a few minutes to change into a blue shirt and dark suit. When he returned to Lucy's sitting-dining room, a knock sounded at the door of her suite. Dimitri and Sergei had arrived, so they could all head to the restaurant together.

A hostess greeted them upon arrival, leading them to their table and handing each of them a menu. Shortly afterward, the headwaiter approached, wished them a good evening, and asked for their drink orders.

Oliver glanced at Lucy as she browsed the beverage menu. "Order something without alcohol, Luce," he reminded her gently.

She nodded and chose an alcohol-free Heineken lager. Oliver thought it was a good choice and ordered the same. Dimitri and Sergei, on the other hand, opted for regular Heinekens.

They studied the menu in silence. Once they had made their selections, they placed the menus down, signaling the waiter, who returned to take their orders and collect the menus.

"Okay, let's talk about what we're here for," Oliver said. "As you know, Prince Alexandrovich assumed control of Morgan Pharma when Bill was kidnapped. During the weeks he was in charge, he appropriated a hundred million dollars under false pretenses. But what is worse is that he has allowed RusPharma scientists to again steal the data on the Alzheimer's cure. So, Lucy and I are here to repair the damage."

"How were you planning to do that?" Dimitri asked.

"The plan we have consists of two parts. The first is to lure the prince into discussions about a joint venture in which Morgan Pharma and RusPharma agree to produce the Alzheimer's medication here in Russia. That in itself wouldn't be enough to interest him because he and his friends would already have taken steps to have the medication produced here.

"The enticement lies in the offer to pay up to a quarter of a billion US dollars to update the production facility. He'll want to add that to the amount he's already embezzled. I'm hoping one of the meetings with him will be in his office. I will eliminate him there after I've made him transfer the hundred million he stole back to the account where it came from."

"What do you mean when you use the word 'eliminate'?"

"Use your imagination, Dimitri. He doesn't deserve to live because he made Lucy take lethal drugs daily to kill her when he had no further use for her.

"The second part of the plan is for me to delete all the files that were stolen. Those files will have been downloaded onto the computers at the RusPharma production facility in Zelenograd where you picked me up to drive me to the border with Belarus."

Oliver stopped explaining his plan when the waiter brought them their appetizers. They ate in silence, thinking of what Oliver had told them. He resumed describing his plan after the waiter had cleared away their plates.

"We should discuss some details now," Oliver said, turning to Dimitri. "I'd like you to be close to Miss Lassiter all the time because the prince might want her abducted or hurt if he finds out we're here under false pretenses. Are you carrying your Glock 22?"

"I am."

"Keep it ready to use at all times. The first meeting with the prince is scheduled for tomorrow morning at ten. He's agreed to meet us at a location of our choosing. Lucy has yet to text him. We have two options: either in the lobby here at the hotel, where it's always busy and relatively safe, or in a conference room. I'd prefer a conference room because that's what we would use for a normal business meeting. What do you think?"

"The conference room. He's smart. He would immediately realize we're not at ease with the situation if we had the meeting in the lobby," Lucy explained.

"I agree. You might want to send a text to him now, informing him we've arrived at the Ritz-Carlton and that we'll organize a conference room here for the meeting."

Lucy took her cell phone from her purse and sent the text. She received an answer almost immediately. All it said was "Welcome to Moscow. I will meet you there."

"If after the meeting the prince decides to enter into the agreement, you, Luce, need to say you want to inspect the intended production site on Saturday. During the visit, you should try to rationalize the amount Morgan Pharma has to invest for the upgrade of the facility. For the signing of the agreement and the payment of the first installment, you must get him to agree to a meeting in his office on Monday. We need Sunday to prepare for that meeting. I'll tell you about that later."

Their entrées arrived just as Oliver finished speaking. Though there were other matters he wanted to discuss—especially with Dimitri and Sergei—he decided they could wait until later. The conversation soon drifted away from the topics Oliver had addressed, and after finishing their coffee, they called it a night. Before parting ways, they agreed to meet for breakfast at eight-thirty the next morning.

Back in Lucy's suite, Oliver called reception to arrange a meeting room for the following morning. With the eight-hour time difference in mind, they went to bed at 11 p.m. local time, hoping to adjust quickly.

28.

PRINCE ALEXANDROVICH

Oliver had set the alarm on his smartphone for seven-thirty, realizing if he hadn't, they might not wake up of their own accord because of jet lag. He kissed Lucy when he exited the shower. She was about to fall asleep again after the alarm had also woken her up.

"Come on, Luce, it's time to prepare for what's to come today. How do you feel?"

"A little uneasy about the meeting. The subject to be discussed isn't that different from my normal work. But I'm nervous about it all going horribly wrong."

"Have faith in me, sweetheart. I'm not going to let anyone hurt you."

"I know, but I can't escape the feeling something is going to go wrong, with terrible repercussions. When we said goodbye to my mother, she told me she has this undefined nervousness as well."

"It's logical for you to feel that way because what we're about to do is far out of your comfort zone, and your mom is simply worried about the outcome. We can still call it off if you want to."

"No. I'm game if you are. Besides, as I said yesterday, I

wouldn't want to be anywhere else without you, which would be the case if I backed out of our plans. I think you'd then want to continue?"

"No, as I said before, I wouldn't be able to get the deal done by myself. Only you or Bill could. Now, please, it's time to get ready."

Oliver wore the same dark suit from the evening before, while Lucy opted for a sharp, business-like look—a dark gray blazer and matching pants, paired with a crisp white top. Black high heels completed the ensemble. Oliver handed her the draft of the joint venture agreement that Bill had instructed the legal team to prepare. She placed it inside a small attaché case alongside her tablet, then slung her purse over her shoulder and turned to Oliver.

"I'm ready," she said.

Dimitri and Sergei were already seated at the restaurant, waiting for them before selecting their choices from the buffet. Breakfast passed with little conversation, the air thick with unspoken tension. After a second coffee, they left the restaurant and made their way to the conference room Oliver had arranged with reception the night before.

At five minutes past ten, a knock sounded at the partially open door. A man stepped inside.

He was impeccably dressed in a dark blue suit, a crisp white shirt, and a light blue tie. His short black hair was slicked back, and a neatly groomed pencil mustache added to his distinguished appearance. His features were regular, almost classically handsome—enough to draw the interest of many women. Yet his short, wiry frame gave him an unassuming presence.

His gaze locked onto Lucy, ignoring everyone else in the room.

A wave of hatred and loathing surged through Lucy as memories flooded back, more vivid than ever. Until now, she had been grateful for certain things he had done—things that once seemed kind, even generous. But she saw the truth now. Every gesture had been calculated, every kindness a deception designed to earn her trust. And once he had it, he had intended to kill her.

"Hello, Lucy. I had no idea I would see you alive and well after I visited your apartment the last time before you left."

The prince kissed the back of her hand when Lucy offered it.

"Hello, Alexander. I'm delighted to see you."

"How did you manage that? I didn't think it was possible without assistance of some sort."

"My mother came to visit. She and a friend helped me to leave New York. I was treated for my alcohol addiction, and I started to be myself again after a week. I want to thank you again for taking command of my responsibilities during my illness. My parents are very appreciative of what you did. They admire your initiative in proposing a joint venture to produce medicines in Russia. Your willingness to have those medicines retailed under the Morgan Pharma brand is greatly appreciated. I understand your visit to Moscow is to implement the agreement you reached with the board?"

The prince disregarded the question.

"Who are your colleagues, Lucy?" he asked, looking at Oliver, Dimitri, and Sergei in turn.

"I'm sorry. I should have introduced them immediately when you arrived. This is Edson Perez. He recently joined our legal department. His field of expertise is acquisitions and joint ventures. I thought it wise to have him work with me on the joint venture we proposed."

Oliver hesitated, unwilling to be the first to extend his hand. He had to suppress the instinct to show just how much he despised the man standing before him. Every fiber of his body bristled with hatred, but he kept his expression neutral. When the prince finally offered his hand, Oliver grasped it briefly, noting the limp, clammy feel of his skin. The touch sent a ripple of distaste through him.

"And this is Dimitri, and that's Sergei," Lucy added. "They're here to protect me. As you know, my stepfather and I were kidnapped some time ago. Let's sit down to talk."

Lucy sat down on a chair on one side of the meeting room table, Oliver two chairs away, and the prince on the other side. Dimitri remained standing just inside the door, while Sergei took up a position outside in the corridor. Lucy removed her tablet from her attaché case and switched it on.

"We need to come to terms, Alexander, on the following issues. First, the brand name under which the Alzheimer's medication is to be retailed. Second, I need to be convinced that RusPharma's production facility is capable of producing the medication in the quality and quantity required. The FDA will want to know everything about its production when we import it.

"Third, I need to determine the investment we need to make for you to build and test the production line. That includes agreeing on the total amount and the timeline for the payment of the installments. Finally, we need to determine the production volume and the respective share of that volume for you and us, as well as the sale price per unit. Are you happy to discuss all that now?"

"Certainly," the prince replied, "but we shouldn't be deciding on the brand name. You and I have capable people in our respective organizations to look into that. But we do need to agree on the principle to be adopted. As I explained in my text, our shareholders will be looking for a brand name that reflects the name of our company as the manufacturer. Can you agree to that compromise?"

"I can. I'll have my staff prepare several alternatives and send them to you for your consideration," Lucy replied.

Nothing was said while Lucy took a minute to make a note on her tablet.

"Now, tell me something about your production facility," Lucy continued.

"RusPharma's production facility is in Zelenograd, a little more than an hour's drive from here. It's the fourth largest in Russia, based on turnover. I own a fifteen percent stake in the company."

"I seem to recall that a pharmaceutical company in Zelenograd was destroyed by an explosion. Was that your company?"

"Yes, we sustained two explosions. The perpetrators are still being sought. Those attacks were not aimed at our production facility, by the way, and we've been able to maintain our profitability. Our research into new medicines has been badly affected, however. We presently have little work for our pharmaceutical scientists because we're undecided about whether we need a new laboratory just now."

"I'd like to visit the facility. I need to see if you've been able to develop systems and procedures for formulation optimization, granulation, tablet compression, coating, in-process quarantine, and acceptance testing. While not all of those processes are required for the current joint venture to produce medication no longer protected by patents, they are for the Alzheimer's medication. Would it be possible to visit Zelenograd tomorrow?"

"Yes. What time would suit you?"

"If it takes, say, an hour and a quarter to drive there, we could be there at eleven. Where in Zelenograd do we need to be?"

"The entrance to the facility is on Georgievsky Prospect, about three hundred yards past the exit leading to the polytechnic university, where the road narrows to a single carriageway. It's easy to find."

Lucy took a few minutes to make the necessary notes on her tablet.

"I propose we discuss the amount we need to invest in the production facility during the visit tomorrow. Do you agree?"

"Yes. I'm surprised you have the knowledge to do that."

"I've lived and breathed the pharmaceutical practices we've adopted since my college days. My stepfather wouldn't have allowed me to come here for these negotiations if that wasn't the case.

"We propose that seventy percent of your production volume is for us to sell in the US and thirty percent for you to sell in Russia, in accordance with the ratio of people living in the US to that living in Russia. We need to discuss exports to other countries at a later stage. Finally, we propose to set the retail price independently of each other, and we won't start paying you a base price for what you can deliver to us until after three years, to allow us to earn back the cost of our investment. How does that sound?"

"You've obviously put significant effort into your proposal. It sounds fair and equitable."

"I'll have Edson complete the draft of the joint venture agreement with what we've just agreed. He will hand it to you tomorrow for you to study in detail before we sign it. Is there anything else you want to discuss at this stage?" Lucy asked.

"I don't think so."

"Stay a little longer to have a coffee with us before you leave," Lucy offered when the prince stood up to leave.

"Thanks for the offer, but I can't. I had to rearrange my plans for today to meet with you. That's led to a tight schedule."

The prince kissed Lucy's hand again before leaving.

***

"You did phenomenal, Luce," Oliver said. "You're a natural in a role like that. You keep surprising me."

Lucy was happy to hear him say that. She smiled.

"Was my comment about the explosion credible? I wanted to make him believe I'm unaware of who caused it and why. Knowing I was in a relationship with Oliver Corbyn until six months ago, he would otherwise assume I wasn't upfront about what happened a year ago. He would then have doubts about our intentions."

"It was brilliant. I should have realized you needed to say what you did to avoid him believing we were hiding something from him. So, what do you want to do this afternoon?"

"I'd like to go to the stores to look for a gift for you. I also want to buy something for Dimitri and Sergei. I feel obligated to them for all they've done for us."

"They're bound to appreciate that enormously, but I don't want you to buy me anything."

"Wait until you see what I have in mind."

Lucy and Oliver returned to their suites to change into casual attire before heading out. Once ready, Sergei drove them to Red Square, skillfully weaving through Moscow's traffic before parking the Mercedes near the GUM shopping center.

They chose one of the many restaurants inside for lunch, enjoying the lively atmosphere and elegant surroundings. As they wandered through the mall afterward, it quickly became clear that Lucy was interested in jewelry.

"This is what I want to buy you, Oliver," she said, pointing to a set of diamond-studded promise rings in the Cartier store, "as a token of my love for you. One for you and one for me. I'd like to have something engraved on the inside of each of them."

"I was going to object when I noticed the price, but I won't because I know how much a ring means to you as a symbol. I remember you wanting to give me a friendship ring the day we confessed our feelings for each other."

"Would the date of that day, November eighth, 2021, be the most appropriate to have engraved, or would you prefer 'Lucy and Oliver,' or 'Lucy and Liam,' perhaps?"

"The date would mean more to me than our names or initials, Luce," Oliver replied.

Lucy agreed and requested that the date be engraved inside each of the rings. Her ring fitted perfectly on the ring finger of her left hand, but Oliver's needed to be resized. While they waited, Lucy took the opportunity to buy Rolex watches for Dimitri and Sergei. At first, they hesitated to accept the gift, but Oliver, with a knowing smile, convinced them.

"Take them," he said. "It'll make her happy."

By the time they returned to the hotel, it was late. After a brief discussion about whether to go out or stay in for dinner, Oliver suggested they order room service. He had noticed Lucy's exhaustion—an accumulation of the long hours spent shopping, the lingering jet lag, the tension of the meeting with the prince, and the fact that she was still recovering from her illness.

After dinner, when Oliver proposed they turn in early, Lucy didn't argue. He thanked Dimitri and Sergei for their protection and suggested they get some rest as well.

Later, when Lucy was ready for bed, Oliver kissed her gently and tucked her in.

"Good night," he murmured.

She gave him a tired but contented smile before closing her eyes.

"I'll come to bed a little later, Luce. I'll try not to wake you when I do."

Oliver closed the bedroom door behind him and reclined on the couch in the sitting-dining room. His mind drifted back to the problem he suspected he would soon have to face—the one he couldn't solve. He turned it over again, searching for an answer, but as before, none existed. Eventually, he let out a quiet sigh and accepted the inevitable.

***

The drive to Zelenograd the next morning was uneventful. They left the hotel at nine-forty-five, giving themselves ample time to reach their destination by eleven. As they approached the facility's gate, Oliver immediately noticed an increase in security. A year ago, only a single guard had been stationed there; now, three stood on duty. The guardhouse itself had been enlarged, providing more space—another sign that things had changed.

Sergei spoke to the guard who stepped forward to greet them, informing him they had been invited by Prince Alexandrovich. After a brief exchange, they were directed to park the Mercedes in the visitors' lot alongside another vehicle and to sign in. Oliver entered their names and affiliations in to the visitor log. Once cleared, the guard escorted them toward the main entrance of a large warehouse-style building—one Oliver knew housed their production activities.

Inside, they stepped into a spacious reception area. Through the large window of an adjoining office, an elderly woman observed their arrival. A moment later, she stood and emerged through a corridor that connected to several other offices.

Her name was Elena. Though her English was limited, she welcomed them warmly. She explained that to maintain the facility's sterile environment, they would need to wear protective gear. She handed each of them coveralls, gloves, and shoe and hair covers, then led them to two dressing rooms off the reception area—one for men, the other for women.

Elena accompanied Lucy into the women's dressing room, and once both had donned their protective clothing, they passed through an air lock. On the other side, they emerged into a wide corridor that seemed to stretch the entire length of the building, lined with multiple doors on either side.

Elena led them to the first door on the left. It stood open, revealing a lecture-style room with seating for about thirty people. At the front of the room, Prince Alexandrovich and Dr. Lenkov stood deep in conversation. The moment their visitors entered, they fell silent, turning their attention toward them.

"Welcome, Miss Lassiter," Dr. Lenkov said as he offered his hand for her to shake. "I didn't think I would ever see you again."

"Why would you think that, Dr. Lenkov?"

"I heard you were seriously ill, which required Prince Alexandrovich to take your place on the Morgan Pharma board of directors."

The prince had meanwhile also said hello, kissing Lucy's hand as he had the day before.

"Yes, I was lucky to have recovered my health. We were also lucky that Alexander was able to provide the leadership the company needed when my stepfather and I were indisposed."

She gestured toward Oliver. "I want to introduce you to Edson Perez. He's a lawyer in our legal department. His specialty is joint ventures. And this is Dimitri, and that's Sergei."

"Alexander tells me you're here for a tour of our facility," Lenkov said, totally disregarding the presence of Oliver, Dimitri, and Sergei. "We thought it to be appropriate to provide you with an overview of the facility before we start. So, please take a seat, and I'll start."

Lucy sat in the middle of the front row, Oliver two seats away on her right, and Dimitri and Sergei on either side of them.

"As you probably know, we have always limited ourselves to producing solid dosage forms of medicine, such as powders, granules, pills, tablets, and capsules. We have production line layouts for three products. These may vary over time, depending on our assessment of what medication is most scarce or most urgently needed.

"One of the production lines is currently fitted out for acetaminophen, and the second for furosemide sodium. The third is being prepared for the Alzheimer's tablet."

"May I ask you the questions that come to mind during your presentation, Dr. Lenkov, or should I ask them after you've finished?" Lucy asked.

"Please ask them as they occur to you."

"Is the preparation of the third production line for the Alzheimer's tablet in anticipation of the joint venture I'm discussing with Alexander, for which we will provide the details, or is the preparation the result of believing you can produce the medication yourself without our assistance?"

"The latter. You might remember that Oliver Corbyn joined our staff last year after the conference in Moscow. He helped us to understand the makeup of the molecule the medication is composed of. Further research by our scientists since has led us to believe we're ready to start its production."

Lucy knew the claim about Oliver's assistance was a lie. He hadn't helped them determine the medicine's composition. It was clear that Lenkov and the prince had coordinated their story, deciding in advance what to tell her when she inevitably discovered they had already begun preparations for production. They couldn't admit the truth—that they had accessed the necessary data from the Boston server two weeks ago.

"What's the purpose of the joint venture if you'll be producing the medication anyway?" Lucy asked.

"It's simple, Lucy," the prince interrupted. "We lack the funds to produce the medicine in the quality and quantity required."

"I appreciate you being so open about it."

Lenkov displayed a floor plan of the building on the screen behind him—a slide from a PowerPoint presentation. The captions were in Russian, and Oliver suspected it had been prepared to brief RusPharma shareholders on their plans for producing the Alzheimer's cure.

Lenkov took his time detailing each stage of the production process. He pointed out where base chemicals were received, quarantined, tested, and approved for use. He explained how formulation scientists would combine the precise proportions of each ingredient to create the tablet, leading into the granulation, compression, and coating stages. He also covered in-process quarantine procedures, acceptance testing, packaging, and final shipping logistics.

Emphasizing the facility's strict environmental controls, Lenkov described how each production step would take place in enclosed spaces equipped with air pressure, temperature, humidity, and filtration systems. He then walked them through a series of photographs, showcasing the specialized machinery and tools used at each stage.

The presentation was long—almost excessively so—leaving the distinct impression that Lenkov was determined to convince Lucy of their need for the funding she had offered.

"So, Miss Lassiter, this is our blueprint for what we have in mind. Part of what I showed you already exists, but we need funds to complete it. I propose we now have a simple lunch before we take you on the tour."

Lenkov left the room and returned a little later with a pot of coffee, cups, and napkins, followed by Elena with a selection of sandwiches on a large plate. She poured each of them a coffee, and they ate the sandwiches while standing.

When Lucy noticed the prince was standing off to one side and that a conversation with him would not be heard by Lenkov, she walked to where he stood.

"Am I correct in assuming that the hundred million we

provided you with is being used to upgrade the production line layouts presently dedicated to the production of furosemide and acetaminophen?"

For a brief moment, Lucy thought she saw anxiety flutter across the prince's face.

"That's correct."

"So the funds we are yet to provide are to be used for the third production line, which is to be dedicated to producing the Alzheimer's tablet?"

"Yes."

"Cool. That means we can finalize the joint venture agreement soon after we've established the amount to be invested by us and when that amount, in installments, needs to be transferred."

"I was hoping we would be able to sign the agreement and transfer the first installment directly after the tour."

"I need at least a day to confer with my people back home about our agreement, so I don't think we'll be able to sign the agreement until late on Monday," Lucy replied.

To Oliver, who was watching closely, it was clear that the prince hadn't anticipated the delay in signing the agreement and receiving the first payment—an issue caused by the need to send the contract back to Lucy's legal team for review.

The tour began shortly after Lucy's brief but pointed exchange with the prince.

"Stay close to me, Edson, and write down my assessment of what we'll invest," she said loudly enough for everyone to hear.

She handed her attaché case to Oliver, who retrieved a small notebook and pencil, ready to record her evaluations.

The tour focused primarily on the third production line, with Lucy methodically assessing each component and calling out the estimated cost of necessary upgrades. The process stretched to nearly two hours, as each assessment prompted discussions on the scope of the improvements. Lenkov protested several times, arguing that some of her proposed upgrades were excessive. But Lucy stood firm, insisting that every enhancement was essential to ensure the medication met the highest standards—particularly when its details would be submitted to the FDA.

After the tour, they returned to the lecture room. Oliver handed Lucy the cost assessment she had requested, the numbers now laid out in black and white.

"Am I correct in assuming that each of the production lines is controlled by a dedicated computer?" Lucy asked Lenkov.

"That's correct," he replied.

"But there was no trace anywhere of an office for your IT specialists."

"Due to the sensitive nature of the data we keep there, those offices are closed to visitors. But I'll take you there before you leave."

"So, the amount we'd need to invest to bring the facility up to our standards, in round numbers, is two hundred and twenty-five million dollars," Lucy said, looking at what Oliver had written down. "I propose we transfer that amount in three equal installments, the first of which is due directly after we sign the agreement. I'm assuming it is you, Alexander, we'll be entering into a contract with on behalf of RusPharma."

Lenkov looked worried when Lucy said this.

"Give Alexander a copy of your draft of the agreement, Edson, and talk him through its contents and the information he needs to provide, such as his bank account details, to effect payment."

Oliver followed Lucy's instructions, retrieving the agreement from her attaché case, which he was still carrying. Carefully, he added the details of Morgan Pharma's planned investment before handing the document to the prince.

"Shall we now decide where and when to sign the agreement, Alexander?" Lucy asked.

"I don't suppose you want to travel to Zelenograd again, so we should do that at my office."

"Sure, but you must first send me your consensus with the details of the agreement or submit changes to it, which Edson here needs to review before sending it to our legal department—and my stepfather because of the amount of money involved. Could you please do that tomorrow, so I can send it in time to receive their reply before the signing of the agreement late on Monday? And you need to tell me where your office is."

With acceptance of Lucy's proposal, it was clear to everyone that their business had concluded. They made their way back through the air lock, removing their coveralls, gloves, and shoe and hair covers in the dressing rooms.

Once back in the reception area, Lenkov led Lucy and Oliver through the adjoining offices, offering a brief tour of the administrative and IT spaces.

"We don't employ IT specialists," Lenkov said. "I usually handle software issues myself. We've simplified matters by using a separate server per production line. The servers are in separate offices next to my office, which is next to Elena's. Because these offices are outside the dressing rooms and air lock, we are not required to wear protective clothing to work there."

Lucy thanked both Lenkov and the prince for the presentation and tour, then extended her hand in a polite gesture. Lenkov shook it, but the prince, keeping with his habit, lifted it to his lips in a formal kiss.

Oliver followed suit, offering his hand to both men. They shook it without meeting his gaze, their disinterest evident.

Elena bid them farewell, watching as they made their way to the guardhouse. There, Oliver signed them out of the visitor log before they stepped outside.

***

"I believe Lenkov isn't aware of the hundred million we paid to upgrade production line layouts for medicines no longer covered by patents," Lucy said after they had turned onto the M10. "When I asked Alexander to confirm that the money would be used for the upgrade, he briefly looked worried, but when he saw Lenkov standing some distance away, he seemed to relax when he confirmed that to be the case."

"And I think Lenkov is worried that the two hundred and twenty-five million will end up in the pockets of the prince," Oliver added. "I noticed him frowning when you proposed the prince to be the party, on behalf of RusPharma, to sign the agreement and receive the funds."

Dimitri shook his head. "I'm ashamed to be a Russian national, Miss Lassiter, when I realize what they're up to."

"Isn't it time for you and Sergei to call me Lucy, Dimitri?"

"Alex won't allow it, Miss Lassiter."

"The next time you see him, tell him I told you to call me Lucy."

"Okay, Miss Lassiter... Lucy."

Throughout the day, Oliver had watched Lucy closely, once again marveling at how effortlessly she played her role. But now, as she leaned into him in the back seat of the car, he could see the exhaustion in her eyes—more so than the day before.

They arrived back at the hotel at six in the evening. Sensing her fatigue, Oliver suggested they have dinner at the Moskovsky restaurant, just a short walk from the hotel, before heading up to their rooms. He figured the restaurant wouldn't be busy yet, ensuring quick service. More than anything, he was intent on getting Lucy to bed as soon as possible.

***

Sunday passed in quiet relaxation. It was late by the time Lucy and Oliver decided to get up, shower, and dress.

Oliver spent extra time in the bathroom removing his beard, washing his face, shaving, and then carefully reapplying it. While Lucy showered and dressed, he ordered breakfast, ensuring everything would be ready when she emerged.

Before sitting down to eat, Oliver called Dimitri, letting him know they had no concrete plans for the day and that he, too, should take the opportunity to rest.

Oliver observed Lucy closely during breakfast. She seemed more refreshed, the lethargy from the previous evening gone.

Still, he wanted to be sure. He set his cup down and met her gaze.

"How are you holding up?" he asked. "You were exhausted yesterday when we returned from Zelenograd. I initially thought it was because of the stress of dealing with the prince and Lenkov, jet lag, and perhaps not having fully recovered from your illness, but I now think it's something else."

"I'd hoped you wouldn't notice. I haven't been able to sleep much these last three nights. I wake up after an hour or so and lie awake for the greater part of the night."

"Is it something you want to tell me about?"

"I resolved not to, but on second thought, I believe I should. We promised each other to not keep secrets."

"I remember, so tell me, please."

"I keep thinking about how you plan to deal with the prince and then with RusPharma because I can't see you doing that without incurring grave risks. I've considered every possible scenario, but in each case, I see you being hurt, and every so often all of us. I'd feel much better if we stopped what we're doing and accepted the loss of the hundred million and the leading role the Russians want in producing the Alzheimer's cure."

"In that case, we should stop what we're doing and fly

home, Luce. I don't want you to have nightmares about what we're doing."

"No, we need to finish this. The consequences if we didn't would simply be too great. But have you thought how exactly?"

"I have, sweetheart, in great detail. Have faith in me, please. I've been trained to think of solutions for problems like those we're facing. As soon as the prince sends you a text stating he's prepared to sign the agreement and confirms the meeting at his office, we need Dimitri and Sergei to drive us to his office after dark to reconnoiter the area. Then I'll explain what we need to do when we visit him. I'll explain my plan for dealing with RusPharma later. Can you live with that for now?"

"Okay. I apologize for not having discussed my concerns with you before."

"Apology accepted. What if I hung the 'Do Not Disturb' sign on the door so you can get some extra sleep? I wish I'd known about your sleeping problem before. I'd have held you close until you fell asleep."

"I'd like that."

Oliver made sure they wouldn't be disturbed, allowing Lucy to sleep for as long as she needed. They both undressed and slipped beneath the blankets, where he wrapped his arms around her, holding her close while ensuring she was as comfortable as possible. Within minutes, she drifted into sleep.

***

The text they had been waiting for arrived late that afternoon.

Lucy was still in bed but awake, nestled under the covers. As the notification sounded, she reached for her phone, read the message, and then reread it aloud.

'Dear Lucy, I am happy with the agreement you prepared for our joint venture. I understand your preference for signing the agreement and the payment of the first installment is late tomorrow afternoon. You said you needed time to consult your legal department if we introduced changes to the agreement, but apart from not deciding on the brand name now, the agreement stands as it was given to me. I've attached it with my additions for you to send to your head office if you think it's necessary. My office is on the second floor of the Voentorg building on Vozdvizhenka Street. I'll be there from four to seven p.m.'

"I need to visit that location," Oliver said, "to determine its layout."

"I'll come with you. Give me fifteen minutes to dress."

While waiting, Oliver called Dimitri and outlined his plan. Twenty minutes later, they met in the hotel lobby. Without wasting time, they set off, the drive to the address the prince had given them taking only a few minutes.

"The first thing we need to check is whether we can access the building by the side entrance on Bolshoy Kislovsky Lane. I believe we can, according to what I can find on the internet."

They had no difficulty finding the side entrance. Sergei parked the car nearby.

Oliver squeezed Lucy's hand. "Do you mind staying in the car with Sergei while Dimitri and I look around? If we were to do that as a group, people would remember us, especially when they were to notice how beautiful you are."

"I can't complain after a comment like that."

"Lock the doors, Sergei, after we leave."

Dimitri and Oliver found the side doors locked. The nearby entrance to what appeared to be an underground parking garage was also secured. Another door, marked with an electricity hazard sign, was equally inaccessible. With no alternative, they had to enter through the main entrance on Vozdvizhenka Street.

Oliver pushed open one of the French doors, stepping into a lavishly furnished reception area. The space featured an ATM, restrooms, an elevator, and a central staircase.

Additional doors led to a small restaurant, a childcare facility, and a dry-cleaning service.

A man in a security company uniform, seated at a desk overlooking the sidewalk, greeted them as they entered.

"*Privyet*," Oliver said. "We were informed that you currently have office space for rent. Would it be possible for you to show us where?"

"I'm sorry, but that's not my job. You need to contact the Offices Dot Co. company if you want to book a tour to see what is available."

"Do you know where the available office space is?"

"On the second and third floors. The office on the second floor is small. The office on the third floor is considerably larger. I'm not aware of the particulars," the security guard explained.

"Will you allow us to take a look at where those offices are located? No one needs to know," Oliver said, extending a hand holding a five-thousand-ruble bill.

The guard accepted the money without hesitation and waved them on.

Oliver and Dimitri ascended the stairs to the second floor, stepping into a corridor that looked more like the corridor of a five-star hotel than an office building. Lined with polished wood paneling and plush carpeting, it led to a series of office doors.

It didn't take long to find the one marked with the RusPharma name and logo.

The building was eerily quiet—it was nearly six o'clock.

"We need to find out how to reach the side entrance from here," Oliver said.

They made their way to the end of the corridor, expecting to find a staircase leading down to the side entrance. A door marked "Fire Escape" stood before them.

Pushing it open, they discovered a metal spiral staircase

stretching the full height of the building, from the underground parking level to the fifth floor. Each floor had a small landing.

Descending to the first-floor landing, they located the side entrance. Oliver turned the handle, and the door swung open—immediately triggering an alarm.

The sharp, piercing sound filled the stairwell. Oliver quickly shut the door, and the alarm cut off as abruptly as it had begun. But in that brief moment, he had recognized the door—it was the same one marked with an electricity hazard sign near where Sergei had parked the car.

Frowning, Oliver stepped closer and examined the wiring of the siren attached to the door.

"When we pass through this door tomorrow, Dimitri, you or Sergei need to pull the electrical lead from the alarm before opening the door."

When they returned to reception, the guard was nowhere to be seen. Oliver looked at his watch.

"The guard's shift must have ended at six," he said.

***

"The details of what we need to do tomorrow are now clear," Oliver told them on seating himself in the back seat next to Lucy. "We need to arrive here after the security guard has left at six. That means that you, Luce, have to send a text to the prince tomorrow at around four in the afternoon to let him know we're running late and that we'll be there at six.

"You need to park the car in the same spot we just did, Sergei. All four of us will then walk to the front entrance. On entering the reception area, we'll walk upstairs to the second floor. Lucy and I will knock on the door of the RusPharma office and enter. You, Dimitri, need to remain outside in the corridor while Sergei takes up a position at the end of the corridor at the door marked 'Fire Escape.' When you meet someone, make sure to turn your head away so he or she doesn't know what you look like when questioned about the disappearance of the prince later.

"After the prince greets you, Luce, you need to propose that both of you sign the agreement. When that's done, congratulate him on the signing as you normally would. You should then say you want to transfer the first installment and suggest he logs in to his bank account to check that the transfer has been received. You need to pretend you're making the transfer, for which you must sit opposite him so he can't see the screen of your tablet. You should then say you want to go to the restroom. In reality, you need to join Sergei and wait for me.

"I'll force the prince to return the hundred million he stole and then eliminate him. When I want to leave with him slung over my shoulder, I'll open the door a fraction for you, Dimitri, to open it all the way when there's no one to be seen. All four of us will then quickly proceed down the fire escape to the first-floor landing and open the door with the exit sign on it after Sergei has pulled the electrical lead from the siren.

"You, Sergei, should check for the presence of people, keeping the door ajar while doing so. When there's no one to be seen, you need to open the door and open the trunk of the car. I'll deposit the body in the trunk. We'll then drive to a secluded spot to bury the body, for which we'll need a spade. I'll leave the details of that part of the operation to you, Dimitri."

No one in the car commented on what Oliver had explained.

"I'm somewhat alarmed by your matter-of-fact tone when you talk about killing the prince," Lucy said. "I think it's also alarmed Dimitri and Sergei."

"I understand, but there's no alternative. The prince was engaged in a sinister plot to murder you. You wouldn't be alive if your mom, Mitch, and I hadn't taken you from your apartment when we did. The doctor who examined you found you'd been given a lethal drug, presumably every day for weeks."

"You're right, Oliver. It's just the matter-of-fact tone you used to tell us about killing the prince that unnerved us."

Oliver considered telling them that he had vowed to kill the prince at the first opportunity, but he knew this was a conversation best left alone. Instead, he let the subject drop. Nothing more was said about their plans for the following day.

They returned to the hotel, where Oliver realized that he and Lucy had skipped lunch. When he asked what everyone wanted to do for dinner, Lucy suggested making reservations at the rooftop seafood restaurant. Dimitri and Sergei agreed, and Oliver arranged a table for four through reception.

Conversation flowed easily over dinner, covering a range of topics. They enjoyed both the food and the company. No one mentioned Oliver's plan for the next day.

**

Oliver chose not to schedule anything for the following morning. He suspected Lucy wouldn't sleep well that night, and he wanted to give her as much rest as possible.

His intuition proved right. When they finally went to bed, Lucy struggled to fall asleep.

Sensing her unrest, Oliver stayed awake with her, refusing to close his eyes until she did. He stroked her hair and gently traced his fingers along her face. When he felt the dampness of tears, he kissed them away, silently offering comfort.

"I'm so sorry, Luce, for having to take you through all this," he whispered.

Lucy didn't respond—she simply let him hold her. It wasn't until well past two in the morning that she finally drifted into a fitful sleep. Oliver, having fought to stay awake, slipped into unconsciousness beside her.

***

When he woke at eight, Lucy was still asleep. Moving carefully, he rose, hung the "Do Not Disturb" sign on the doors of both their suites, and returned to bed.

He lay beside her, watching her, a deep wave of compassion tightening in his chest. She had endured so much—because of him. And the worst was still ahead.

As if sensing the weight of his thoughts, Lucy stirred. Her lashes fluttered, and when she opened her eyes, she found him watching her. A soft smile touched her lips.

Without a word, she reached for him, slipping an arm around his neck and pulling him close. Her lips met his in a kiss—gentle, reassuring, and filled with quiet understanding.

"It's early, sweetheart," he whispered. "We should sleep some more."

***

By lunchtime, they finally decided to shower and get dressed.

As Oliver buttoned his shirt, he called Dimitri, inviting him and Sergei to join them for lunch at a nearby restaurant.

When they met, Dimitri wasted no time in addressing the previous day's conversation. Apologizing, he admitted he hadn't given Oliver his agreement with the plan for what needed to be done.

"There's nothing to apologize for, Dimitri. My unemotional tone is the result of having spent a full week thinking and planning what we need to do. The emotion I might have felt about eliminating the prince at the beginning of the week is now nonexistent. All I feel is pure determination to do what is necessary."

***

The afternoon dragged on, each passing minute heightening their apprehension.

At four o'clock, Oliver turned to Lucy. "You should now send the prince a message. Tell him we're running late and that we should be at his office around six."

She nodded and typed out the text.

By five, Lucy and Oliver decided to dress formally—if only to send the prince a clear message that they regarded the signing of the agreement as significant.

At six, they left the hotel. As before, Sergei parked near the side door. The four of them walked toward the front entrance.

Oliver suggested they first walk past the entrance to ensure no one was at reception. Finding it empty, they retraced their steps. Just as Oliver reached out to push open one of the glass doors, a sudden wave of disillusionment washed over him.

The doors were locked.

"I'm sorry, everyone. I forgot that when the guard leaves, he locks these doors so people can't enter from outside. Since we were able to leave through these doors after the guard left yesterday, I assumed they wouldn't now be locked. We need to wait until someone leaves the building without showing that person our faces. Sergei, why don't you light up one of your cigarettes so it looks like we're having a smoke before we leave to go our separate ways?"

Sergei followed Oliver's suggestion. They didn't have to wait long.

Two men stepped out of the elevator into reception, their

conversation so engrossing that they paid no attention to the four of them.

Oliver acted quickly. He caught the door just before it shut, slipping inside and allowing it to close and lock behind them.

They moved swiftly up the stairs to the next floor. At the end of the corridor, Sergei took up position, standing watch.

Oliver approached the RusPharma office and knocked before opening the door, stepping aside to let Lucy enter first.

The door led into a small foyer, which opened into the main office. Like the rest of the building, the furnishings were extravagant—an opulent display of power and wealth.

"I'm terribly sorry, Alexander, for being late," Lucy said. "I had to take care of some other business before coming here. That took longer than I anticipated. I'm glad you're happy with the agreement."

The prince stood, took Lucy's hand, and pressed a customary kiss to it before settling back behind his desk.

Lucy took the only other available chair in front of the desk, while Oliver remained standing.

When the prince handed Lucy the original paper version of the agreement—now updated with his bank account details, the address of the RusPharma office, and other administrative information—she glanced at it briefly before passing it to Oliver for review.

"The agreement is now indeed complete, Miss Lassiter," Oliver said after flicking through the pages and returning it to her.

"Can I ask you to make two copies so you and I each have one, Alexander? Edson is to hand the original to our legal department when we return."

The prince complied with Lucy's request. Together, they initialed each page and signed the last page of all three copies, adding the date and Moscow as the place of signing.

With the formalities complete, Lucy retrieved her tablet

from her attaché case and switched it on.

"I'll now transfer the first installment to your bank account as specified in the agreement. I need your Wi-Fi password for that. It might take a few minutes because of the codes I need to input to make a transfer as large as seventy-five million dollars. May I suggest you access your bank account when I've finished, to ensure the amount has been transferred?"

Oliver caught the fleeting smile that crossed the prince's face. In that instant, he knew—the prince had taken the bait—hook, line, and sinker.

Lucy went through the motions of making the transfer, her every move calculated. She waited just long enough for it to seem plausible that seventy-five million dollars had been transferred into his account. Then, without hesitation, she switched off her tablet and returned it to her attaché case, along with two of the signed agreements.

"It's done, Alexander. Let me congratulate you on what we've achieved."

Lucy stood and extended her hand to the prince just as he finished logging into his account. This time, he shook her hand—his eyes glued to the monitor.

"I need to go to the restroom," Lucy announced. "I'll return to check the transfer with you before I leave."

She picked up her purse and attaché case and walked out without a backward glance.

***

Oliver settled into the chair Lucy had just vacated, his gaze fixed on the prince, who remained absorbed in the computer screen.

A wry smile crossed Oliver's face.

"Did you really think you could get away with what you're doing?" Oliver asked in a soft voice, relishing the moment he had so often thought about.

"What do you mean?" the prince answered, now looking at him with a concerned expression on his face.

"Did you really think you could get away with the attempted murder of Lucy, the theft of one hundred million dollars, and the theft of vital information for the production of the Alzheimer's cure?"

"I don't know what you're talking about," the prince replied, fear now showing on his face. "I want you to call Miss Lassiter back here. She'll dismiss you from her staff because of what you're saying."

"She's fully aware of what I'm doing. She feels no remorse for your plight."

The prince pulled open a desk drawer. Oliver had anticipated the move.

Before the prince could reach inside, Oliver sprang to his feet, seizing his wrist in a firm grip, his eyes never leaving the man's face as he retrieved the gun from the drawer and placed it on his side of the desk—out of the prince's reach.

"I'm not who you think I am," Oliver continued. "You will have heard of me. I destroyed the RusPharma laboratories in Zelenograd and Voskhod and rescued Bill Lassiter, killing all three of his captors. I am now your judge, jury, and executioner. Have you anything to say in your defense?"

The prince was speechless, unable to muster a single word in his defense.

Oliver knew he had no time to waste—Lucy, Dimitri, and Sergei were still in the corridor, and their presence couldn't be risked.

Without hesitation, he moved around the desk, seized the prince by the neck, and yanked him from his chair.

"Let me go!" the prince screamed.

"The worst of your crimes is your attempt to murder Lucy by giving her a lethal drug, day in and day out. If you'd been allowed to continue with what you were doing, she wouldn't be alive today. When I found out what you'd done, I vowed to kill you. But before I do, you will transfer the hundred million to the bank account it came from."

"I won't!" the prince yelled.

"Make that transfer!"

Having noticed before the prince was right-handed, Oliver broke the prince's left arm. The pain made him yell at the top of his voice.

"Make that transfer!" Oliver said decidedly.

"I won't!" the prince screamed.

Oliver knew he needed to apply more force to make the prince comply. Without hesitation, he drove the flat of his right foot into the prince's kneecap. A sickening crack echoed through the office as the joint gave way, the leg twisting at an unnatural angle.

The prince collapsed in agony, his screams piercing the room. Oliver hauled him back into the chair.

"Now make the transfer!"

The prince sobbed, whimpered, and muttered incoherently, but his hands trembled toward the keyboard. Oliver kept a sharp eye on him, watching every keystroke. When the prince entered the account details, Oliver double-checked them, matching them against the information Lucy had shown him.

The moment the screen confirmed that a $100 million withdrawal had been made, Oliver acted.

He clamped a firm hand over the prince's mouth and nose. The man thrashed weakly, his already broken body too spent to fight back. Within three minutes, he was still.

Oliver shut down the computer and emptied the prince's pockets. The desk was bare except for a key and the gun. He wiped the firearm clean of prints before returning it to the drawer. Pocketing the key—likely to the office door—he also retrieved the prince's copy of the agreement, powered down his cell phone, and gathered everything into a shopping bag he found in the corner.

With methodical precision, he slung the lifeless body over his right shoulder, switched off the lights, and cracked open the door.

Moving swiftly, he wiped down everything he had touched.

"We haven't seen anyone, Oliver," Dimitri said.

Oliver entered the corridor. Dimitri closed the door and wiped the door handle clean. Oliver locked it with the key he was holding in his left hand. They walked briskly to the end of the corridor, where Lucy and Sergei opened the door to the fire escape and preceded them down the stairs to the first-floor landing. Sergei pulled the electrical lead from the alarm and opened the door far enough to check if anyone was nearby or watching.

They needed to wait a minute before Sergei opened the door for them to exit. The four of them hurried to the Mercedes, where Oliver dropped the body into the trunk. Dimitri had meanwhile allowed the side door to lock behind them.

"The rest of the operation is yours, Dimitri. These are the contents of the prince's pockets, his cell phone, and the key to his office—you should also bury those. I want to sit next to Lucy and not do anything for a while."

Lucy turned to Oliver when he spoke. In the dim light of the back seat, she thought she caught a flicker of emotion on his face—brief, fleeting, but unmistakable.

Without a word, she slipped an arm around him. He hesitated for only a moment before reciprocating.

Oliver barely registered where Sergei was taking them. The drive stretched for thirty minutes, the last five spent bumping along a sandy, uneven road.

When they finally stopped, Dimitri and Sergei stepped out without a word. They moved to the trunk, heaved out the body, and disappeared into the trees. The moon cast long, shifting shadows as they carried their burden deeper into the dense foliage.

Twenty minutes later, they returned.

No one asked any questions. There was nothing left to say.

29.

THE SECOND HURDLE

The car ride back to the Ritz-Carlton was steeped in silence, each of them lost in their thoughts. The weight of what had transpired pressed heavily upon them. Though they had succeeded, that victory was overshadowed by the grim reality of their actions—their role in the prince's demise and disposal.

As they waited for the elevator in the hotel lobby, Oliver broke the silence. "Let's each make our own plans for dinner," he suggested. "We'll meet for breakfast at nine."

Lucy and Oliver opted for room service, their appetite subdued at first. But the food was good, and the tension began to lift. Slowly, their thoughts shifted from the unsettling past to the milestone they had crossed. By the time their plates were cleared, the weight of their success had begun to take precedence over the shadows that had accompanied them.

"Where do we go from here, Oliver?" Lucy asked as they were preparing for bed later.

"We need to have a meeting with Mitch, Dave, Dimitri, and Sergei after breakfast, either here or at the hotel where Mitch and Dave are staying."

"Why? What are your plans?"

"We have a difficult decision to make tomorrow, Luce, and

I want the six of us to make it together after considering the options. Would you mind if we were not to discuss it now?"

"That frightens me. What decision?"

Oliver realized there was no alternative but to tell her what he had been worried about for days, particularly since visiting the production facility on Saturday.

"Okay, sweetheart, please be patient and hear me out. As you know, I need to gain access to the production facility in Zelenograd to download the files on the hard drive Will Bryce gave me. I'm no longer confident about the outcome of that task. The security measures, compared to when I was there last year, have been upgraded considerably.

"I can't ask you, Dimitri, and Sergei to wait for me in the car near the site somewhere while I break in. If I'm caught, they'll organize a search for accomplices. They'd discover the car, and all of us would be arrested. I made a solemn promise to Bill before we left that I would return you safe and sound, whatever happened. So, I want Mitch to fly you home at around the same time I plan to break in."

"No, Oliver, no! If you're captured, I want to be with you to face whatever comes our way."

"That's not possible, Luce. If we're both caught, the FSB will send us to different prisons."

"I was afraid something like this would happen during the nights I couldn't sleep. You promised never to leave me again, and I tried to convince myself that if we failed in what we needed to do, you and I would at least be together to face whatever awaits us."

"I know, and I apologize for now needing to insist that Mitch fly you home tomorrow evening."

"How are you going to leave Russia if you're successful in destroying RusPharma's capability to produce the Alzheimer's cure after Mitch has left?"

"That's something we need to discuss tomorrow, but I was

thinking of asking Dimitri and Sergei to wait somewhere close to the production facility after having driven you to the airport. I'll ask them to drive me to Helsinki via Saint Petersburg and catch a flight from there."

"If it's safe for Dimitri and Sergei to return to Zelenograd to wait for you, why can't I be in the car with them?"

"Because that's not without risk. Even your presence at the airport, if I'm caught before Mitch can take off, is too much of a risk. Our presence in Moscow since last Thursday afternoon will have been noticed by the FSB. If they capture me at the production site, they'll automatically be looking for you, so I was thinking of dropping my Edson Perez identity tomorrow evening to go back to being Oliver Corbyn. You and Oliver Corbyn haven't been seen together for more than a year."

Oliver felt a sense of relief seeing that Lucy was gradually coming to terms with his decision. Yet he could tell she was deeply unsettled by his plans to have Mitch fly her home. As they slipped under the blankets, he pulled her close, holding her tightly. She buried her face against his chest and wept.

***

The next morning, before breakfast, Oliver brought up the need for a meeting with Mitch and Dave. Using the hotel phone, he called Mitch and emphasized the importance of finding a discreet location. Mitch suggested his hotel room, explaining that the Radisson Blu at Sheremetyevo Airport primarily catered to flight crews—making it unlikely to draw FSB attention. Oliver agreed, and they set the meeting for eleven that morning.

After breakfast, Sergei and Dimitri drove Oliver and Lucy to the Radisson Blu. Upon their arrival, Mitch arranged for coffee as they settled in for the discussion.

"The first thing I want to say is for the benefit of Mitch

and Dave," Oliver began. "We successfully retrieved the hundred million dollars from the prince yesterday. You also need to know that he's been punished for his attempt to murder Lucy. I prefer not to say more than that. The less you know about what happened yesterday, the better."

"That's great news, Oliver," Mitch said. "I take what you said to mean the prince is no longer among the living?"

"That's correct, Mitch. I now want to explain what we need to do to stop RusPharma from producing the Alzheimer's cure. I'm planning to break into the production facility at midnight tonight. What you need to know is that security measures there have been upgraded since a year ago. The prince arranged a tour of the site for us last Saturday. We found there are now three guards on duty instead of one, and the building is now equipped with surveillance cameras.

"If I'm caught breaking in or deleting files from their computers, Lucy, Dimitri, and Sergei will run the risk of also being captured if they're sitting in the car waiting for me outside on the road somewhere. I therefore believe Lucy needs to be flown home before I break in. We talked about her flying home last night. She finds it difficult to accept. She wants to face what I might be in for with me. Knowing the FSB as well as I do, I'm certain they'll separate us on capture and treat us differently. They'll lock us up in different prisons, for starters.

"I hate to say this again, Luce, but I insist Mitch flies you home this evening at eleven. I promise never again to insist on something involving you. Your role in what we've achieved up to now was indispensable. We couldn't have achieved what we have thus far without you. But the second hurdle we need to clear is something I must do alone, so don't think you're letting me down by going home early."

All eyes were on Lucy when Oliver paused to wait for questions or comments. They knew how much Lucy and Oliver loved each other. Lucy struggled to hold back her tears.

"I agree with Oliver, Lucy," Mitch added. "What you also need to consider is that if Oliver is caught, his chance of escaping from wherever they lock him up while awaiting the farce they refer to as a trial will be very much greater than if he has to also find and rescue you. I've gotten to know Oliver well during this last year, and I have faith in his ability to turn all this into a happy ending."

Mitch had greatly overstated Oliver's ability to ensure a happy ending, but Oliver chose not to comment. He knew saying anything would only unsettle Lucy. She held Mitch in high regard, and his words carried weight—more than Oliver was willing to risk undermining.

"I know, Mitch," Lucy said. "I'd already aligned myself with Oliver's logic last night to let you take me away from here, but I can't come to grips with the possibility of him getting caught and its consequences. I've spent many a sleepless night thinking about what could happen."

"I know, Luce. Please have faith I can do this."

"I have, Oliver."

"Shall I explain what else we need to do today?"

Lucy nodded.

"We need to pack and check out of our hotel after our evening meal," Oliver continued. "Sergei and Dimitri then need to drive us to the airport for an arrival at around ten-forty-five. You, Mitch, should then take responsibility for Lucy. The drive will take about forty-five minutes, so we should leave the hotel at ten.

"Sergei then needs to drive Dimitri and me to Zelenograd. That will take about thirty minutes. You, Sergei, need to park the car some distance from the site so it won't be immediately found when the area is closed off in search of those responsible. A possible location is the parking lot opposite the entrance to the university. You and I, Dimitri, will walk from there to the entrance of the RusPharma plant, which is about three hundred yards past the parking lot, hugging the trees and shrubs on the right-hand side of the road. Please wear black clothing to make it difficult for people to see you.

"I'll cross the road from there and climb over the fence at a location where I believe the cameras won't spot me. I'll discard my present identity and enter as Oliver Corbyn to avoid drawing attention to Lucy or to Morgan Pharma if I'm caught. The Russians haven't seen Lucy and Oliver Corbyn together since the Alzheimer's conference a year ago.

"At the first sign of trouble, such as a scramble by the guards to run to the production building, you need to run to where Sergei parked the car and return to Saint Petersburg. If nothing like that happens, stay and wait for me. If all goes according to plan, you and Sergei have to drive me to Helsinki. We'll cross the border where we did before when we freed Bill from his captors."

"What if I fly Lucy to Helsinki and wait for you there?" Mitch suggested.

"Yes, Oliver, I'd like that," Lucy replied while Oliver was still considering the question.

"You'd have to wait at least a day because it's a long drive, right, Dimitri?"

"About fifteen hours if we only stop for gas and meals."

"I could call Alex on our return from Zelenograd to inform him whether Oliver is with us or not. He would then call you, Mitch," Dimitri proposed.

Lucy nodded, her spirits lifted by the new plan. Oliver knew exactly why—just the thought of seeing him as soon as the next day had brightened her mood. He felt reassured by Mitch's proposal and the effect it had on her, but deep down, he knew it wouldn't change the one thing he dreaded.

This mission was different. Unlike every assignment before, he hadn't had the luxury of meticulous preparation. His past successes had depended on carefully crafted plans, built on deep infiltration—knowing his targets inside and out before striking. This time, he was walking in nearly blind. Apart from what he had glimpsed during Saturday's tour, he had little intelligence on the facility's security systems. He didn't even know if the site was guarded around the clock or how many men would be on duty when he attempted to break in.

Oliver estimated that his chances of success were no better than fifty percent. The risk of being caught had never been as high. That alone didn't extremely trouble him—he had always accepted the danger of his work. But Lucy? If he were captured, she would be inconsolable. Every possible strategy had led to the same dead end, except for one—giving up the fight for the Alzheimer's cure. And that was something he now didn't want to do.

"Any questions or anything to add, anyone?" Oliver asked, wanting to end the discussion.

There was nothing left to say. A heavy silence settled over them.

***

After lunch in Mitch's room, Sergei drove Dimitri, Lucy, and Oliver back to the hotel. Without discussion, they each retreated to their respective rooms and suites.

To pass the time, Lucy began packing. When Oliver went to the bathroom to wash the dye from his hair, she followed, wordlessly joining him.

"I apologize again for causing this whole thing to end in this way, Luce," he said as Lucy washed his hair. "I had a clear idea of what we needed to do before leaving my apartment. I believed that dealing with the prince was going to be the most difficult, not realizing that security at the RusPharma site had been upgraded to the extent it has."

There was nothing left to say. Oliver felt a quiet relief—

Lucy had not only accepted his plan but had come to believe it was their only choice.

The somber mood that had settled over them after their meeting with Mitch and Dave gradually began to lift as the afternoon wore on. With no further need for the Edson Perez disguise, Oliver discarded it, then changed into dark clothing, preparing for the night ahead. He placed his belongings into his suitcase and the backpack for Lucy to take with her when she left. The only things he kept were the essentials—securing Will Bryce's hard drive and a box of matches to his stomach and pocketing the Russian cash to enable him to make his way to the Morgan Pharma office in Saint Petersburg in the event Dimitri couldn't wait for him.

Lucy sat in silence, watching as he readied himself, the weight of the moment hanging heavily between them.

For the last time, Oliver ordered dinner from the room service menu. They talked—about everything and nothing—filling the space with words that neither of them would remember but both needed to say.

And then, softly, Lucy confessed, "I've been thinking about making love to you all afternoon. But I didn't mention it because of the feeling I had of that not being the way I should say goodbye to you. As if making love is the pinnacle of what we mean to each other."

"I agree, but out of curiosity, what is the high point of what we mean to each other?"

"For me, it's our closeness," Lucy replied. "The comforting feeling of being with you. Either holding hands or putting our arms around each other when we venture outside to go somewhere. The tenderness that overwhelms me when you hold me close and when I cuddle up to you. I then feel safe and secure and able to share my deepest thoughts with you. I told my friend Zoey once that you're my soulmate. That says it all, doesn't it?"

"It does, sweetheart, but I think our lovemaking is the result of how much we love each other, especially when it's so pure, sincere, and unselfish."

"Does that mean you would have wanted me to make love to you today?"

"If you had, I wouldn't have thought it to be inappropriate. I love you. I will always love and cherish you. I will always believe in the good of what you do and say. I would have thought you wanted us to hold each other close one more time, and if that ended in lovemaking, I'd then revere that moment forever."

Oliver's words left Lucy with mixed feelings. She embraced him and asked him to forgive her for not having made love to him.

"There's nothing to forgive, Luce. If the shoe was on the other foot, I wouldn't have made love to you this afternoon either, partly because it would indeed seem as if that's the most important facet of our relationship, which it isn't, and partly because I feel that the moment to make love should arise spontaneously, not planned. Does that make sense to you?"

"It does, Oliver."

It was to be their last conversation.

***

Oliver called Dimitri, asking for help with their baggage. While Dimitri assisted, Lucy handled the checkout. Sergei opened the back door of the Mercedes, and Lucy slid in beside Oliver. He had already taken advantage of the car's cover before Lucy arrived, a necessary precaution now that his identity had changed.

The drive to the private aviation terminal at Sheremetyevo Airport took just over forty minutes. When they arrived,

Mitch was waiting with a baggage trolley, swiftly loading Oliver and Lucy's belongings for Dave to stow in the Lassiter jet's cargo hold.

Lucy's farewell to Oliver was raw and wordless, an ache neither could ignore. She clung to him, unwilling to let go, her grip tightening as if she could keep him with her through sheer force of will. He kissed her over and over, savoring every last moment until finally, he loosened her arms from around him. Mitch took her hand, gently guiding her away. She kept looking back, her eyes searching for him even as she disappeared from view.

***

The drive to Zelenograd took forty-five minutes, slowed by heavy congestion caused by an accident on the M10. When they reached the university, Oliver pointed to the parking lot across the road. Sergei maneuvered the car into position, ensuring a quick getaway if necessary.

Oliver and Dimitri set off toward the RusPharma plant, moving under the cover of trees and shrubs lining the right-hand side of the road. It was nearly 11:45 p.m. They decided to remain hidden until after midnight, watching for a shift change in the guardhouse.

From his position, Oliver spotted two guards inside. A single light illuminated the long desk they sat at. One of the men leaned back in his chair, hands folded behind his head, periodically glancing at four computer monitors. The monitors displayed the facility's security camera grid. Oliver had counted twenty-four feeds, two of which provided glimpses of the interior.

The second guard was absorbed in a document, seemingly uninterested in the screens. In the employee parking lot, Oliver counted ten vehicles—evidence that Lenkov had ordered round-the-clock shifts.

At precisely midnight, two others replaced the guards. The new arrivals were locked in a heated argument, one gesticulating wildly as if vehemently disagreeing with the other. Their focus was entirely on their dispute, with little concern for the monitors in front of them.

Oliver knew this was his moment.

"Remember, Dimitri, you need to return to the car at the first sign something is wrong. Keep watching the behavior of the guards for anything unusual."

Without hesitation, Oliver slipped from the shadows, making his way toward the production building. Sticking to the tree line along the right-hand side of the road, he moved with calculated precision until he reached the rear of the facility.

He crossed the road to the location where, on Saturday, he had noticed what appeared to be a faulty camera—one that hadn't yielded a clear image. He could only hope his observation had been correct. Accepting the risk, he climbed the fence and dropped silently to the other side. Flattening himself against the building, he waited.

Minutes passed. The night remained still.

When he was certain he hadn't been detected, he crept along the building's exterior. He knew the outdoor cameras were angled toward the perimeter fence, meaning that as long as he stayed low and close to the walls, they wouldn't see him.

Oliver made his way to the loading bay, where trucks would normally pick up and drop off shipments. As expected, it was securely locked. The facility had few windows, leaving him with only one viable point of entry—the same way they had entered on Saturday.

The mission had now reached its most critical phase. The fact that only two security cameras monitored the building's interior told him one thing—those areas were important.

One of the cameras covered the corridor leading from reception to the offices of Elena and Lenkov and where the servers controlling the production lines were housed.

The second monitored the formulation room, where Oliver had observed two women manually preparing small batches of an early-stage Alzheimer's tablet on Saturday. Each batch would have varied in properties such as hardness, thickness, and dosage mass—small refinements in what would eventually become a finalized formula. Oliver understood the significance of this phase in drug development. Lenkov, knowing its importance, had decided to keep that room under surveillance.

The formulation room was large, equipped with tablet presses, roller compactors, blending machines, and storage for base chemicals. It also housed a system for testing the chemical properties of newly produced batches. Simply deleting the files from the server wouldn't be enough—RusPharma's scientists had already made notes and progress reports based on the stolen Morgan Pharma data. If he wanted to cripple their ability to produce the cure, he needed to destroy everything in that room.

Oliver found the main entrance unlocked. Inside, the lights blazed, and the hum of activity echoed through the corridors—proof that Lenkov had ordered round-the-clock operations.

He turned his attention to the security camera covering the hallway leading to the offices. Initially, he had planned to disable or redirect it, but with personnel inside the building, he reconsidered. Any tampering could raise immediate suspicion. Instead, he decided to take the risk—hoping that if he was seen, the guards would assume he was a staff member.

Moving quickly, Oliver entered the server room that controlled the third production line. As expected, the computer was powered on. He swiftly navigated to the Morgan Pharma folder, permanently deleting all its contents. Then he copied the files from his hard drive into the now-empty folder.

As the data transfer progressed, he remained tense, straining to hear any movement in the corridor. If the guards were actively monitoring the security feed, this was the moment they would react.

Nothing happened.

Oliver exhaled quietly. The guards weren't paying attention to the cameras.

Emboldened, he unplugged the hard drive, tucked it away, and turned toward Lenkov's office.

Lenkov's computer was also powered on. Oliver quickly scanned the folders and, as expected, found the stolen files. He deleted them without hesitation, then began transferring the files from his hard drive, just as he had done before.

Then he heard it.

A noise.

He stood abruptly, his pulse spiking. His worst fear materialized in the open doorway—a guard.

Oliver reacted instantly. Before the man could reach for his weapon, Oliver lunged, clamping his right hand over the guard's mouth and nose. With his left, he ripped the gun from the holster and let it drop to the floor. The guard thrashed violently, trying to pry Oliver's grip loose, but Oliver seized one of his hands, preventing him from breaking free. The struggle was brutal, the guard's strength formidable. Every second felt stretched and unbearable.

Five minutes passed.

Then the man went still.

Oliver hadn't planned to kill anyone. The realization settled over him in a grim wave. But now, an opportunity presented itself—one that could increase his chance of success. Wearing the dead guard's uniform would allow him to move more freely. The second guard in the guard room wouldn't think twice about seeing him in the corridor.

He worked quickly, stripping the uniform and pulling it on over his sweater and pants. He strapped the holster with the gun around his waist, then turned back to Lenkov's desk. Searching the drawers, he found what he had been looking for—the original hard drive containing the Boston files. He swapped it with his own, slipping Lenkov's drive into a pocket of his uniform.

Time was running out.

Oliver moved to reception, keeping his head low to avoid the cameras. He entered the men's dressing room and quickly pulled on sterile coveralls, gloves, and shoe and hair covers—ensuring he blended in with any lab personnel. From there, he passed through the air lock and into the main corridor.

His destination: the formulation room.

He pushed open the door. It was empty. Relief flooded him—but only for a moment. He was on camera. He needed to move fast.

He hurried to the desk against the far wall, gathering every report and document in sight. These notes held the key to RusPharma's ability to recreate the stolen Alzheimer's formula. Without them, their research would be set back years.

He rifled through the drawers, finding even more notes. He scooped them up and dumped everything into a garbage bin. Then, he dragged it into the storage area, where shelves of chemicals and compounds had been placed. Some were highly flammable. Others highly explosive. He knew which ones were the most destructive.

With swift precision, Oliver pulled the hard drive from his pocket and tossed it into the bin. He reached under his uniform, withdrew the box of matches, and struck one.

Flames leaped to life, devouring the paper and spreading hungrily toward the chemicals.

It was time to go.

Retracing his steps, Oliver discarded the sterile clothing and emerged into reception, gun in hand. As he reached the exit, his breath caught.

The second guard.

Ten feet away. Gun drawn.

They fired at the same time.

The shots cracked through the air—both men collapsed.

And then a deafening explosion. The building erupted, flames and debris tearing through the night.

Then—silence.

30.

THE AFTERMATH

Dimitri remained hidden among the trees opposite the guardhouse, watching intently. He saw Oliver slip into the building. Minutes later, one of the guards left the guardhouse and followed suit. Dimitri hesitated, debating whether he should return to the car.

Then the second guard exited the guardhouse—this time with his gun drawn.

Dimitri's pulse quickened. That was his cue to leave.

As he sprinted toward the car, gunfire cracked through the night. Then, a deafening explosion tore through the silence, shaking the ground beneath him. He briefly looked back.

***

Once they reached the M10 on their drive to Saint Petersburg, Dimitri called Alex, rousing him from his sleep. He briefly explained what had happened.

"Please contact Lucy. She's on her way to Washington, D.C.—currently en route to Helsinki. Tell her Oliver never made it out. We had to leave to avoid being discovered."

Dimitri hesitated briefly before adding, "We heard gunshots. Then an enormous explosion."

***

Lucy's breath caught when Alex relayed the message. Fear gripped her, raw and unrelenting. She had prayed—desperately—that Oliver would return with Dimitri and Sergei, that they would escape together.

Mitch tried to reassure her, but she was inconsolable. For a fleeting moment, he even considered turning back to Moscow to uncover what had happened. But in the end, he forced himself to heed Oliver's words. His mission was to get Lucy to safety.

By sunrise, they were in the air, bound for Dulles. There was no point in waiting any longer for further news.

***

When the Lassiter Jet touched down at 5:30 a.m. on Wednesday, Jacky and Bill were waiting.

Mitch had called Bill before departing Helsinki, warning him of Lucy's fragile state. The moment she saw them, she collapsed into their arms. The three of them held each other, grief and fear thick in the air.

Mitch escorted them to Oliver's apartment. Once there, Lucy recounted everything—the events of each harrowing day in Moscow, the mission, the explosion.

***

After breakfast, Bill called Ken Rivera. He requested an urgent meeting. The CIA director wasted no time clearing his schedule, setting the meeting for 2 p.m.

Seated across from Ken Rivera, Lucy took a steadying breath before speaking.

"Oliver never made it out," she said, her voice tight with

emotion. "He broke into the RusPharma production plant but never returned. We need to know what happened."

She met the director's gaze. "I know the CIA monitors Russia with satellites. Is it possible for you to have someone check if you've captured anything that would shed light on what happened?"

Ken signaled to an aide, who promptly summoned the data analyst responsible for Moscow Oblast. The analyst arrived minutes later, laptop in hand.

"One of our satellites captured the explosion," he confirmed, his tone professional but grave. "It destroyed at least half of the RusPharma factory."

Lucy leaned forward, hands clenched. "And Oliver?"

The analyst's fingers moved across the keyboard, pulling up the data.

"Two men came face to face at the entrance just before the explosion. Both fell to the ground after what looks to be a shooting." He shook his head. "That's all we have."

Lucy sat frozen, her mind racing through the implications.

Bill exhaled sharply. The data analyst closed the laptop with a heavy sigh.

"I'll have one of our operatives in the region dig deeper," Ken assured them. "We'll find out what we can."

Bill nodded. "Please let us know the moment you hear anything."

With nothing more to be done, they left—Lucy clinging to the sliver of hope that Oliver might still be alive.

***

Later that afternoon, Lucy called Will Bryce.

"Can Sasha be trusted?" she asked.

Will confirmed that Sasha had proven reliable.

"I need to speak with her," Lucy said. "I'll be flying to

Boston first thing tomorrow."

The next morning, Mitch flew Lucy to Logan Airport and accompanied her to the Boston lab. There, she told Will everything—Oliver's mission, his disappearance, and the explosion that had destroyed a significant part of the RusPharma production building. Then she asked him to call Sasha into his office.

When Sasha arrived, Lucy wasted no time.

"Oliver went back into the RusPharma plant Tuesday night," she said. "He was trying to undo what Lenkov did. But he never returned. I need your help."

Sasha listened, her expression grave.

Lucy leaned forward. "I need you to reach out to someone—anyone—who might know what happened."

Sasha hesitated only a moment before pulling out her phone. She called Anatoly, who was now working at the RusPharma production facility.

When she ended the call, her face was pale.

"The explosion destroyed the formulation room," she said. "Everything in the surrounding area as well—including the computer data on the Alzheimer's medication. The files on the computers that had survived the blast were found to have been tampered with."

Lucy's heart pounded. "And Oliver?"

Sasha swallowed. "Anatoly said that when he was finally allowed to leave the facility, he saw both guards lying on the ground—killed in a face-to-face shooting. An FSB agent on site asked him to confirm that one of the bodies was that of Oliver Corbyn."

Lucy went cold.

"The FSB said they were waiting for someone from Moscow to examine the bodies before they could be removed," Sasha continued. "The second guard's body was later found in the director's office. They took all three bodies away that afternoon. Meanwhile, emergency services transported six wounded staff to the hospital. Three employees died in the explosion."

Lucy barely registered the rest of what Sasha said.

"The Kremlin is in a fury. Prince Alexandrovich's disappearance has dominated the headlines, with threats of severe retaliation against those responsible."

***

Back at Oliver's apartment, Lucy, Mitch, Bill, and Jacky tried to piece everything together.

They compared the CIA analyst's satellite data with Anatoly's account, searching for an explanation—how Oliver had ended up in a guard's uniform, why the bodies were left untouched for more than twelve hours.

One conclusion haunted them all: If Oliver had still been alive after the shooting, he would have been taken to the hospital, not left on the ground.

Lucy couldn't take it.

The realization shattered what little composure she had left. She broke down completely, inconsolable, her grief all-consuming.

***

For two weeks, Jacky and Bill did everything they could to comfort her, but nothing helped. She barely ate, barely spoke. Every so often, she seemed to drift into a numb silence, lost in a place no one could reach. Bill tried to convince her to return with them to LA, hoping a change of scenery might help. She refused.

Mitch had been watching her closely. The weight of her loss had affected him more deeply than he expected. When she came to be alone in Oliver's apartment, he made a decision.

He called Bill. "Let me work for her," he said. "From now on. Wherever she wants to go, I'll fly her. I'll stay with her. She shouldn't be alone."

Bill agreed. He was worried too.

They both feared Lucy wasn't just grieving.

They feared she was losing the will to live.

***

Bill resumed his role as chairman of the board. One of his first actions was to promote Will Bryce to CEO of the Boston office and lab. He tasked him to do everything in his power to fast-track the Alzheimer's cure through the FDA approval process.

Meanwhile, the CIA uncovered that Keith Dunbar, Barry McKenzie, and Ellen Wright had been paid to side with the prince. Bill wasted no time in terminating their board memberships. The three were later tried and sentenced to two years in prison.

Lucy's grief consumed her. Every thought, every action was weighed down by the loss. It took her two months before she could partially resume her work at Morgan Pharma. New York held too many painful memories. She sold her apartment, choosing instead to live in Oliver's.

Her friend Zoey tried to pull her back to life, inviting her to rejoin their circle. But Lucy declined, remembering how much it had taken Oliver to help her break free the last time. She couldn't go back.

***

Ten weeks after their meeting, Ken Rivera called Bill with an update.

"One of our operatives confirmed that the person responsible for the explosion at the RusPharma facility is dead," he reported.

Bill absorbed the information, weighing its implications.

He decided not to tell Lucy.

For months, she'd clung fiercely to the one thing that kept her going—the promise she had made to Oliver to believe in his mission. Telling her now that Oliver's death had been confirmed might shatter her completely. She had fought too long, too hard, to abandon the fragile hope that Oliver was still alive, imprisoned somewhere.

Bill couldn't be the one to take that from her.

***

Eight months after taking over the Boston facility, Will Bryce succeeded. He had secured a priority review from the FDA, ensuring the Alzheimer's medication moved swiftly through the approval process. When it was released on the US market, it was hailed as the greatest medical breakthrough in recent history.

Will Bryce and Liam Richards were awarded the Nobel Prize in Physiology or Medicine for their work. To circumvent the rule that prohibited posthumous awards, the Nobel Committee argued there was no definitive proof that Liam Richards was dead.

A year after RusPharma's ability to manufacture the drug had been destroyed, the president invited Bill, Jacky, and Lucy to the White House for an informal lunch. When they arrived, he told them of his decision.

"In recognition of extraordinary service to this country," the president said, "Liam Richards has been awarded the Presidential Medal of Freedom."

They accepted the medal in his absence.

***

Fourteen months after becoming CEO, Will Bryce married Sasha.

By then, Sasha and Lucy had grown close. What had started as brief updates about Russia had turned into long conversations, shared confidences, and, eventually, a true friendship.

So when Sasha asked Lucy to be her maid of honor, she didn't hesitate.

For the first time in a long time, she said yes—to something, to anything, to life.

31.

RESILIENCE

Lucy had settled into the habit of visiting Sasha at the Boston lab every two or three weeks. During each visit, she would ask Sasha to reach out to her former colleagues—just in case there was any news about Oliver.

On Wednesday, September 18—three months after Sasha's wedding and more than twenty-one months since Oliver was shot—Sasha handed her a newsletter.

"Turn to the photo on page three, and tell me what you see," she said.

The photo showed twenty men and women, dressed in tattered clothing, posing for the camera. Their hardship was evident in their faces—in their posture.

Lucy's breath caught. She wasn't just surprised—she was shaken by the stark reality of their suffering.

"How terrible, Sasha," Lucy commented, turning to the front page to determine the origin of the newsletter.

"It's a trimonthly publication issued by the Kazan Specialized High-Security Psychological Hospital in Tatarstan," Sasha added when she noticed Lucy wanted to identify the organization that produced the newsletter.

"Look at the photograph again, and tell me what you see," Sasha repeated.

Lucy turned to the photograph again and now studied it in detail.

"The tall man in the back row...he looks a lot like Oliver," Lucy said, her voice catching as she took in the likeness.

"That's exactly what I thought," Sasha replied. "Cover his beard with your finger—just for a second. The resemblance is uncanny."

Lucy hesitated, then placed her finger over the lower part of the man's face.

Her breath hitched. Without the beard, the resemblance wasn't just striking—it was undeniable.

"Where did you get this?"

"I have an older brother who has a history of violence. Whenever he was upset about something, he would react violently and hurt everyone around him, including my parents, my younger sister, and me. He was committed to the Kazan Psychological Hospital when he killed a neighbor who attempted to stop him from hurting my sister. My parents send me the newsletter from time to time so I can keep up with news about him and the hospital. The hospital is a prison for perpetrators of hideous crimes when they are found to possess a psychiatric disorder. The conditions there are horrendous."

"We should try to find out who that man is," Lucy said, keeping her eyes focused on the photo.

"I thought so too. I'll ask my parents to find out who he is the next time they visit my brother. You can keep the newsletter."

On the way to Boston Logan, seated in the back of a taxi, Lucy handed the photograph to Mitch.

He barely needed a second glance.

"Incredible," he muttered, his grip tightening on the edges of the paper. "He looks just like Oliver."

"I can fly you to Kazan, if you like, to investigate who he is," he told her.

"Sasha promised to make inquiries. We should wait to see what she can find out. But you might want to renew our Russian visas just in case."

***

Two weeks later, Sasha called.

For fourteen days, Lucy had lived in a whirlwind of emotions—hope battling doubt, fear clashing with the desperate belief that somehow, against all odds, the man in the photograph was Oliver.

Now, as she answered the call, her heart pounded.

"My parents asked about the tall man in the photograph. They were told he was committed to the hospital nineteen months ago. He has lost his memory of the time before he was arrested. He doesn't know his name or where he comes from. What he knows is what he's learned since his incarceration. He only knows a little Russian."

Lucy was stunned by what Sasha had uncovered. The details shook her, yet logic told her it couldn't be Oliver—he spoke fluent Russian, after all. But that realization did nothing to stop her growing obsession with the mystery surrounding him.

When she told Mitch what she had learned, he once again suggested they travel to Kazan. This time, Lucy agreed.

The next morning, after a restless night, she called Sasha. "Will you come with us?" she asked. "We need an interpreter."

Sasha conferred with Will, who, knowing how important this was to Lucy, readily agreed. They decided to take the Gulfstream to Kazan later that week.

***

On the day of departure, they left Dulles Airport at 10 a.m., stopping at Boston Logan to pick up Sasha. She was already waiting, allowing them to take off again by noon. They landed at Kazan International Airport at 5:30 a.m. local time the following day.

Lucy had booked rooms for the three of them at the Double Tree Hilton Kazan City Center, while Dave and Annette, as usual, stayed at a hotel near the airport.

Lucy and Sasha had managed to sleep during the flight, but Mitch hadn't. Notwithstanding her eagerness to get to the hospital, Lucy suggested they rest for a few hours after checking in. Mitch, grateful for the consideration, agreed.

***

At 3 p.m., they arrived at the hospital.

Sasha explained their purpose to a woman who had been called to meet them. "We've traveled halfway across the world," she said, "to find out if a particular patient is someone we've been searching for."

The woman introduced herself as Dr. Karina Sokolova, head of the medical staff. Lucy was immediately struck by her appearance—she wasn't dressed like a doctor. Her colorful dress, high heels, and heavy makeup seemed out of place in a hospital setting. With her hair pulled into a tight bun, she looked more like an administrator than someone directly involved in patient care.

Dr. Sokolova looked at each of them in turn. "Who is it you wish to see?"

Lucy handed Sasha the newsletter. Sasha turned to page three, her finger resting on the tall man in the photograph.

Dr. Sokolova's lips curled into a knowing smile.

"Ah," she said. "Pavel."

"Pavel?" Sasha echoed.

She nodded. "That's what we call him—he has no memory of who he is." Her tone softened. "We'd be grateful for any information you can provide."

Lucy's heart pounded.

Without a word, Dr. Sokolova gestured for them to follow. They navigated a maze of endless corridors, each step tightening the knot in Lucy's chest.

Then they stepped into a small courtyard garden.

There, crouched on the ground with his back to them, was the man from the photograph.

Dressed in the same tattered clothing, he moved slowly, methodically, pulling weeds from between the flowers. He hadn't noticed them.

Lucy held her breath.

This was it.

"There are some people here who want to talk to you, Pavel," the woman called out.

Sasha translated Dr. Sokolova's words for Lucy and Mitch, but the man gave no response. He remained focused on his task, pulling weeds as if he hadn't heard a thing.

Lucy couldn't wait any longer.

She stepped past him, moving to where she could see his face. Her heart pounded violently in her chest. Every breath felt shallow, unsteady.

Then, just as she turned to look at him, he looked up at her.

The shock hit her like a physical blow.

Oliver.

Her vision blurred. A wave of dizziness crashed over her. Her heart skipped a beat.

Without thinking, she rushed to him, falling to her knees. Tears spilled down her face as she flung her arms around his neck, clinging to him as if letting go would make him disappear.

A sob tore from her throat. Then another.

Lucy wept openly, her body shaking with the force of her emotion.

Around them, everyone stood in stunned silence, moved by the rawness of the moment.

But Oliver—Pavel—remained still.

For a long time, he didn't react. Then, slowly, he raised a hand and ran his fingers through her hair. His expression barely changed, though there was something—something like concern—in his eyes.

When Lucy finally loosened her grip and pulled back, desperate for recognition, he simply turned away.

Without a word, he went back to pulling weeds.

"I want to take him away from here," Lucy said with a loud sob. "Please ask how we can make that happen, Sasha."

Sasha relayed Lucy's request.

Dr. Sokolova shook her head immediately. "That's out of the question," she said.

Through Sasha's translation, she explained that the man—Pavel—had been committed to the hospital for life nineteen months ago after being found guilty of serious crimes.

Lucy's stomach twisted.

But then, Dr. Sokolova hesitated, her tone softening. She admitted she had a certain sympathy for him—he was unusually docile, always following orders without resistance, something few patients did.

"Our tests show that his memory is completely blank before the incident that caused his amnesia," she continued. "Everything he knows—everything he remembers—is only from the time after that event."

She paused, then added, "His thoughts and actions are, for all intents and purposes, those of a child. Seven, maybe eight years old."

Lucy felt the floor drop out from under her.

She couldn't accept this. Wouldn't.

Her mind raced. Then it struck her—Dr. Sokolova wasn't refusing out of cruelty. If she was responsible for her patients, she could be held personally accountable if she released Oliver into their care.

Desperation clawed at her.

She turned to Sasha, gripping her arm. "Offer her money," she pleaded. "Anything. Whatever it takes."

Sasha hesitated, then spoke.

Dr. Sokolova again looked at each of them, lingering on Lucy's tear-streaked face.

Then she answered.

"We are terribly short of means to carry out what we are supposed to," she replied. "The budget we receive from the ministry decreases every year. Since we are never visited by officials to check on whom we have imprisoned here, I am inclined to say yes to your request to take Pavel from here in exchange for money. But the amount would need to be substantial—at least a hundred million rubles."

"Ask her if she's prepared to accept a check for that amount," Lucy said, opening her purse to take out her checkbook after Sasha had interpreted what the woman had said.

Dr. Sokolova hesitated only briefly before nodding.

"I'll release him," she said. "Once the check clears."

She instructed them to return in three days, in the afternoon, to collect him.

Lucy turned to Oliver—Pavel—her heart aching. She crouched beside him, pressing a gentle kiss to his cheek before they left.

He didn't react.

He simply continued tending to the garden, his fingers carefully plucking weeds as if nothing had changed.

As they rode back to the hotel in the same taxi, Lucy, Mitch, and Sasha exchanged thoughts, dissecting every detail of Oliver's appearance and behavior.

But no matter how much they analyzed, one truth remained unshakable.

Oliver was alive.

But he wasn't the same.

"He has a terrible scar on the side of his face," Mitch said, "and he's lost perhaps as much as a third of his weight. He looks frail, if not sick."

Lucy started to cry again. She had also seen the scar and noticed how pale and thin he looked.

***

Lucy barely slept during the agonizing wait for the check to clear. Her mind never stopped racing—how would she take care of him? What would his future look like? No matter how uncertain things seemed, one resolution remained firm in her heart: She would do everything in her power to provide for him for as long as she lived.

***

Three days later, they returned to the hospital.

Sasha had arranged for two taxis to take them, along with their baggage, instructing the drivers to wait.

Dr. Sokolova met them in the front office, greeting them with a satisfied nod. "The money has been received," she confirmed. "It will go a long way in improving conditions for our patients."

Then she pressed a call button. Moments later, a young man in a nurse's uniform entered.

In a clipped, commanding tone, she ordered him to bring Pavel. For Sasha's benefit, she added, almost as an afterthought, that her staff had found him more appropriate clothes for traveling.

Nothing could have prepared them for what they saw when Oliver was brought out.

He was dressed in little more than rags—baggy pants with holes at the knees, an old sweater, frayed at the elbows, and worn-out sandals barely holding together.

Lucy's breath caught. Her hands trembled, rage and heartbreak battling within her.

She said nothing. She simply took Oliver's hand and led him outside, not bothering with goodbyes.

As they stepped into the sunlight, something shifted.

Oliver's face brightened. His eyes lit up with childlike excitement as he realized they were about to travel by car.

***

The taxis took them straight to Kazan International Airport.

Lucy had thought ahead, bringing Oliver's real passport—the one identifying him as Liam Richards—just in case. It turned out to be a wise decision. They passed through passport control without issue.

But as they approached the jet, Oliver suddenly stopped.

His hand slipped from Lucy's grasp. He shook his head violently, taking a step back. Then, in Russian, he spoke—his voice urgent, laced with fear.

Lucy's stomach twisted. She didn't understand his words, but the message was clear.

Oliver had never seen an aircraft before.

To him, the massive jet resembled something unnatural, incomprehensible—something to be feared.

"He's frightened," Sasha said.

Tears welled in Lucy's eyes. She turned to Oliver, placing her hands gently on his arms, and tried to guide him toward the aircraft.

He hesitated, his gaze searching hers—the same way he

had three days ago. Then, slowly, he reached out and stroked her hair again, as if trying to understand her distress.

Finally, he let her lead him up the cabin stairs.

Inside, Lucy pointed to a seat, indicating where he should sit. But the confined space unsettled him. His eyes darted around, tension building in his posture. He remained standing, uneasy, until Lucy took a seat across from him.

Only then did he lower himself hesitantly into the seat.

But his unease wasn't over.

The moment Dave closed the cabin door and Mitch started the engines, Oliver stiffened, his hands gripping the armrests. His breath quickened, his eyes wide with alarm.

Lucy reached out, trying to reassure him.

The journey home had only just begun.

"It's okay, Oliver," Lucy said repeatedly, tears filling her eyes as she held his hands.

As the aircraft gained altitude, Oliver pressed his face to the window, his unease gradually fading. When Lucy forced a reassuring smile, he seemed to relax further, though his eyes remained wide with curiosity.

Twenty minutes into the flight, Annette offered them a plate of sandwiches. Lucy took one and began eating, hoping Oliver would follow suit, but he shook his head violently. The same happened when Annette offered them a selection of juices.

Lucy and Sasha exchanged a glance. What did it mean?

Determined to understand, Lucy took him to where Annette had prepared the food and drinks, allowing him to choose for himself. She was startled when he reached for nothing but a slice of dry bread and a glass of plain water.

Back in their seats, Oliver devoured the bread in seconds, then stood, retracing his steps to fetch another slice and another glass of water.

It hit Lucy then.

This was what he had survived on in captivity—bread and water. His frailty, his sunken frame, it all made sense. He wasn't just being selective. He was choosing what was familiar, what had been forced upon him.

Determined to show him there was more, she picked up a glass of orange juice. When he refused, she took a sip, smiled, and handed it to him again. This time, he mirrored her action—taking a sip, then handing it back. She repeated the gesture, this time motioning that it was his. He hesitated but drank it all in a few gulps.

Encouraged, Lucy selected a wholesome tuna sandwich, took a small bite, and offered it to him. Oliver studied it for a moment before mimicking her action, taking a small bite before returning it.

She shook her head, pointed at him, and gave it back.

Slowly, he ate.

The taste must have pleased him because, to Lucy's astonishment, he got up and selected another tuna sandwich from Annette's tray. Then another. And another. He ate four more before settling into his seat, his gaze returning to the lights flickering below.

***

A few minutes later, Lucy noticed Oliver placing a hand on his crotch while still watching out the window. She waited. He shifted uncomfortably, glancing at her, then around the cabin, as if trying to decide where he should relieve himself.

She understood immediately.

Taking his hand, she led him to the bathroom.

Inside, it became clear—he had no idea what to do.

Lucy lifted the toilet lid, pulled down his pants, and gently guided him to sit, unsure if he needed more than just to pee. As she helped, she made another discovery.

He wasn't wearing underwear.

It dawned on her that, for some reason, he had likely never been given any in captivity. When he looked down at where his urine went, the confusion on his face told her something else—he had never done this sitting down before.

She swallowed hard, willing herself to stay composed.

***

Determined to do more for him, Lucy made her way to the cockpit.

"Mitch," she said softly, "do you have any spare clothes? Like before?"

He nodded without hesitation and handed her everything she needed—except shoes.

"I might have something," Dave offered. "My running shoes, if they fit."

Armed with fresh clothes, Lucy returned to Oliver. She led him back to the bathroom, undressed him, and guided him into the shower. He didn't resist.

As she washed him, her breath caught.

Under the grime, his body was covered in scars.

Some were thin and crisscrossed over his back, the result of sharp, repeated wounds. A deep, badly healed puncture wound sat beneath his left collarbone. His stomach bore burn scars, and the backs of his legs told the brutal story of severe beatings.

Tears blurred her vision. She let them fall freely.

Oliver noticed.

He raised a hand and stroked her hair.

Lucy's chest tightened as she continued washing him, careful and reverent.

After drying him off, she helped him into the fresh clothes. When she tried to pull up the boxer shorts Mitch had given her, he stopped her.

She met his eyes, took hold of his arms as she had before, and shook her head.

Again, he simply obeyed, allowing her to dress him as she wanted.

***

With a pair of scissors and her shaving kit, Lucy began trimming his overgrown hair and beard. As she worked, she uncovered yet another scar—this one on his forehead.

She hesitated.

She decided to leave his hair and beard long enough to soften his appearance while keeping the worst of the scars concealed.

When she was satisfied with how he looked, she led him back to his seat.

Oliver sat down, watching her for a long moment, a puzzled expression on his face. Then, silently, he turned back to the window.

Later, when Annette brought another plate of food and juice, he reached out and made his own selection without hesitation.

Lucy took note. He was still hungry. But this time, he was learning that there was more.

***

When Lucy signaled that they were ready to sleep, Annette swiftly rearranged the seats into beds.

Taking Oliver's hand, she led him to the bathroom. She guided him through the now-familiar routine—sitting him on the toilet, letting him take care of his needs, then removing his shoes, socks, shirt, and pants. She washed his hands, brushed his teeth, and finally, when he was clean and ready, led him back to his bed.

Gently, she pulled the blankets over him and pressed a soft kiss to his forehead.

He didn't react, but he didn't resist either.

Lucy then retreated to the bathroom to change into sweatpants and a pajama top. When she returned, she found Oliver watching her, his eyes tracking her every movement.

She lay down on her bed across the aisle, then reached out her hand to him.

For a moment, he hesitated. Then he took it, holding on for a long, silent minute before finally letting go.

Oliver closed his eyes.

Lucy did the same.

***

Exhaustion and the weight of the past few days made Lucy sleep deeper than she had in weeks.

When she finally woke, the cabin was basking in the glow of the sun.

She turned her head and looked across the aisle.

Oliver was awake.

Lying on his back, his eyes were fixed on the ceiling—motionless, lost in thought.

Something inside Lucy clenched.

She had found him.

But she still didn't know how much of him remained.

"I've been watching him, Lucy," Sasha said from the bed she was in. "He's been awake for half an hour or so, all the while staring up at the ceiling. I think it's because he wasn't allowed to get out of bed in Kazan until he was told, and he's now waiting for someone to let him get up."

Tears of compassion welled in Lucy's eyes as she processed Sasha's words.

She stood up, wiping the tears away with the back of her hand so she could see him clearly. Then, without hesitation, she leaned down and kissed him.

Gently, she pulled back his blankets and helped him to his feet.

Oliver, moving with quiet precision, folded the blankets neatly and placed them on his pillow.

Lucy's heart clenched.

He was following prison routine.

***

They landed at Boston Logan at eight-thirty that evening.

At the terminal, Lucy embraced Sasha, thanking her for everything. She watched as Sasha disappeared into the crowd, knowing Will was waiting for her—Sasha had called him with their ETA before they left Kazan.

Meanwhile, Mitch wasted no time. The moment they completed formalities, he applied for a slot for their immediate departure to Dulles.

***

Mitch arranged for a taxi to take the three of them and their baggage back to Oliver's apartment.

As they settled into the ride, Lucy turned to Mitch.

"Stay," she said.

She had always trusted him to be there, but now more than ever, she needed his support—in case something unexpected happened with Oliver.

Mitch nodded. "Should I sleep on the couch?" he asked. "So Oliver can use the guest room?"

Lucy shook her head.

"No," she said softly. "In Kazan, the beds in the inmates'

rooms were lined up side by side, barely any space between them."

Mitch frowned, listening.

"If we put him in a room by himself now, he'll be frightened," Lucy continued. "I want him to sleep in his own bed. And if he doesn't seem disturbed by me being there, I'll sleep beside him."

Mitch didn't argue. He understood.

Oliver had lost everything once. The last thing Lucy wanted was for him to feel alone again.

***

Lucy decided to leave unpacking for the following day.

For now, Oliver needed her attention.

She led him to the bathroom, sat him on the toilet, and used hand gestures to explain that he could relieve himself whenever he needed to. As before, he studied the toilet with quiet curiosity.

Once he was done, she helped him clean up, washed his hands, brushed his teeth, and removed his clothes—leaving only his T-shirt and boxer shorts. Then, she took his hand and guided him to his bedroom.

Pulling back the blankets, she motioned for him to lie down.

When he did, she tucked him in and pressed a gentle kiss to his forehead.

Then she undressed, went to the bathroom, and slipped under the blankets on the other side of the bed.

The reaction was immediate.

Oliver shifted as far away from her as possible, a distressed sound escaping his throat—an unmistakable objection to her presence.

Lucy froze.

The realization hit her like a punch to the stomach.

Someone had hurt him.

In prison, in a bed—maybe in a moment just like this.

Tears burned in her eyes, but she forced herself to remain still, respecting the distance he had created.

She didn't sleep. Not until the sun peeked over the eastern horizon.

All night, she lay there, thinking of everything she had learned since pulling him from the life he had been forced into. The scars, the starvation, the obedience...the suffering no one could erase.

Her face was damp with silent tears when exhaustion finally took over.

***

When Lucy woke, Oliver was already awake.

Lying on his back, he stared at the ceiling, motionless.

A pang of regret struck her—she had forgotten to show him he could get out of bed whenever he wanted.

She hesitated, then sat up, walked around the bed, and pointed at him. Then at the blankets, miming pulling them down.

She repeated the gesture twice.

This time, he understood.

He started to pull the blankets away—but she had to stop him before he folded them and placed them neatly on his pillow.

Instead, he hurried straight to the bathroom.

Lucy exhaled.

It was a small step. But it was something.

During the sleepless nights in the hotel after finding Oliver in Kazan, Lucy had made a decision. If she was going to care for him, she needed to establish a predictable daily routine. Structure, she believed, would help him regain independence—learning to use the bathroom, shower, wash his hair, get dressed, without her help.

She had discussed this plan with Mitch on the flight to Dulles, confiding in him about the scars that covered Oliver's body. Now, she was ready to put her plan into action.

Lucy led Oliver to the bathroom, gently removed his T-shirt and shorts, and guided him into the shower. She demonstrated how to lather shampoo into his hair, how to use shower gel on his body, and then handed him the bottles to try for himself. When he was done, she dried him, brushed his hair, and showed him how to wrap a towel around his waist.

In the walk-in closet, she showed him how to select his own clothes. She picked a clean pair of shorts, a T-shirt, a long-sleeved shirt, jeans, and sneakers. She helped him dress, once again patiently convincing him to wear the shorts under his jeans and the T-shirt beneath his long-sleeved shirt.

Afterward, she led him to the kitchen and turned on the TV, selecting a cartoon channel. If he had never seen television before, she knew it would captivate him.

While he watched, Lucy finally took a moment for herself—showering, dressing, and mentally preparing for the day ahead.

When Mitch entered the kitchen a little later, Lucy explained her next goal: ensuring Oliver ate a nutritious breakfast every morning. Since there was nothing in the fridge, she asked Mitch to go grocery shopping.

"Get whole-grain rolls and bagels, bread for toast, milk, cereal, eggs, pancake and waffle ingredients, maple syrup, fresh fruit, sandwich spreads, cheese, ham...and anything else you think we'll need."

Mitch nodded and left. When he returned, he carried enough groceries for several days.

Lucy was determined to introduce Oliver to different breakfast options until she learned what he liked. She switched off the TV—earning an immediate frown from Oliver—then poured milk into a bowl of cereal, motioning for him to eat with a spoon.

While he hesitated, she prepared scrambled eggs on toast and poured coffee for all three of them. She took a seat beside Oliver, eating first, then gesturing for him to follow.

After a long pause, he finally mimicked her movements.

When they finished, she took the opportunity to teach him how to store the food. She showed him which ingredients belonged in the fridge and which went into the cabinets. It was a lot to take in, but through daily repetition, she hoped he would eventually be able to prepare breakfast on his own.

Finally, she switched the TV back on.

Oliver smiled.

That small reaction made Lucy's heart swell.

After an hour, Lucy turned the TV off again and sat beside him.

It was time to teach him English.

She started with the simplest words.

Pointing to herself, she said, "Lucy."

Then she pointed at him. "Oliver."

She hesitated for a moment, wondering if she should call him Liam instead. But no—he had always been Oliver to her.

She repeated the names three times before gently placing his index finger against her chest and mouthing her name, encouraging him to say it.

After two attempts, something clicked.

"Lucy," he said, his Russian accent thick but unmistakable.

Her chest tightened.

She repeated the process, this time placing her finger against his chest. "Oliver."

He watched her mouth form the word before repeating, "Oliver."

From there, progress came easily.

She pointed at a vase on the dining table, its flowers long withered. "Flowers."

He echoed, "Flowers."

Lucy continued through the morning, introducing new words until she noticed signs of fatigue. She didn't want to overwhelm him, so she turned the TV back on, rewarded again with his small, pleased smile.

Lucy and Mitch agreed that Oliver needed a high-calorie diet to regain his strength.

"We should all eat the same thing," she said. "Let's order lasagna for lunch, have a snack in the afternoon, and beef with vegetables for dinner."

Mitch placed the order, and when the food arrived, Lucy once again turned off the TV.

Sitting down at the table, she began eating.

Mitch followed.

Oliver watched them both for a while, uncertain, before finally picking up his fork.

For the first time, he ate without needing encouragement.

It was another small step.

But for Lucy, it meant everything.

***

Lucy decided that their afternoons needed variety. Repeating the same routine every day risked boredom, which could interfere with Oliver's progress. She wanted to keep him engaged, curious, and learning.

That afternoon, she took him to the apartment building's outdoor pool.

She had once known Oliver as a strong swimmer. Today, she wanted to find out if that was still the case.

After finding his swimsuit, she helped him put it on. Then, she changed into her black bikini.

Hand in hand, they walked to the pool, Lucy carrying towels and T-shirts for both of them. The mid-October sun was unseasonably warm, making the water look inviting.

Lucy tossed their things onto a sun lounger before diving in.

Turning back, she waved for Oliver to follow.

He hesitated.

His eyes scanned the water, filled with uncertainty—as if he had never seen as much water.

Lucy's heart clenched.

She beckoned him again, and after a long moment, he stepped forward, lowering himself hesitantly into the shallow end.

The truth hit her instantly.

He couldn't swim.

Not anymore.

She had prepared for many possibilities—but not for this.

Tears burned the back of her eyes, but she forced them down. This was just another step in his recovery. Another piece to rebuild.

She gently led him out of the water and onto the sun loungers, letting him rest before they returned to the apartment.

Before taking Oliver to the pool, Lucy had asked Mitch to pick up a variety of snacks and candy bars. She knew they weren't the healthiest option, but her goal was to get Oliver to put on weight.

More importantly, she wanted him to know that food—tasty, enjoyable food—was always available whenever he was hungry.

Mitch had stocked up before they returned.

Once inside, Lucy unwrapped a Mars bar and handed it to Oliver, taking a small bite first to encourage him.

He mirrored her action, chewing slowly.

She watched as his expression shifted.

He enjoyed the taste.

Relief washed over her. She handed him another.

Later, she guided him to the bathroom, helping him through the same shower and dressing routine she had established that morning.

Once again, he was completely passive.

Lucy's fingers trembled slightly as she buttoned his shirt, struggling to reconcile the man in front of her with the Oliver she had known.

He had always been decisive. A man who knew exactly what he wanted and pursued it relentlessly. Someone who wouldn't accept anything less than the best, refusing substitutes unless they had superior merit.

Now, he simply obeyed.

It was as if his captors had erased the part of him that questioned, that pushed back, that chose.

They had broken him into total submission.

And submission had become his survival instinct.

Lucy swallowed against the knot in her throat.

This wasn't just about reteaching him how to eat or dress.

It was about helping him find himself again.

As soon as he was dressed, Oliver left the bathroom and walked into the kitchen.

He picked up the remote.

Then, without hesitation, he turned on the TV.

Lucy paused.

It was a simple action. But it was his choice.

She smiled softly.

Maybe it didn't seem like much, but to her, it was a small victory.

From now on, she would let him turn on the TV whenever it fit into their growing schedule.

He needed structure.

But more than that, he needed freedom.

***

Exhausted from restless nights, Lucy decided to take a nap on the couch, asking Mitch to keep an eye on Oliver. Mitch let her sleep until dinner arrived.

At the table, Lucy carefully cut Oliver's steak into small pieces before they ate together. She opened a can of sports drink, took a sip, and handed it to Oliver. He drank, then pointed to another can and gestured to himself. She smiled, opening it for him.

After dinner, they settled in front of the TV with coffee. Lucy deliberately chose a program free of violence or anything that might disturb him. As the evening progressed, she noticed his eyes drifting shut, only to reopen moments later.

At first, she thought he was simply tired—but then realization struck.

Jet lag must have affected him far more than it had affected her or Mitch. In captivity, his days had followed an unchanging routine—waking and sleeping at the same time every day. This sudden disruption was overwhelming.

She felt a pang of guilt for not realizing it sooner.

Lucy switched off the TV and explained the situation to Mitch before taking Oliver to the bathroom. She repeated the same bedtime routine as the night before, guiding him through every step.

In his bedroom, she hugged him, kissed his forehead, and tucked him in.

Then, turning to Mitch, she admitted, "I don't want him to be alone tonight. I'll go to bed too."

She slipped under the blankets beside him, careful not to disturb his space.

As soon as she lay down, he turned his back to her and edged as far away as possible.

Lucy understood.

And it broke her heart.

She lay awake for hours, thinking about everything that had happened—how much he had endured, how much he had lost. When sleep finally came, it was only when exhaustion overtook her thoughts.

When Lucy woke the next morning, Oliver was already gone.

The faint sound of the TV echoed from the kitchen.

She found him seated, watching cartoons, just as he had the day before.

Smiling, she set their morning routine into motion. She helped him shower, dress, and then prepared a different dish for breakfast.

When they had gone through all the everyday objects she could point to and name, she turned to Mitch.

"I need picture books—ones that show people doing things," she said. "I need to start teaching him verbs."

Mitch nodded and left for the store.

***

With their daily routine firmly in place, Lucy remained unwavering in her efforts to teach Oliver the world around him—her world.

But she knew that hugs and kisses weren't enough to make him understand concepts like love, respect, or empathy.

His past had been filled with cruelty and deprivation.

If he had never received kindness, how could he recognize it?

How could he trust it?

She was convinced that before he could understand emotions, he needed to understand words.

***

Each afternoon, she and Mitch introduced him to something new.

On the second day, they took him to the Botanic Garden on Maryland Avenue. Other days, they visited landmarks— the Lincoln Memorial, the Capitol, the White House, the Smithsonian, the National Mall—places filled with history and meaning.

They knew he couldn't yet understand what these places represented. But maybe, just maybe, their sheer presence would awaken something in him.

And something did.

Oliver began looking forward to their outings. Every afternoon, his eyes would light up in anticipation.

It was a small victory—but to Lucy, it meant the world.

***

Two weeks after their return from Kazan, Lucy picked up her phone and called Ken Rivera.

His reaction was immediate. "Lucy?"

"We found Oliver," she said, her voice steady. "He was committed to the Kazan Specialized High-Security Psychological Hospital nineteen months ago."

She took a breath before continuing.

"He's lost his memory, Ken. His body is covered in scars from unbelievable beatings and torture. We were able to get him released by paying off the people in charge. He's here, with me, in his apartment."

There was a long silence on the other end.

Then Ken spoke. "Lucy...one of my operatives in Russia informed me a long time ago that he had been killed. I told Bill."

Lucy's grip on the phone tightened.

"I'm glad Bill never told me," she said. "If he had, we

wouldn't have fought so hard to find him. We wouldn't have searched for him, dead or alive."

Ken exhaled heavily. "I understand. Do you need anything?"

"Yes. I need an expert on memory loss. Someone who can help him. Can you recommend a doctor?"

"I'll have my team find the best people for Liam," Ken assured her. "I'll call you as soon as I have a name."

Ken called back the next morning.

"You need to take Liam to the Memory Disorders Center at Johns Hopkins University School of Medicine in Baltimore," he told her. "One of my staff spoke with Dr. Ingrid Bell. She's a leader in her field. When we explained that the case was important to us, she agreed to see you tomorrow at three p.m."

Lucy let out a breath of relief. "Thanks, Ken. I'll let you know what she has to say."

She ended the call and turned to Oliver, watching him across the room.

This was the first real step toward answers.

Toward healing.

And maybe—just maybe—toward getting him back.

**

The daily routine was now set.

Lucy pressed on, undeterred, teaching Oliver her way of life—showing him, in every possible way, that she loved him.

But love was something he had never known.

The brutal beatings at the hands of men, the cold indifference of his captors, the emptiness of his imprisonment—none of it had allowed for warmth, for kindness, for human connection.

She struggled with how to show him that things like respect, empathy, and love existed.

Hugs and kisses weren't enough.

Before she could describe love in words, she had to teach him English.

***

Lucy immediately found Dr. Ingrid Bell to be kind and understanding—someone she felt at ease with from the start.

As they settled into her office, Lucy introduced her to Oliver and Mitch.

Dr. Bell offered Oliver a warm, reassuring smile.

"Hello, Oliver," she said gently.

He didn't respond, his gaze flickering between her and the unfamiliar surroundings.

Lucy reached for his hand, giving it a soft squeeze. "We're here to help you," she whispered.

Dr. Bell nodded, her expression calm and patient. "Let's take things one step at a time."

Lucy exhaled, hoping this was the beginning of the answers they had been searching for.

"I was told the name of the patient is Liam Richards, not Oliver Corbyn," Dr. Bell said.

"Liam adopted Oliver Corbyn as an alias when he was tasked by the CIA to prevent the Russians from using data they had stolen from our Boston lab more than three years ago. That name has stuck ever since."

Dr. Bell asked Lucy how Oliver sustained the conspicuous head injury.

"All we know is that Oliver was shot, beaten, and tortured when he was on his last assignment in Russia twenty-two months ago to destroy their capability to produce the Alzheimer's medication he helped us develop. The Russians had stolen the information they needed from our lab."

"Do you mean to say that this man is the same Liam

Richards who is to be awarded the Nobel Prize with Will Bryce in eight weeks' time on December tenth?"

"One and the same," Lucy confirmed. "Our efforts to find him after he didn't return from the assignment have only recently led to success. We discovered he was committed to the Kazan Specialized High-Security Psychological Hospital more than nineteen months ago, while the shooting I referred to took place more than twenty-two months ago. We know he incurred the wounds that caused the scars on his body before he was taken to Kazan."

"Can I see them?" Dr. Bell asked.

Mitch, Oliver, and Lucy sat in the consultation room adjacent to Dr. Bell's office. The sterile, clinical space felt heavy with anticipation.

Lucy gently guided Oliver to his feet.

"We have to take off your clothes, Oliver," she said softly.

As soon as she reached for his shirt, he recoiled.

His body tensed. His head shook violently—the same way it had before.

Lucy stopped him, placing her hands on his arms. She leaned in and pressed a soft kiss to his temple.

"It's okay, Oliver. It's okay."

Her voice was steady, soothing.

Slowly, his body relaxed.

Dr. Bell approached, her eyes filled with quiet reassurance. She began inspecting the scars that marred his body.

Then she inhaled sharply.

The disbelief on her face was unmistakable.

Lucy felt her chest tighten.

She had seen those scars before, traced them with her own hands. But to witness someone else—someone with medical expertise—react in horror only reaffirmed the brutality Oliver had endured.

Dr. Bell exhaled, steadying herself.

"These injuries..." she murmured, her voice tight. "Whoever did this to him—" She cut herself off, pressing her lips together.

Lucy already knew what she was going to say.

She reached for Oliver's hand, holding it tightly.

The scars told a story of pain, survival...and unimaginable cruelty.

And now, they were finally being seen.

"Will you let me take a close-up photograph of the two gunshot scars, Miss Lassiter?"

"Yes, of course, but what scars are you referring to?"

"The one below the left collarbone and the one on his forehead, which, I believe, is the cause of his memory loss."

It was Lucy's turn to be surprised. She dressed Oliver as Dr. Bell made notes on her computer.

"We need to take a CT scan of Oliver's head. Will he allow us to do that?"

"I'm not sure, but if it's important, I'll do my best to make him believe it's okay."

Dr. Bell led them to the nearest CT scan room.

After the previous patient left, she turned to Lucy, explaining how she needed Oliver to lie down on the exam table.

But the moment Lucy gestured for him to do so, he recoiled once again.

His body tensed. He shook his head violently.

Lucy hesitated.

Then, thinking it might help, she climbed onto the table herself, lying down to show him.

But he didn't move.

He just stood there, his eyes darting between her and the unfamiliar machine, his breath uneven.

Lucy sat up, feeling helpless.

She had no idea what to do.

Dr. Bell placed a gentle hand on her shoulder.

"I can't properly diagnose his memory loss without the

scan," she said softly. "If all else fails...we can sedate him."

The words hit Lucy like a blow.

Her eyes welled with tears as the gravity of the situation became undeniable.

Then something unexpected happened. Something Lucy and Mitch would never have believed if they hadn't seen it with their own eyes.

Oliver moved toward her.

Without hesitation, he stroked her hair—the way he always did when he saw her cry.

Then, in an awkward, hesitant manner, he climbed onto the exam table and laid down, mimicking the way she had done moments before.

Tears filled his eyes.

And then—he closed them.

Lucy couldn't stop herself.

She leaned over him, pressing a soft kiss against his damp cheek, her lips lingering for a moment longer than necessary.

Dr. Bell gave a quick nod to the CT technologist.

"Start the scan," she ordered.

The machine whirred to life.

As soon as the table moved and Oliver's head entered the circular scanner, his eyes flew open in panic.

The buzzing, clicking, and whirring sounds surrounded him, growing louder as the scanner rotated.

He flinched. His head moved—causing the scan to be ruined.

The technologist had to start over.

The second attempt was no easier, but Lucy whispered soft reassurances through the intercom, her voice the only thing grounding him.

By the time they returned to the consultation room, Oliver was visibly drained.

Dr. Bell had stayed behind in the CT control room, studying the images.

Lucy, Mitch, and Oliver sat in silence, waiting.

Ten minutes later, she returned.

Without a word, she sat down at her desk, made a few notes on her computer, then looked up at them.

Her expression was unreadable.

Lucy's heart pounded.

"Oliver has incurred a traumatic brain injury. The bullet that struck him on his forehead is still lodged in his brain. It passed through the lower part of the prefrontal cortex, the amygdala, and the hippocampus, the last two of which are areas involved in what we call explicit memory. More than ninety percent of people who are thus shot die immediately afterward or in the hospital later.

"After he incurred the injury, he would have been in a coma for a considerable length of time. It's likely that a superficial inspection by the people around him would have led to the thought he was dead, which isn't all bad because the brain would have been able to release small proteins we call cytokines to initiate neuroprotective processes. Believe me, Oliver is lucky to be alive."

"We found out the Russians had left his body where he had been shot for more than twelve hours before taking him away," Lucy said. "What are his chances of recovering from his memory loss?"

"I'm sorry, I don't know. We first need to study the possibility of surgical removal of the bullet. That in itself is a dangerous operation, but the opinion of most specialists in a case like this is to remove the bullet and then wait and see how the brain reorganizes itself by the process we refer to as neuroplasticity. Neuroplasticity allows the nerve cells in the brain to compensate for injury and to adjust their activities in response to new conditions.

"You also need to know that the bullet that struck Oliver below the left collarbone is also still lodged in his body. I took the liberty of taking some additional scans of that part of his body to check."

Lucy couldn't hold back her tears.

The weight of it all—the reality of Oliver's condition—hit her like a tidal wave.

She had known this wouldn't be easy. She had braced herself for bad news. But seeing the concern in Dr. Bell's eyes, the way she hesitated before speaking, made it all feel so much more real.

Her chest tightened, and before she could stop it, tears spilled down her face.

This wasn't just a memory problem.

This was something far worse.

"As I see it, Miss Lassiter, you have a difficult decision to make. Oliver has shown considerable resilience in living through everything that's happened to him—specifically the bullets that struck him and the beatings and torture he was subjected to during his imprisonment.

"He's alive, and because his memory appears to be intact from when he awakened from his coma after being shot, he should develop further—initially as a young boy. We'll need to keep him under surveillance while he does.

"If we decide it's technically possible to surgically remove the bullet from his brain, we'd be willing to operate on him if you give us permission to do that. If the operation is successful, the chance of at least partially regaining his memory from before the shooting is greater than if we do nothing.

"Please don't decide now. We'll need about two weeks to properly investigate the possibility of surgical removal. If you decide on surgery, we should be able to plan that for a month from now."

Lucy turned to Mitch, her eyes silently pleading for him to

respond to Dr. Bell's proposal.

He understood immediately.

"We need to discuss everything we've learned," Mitch said, his tone steady but firm. "Let's schedule another consultation in two weeks."

Dr. Bell nodded in agreement, and after settling on a date and time, they stood to leave.

Lucy and Mitch thanked her before stepping out into the hallway, Oliver following quietly behind them.

The ride home was quiet.

Lucy sat in the back seat beside Oliver, her heart aching with the weight of everything Dr. Bell had revealed.

She couldn't hold it in—the pain, the helplessness, the sheer unfairness of it all.

Tears welled in her eyes. She turned her face toward the window, hoping Oliver wouldn't notice.

But he did.

For the first time, he didn't just observe—he reacted.

He watched her with growing unease, shifting uncomfortably beside her. Unlike before, when he would simply stroke her hair and return to whatever he was doing, this time, he seemed distressed.

And then it hit her.

He understood.

Not just that she was upset—but that it had something to do with him.

The realization struck deep.

His willingness to lie down for the scan, despite his fear, had been because of her. Because seeing her break down had mattered to him.

It was progress, in the most unexpected way.

But it also shattered her heart even more.

***

Lucy called Ken Rivera the following day to tell him what Dr. Bell had discovered.

"Dr. Bell examined Oliver yesterday. The memory loss was caused by a gunshot to the head. The bullet is still lodged in his brain. He also has a bullet lodged in his body below the collarbone, above the heart."

"Is there anything they can do for him?" Ken asked.

"She needs two weeks to determine if her neurosurgeons can operate on him to remove the bullet from his brain. It's a dangerous operation, and we've yet to decide whether he should undergo surgery. Dr. Bell believes he's not in danger of something life-threatening at present because he's lived for twenty-two months since the shooting. We need to decide in two weeks when we'll see her again. She told us Oliver is lucky to be alive."

"Is Oliver aware of the situation?"

"I don't know. He behaves like a young boy, so I don't think he is. He's only aware of the things that have happened to him after the shooting. His memory loss is complete. His command of the English language has gone, and he can no longer swim. He only speaks a little Russian because of having been exposed to that language during the past twenty-two months. I'm teaching him English to be able, at some stage, to talk to him.

"What you and the CIA should know, Ken, is that the scars Oliver has all over his body indicate he was tortured over an extensive period. The scars on his stomach were caused by fire. Numerous other scars were the result of having been cut with a knife or a sharp instrument. Still others are the result of having been hit hard with a blunt instrument. The beatings and torture will have happened during the latter part of those three months before he was incarcerated in Kazan. Dr. Bell believes he would have died if they had started to torture him directly after they found him."

"I agree," Ken said. "The explosion that occurred immediately after the shooting would have been reason enough to either leave his body where it fell or to remove it to some location and leave it there, thinking he was dead or about to die. They wouldn't have dealt with him until after he regained consciousness, and on knowing who he was, they would have allowed him to recover to some extent before starting the beatings and torture as revenge for destroying the RusPharma facility. More specifically, the torture may have been intended to get him to talk because they wouldn't have realized he had lost his memory. He wouldn't have understood what they were asking, having lost his command of both English and Russian."

"Shall I keep you informed of developments?" Lucy asked.

"Please do."

***

Following their first visit to the Memory Disorders Center, Lucy pressed on, tirelessly teaching Oliver.

Every day, she worked with him—guiding him through English lessons, showing him how to care for himself, how to use the bathroom, dress, and prepare breakfast.

And, above all, she continued to show him love.

As time passed, he improved.

Slowly, he became more independent.

And two weeks later, something changed.

For the first time, when Lucy joined him in bed, he didn't move away.

He no longer curled up at the edge, no longer put as much distance between them.

It was a small thing, but for Lucy, it meant everything.

***

The evening before their second consultation with Dr. Bell, Lucy sat down with Mitch.

She took a deep breath, knowing the question had been weighing on her for days.

"If surgery is an option..." She hesitated, searching his eyes. "Should we do it?"

"I've been thinking of nothing else," Mitch said, "as I'm sure you have too. It's possibly the most difficult decision you'll ever have to make. As I see it, the operation, if feasible, isn't without significant risk. The thought of Oliver regaining some of his memory afterward is difficult to discount, but you're making remarkable progress in what you're doing, and it's possible that, in time, he'll be able to take some sort of role in life next to you."

"I'm frightened the operation will kill him. We need to know what the consequences are of leaving the bullet in his brain untouched before we can decide."

"You're right. We didn't ask Dr. Bell that. I suspect the consequences aren't that serious. Otherwise, he wouldn't have made it through these last twenty-two months."

"So we shouldn't have him undergo surgery if the operation is as dangerous as we think it is unless the bullet needs to be removed to avoid complications at some point. Do you agree?"

"I agree," Mitch replied.

***

The following day, Lucy, Mitch, and Oliver sat across from Dr. Bell once more.

She wasted no time getting to the point.

"I spoke with our neurosurgeons," she began. "They believe surgery to remove the bullet from his brain is feasible—but the risks are considerable."

Lucy swallowed hard. She had been bracing for this, but hearing it out loud made it more real.

"What happens if we don't operate?" she asked.

Dr. Bell folded her hands on the desk. "Without surgery, we can't expect any of his long-term memory to return."

Lucy felt the words sink in.

"But," Dr. Bell continued, "not removing the bullet won't be life-threatening. He's lived with it for nearly two years without complications."

A heavy silence settled over the room.

Mitch glanced at Lucy, waiting for her to process everything.

After a long pause, she shook her head.

"No surgery," she said, her voice quiet but firm. "I won't put him through that."

Dr. Bell nodded in understanding but then shifted the conversation.

"There's another procedure I'd like you to consider," she said. "We could at least remove the bullet in his shoulder, near his left collarbone. And..." She hesitated before adding, "Our plastic surgeons could treat some of the scars on his body."

Lucy's heart clenched.

Another decision to make.

She glanced at Oliver, who sat quietly beside her, unaware of the weight of the choices being made for him.

Once again, she had to decide what was best.

"We need to have advanced a lot further in the way we're treating Oliver before we want to consider that, Dr. Bell," Lucy answered. "It would create tremendous stress, which could lead to a lapse into the state of mind he was in before he was committed to prison. He might interpret what we want to do as inflicting pain, which he might see as torture."

Dr. Bell said she understood. "Please know we're prepared to go a long way in treating Oliver. We consider him a hero for his role in developing the Alzheimer's cure. You need to know that more than half of our patients suffer from memory loss caused by Alzheimer's, and the cure he helped develop has lessened the suffering of most of those patients."

They said goodbye to Dr. Bell and left.

32.

COMPLICATIONS

Lucy's dedication to Oliver's recovery was boundless. Days turned into weeks and weeks into months. With each passing day, Oliver continued to make progress. After three months, Lucy shifted her focus. Now that he had mastered everything else she had taught him—bathing, dressing, preparing meals—she decided it was time to concentrate fully on teaching him English.

He had grown remarkably independent. Each morning, he prepared his own breakfast. For lunch and dinner, Lucy let him decide what they would eat, showing him photos on her iPhone of every dish they had ordered before so he could choose.

She kept an ample supply of snacks, mostly healthy options, knowing he liked to eat between meals. But she also stocked a few candy bars, recognizing his preference for sweets.

Still, she was never far away. She would watch over his choices, sometimes gently gesturing that he shouldn't always want the same candy bar or subtly correcting him when he made other mistakes.

The extra food had worked. Oliver had gained most of the weight he had lost. His once-pale complexion was now replaced with a tan.

Lucy had even adjusted his hairstyle—letting it grow just enough to conceal the scar on his forehead. Similarly, she kept his beard slightly longer to cover the scar on the right side of his face.

She gave him full control over when he wanted to go to bed; though, for some reason, they always ended up going to bed at the same time.

Each morning, he would wake up early to watch cartoons.

Yet despite all the progress, something troubled Lucy deeply. Oliver still showed little emotion. He continued to stroke her hair when he noticed she was upset. Occasionally, he would wipe a tear from his own eyes when she cried about something involving him. But he never hugged her. Never kissed her. Never reciprocated any gesture of affection.

She longed for acknowledgment—even the simplest sign that he cared for her in some way. But it never came.

During one of their visits to Dr. Bell, Lucy finally asked the question that had been haunting her.

"Is there a reason for his lack of emotion?" she asked carefully. "His inability to love me—even in the way a child might love a parent or a caretaker?"

Dr. Bell's expression softened.

"I should have mentioned this before," she admitted. "The bullet damaged the amygdala. That part of the brain is critical for processing emotions. His injury probably impairs his ability to feel or express them...especially love."

The words hit Lucy harder than anything else ever had. She sat there, numb, absorbing the devastating truth.

He couldn't love her. Not in the way she loved him. Not in any way at all.

Despite knowing this, Lucy refused to give up. She desperately tried to reach him—to win his love. But no matter how much she persisted, there was no change.

Although he no longer moved away from her when she

climbed into bed beside him, he still maintained his distance. On many nights, she had to fight the overwhelming urge to touch him, to be closer to him. But she never did. She knew the truth—inside his body, he was still just an eight- or nine-year-old child. She would never cross that line.

Lucy's entire world became Oliver. She never left the apartment without him. They were inseparable. She even quit her job at Morgan Pharma, devoting every waking moment to his care.

Jacky and Bill, who flew in from LA every few weeks to visit, begged her to reconsider. They suggested hiring private caretakers and a teacher so she could resume her life. She flatly refused.

"Oliver is my priority," she told them, her voice unwavering. "He is my destiny. For as long as I live."

Bill and Jacky returned to Beverly Hills, deeply concerned. They feared the daughter they loved so much had taken on an impossible task—one that would forever deprive her of happiness.

Lucy's old friends reached out too. Zoey called one day, suggesting they go out to have some fun. Lucy didn't hesitate. "Disappear from my life," she said.

They would never see or speak to each other again.

Through it all, Mitch remained by her side. He often flew Lucy and Oliver to Boston, where she spent time with Sasha and where Will sat down with Oliver, trying to talk to him.

Mitch never questioned her. Never doubted her. He believed in her mission. And, in his own quiet way, he made sure she was never alone.

***

The time Lucy had spent teaching Oliver English had been rewarding. After four months, they could finally talk about a variety of subjects.

One afternoon, as they sat together, Lucy took a deep breath. She knew she had to ask. But she also dreaded the answer.

Looking into Oliver's eyes, she finally said the words.

"Tell me, Oliver, who hurt you before you were taken to Kazan?" Her gaze dropped to the scars that marked his body.

"Bad man."

"What did he do?"

"Man hit."

"Where did he hit you?"

Oliver didn't reply but pointed to the right side of his face, his stomach, his back, and his legs.

"What did he hit you with?"

"Big knife."

"Did he hit you or did he cut you?"

"One man hit, one man cut."

"What happened to your stomach?"

"Fire."

"What do you mean?"

"Fire from bottle."

Lucy understood this to mean he had been burned by the flame of an acetylene torch.

"Who shot you?" Lucy asked, pointing to his forehead and his collarbone.

"Oliver not know."

Lucy decided to change the subject. "Are you happy here?"

"Oliver not know happy."

Lucy needed to think hard about how to describe happiness. "Do you like it here?"

"Oliver not know like."

"Do you want to stay here?"

"Oliver stay!" he said emphatically.

"Lucy stay here too, Oliver?"

"Oliver stay! Lucy stay!"

"Mitch stay here too?"

"Oliver stay! Lucy stay! Mitch stay!"

Lucy's heart lifted when she heard Oliver express that he wanted to be with her and Mitch. It was a small step, but a meaningful one.

This conversation made her realize something—it was time to teach him about emotions. She remembered one of the picture books Mitch had bought months ago contained drawings of faces showing different emotions—sad, happy, angry, fearful, surprised, disgusted, and more. Determined, she found the book, sat down beside Oliver on the couch, and began explaining each one.

***

As the days passed, Oliver's English skills flourished. Each morning, they dedicated time to expanding his vocabulary, and his ability to communicate grew quicker than Lucy had expected.

After two more months, Lucy decided it was time to quiz him.

She wanted to know if he understood feelings—not just as words, but as something he could recognize within himself.

Sitting beside him, she gently asked, "Are you happy, Oliver?"

"Yes. Lucy not happy."

Lucy was surprised by his answer. "Why do you think that?"

"Lucy cry much."

"Lucy is sad because bad people hurt you."

"Oliver not pain now."

Lucy was stumped, not knowing how to address his indifference to having been beaten and tortured and her reason for crying.

"Lucy wants to hold and kiss you, Oliver, but you don't want that," she said instead.

Oliver now looked at her inquisitively. "Hold and kiss hurts."

"No," she said. "Holding and kissing each other is cool. Why does it hurt?"

"Man in Kazan hold Oliver—much hurt."

Lucy had suspected all along he was abused in prison, and to now hear him confirm that overwhelmed her. She realized it was important to immediately disprove his belief that holding and kissing someone resulted in hurt.

"That was a bad man. Lucy is a good person. Lucy will not hurt Oliver. Lucy likes Oliver, and Lucy wants Oliver to kiss Lucy."

Lucy didn't know of another way to say what she wanted. She was surprised when Oliver kissed her on the cheek in a shy sort of way. She couldn't help herself, and she responded by throwing her arms around his neck and kissing him on the lips.

"Did that hurt?"

"No...Lucy happy now?"

"Yes, Lucy is happy now."

That night, as they lay in bed, Oliver reached out. His fingers gently brushed Lucy's shoulder. She turned to look at him, expecting nothing more than the usual silence. Instead, he leaned in—and kissed her softly on the cheek.

Lucy's breath caught.

Tears welled in her eyes as she looked at him, her heart aching with emotions she couldn't put into words.

For the first time, he had initiated affection. For the first time, he had chosen to give, not just receive. She turned away, unable to stop the quiet tears from falling.

***

Around the same time, Mitch offered a suggestion.

"Let's take Oliver to the gym," he said. "It'll help him regain some of his strength and fitness."

Lucy agreed, and from that day forward, the three of them committed to regular gym sessions, visiting the well-equipped fitness center in their apartment building every second afternoon.

Mitch guided Oliver through the equipment, starting with a modest program in the first week. Gradually, he increased the intensity, pushing Oliver little by little as his strength and endurance improved. After every workout, they returned to the apartment, where Oliver and Mitch each took a shower before settling back into their usual routine.

During the fourth week, after Mitch once again raised the intensity of Oliver's workout, something changed.

"Oliver head hurt," Oliver murmured, rubbing his forehead.

Lucy immediately took notice.

"Let's go home," Mitch said, exchanging a glance with Lucy.

They cut the session short and returned to the apartment. As always, Oliver went straight to the bathroom to shower while Mitch took a shower in the second bathroom.

Fifteen minutes later, Mitch stepped into the living room. Lucy looked up expectantly, waiting for Oliver to appear. But he didn't. He was always the first to finish showering and join them. Something wasn't right. A chill ran down Lucy's spine as she stood up and hurried toward the bathroom. Her heart pounded as she pushed the door open. Oliver lay on the floor, still dressed in his T-shirt, shorts, and gym shoes. Motionless.

Lucy's breath hitched in her throat. Her worst fear had come true.

"Mitch!" she screamed. "Call 911—Oliver's unconscious! Hurry!"

Mitch wasted no time. As soon as he reached an emergency dispatcher, he answered her questions impatiently, urgency lacing his voice.

Fifteen minutes later, when the paramedics arrived, Mitch made a request.

"Take him to the Memory Disorders Center at Johns Hopkins in Baltimore—he's a patient there."

One of the paramedics exchanged a glance with his partner before responding.

"The fastest way to get him there is by helicopter. We'll transport him to the Walter Reed National Military Medical Center in Bethesda first. From there, he'll be airlifted to Johns Hopkins."

Mitch nodded. "Do it, please."

He arranged for Lucy to accompany them, then quickly called a taxi for himself.

"I'll meet you there," he told Lucy. "I'll also call Dr. Bell and let her know what happened."

When the helicopter landed at the hospital heliport, Dr. Bell and two nurses were already waiting. Lucy barely registered their presence—her eyes were fixed on Oliver as he was transferred to another wheeled stretcher and rushed toward the emergency room.

She followed closely behind, her heart pounding. At the door, Dr. Bell stopped her.

"Wait here," she said gently, motioning toward a waiting room.

Lucy hesitated but reluctantly nodded, knowing she had no choice.

The examination lasted two hours. Two agonizing, unbearable hours. Lucy's anxiety grew with every passing minute. She paced, wrung her hands, and tried to sit still, but all failed to lessen her fears. When Dr. Bell finally appeared, Lucy shot up from her seat, meeting her halfway across the room. One look at the doctor's face, and Lucy knew. Something was wrong.

"Sit down, please, Miss Lassiter," she said. "What was Oliver doing when he lost consciousness?"

"He and Mitch had just completed part of a program in the gym when Oliver told us he had a headache. When we returned to the apartment, Oliver went to the bathroom to take a shower. When he didn't return when I thought he would, I went to look for him and found him on the floor, still wearing his exercise clothes. He must have lost consciousness fifteen minutes before I found him. How is he? Tell me, please."

"We performed a CT scan of his brain because we suspected his condition was related to the bullet lodged there. We were shocked to find internal bleeding in the region around the bullet. The increase in blood pressure associated with working out in the gym will have caused that. I have bad news, Miss Lassiter," she added. "We now need to carry out the operation we've discussed several times. We must relieve the pressure in that part of the brain, which, among other things, requires we remove the bullet. He won't make it through the night if we don't."

"No, God, no!" Lucy cried.

"May I assume you'll want us to do that now?"

"Yes, yes, of course," Lucy said with a sob.

"Good. I'll have someone bring you a form to sign. I apologize for not being able to stay to talk to you in detail about what we're about to do. Oliver will now be transferred to the neurosurgery department. I've already begun preparations for surgery. One of our neurosurgeons has arrived to take charge, and two others have been called to assist.

"I'll be watching them all the time, and when there's something to report, I'll let you know. Please follow me. I'll show you to a comfortable waiting room near the OR. The operation could take as much as nine hours. One of the nurses will bring you coffee or tea and something to eat."

Dr. Bell showed Lucy to the waiting room. As the door clicked shut behind her, something inside her broke. The stress, the worry, the anxiety—all the weight she had carried since that moment at Sheremetyevo Airport more than two and a half years ago—finally crashed down on her.

She crumpled, tears flooding her eyes as she wept uncontrollably.

When Mitch found her, his heart ached at the sight of her grief. He pulled her into his arms, but there was nothing he could say to comfort her. She wept, and Mitch held her, offering only the comfort of his presence. She cried until there were no more tears left.

"It's my fault," Lucy whispered between sobs. "The stress... I've put him through so much."

Mitch didn't know how to respond. He knew she was carrying the weight of everything, but hearing her voice that guilt made him feel responsible too. The workouts, the strain, the risk. He had been the one to suggest it.

The waiting was unbearable.

Mitch and Lucy were brought food and coffee by friendly nurses, but it did little to ease the tension gnawing at them. Dr. Bell didn't return with updates until early that evening. When she finally did, she explained about their decision.

"We've opted for open brain surgery," she said, her voice steady but laced with concern. "We were able to access the area affected by the bullet. His vitals are stable, but the riskiest part of the operation is still to come."

Lucy and Mitch nodded, trying to process the gravity of the situation. They thanked Dr. Bell, their thoughts overwhelmed with the news.

The hours stretched on, the waiting room feeling like a weight pressing down on them. Then, several hours later, Dr. Bell returned with more news.

"We successfully removed the bullet," Dr. Bell said, her voice steady but filled with a note of surprise.

She hesitated for a moment before continuing.

"But what's truly remarkable...is what we discovered from the MRI."

Lucy held her breath.

"Oliver's brain has shown an extraordinary level of neuroplasticity," Dr. Bell explained. "It has begun to repair some of the damage caused by the bullet."

Mitch exhaled sharply. Lucy felt her pulse quicken. Hope... the first in all that time. It felt real.

"He's...he's going to be okay?" she asked, barely able to breathe the question.

Dr. Bell smiled faintly. "We're cautiously optimistic. The next part will tell us more, but he's stable."

Hours passed, and it wasn't until 2 a.m. that Dr. Bell returned. She stepped into the room, her expression softer this time.

"The operation is over," she said, her voice full of exhaustion and relief. "We were all taken aback by how well things went. He's now being transported to the Neurosciences Critical Care Unit. They'll monitor him closely there, but for now, the worst is behind him."

Lucy's body relaxed for the first time in hours. The anxiety hadn't gone away entirely, but this was the news she had needed to hear. They had made it through.

"We need to talk about the recovery process," Dr. Bell continued. "I want him to stay with us for ten to twelve weeks. His precise injury is uncommon, and the degree of neuroplasticity his brain is developing is also uncommon. We don't know how that's going to affect him. It remains to be seen to what degree he requires rehabilitation specialists to help him walk, carry out daily tasks, and assist him if he were to develop a speech disability. Can you agree to that?"

"Only if I can stay with him all of that time. His feelings are those of a young boy. He would become distressed if I were not here. Moreover, he was sexually abused when he was in prison, and that has caused him to build up a wall around himself. My interaction with him is only now leading to a more normal relationship, in which he's no longer afraid of being touched. He wouldn't kiss me on the cheek, for example, until recently."

"We can cater for an arrangement in which you have your own room, and if you want to sleep in the same room as Oliver, we can arrange for your bed to be rolled next to his once he regains consciousness. Would that satisfy your requirements?"

"Yes, thank you," Lucy responded. "Can I see him?"

"Do you think you should?"

"Yes, why shouldn't I?"

"Because he's in a state we call a postoperative coma. He's connected to various life-support systems. It's not a pretty sight. His coma could last a week. It might be better to see him for the first time after he regains consciousness."

"I want to see him now, please."

"I'll take you to him. The doctor in attendance and one of the nurses will be making him as comfortable as they can. I'll ask them to prepare a room for you as close as possible to where Oliver has been taken. Mitch can come with us, but I would prefer to only let you see him if you don't mind."

When Lucy entered Oliver's hospital room, she was shocked to see him.

He lay motionless, attached to several life-support and monitoring systems—a ventilator, IV drips, a urinary catheter, and monitors tracking his blood pressure, heart rate, respiratory rate, and temperature.

His hair had been partially shaved, revealing the sutures that had been made along his scalp.

A doctor stood beside him, carefully applying a dressing and bandages to the incision.

But what struck Lucy the most was his appearance. He looked pale and frail, just as he had the day she found him in Kazan. Her heart ached for him. She wanted to take his hand, to hold him, to remind him she was there. But for now, all she could do was watch—and wait.

When Lucy finally stepped out of Oliver's room, a nurse greeted her with a kind smile.

"There's a room across the corridor for you," she said, leading Lucy to a small, private space.

The room was simple but functional—a hospital bed, an adjustable rolling overbed table, a small closet, and a table with two chairs near a window. An internal door led to a bathroom.

"This will be yours for the duration of his stay here," the nurse said.

Lucy nodded gratefully. It meant she wouldn't have to leave him.

***

Lucy and Mitch left the hospital to return to the apartment. She packed lightly, bringing only what she absolutely needed. When the taxi arrived, Mitch placed a steady hand on her shoulder.

"I'll be on standby for anything you need," he assured her.

She gave him a small, tired smile. "I know."

Then she climbed into the taxi, heading back to the hospital. When she returned to the Neurosciences Critical Care Unit, she walked into her new space, placed her bag on the bed, and took a moment to breathe. She slowly unpacked, placing her things in the small closet, then familiarized herself with the space.

This would be her home for as long as Oliver needed her. She wouldn't leave his side.

Not now.

Not ever.

33.

FINALE

Oliver's vital signs remained stable. Every day, Lucy sat by his bedside for an hour each morning, afternoon, and evening. There was little else for her to do. Occasionally, she would visit the Cobblestone Café in the food court for lunch or dinner, but more often than not, she stayed in the Neurosciences Critical Care Unit, eating whatever the nurses offered her. She made each nurse promise to call her—no matter the hour—the moment Oliver showed any sign of regaining consciousness.

Nearly a week passed before, at last, a nurse told her that Oliver was showing signs of awakening from his coma. Heart pounding, she rushed to his room, where a doctor and a nurse stood by his bedside, watching him closely. The doctor turned to her and began explaining why they were monitoring him so intently.

"The eye movement he's displaying is either due to regaining consciousness or autonomic responsiveness, as we call it. To decide which, we have to find out whether he's regained a sense of awareness of what's happening around him. He should be able to demonstrate an ability to act with intent on truly regaining consciousness."

Lucy was glad for the doctor's explanation. She stood back

from the bed to avoid interfering with what he and the nurse were doing. When, after some time, Oliver's eyes remained open, Lucy felt a feeling of anticipation pass through her body, which turned into joy when his eye movement indicated he was aware of what was happening around him. This caused the doctor and the nurse to remove the intubation tube and the ventilator.

"Take a deep breath and exhale, please," the doctor instructed Oliver.

Lucy had been told that the transition to normal breathing after extubation often required assistance, such as forcing the patient to take a deep breath.

There was no response. Oliver's gaze drifted around the room, unfocused and distant. The doctor repeated his request several times, but Oliver remained unresponsive, as if he hadn't heard a word.

Lucy's joy quickly gave way to unease. She watched as the doctor and nurse exchanged a glance—silent, yet telling, as if questioning why Oliver wasn't reacting.

And then, finally, a sign of progress. Though he still hadn't responded to their commands, it was clear he was breathing on his own. A few ragged coughs escaped his throat, as though his body was instinctively trying to clear his windpipe.

"What is your name?" the doctor asked him.

The doctor repeated the question three times.

"Pavel," Oliver said suddenly, with a Russian intonation and a croaky voice.

A feeling of trepidation filled Lucy. The doctor looked at her, not understanding Oliver's answer to his question.

"He was called Pavel by the staff and inmates of the psychiatric hospital in Russia he was imprisoned in for nineteen months. But why would he remember that name when we've been calling him Oliver ever since we freed him nine months ago?"

"If he was called by different names, he would answer my question with the first name his brain recalls. For now, we should be happy he's regained consciousness and that he's able to remember his name."

The doctor and nurse kept most of the monitoring systems and IV drips in place before quietly exiting the room. As soon as they were gone, Lucy pulled up a chair and sat beside Oliver's bed. Gently, she took one of his hands in both of hers. She had noticed—ever since he became aware of his surroundings—that his eyes had been on her, watching.

"Do you know who I am, Oliver?"

"My name is Pavel."

"The people you were with in Kazan called you Pavel, but your name is Oliver."

Oliver didn't immediately reply, as if he was trying to recall what Lucy had referred to.

"Yes, I remember, and you are Lucy," he continued after a pause.

Lucy was surprised to hear him use the first-person singular because he had always referred to himself as Oliver.

"Do you remember Mitch, Sasha, and me taking you out of prison in Kazan?"

"Yes, we went in a car to an airplane."

"And do you remember living with Mitch and me in the same apartment, watching TV, and doing other things you like?"

"Yes, I remember."

Lucy wished the doctor and nurse were present while Oliver slowly remembered the events of the last nine months. Their conversation lasted more than an hour.

"How do you feel, Oliver?"

"My head feels strange."

In saying so, he used his free hand to feel the bandages covering his head.

"Do you remember falling down in the shower?"

"Yes, I felt dizzy."

Lucy was again surprised to hear him use the words *strange* and *dizzy* because she couldn't remember having taught him those.

"The exercise in the gym with Mitch caused that. Do you remember doing those exercises with Mitch?"

Oliver looked at her with an expression that led Lucy to believe he wanted to say something without knowing what exactly.

"Do you remember Dr. Bell, Oliver?" she continued when he hadn't answered her question.

"Yes."

"She and some nice people took away the pain in your head."

"Can we go home now?" Oliver asked, disregarding what Lucy had said and looking at the IV drips as if to find out how to free himself from them.

"No, you and I must stay here until you feel better."

Oliver looked around the room he was in. "Where will you sleep?"

"In a bed next to your bed."

Dr. Bell walked into the room. She had been informed that Oliver had regained consciousness. She allowed the conversation between Lucy and Oliver to proceed while she listened.

"A big bed like we have at home is better."

This again startled Lucy because it was said in perfect English.

"I'll be close to you when we go to sleep."

"I like you, Lucy."

Lucy was dumbfounded on hearing him say that.

Dr. Bell asked Lucy to step outside into the corridor.

"I want to talk to Dr. Bell, Oliver. Is that okay?"

He didn't answer. Lucy recognized his wish for her to stay.

She planted a kiss on his cheek and left the room anyway.

"I've seen this happen before," Dr. Bell explained. "His knowledge of the English language is returning. General facts and information are stored in a different part of the brain than where explicit memories are stored. The latter part of the brain has been damaged, and he might not recover that part of his memory, but the part in which semantic information is stored, such as knowledge of a language, is relatively intact, and he's now remembering that."

Lucy was deliriously happy to have Dr. Bell explain that to her. She embraced her before returning to Oliver's room.

"Don't tire him, Miss Lassiter," Dr. Bell called out after her. "It's taking him significant effort to remember the appropriate words at the right time. We should now allow him to sleep."

When Lucy returned to her chair next to Oliver's bed, she told him that Dr. Bell wanted him to sleep.

"I feel tired," Oliver replied.

He closed his eyes and was asleep within minutes.

Lucy stepped out of the room to call Mitch, unable to contain her excitement. Oliver's command of English was returning, and she wanted to share the good news. The moment Mitch answered, he could hear the joy in her voice.

***

From that day on, Lucy and Oliver spent hours in conversation. The topics were often trivial, but that didn't matter to her. What fascinated her was how he continued to use words she never taught him. Yet despite his eagerness to talk, he tired quickly, and more often than not, she was asked to let him rest.

A week later, Oliver was finally permitted to get out of bed for short periods. He was transferred from the Neurosciences

Critical Care Unit to the Neurosciences Care Unit. A physical therapist assessed his ability to walk and climb stairs before guiding him through exercises designed to rebuild his strength and fitness.

Afterward, an occupational therapist evaluated how well he could manage essential daily tasks—getting dressed, using the restroom, and taking a shower. Finally, a speech and language therapist worked with him, tracking his progress in recalling and using English.

Every other day, Dr. Bell stopped by to speak with Lucy, updating her on Oliver's steady improvement.

"I'm satisfied," Dr. Bell said, "to find that Oliver's ability to perform the assessed activities hasn't suffered because of the operation. We now need to see to what degree he can regain his explicit memory."

"Would knowledge that he used to love me be a part of what you call explicit memory?" Lucy asked.

"That's a difficult question to answer. I believe emotional events like a stressful goodbye, a kiss after a major argument, or making love for the first time would, but not necessarily minor events."

"Should I start asking him about specific events that occurred before he was shot to determine if he's regained that part of his memory?"

"Yes, but as soon as you find he doesn't remember the event, change the subject to something he does to avoid him worrying he can't remember."

When Lucy started talking to him according to this plan, he was no longer confined to his bed. They would start their chats in the morning at the table in his or her room. One of these conversations was remarkable in more ways than one.

"Will you let me ask you questions about what you can remember, Oliver?"

"You have already asked me questions about what I remember."

"Yes, I know, but I want to know if you can remember more things."

"I will answer your questions," Oliver said in perfect English.

"Are you aware that you are now remembering more English? You're using words I didn't teach you."

"I sometimes remember many English words."

"That's cool. Dr. Bell told me you'll soon remember even more English words."

"What did Dr. Bell do to me?"

"You were shot twice. One bullet damaged your head, and another bullet hit your shoulder. Both bullets remained in your body all this time. The pain you felt in your head when we were in the gym with Mitch caused you to fall on the floor in the shower. Dr. Bell took the bullet out of your head to make you feel better. Do you remember having pain in your head?"

"Yes. I called you in the shower because of pain in my head."

Lucy hadn't realized he had called her before he collapsed on the floor. It made her feel guilty because she hadn't realized the headache he complained of was indicative of a serious problem.

"I'm sorry. I didn't hear you."

They remained quiet for a while. Lucy thought this would be a good time to ask him if he remembered anything before he was shot.

"What other things can you remember?" she asked.

His answer came quickly, as if the question had lingered in his mind for a time. "I can see things when I close my eyes."

"What things?"

"Many bad things."

"Tell me."

"I see you when you were angry and when you were sick."

Lucy was taken aback when Oliver described what he saw when he closed his eyes. His vision of her—angry with him—left her feeling uneasy. She knew it had happened once—on the morning after she had barricaded herself in the guest room of his apartment when she refused to speak to him. Now, as she sat beside him, she considered how best to explain what had led to that moment.

"I'm so sorry, Oliver. I was angry with you because you wanted to go away for a long time, and I wanted you to stay with me. I'll never be angry with you again."

Lucy decided not to talk further with him about what he saw when he closed his eyes until she could talk to Dr. Bell about it.

When Lucy saw Dr. Bell enter the unit late that afternoon, she told her what Oliver had said.

"That's good news once again," Dr. Bell said. "It means that part of his explicit memory is returning. It's common in that case for the patient to first remember events that caused great stress or worry at the time. You now need to prompt him to tell you about every one of his pictures or visions and, if you can, explain to him the way those are connected or related. It will help him remember more of the events that happened. We refer to that process as tests of recall and recognition."

The next morning after breakfast, Lucy resumed talking to Oliver about his pictures. Once again, he explained that there were many more, and she encouraged him to describe each one. Some she couldn't relate to—either because they occurred before she met him or were tied to his CIA assignments. But one thing became clear: Every one of his "pictures," as he called them, was linked to a stressful or worrisome event.

Over the next week, Lucy carefully pieced together the connections between many of the memories he described. When she finally shared her observations with him, she watched him closely. In some cases, he nodded in recognition; in others, he simply said, "Yes."

Then something shifted. Oliver began recalling other events—ones untainted by stress or anxiety. Some, he said, made him happy. But as he spoke, Lucy found herself perplexed by some of the memories he held dear.

"I was happy when I saw you waiting for me, when you kissed me unexpectedly, when I kissed you, and when you and I were in bed kissing and holding each other," he said.

Lucy could have jumped for joy when she realized that, in recalling the memory of them being in bed together—kissing and holding each other—as a happy event, Oliver might finally be able to let the trauma of his past fade into the background. Perhaps now, the abuse he had suffered would no longer stand in the way of his ability to touch her in bed—or allow her to touch him.

Another week passed, and Lucy became convinced that Oliver had developed a reasonable grasp of the events in his life since they first met. She knew that, in time, more details would surface. What she didn't yet know was the state of his semantic memory—his ability to recall factual knowledge like the details of the Alzheimer's cure or, for that matter, everything he had learned in school about the world and the people in it.

Still, his progress in reclaiming the English language was undeniable. And since language was stored in semantic memory, she held on to hope that, in time, his recovery would extend to other areas as well.

***

Lucy raised the subject of going home with Oliver in the tenth week of their stay at the Neurosciences Care Unit after Dr. Bell informed her there was presently little else they could do for him.

"Shall we go home now, Oliver?" she asked him.

"Yes, I want to go home now," he replied. "Is Dr. Bell happy with my progress?"

Lucy had noticed that during the past two weeks, Oliver rarely made language errors.

"Dr. Bell is pleased with your progress. We'll need to see her every two weeks after we go home. You are her favorite patient, and she wants to regularly check on you. Is that okay?"

"Yes."

"I'll call Mitch to ask him to pick us up."

***

They returned to Oliver's apartment on a Friday afternoon. As they unpacked, Mitch busied himself in the kitchen, brewing coffee and preparing something to eat—both of them had skipped lunch.

While they settled in, Lucy filled Mitch in on the extent of Oliver's recovery. Oliver listened closely, occasionally correcting her or adding details she had missed.

Mitch had only visited the Neurosciences Care Unit three times, mostly during the early days of Lucy's stay. Seeing Oliver now speaking fluent English and recalling so much of his past left him astounded.

To celebrate their homecoming, Lucy suggested they go out to a nearby restaurant for dinner. Mitch and Oliver agreed.

After they were seated, the waiter handed them menus and asked what they'd like to drink. Lucy reached for the wine and beverage menu—but before she could open it, Oliver surprised them both by taking it from her.

"I'm sorry, Luce, but I can't allow you to choose anything containing alcohol," he said.

It was the first time he called her "Luce" since they rescued him from the prison in Kazan, and it was the first time he referred to the time of her alcohol addiction, apart from having said before he remembered she was very sick. She was secretly thrilled by what he had said, as it demonstrated his closeness to the person he had been before the destruction of the RusPharma production facility.

It was late when they returned to the apartment. Lucy stretched and announced she was tired and ready for bed. Oliver echoed her sentiment, and together they wished Mitch good night before heading to their room.

As they settled in, Lucy couldn't help but notice Oliver's familiar habit—going to bed whenever she did. It made her wonder if he still struggled to sleep without her presence—if the scars of his past trauma would continue to keep him from letting her touch him in bed. But something had shifted. Their relationship had changed. He was no longer the boy he had been before the operation.

For the first time, she allowed herself to consider the possibility of making love to him. But uncertainty lingered. Would he share that desire? Or would she be met with hesitation, perhaps even rejection? She knew she would have to tread carefully, moving forward only if the moment felt right.

They slipped beneath the blankets at nearly the same time. As always, Lucy left the lamp above the vanity on, casting soft shadows on the walls—the same ones Oliver had studied so intently during his first nights back from Kazan. Now he lay on his back, his gaze flickering over them once more.

Lucy turned onto her side, watching him. Then, tentatively, she inched a little closer—closer than she would have before the operation.

"I love you, Oliver," she said.

"I love you too, Lucy."

He turned on his side to look at her. This encouraged her

to throw caution to the wind and she crept a little closer to him yet again.

"I don't know how to ask, but will you let me touch and feel you? I've wanted to do that for a long time, but I was afraid you wouldn't let me."

"I don't like being touched in bed. A man would often come into my bed in Kazan after the lights were turned off. He hurt me, but he was an important person, and there was nothing I could do to stop him. But you taught me it's different between two people who love each other—that two people will make each other happy when they kiss and hold each other. But I don't know how."

"It's called making love. You made love to me many times before you were shot. Now I want to make love to you and make you happy! When it becomes difficult to lie still, you should do whatever your feelings tell you. Is that okay?"

"But that sounds as if making love only makes one of us happy. I don't want you to be unhappy when you make love to me."

"It won't make me unhappy, Oliver. It will excite me beyond belief to know I'm creating special feelings of desire in you for me."

"I think I understand. But I'll make love to you afterward to create those feelings in you."

Lucy didn't reply to his last statement. Instead, she cuddled up to him and tenderly kissed him on the lips, eyes, ears, and neck. She pulled up his T-shirt and stroked his chest, softly and teasingly. She followed with a series of very tender kisses on his body. She then pushed back the blankets, sat up on her knees, and took off her pajama top and panties and helped him take off his T-shirt and shorts.

She lay back down next to him again and pulled the blankets back up. She pushed her body against him to feel him completely. She knew the excitement it produced would be mutual. Lucy noticed he had now lost his ability to lie still, and she suspected he wouldn't have the sexual stamina he had possessed before. She hurried to keep up with him.

Lucy straddled him, initially to sit upright so he could feel her breasts, but then she leaned forward to kiss him again. She knew that the thought of entering her would now come naturally. She was surprised when he did, almost immediately.

Lucy held on to him. She worked her pelvic muscles to hold him fast. She knew by doing so, she could delay his point of no return until she was ready. When that moment came, she was no longer able to support her weight with her arms. Waves of ecstasy she hadn't experienced in a long time drowned her as she collapsed onto him.

She remained lying on top of him. She kissed him everywhere on his upper body and his face. He closed his eyes when she lingered with long kisses on his eyelids.

"I longed to make love to you like that for a long time. Do you now remember us making love like that before?"

"Yes, the memory of it came when you sat up on your knees. I remembered the first time you did—when we were in Russia together for the conference. It was a powerful memory, and I suddenly fully understood what you said about excitement and desire."

Lucy continued to lie on top of him. She relished being able to feel him completely. Peace engulfed her. She was particularly elated about his ability to now rid himself of the consequences of the sexual abuse. She also knew that his memory of who he was before he destroyed the RusPharma production facility had automatically restored the qualities in him she fell in love with. He would now have no difficulty in having respect, sympathy, empathy, compassion, and love for others.

***

Lucy and Oliver woke up late the next morning. In the kitchen, they found a note from Mitch on the table. It was short and to the point—he had left to fly to Boston to pick up Sasha and Will, who planned to visit that afternoon. A postscript at the bottom mentioned that Jacky and Bill would likely be joining them as well. The pilot assigned to the Lassiter jet told him they would be flying them to Dulles that day.

Lucy checked their kitchen supplies and realized they were missing key ingredients for the lunch she had in mind. She suggested a trip to the store. Oliver readily agreed, and the rest of the morning was spent preparing a spread of delicacies.

Sasha, Will, and Mitch arrived first, followed by Jacky and Bill an hour later. From the moment they stepped inside, it was clear they were particularly eager to see how Oliver had fared after surgery. They were astonished at how much of his memory he had regained.

When the opportunity arose, Lucy asked Will to join her in the kitchen. She asked him to subtly gauge how much Oliver remembered about the Alzheimer's cure and his broader knowledge of pharmaceutical research. She kept a close eye on Oliver as Will returned to his seat and steered the conversation toward the cure. To her surprise, Oliver not only joined in the conversation but contributed more to the discussion than Will himself. Bill, Jacky, Mitch, and Sasha listened intently.

An hour later, when Lucy returned to the kitchen, Will joined her, his expression one of quiet amazement. He assured her that Oliver's memory seemed fully intact—he still knew everything they had done and what was needed to continue the research on dementia. Relief washed over Lucy.

That evening, Jacky and Bill checked into a nearby hotel, as they always did when visiting. Not wanting to impose further, Sasha and Will decided to do the same. It also meant they could spend more time together the next day without feeling like houseguests.

***

An incident the following afternoon would drive a wedge between Jacky, Bill, and Lucy for months.

During lunch, which they had ordered in, Bill suddenly turned to Oliver.

"Are you prepared to accept the position of CEO of all of Morgan Pharma?"

The question caught everyone off guard—Lucy most of all.

Oliver didn't answer. Instead, he turned and looked at Lucy.

"How could you ask Oliver that?" she asked.

"Because I was listening closely to the conversation between Oliver and Will yesterday, and I heard Oliver say things that tell me he's more than capable of becoming company CEO. As you know, we've been searching for someone to fill that position for a long time, unsuccessfully. I spoke to your mother about it, and she agrees with me."

Lucy was deeply upset by Bill's proposal. She stood up from the table.

"Oliver has a long way to go before he should be approached about something like that. He still has to undergo six operations. He has a bullet in his shoulder that needs to be removed, and he needs to undergo plastic surgery to remove the scars on his forehead, face, back, stomach, and legs. That's going to take considerable time.

"Besides, Dr. Bell wants to see him every two weeks. Apart from all that, I want to talk to him about our future together in a peaceful setting without pointers from you."

Oliver smiled and also stood up. After kissing her, he sat her down and told Bill he first needed to undergo the surgery Lucy had mentioned and to have a discussion with her about their future together.

"Thank you, Oliver," Bill said. "Why don't you and Lucy take a long holiday on *Artemis* when you're ready to discuss your future?"

"Thanks for the offer, but I'll leave that up to Lucy to decide."

***

Over the next thirty-two weeks, Oliver underwent six surgeries. Dr. Bell supervised each procedure. Only one required a general surgeon; plastic surgeons performed the remaining five. Each extensive surgery demanded a six-week recovery period. Throughout it all, Lucy stayed by his side whenever he was hospitalized for observation.

Between operations, Oliver spent much of his time reflecting on his future with Lucy. The uncertainty weighed on him, growing heavier with each passing week.

When they returned to their apartment after his final surgery, he decided to talk about it.

"We need to talk about our future, Luce," he said.

Lucy had sensed for weeks that something was troubling him. She had attributed his restlessness to boredom—a lack of anything meaningful to occupy his time. Even Mitch had noticed, mentioning his unease to her twice.

Now, as she looked into Oliver's eyes, she realized it was more than that.

"I've been waiting for you to tell me when you want to discuss that. I've thought about it a lot," she replied.

"Can we go somewhere for a few weeks to collect our thoughts and discuss it?" he asked. "We don't need to see Dr. Bell for five weeks, and it would be good to escape the apartment for a while."

"I agree," Lucy said.

She got up from where she was sitting to sit on his lap and put an arm around him.

"I remember Bill saying we should go on a holiday on board *Artemis* for a few weeks," Oliver said. "It would allow us to return to the place where we first met and revisit the conversations we had almost five years ago."

"I think a holiday on board *Artemis* is an excellent idea," Mitch said when Lucy and Oliver told him about possibly taking the holiday Bill had suggested. "The weather along the coast of Sardinia is perfect this time of year. I'll make all the arrangements if that's what you want to do."

"You decide, Luce," Oliver said.

Lucy agreed. Mitch made the arrangements the following day.

***

Two days later, on June 1, Mitch, Dave, and Annette flew them to Nice Côte d'Azur Airport. From there, they took a helicopter to the Monaco Heliport, where Armand, the bosun, was waiting for them. He drove them to a quay in Port Hercules, where the yacht's tender awaited. After transferring their baggage, they sped across the water toward *Artemis*, anchored just offshore near the entrance of the port.

Upon arrival, Lucy and Oliver were warmly welcomed by the captain and the entire crew. Lucy knew them well. Oliver quickly realized that despite never having met most of them, his reputation had preceded him. The captain and longtime crew members were well aware of his past—how he had rescued the Alzheimer's cure from the hands of the Russians and, eighteen months earlier, had shared the Nobel Prize with the chief pharmaceutical scientist of the Boston lab. There were even whispers that he had been awarded the Presidential Medal of Freedom.

Mitch, who had accompanied them on the tender, bade them farewell as they stepped aboard. Lucy invited him to stay, but he declined with a smile, insisting they should enjoy this time alone. The crew then returned Mitch to Port Hercules before bringing the tender on board.

***

Lucy and Oliver fully embraced the serenity of life on *Artemis*. At her request, the captain anchored off the east coast of Sardinia, near secluded beaches nestled between headlands that jutted into the sea—hidden gems unreachable by road. Each morning, after a leisurely breakfast, the crew would take them ashore by tender, setting up sun loungers, beach umbrellas, and anything else they needed for the day.

They spent their mornings exploring and taking long walks while Dorothy, the head stewardess, had lunch prepared and delivered to them. Afternoons were filled with laughter, playful teasing in the water, and gentle flirtation. It was here that Lucy discovered that Oliver's swimming ability had returned—not yet with the powerful strokes he once was capable of, but strong enough. His body was still recovering from the effects of multiple surgeries and lost physical condition, but she could see his strength slowly returning.

As the sun dipped lower, they would relax, talking about everything and nothing. More often than not, their afternoons ended in each other's arms before returning to the yacht. Later, Lucy would call those twenty days their honeymoon.

***

During their second week on *Artemis*, Oliver finally broached the subject that had weighed on his mind. He had spent days considering how best to approach it, waiting for the right moment.

Lucy had just reclined on her lounger after their swim, her

eyes drifting closed for a nap. Oliver, lying beside her, sat up. She noticed immediately—he was nervous.

"Shall we now have a talk about our future, Luce?"

Lucy's inclination to allow herself to doze off disappeared immediately, and she gave him all of her attention.

"Sure."

"I've given the matter considerable thought, and if you'll let me ask you some questions, your answers will point to a future I would be happy with."

"That's not fair. I'd be deciding our future with no input from you apart from the questions."

"I know, sweetheart, but I've decided that you and you alone should decide on the issues I want to talk about. I want you to be happy. I'll be happy when you are. You're my rescuer, my redeemer. I would still be in prison, tending to my flowers during the day and dreading the night if you hadn't persisted in looking for me. I want to do no less than be there for you for as long as I live."

Oliver's confession amazed her. To want her to determine their future and for him to comply with whatever she was to suggest was totally unfair. She realized she needed to object.

"No, Oliver, we'll discuss your questions and arrive at answers together."

Oliver looked at her for just a moment, unsure about how to proceed.

"Okay. I thought you might say that. My approach was too much to hope for. Let's see where your approach leads us. The first question is related to our life as it is today. We need to decide if it's fulfilling enough to want until we become old and frail."

"Define *fulfilling* for me," she said.

"A fulfilling life is sometimes described as filled with purpose and satisfaction and highly meaningful," Oliver explained.

"I told my mother and Bill once that you're my priority in

life for as long as I live. I said that when they proposed hiring people to take care of you to allow me to get on with living my life. The fact you've recovered from your memory loss makes no difference to how I feel about my commitment to you and our relationship, but I believe that while I'm totally happy, there's room for something else—something that involves both of us in the same measure, something that will provide meaning and purpose."

"I agree. So, what would you say to look at the possibility of working for the company in roles we'd both want? The last time I spoke to Will, he explained he wanted a budget and people to start a new research project on dementia. As you know, Alzheimer's is just one type of dementia. There are seven more. I'd like to work with him on that. Can you see yourself working for the company in a role that would also provide motivation and satisfaction?"

"I was responsible for PR and marketing. I was based in New York because our head office is there. I don't want to go back there because nearly all of my bad memories concern things that happened there."

"I thought as much. So, why not try to get Jacky and Bill to move the head office to Boston—close to the Boston facility? We could buy a nice home there and work virtually in the same office. If that appeals to you, we should then solve the problems your travels to the Morgan Pharma offices around the world create. I don't want you to do that anymore. I'd want to die if something happened to you."

"I like the idea of moving the head office to Boston. But let's set aside the question about how I can obtain satisfaction from working for the company for the moment. There are other possibilities than to manage the team responsible for PR and marketing."

"But do those possibilities offer a solution for limiting travel to allow us to be together?"

"We'd need to discuss that with my mother and Bill, but their happiness when they learn we both want to work in meaningful roles in the company will likely make them accept any condition we propose."

"I believe you're right. The last question I want to ask you involves the nature of our relationship. There's only one way to give recognition to what we mean to each other. I love you and you love me. My life wouldn't be worth living if I were to lose you, and your dedication to me these last eighteen months has been of an extraordinary nature. I wouldn't be here talking to you like this if you hadn't persisted in returning my life to me—no, to us, in the way you have."

Oliver's voice wavered, now thick with emotion. As the weight of his words settled between them, his composure broke. His eyes filled with tears, and at that moment, Lucy saw the man he truly was—vulnerable, unguarded, stripped of all his formidable masculine traits.

"I'm sorry, Luce, for becoming emotional. But I simply don't know how to show my thankfulness and feelings for you. Every time I think of what you mean to me, I'm at a loss for words, like now."

Lucy felt her emotions swell as she listened to him pour out his heart. His words, raw and unguarded, stirred something deep within her. She rose from her lounger and sat beside him on his. Gently, she ran her fingers through his unruly hair, then pressed her face against his, feeling the warmth of his skin.

She had never seen this side of the man she loved. And at that moment, she knew—this was happiness unlike anything she had ever felt before.

"I love you deeply, Oliver. I know you love me as much as I love you. I can't live without you."

"Let me carry on, sweetheart, with what I was about to ask before I became emotional."

Oliver looked at her and smiled. She had no idea what else he wanted to ask and talk about.

Oliver cleared his throat before continuing. "There's only one way in which we can solidify the feelings we have for each other, and that is for us to marry."

Oliver left the sun lounger and kneeled on one knee in front of her.

"Will you marry me?" he asked.

Lucy was startled when he asked, not having expected it.

"I will, Oliver," she said with tears in her eyes.

"I haven't got a ring to give you, Luce. You're the expert on rings. We'll be in Olbia the day after tomorrow, and I was thinking of buying you a ring there that you'll help me choose. I hope you're not disappointed I haven't bought you a ring to give to you now."

As Oliver spoke about not having bought her a ring, Lucy slipped her arms around his neck, holding him close. A tender smile touched her lips before she kissed him softly.

"We don't need a new ring," she whispered. "We could have our promise rings engraved differently—maybe with our wedding date."

Her words were gentle, reassuring. To her, the ring didn't matter. What mattered was the promise they had already made—and the future they were about to build together.

"No, Luce, I want to buy you a true wedding ring of your liking."

***

Later that afternoon, they returned to the yacht, showered, and dressed for dinner on the aft deck. Dorothy, who had been observing them closely since their arrival in Monaco, couldn't help but notice a new closeness between them. There was something different now—something unspoken but undeniable.

Her curiosity got the better of her later that evening. When she found a quiet moment with Lucy, she leaned in and asked, "Did something special happen today?"

Lucy smiled, unable to hide the happiness in her eyes. "Oliver asked me to marry him," she admitted.

Word spread quickly among the crew, and before long, it became a cause for celebration. The chef, inspired by the news, prepared a surprise engagement cake, which Dorothy served to them after dinner.

***

Two days later, *Artemis* docked stern-to at the quay in Marina di Olbia. That afternoon, Lucy and Oliver strolled through the town's charming streets, stopping at jewelry stores, searching for the perfect rings. They found them at MEG Jewels, a boutique where every piece was designed and handcrafted by its owners. With quiet smiles and a shared understanding, Oliver purchased Lucy's ring and Lucy chose Oliver's.

***

Six weeks after their holiday, they were married.

The ceremony was intimate, attended by only a select few. Lucy had asked Sasha to be her maid of honor while Oliver chose Mitch as his best man. They had selected President Lincoln's Cottage on Rock Creek Church Road in Washington, D.C., as their venue—a place that felt meaningful and private.

Beyond their close friends and the Lassiter family, word of the wedding had reached both the CIA and the White House. Ken Rivera and the White House Chief of Staff attended, as did Dr. Bell.

Before the wedding, Oliver had told Lucy that they needed to embrace his true identity. She had objected at first, but he had explained there was no other way for them to be properly married. And so they became Mr. and Mrs. Liam Richards.

It took Lucy a long time to start calling him Liam.

At the ceremony, they insisted on reciting their own vows. As they stood before their loved ones, Liam took Lucy's hands in his and gazed into her eyes.

"I love you, Lucy. My love for you will last for as long as I live. I give myself to you today in marriage, to share the good and the bad at your side. I will always respect you, be understanding, and trust you. I promise to be faithful and to hold you in the highest regard. I accept you unconditionally as my partner for as long as I live. I give you this ring as a symbol of my everlasting love for you."

Mitch handed Lucy's ring to Liam for him to slip onto her finger.

Lucy replied. "Liam, I promise that my love for you will last forever. I take you to be my husband from this time forward until I die, to share with you all that is to come. I give you my hand and my heart. I promise to always be by your side to achieve the things we both hold important. I vow to respect you and trust you unselfishly. I pledge all these things from the bottom of my heart. I give you this ring as a token of my love for you."

Sasha handed Liam's ring to Lucy, which she slipped onto his finger.

They returned to Liam's apartment afterward and spent a week alone.

***

Jacky and Bill came to visit the following Saturday afternoon. Over coffee, Liam took the opportunity to share his plans—he wanted to work with Will Bryce on dementia, which meant relocating to Boston.

Lucy, in turn, made her feelings clear. "I never want to be separated from Liam again," she said firmly. Then she proposed something neither Jacky nor Bill had expected.

"What if you moved Morgan Pharma's headquarters to Boston?" she suggested. "It would put the company closer to the Boston lab, and it would allow me to return to work for the family business."

Jacky and Bill exchanged stunned glances. They had never imagined that either Lucy or Liam would consider working for the company again—let alone propose such a significant change.

"It will be a costly move, but we agree. What would you want to do after the move?"

"I'm not sure," Lucy answered. "I could take charge of the PR and marketing department again, but that would require a lot of travel, which Liam won't allow me to do if he can't join me."

"I've played with the idea of appointing Oliver—sorry, Liam—as CEO of the whole of Morgan Pharma, but I've learned he's more interested in the scientific aspects of what we do. Will Bryce recently sent me a very detailed proposal for making a budget available for a wide-scope research program on dementia. He told me that Liam assisted him in writing it, so why don't we change things around—for you, Lucy, to become CEO of the company, and for Liam to become director of research and development?"

Liam hadn't wanted to interrupt the discussion between Lucy and Bill, knowing she was perfectly capable of arguing her case. He was surprised to hear Bill formulate a perfect solution to their problem.

"What do you think, Liam?" Lucy asked.

"That's a perfect plan. I'm assuming you'll have assistants and staff to take care of most of the traveling in that case."

The issues that had worried them were resolved.

Bill announced the closure of the New York head office as soon as a suitable alternative had been found.

***

From that point onward, things moved quickly. Lucy and Liam bought a beautiful home in Boston, not far from Morgan Pharma's new headquarters. They decided to keep Liam's apartment in Falls Church. That place held too much history to let go—it was where Liam had cared for Lucy through her battle with alcohol addiction and where she, in turn, had nursed him back to health after finding him in Kazan. It was a place of struggle, but also of healing. Whenever they needed a break from work, they would have Mitch fly them there for a few days of respite.

Given their past encounters with the FSB and others who might seek revenge for having lost the battle for the Alzheimer's cure, they hired a private security firm to ensure their safety, providing protection around the clock.

Not long after settling into their new home, Lucy made an announcement that changed everything—she was pregnant.

They had talked about raising a family before they were married, after returning from their holiday. They both knew they wanted children but hadn't decided when. That uncertainty had led Lucy to make her own quiet decision—to stop taking her birth control pills.

When she told Liam, he was overcome with emotion. His eyes shone as he pulled her close, vowing to stand by her through every moment of the journey ahead.

Months later, the day finally arrived. When Lucy turned to him and said it was time, a mixture of excitement and fear surged through him. He drove her to the hospital, staying by her side, holding her tightly as she labored.

And then the reward—their son.

When the attending nurses asked if they had chosen a name, he and Lucy looked at each other and answered in unison: "Oliver."

THE END

ACKNOWLEDGMENTS

This novel has traveled a long and winding road to publication. Initially believing that traditional publishing was the only viable path, I dedicated myself to researching literary agents, carefully selecting those I thought would be interested in reviewing a romantic suspense manuscript. The responses I received were mixed—ranging from definitive rejections to encouraging feedback that praised the storyline, plot, and characters, yet ultimately declined to proceed.

Disheartened, I sought guidance from Mark Malatesta, a former literary agent turned consultant who offers advice on navigating the publishing world. Following his recommendations, I submitted my manuscript to numerous other agents. While most responses remained disappointing, Robert G. Diforio of D4EO stood out. After having his staff read the entire manuscript, they reported back with enthusiasm:

"This was a wonderful read! Definitely attention-getting. I love Lucy and Oliver. They had this interesting banter that I quite enjoyed. Their relationship was complex, and I craved every moment they spent together while they pursued a revolutionary cure. Well done, Peter! I would proceed with *The Alzheimer's Cure*."

Encouraged by this feedback, Bob offered me a contract and submitted the book to fifteen publishers. The outcome was again mixed—three publishers expressed strong interest but ultimately chose not to proceed.

At this point, I discovered hybrid publishing—a model where authors invest in the publication process in exchange for retaining a significantly higher percentage of the profits (typically 85% to 90%) compared to traditional publishing (which offers 10% to 15%). After carefully reviewing author feedback, I identified one hybrid publisher that stood out: Atmosphere Press.

Working with Atmosphere Press has been a rewarding experience. Over five months, my manuscript underwent two rounds of developmental editing, accompanied by multiple video meetings in which we discussed ways to enhance the manuscript. The book was also proofread twice. I collaborated closely with their team on the design of the cover. My ideas were taken seriously throughout the process. Every stage was handled by professionals, which convinced me to entrust them with three additional novels I had been working on. I am pleased to have contracts in place for all four books.

I am deeply grateful to the following members of the Atmosphere Press team:

- Dr. Kyle McCord, Acquisitions Director, for reading the manuscript carefully and choosing to publish the book.

- Dr. Nick Courtright, Founder and CEO, for his involvement in the acquisition process and investment in my book's success.

- Alex Kale, Publishing Director, for expertly guiding me through the publishing journey. Her consistent support is invaluable.

- Charlie Westerman, Developmental Editor, for his remarkable insight and dedication—likely the single most impactful collaborator on my manuscripts.

- Ronaldo Alves, Art Director, for working closely with me on the cover design and visual elements of the book.

- Karli Fitzgerald, Social Media Manager, whose role will become increasingly crucial as we work to promote the book.

- Dakota Reed (and others), Proofreading and Interior Design, for meticulous proofreading and thoughtful design contributions.

I also wish to extend my heartfelt thanks to Mark Malatesta, who stood by me during moments of doubt and encouraged me to persist. His belief in my manuscript proved vital.

Lastly, my gratitude goes to Bob Diforio, my literary agent, a role he relinquished when Atmosphere Press and I entered a publishing contract. He provided unwavering support. While three major publishers came close to offering a contract, the reasons they ultimately declined remain a mystery—especially given the positive feedback Bob shared with me. I firmly believe their decisions had nothing to do with the quality of the manuscript itself.

This journey has been challenging yet deeply rewarding, and I am immensely grateful to all who believed in *The Alzheimer's Cure* and helped bring it to life.

ABOUT ATMOSPHERE PRESS

Founded in 2015, Atmosphere Press was built on the principles of Honesty, Transparency, Professionalism, Kindness, and Making Your Book Awesome. As an ethical and author-friendly hybrid press, we stay true to that founding mission today.

If you're a reader, enter our giveaway for a free book here:

SCAN TO ENTER
BOOK GIVEAWAY

If you're a writer, submit your manuscript for consideration here:

SCAN TO SUBMIT
MANUSCRIPT

And always feel free to visit Atmosphere Press and our authors online at atmospherepress.com. See you there soon!

OTHER TITLES BY PETER VAN OOSSANEN

WWW.PETERVANOOSSANEN.COM

The Science of Sailing, Part 1: The Attainable Speed Under Sail, Van Oossanen Academy publishers (www.vanoossanenacademy.nl), ISBN 978-90-827682-0-6.

The Science of Sailing, Part 2: The Origin and Nature of Fluid-Dynamic Lift and Drag, Van Oossanen Academy publishers (www.vanoossanenacademy.nl), ISBN 978-90-827682-1-3.

The Science of Sailing, Part 3: Phenomena and Drag Originating from the Boundary Layer, Van Oossanen Academy publishers (www.vanoossanenacademy.nl), ISBN 978-90-827682-2-0.

The Science of Sailing, Part 4: Phenomena and Drag Originating from the Air-Water Interface, Van Oossanen Academy publishers (www.vanoossanenacademy.nl), ISBN 978-90-827682-3-7.

The Science of Sailing, Part 5: Sailing Fundamentals, Foils and Foil Sections, Hull Forms, and Australia II, Van Oossanen Academy publishers (www.vanoossanenacademy.nl), ISBN 978-90-827682-6-8.

The Extraterrestrial, Atmosphere Press (www.atmospherepress.com)

When Mercy Died, Atmosphere Press (www.atmospherepress.com)

Removal of the President, Atmosphere Press (www.atmospherepress.com)

ABOUT THE AUTHOR

Peter Van Oossanen is a distinguished Dutch scientist, naval architect, and author. After earning his PhD from Delft University in 1974, he served as a principal scientist at the Maritime Research Institute Netherlands (MARIN) until 1991. During this time, his groundbreaking research on sailing yachts contributed to the design of *Australia II*, the yacht that famously won the 1983 America's Cup—marking the first time a challenger had defeated the USA since the competition's inception in 1851.

In 1992, Peter founded the Van Oossanen Group of companies, specializing in yacht and ship design. His 1988 publication on the resistance and propulsion of ships became a definitive text in ship hydrodynamics, solidifying his reputation as a leading authority in the field—a distinction that earned him numerous awards and accolades.

Following his retirement in 2013, Peter turned his focus to writing, authoring five books that explore the science behind sailing. In 2020, he embarked on a new creative journey, transitioning to fiction and launching his career as a novelist.

(www.petervanoossanen.com)

Made in United States
Troutdale, OR
12/21/2025